Margaret's Secret

A Novel by

Vivienne Makepeace

ISBN: 0987458604
ISBN-13: 9780987458605

Chapter 1

*W*HEN YOU WRITE *down your own story, it is with a great deal of vanity that you consider that your life was worth the time to read. Does anyone desire to read The Life and Times of the Local Janitor or The Definitive Works of Mary, the Seamstress? But the life of Napoleon would have no greater value, I would wager, than any of these humble ones. Still, our common man does not rate an ink spot in the vast halls of history books, though every breath of their simple lives has turned the huge rudder of the ship we call time, and taken us far out to sea...*

I wrote these words, and a good many others, before I realized that there was only one way to tell this story.

In the warm sunlight of this new day, I sit in front of the window that faces the esplanade and the shore of the Coral Sea. I have found myself in no stranger place, as any young woman could have imagined, and now recount my journey from the shores of England to this rich and primeval land in Australia.

Queensland, as this new northern state is named, is one of six in this vast continental island and it is built of tall mountains and dense jungles where the little known Yidinji rainforest aborigine live. It is quite apart from the rest of Australia that is so vast and with many desolate deserts of scrub and red sand sweltering under the blazing sun. But here it is lush and green and akin to paradise.

As I sit here contemplating my task, I can hardly fathom the events that came upon me in this wondrous place. Indeed, my long months of isolation all but destroyed me. Yet, such trials also gave me a new birth and a new beginning. Oh, how I desire to pull those precious memories close to my breast again and make them real. But knowing time shows no mercy for our fault, I suffer an interminable ache and oft times beg heaven above to hide such things away where even I, might not find them and some measure of peace could return to me.

Yet now, here I sit amidst the tidy clutter of my room, staring out beyond the roof tops toward the sea and can do little more than fill the pages of this journal with the burden of truth that I cannot seem to shed in any other way without bringing on myself terrible judgment—that I am sure I shall not be fit to bear. I am at a loss as to whether I shall manage this duty well but these blank pages frown at me and remind me that I must do this for your sake, and those who come after... and for the memory of this place that is fast fading into time before any should catch sight of its leaving.

So I begin to fill this soft, leather bound book with the voice that is nearer to the truth than future history may tell it. Indeed, it is well known that when it is expedient, the official record is kindly dealt with by those who claim a better memory than may have been. I imagine that my account may well defy the pens of many others who sit in their own windows, gathering up words and stringing them like shells to rattle on blank, white pages of their own. Some will be without a care for the true and secret things I have known firsthand—my most gentle observations of this burgeoning new world and the first people who lived here and who rightly belong to it. Yet I care not. It is enough that I write what I have known and ask none but God to judge me.

My name is Margaret, which was given me by my dear and long-dead father in England. It means *a pearl*, and the words I shall string will echo that meaning—but also the name this land has given me, Guli, *the mother of pearl*. Every letter I shall write will try to emulate those lustrous spheres and hope to reflect the true light of this place and the real people in it. Indeed, should I manage it, you shall see as I do, the wonder of the Rainforest Cathedral and the home I now call my own.

It seems so long ago that we first left London, though as I begin, only a little more than two and a half years have passed and I am only in my nineteenth year. Now, narrowly brought back to life from my ills and having taken leave of the hospital that is newly built, I wake to find it is well into 1879. All around me the new town is buzzing with busy streets, filled with carts and horses and white-linen-dressed women twirling their parasols under the fierce tropical sun.

It's the end of the dry season and the days are perfect, as they have been for many months. There are only two seasons in this magical place, unlike my home in England. Here, the wet is endured for five torturous and steamy months and then the dry season comes, the Gurraminya Minya. For seven more, our Lord shows the greater part of mercy and indeed, what heaven should surely be like.

I have been living at the new-whitewashed address of my dear Mrs. Steadman in Matthews Street and I could not be more grateful for her Christian hospitality, having abandoned our distant farm some forty miles south from the town. I am now housed safely and have recovered well from my desperate illness that, were it not for the kind intervention of Mrs. Steadman and her fellowship, would have certainly claimed my life. And none would have known it, being that I was alone and so far from society and my husband still unheard of.

Today, the first sounds of morning woke me more urgently than the former days. I dressed quickly and sat with Mrs. Steadman to eat my toast and wild honey, washed down with a cup of tea she often makes so strong, it rivals the look of the coal bucket and tastes much the same. After which, I sought to make some excuse to visit Mr. McKenzie at his mercantile store so that I might buy some lavender soap as a gift to my kind hostess, as it is her favorite and she had some time since, used all her own.

I consider Mr. McKenzie not just a businessman of some notoriety among the townsfolk but he may well be the only one who has the slightest sympathy for the matters I now know beyond the trappings of my so-called civilized world. For this reason, it was no burden to visit him to make his acquaintance again even without excuse.

As the day sparkled before me, I took the short walk along the golden clay and sand of Abbott Street toward his address.

A flock of rainbow lorikeets sped across the wide thoroughfare and darted through the gap between the livery and the Empire Hotel, and I looked up across the roadway and followed them with my gaze before returning my eyes to my next step on the wooden planked pathways that stood along the roadside.

The carriageway was unusually wide for a northern settlement because, from the town's first inception, the main streets had been designed to accommodate fully loaded carts to turn about. This had attracted some criticism among those of a conservative nature. Many said such a small parish had no need for grandiose thoroughfares but now the planners are hailed as visionary for having such sensible foresight. The width so loved by horse and bird alike, is a Godsend, since the port is far exceeding all expectations and the populace is now reaching 1,500 souls already.

As I walked, another flock of small and noisy parrots dived in unison, loudly screeching as they sped around the corners of the buildings. They disappeared too, into the tall fig trees still standing behind the main town and sheltering the tent city that had grown up beyond its fringes. They were like bejeweled green and orange bullets and how I would have wished to follow them, but my former days of freedom are cut short. Yes, I must be what I must be, having returned to the tame and constant appearance that is claimed by decent folk to be essential to one's conscience and one's kind. Yet beneath my propriety is the memory of those secret things that still call with the sight of those pretty birds, speeding off to the distant mountains, as though they might yet tempt me to follow—even now.

As my shoes clacked on the walkway, I could see Mr. McKenzie's store in the distance and it still had its sign made from the side of a wooden crate. It was roughly painted in fading white with the words *General Store* and hung haphazardly from the tin roof of the veranda, having survived the year's monsoon and tempests. It had been there from my first arrival, when there was almost no town at all. Mr. McKenzie resisted all suggestion that he should upgrade his store's frontage or the sign. The town's menfolk of distinction had pointed out that the new Bank of Queensland was now built in stone and brick, and so much progress required a better presentation and that he should oblige them with improvements.

Mr. McKenzie would have none of it, for he was of a mind that "needs must dictate action" and there was no need for pretentious acts, in his opinion. "A man's name is good or nay, no matter the size of sign he has," he would loudly say in his heavy Scottish accent so that the whole street should hear and those that might object could only say he was, "Indeed, a stubborn man!" I knew from my dealings with him, that "stubborn" he was not. Rather, he was one who's certain faith had brought about that change which made him least like the character of this world and closer to the beauty and truth I had discovered far from civilization—where no sign could be nailed.

When I stepped into the slightly cooler and shadowy interior, stacked high with all manner of implements and rough sacks printed with Corn, Tea, Tobacco or some such other staple, Mr. McKenzie saw me from behind his counter. Without a moment's pause he closed his notebook, stepped from the bench end and waved for his young assistant to take his place.

"Ah, Mrs. Bermingham. Aye, 'tis good to see ye out and about at last." He smiled broadly and I noticed that his waistcoat only barely hid the striped shirt with shiny buttons underneath. He had gained some weight since last I'd seen him but his voice was warm and friendly, just as it had been as he said, "Dear Lass, come... sit with me here, have some tea and tell me how ye fare."

I followed him, stepping carefully past a grinding mill made of iron, its swirling decorative spokes shining with blacksmith's polish in the light from the door. A ticket twirled from the top spoke in the slight breeze that sped past me; I spied it read *thirty shillings* in Mr. McKenzie's own handwriting.

As I walked toward him, he picked up a set of cups and placed them on the table at the back of the store before pulling out a somewhat battered chair for me to sit upon. Soon he had poured a strong brew of tea from the tin teapot that sat and stewed constantly on a potbelly stove against the back wall. The black liquid seemed near as good as Mrs. Steadman's, though the pot was dented and reflected a distorted image of our surroundings. He replaced it on the stove and I wondered how I might drink as little as could be considered polite before he brought a small, chipped, porcelain jug to the table and said, "A drop of milk, Lass?"

I waved it away and said, "No thank you sir." Having long since forgotten the taste from my many months of deprivation and not wanting to waste it in the tea I should only like to sip.

"So Lass, those of us from the mission have heard a whisper of ye plight. Very hard, aye, very hard to be sure. 'Twas such a pity we didnae know of ye earlier, stuck out there on your own in the wilderness."

He shook his head and, somewhat realizing his lack of judgment in bringing it up at all, quickly patted my hand.

"We all offered up a good few prayers for ye, three Sundays hence, aye, we were very sorry to hear of those troubles happening to such a young and pretty Lass. Still, praise be, I can see ye are already getting the benefit of the Lord remembering ye—and answering us all by bringing ye back alive and well again. He looked at me closely and said gently, "... Aye, is true enough, the Lord rescues his own good flock from the wilderness and good many places besides!"

I felt shy of the kindness he was showing, as it reminded me of what I concealed and I am certainly undeserving. I felt sure he would see my hidden shame as though it were written on me, so I swept an imaginary hair from my forehead to hide my eyes and chanced a glance toward the door as though I might escape.

He must have felt and misunderstood my discomfort and wanted to relieve me of it, as he was a kind man and this was well known by all.

"Oh dear ..." he whispered, "think nae that I be carin' a thing about it when I heard such rumors that ye had been havin' some connection with the natives in them parts." He placed one hand over the other as though hiding away such an unseemly association for a white Englishwoman to have had.

I could not help but focus on his gold signet ring glinting in the dusty shadows so far from the light of the door and replied a little shyly, "They are the Malanbarra bama and the name means The River People, sir."

"Does it, Lass? I confess I know little of them down that way. Be it true, they camp on your land up river from Pyramid Mountain?"

I nodded cautiously, "Aye, and some say, they are a mite too friendly to be meaning any good, but what say ye?"

I could barely speak, and coldness filled my stomach. I felt sure my whole face had filled with blush as things I had thought were not known, opened as easily as a can of peas.

"Did ye nae' have trouble with them?" he went on with a frown on his face before it was flicked away and he said, "If they left ye well enough alone, it be a blessing, sure enough! Oh aye, especially while ye husband be gone to the Thorn Borough goldfield and ye be left on your own out there."

He lifted the hand with the signet ring and briefly patted mine, as I held onto the table top hoping it would keep me from spinning into the black pit that had opened up beneath me with his inquiry.

Pressing on and desiring to engage me, he said, "So Lass, what manner of people are they? How did ye find them to be living? Aye, I have an interest in our native neighbors. Alas, I am outnumbered; more's the pity, for most in these parts care nae to admit to having them as neighbors at all—and nae many have a good word to say about any God fearin' folk that should try to call them such, neither!"

Now realizing I was far from a hidden subject in the town, but sensing his curiosity was in no way malicious as others might be, I said, "I have to say, sir, it is utterly true, that the Malanbarra clan is responsible for saving me from certain death during... that time. I should say, they are the most noble of race, no matter the opinion of the less informed."

I suppose there was a tinge of defensiveness in my tone and Mr. McKenzie looked at me over his glasses and smiled slightly as he said, "Aye? Is that so?" He cocked his head and frowned with some internal consideration of the matter. "Well, you know… I confess to you, even as I have to our brethren on occasion, that I am concerned to me core for the aboriginals in all these parts. All the clans of this Yidinji tribe are reacting badly and are being very worrisome to the new settlers even though ye have such a favorable report. A good deal of trouble comes to them because they will not come in and be civilized as some would say is best for them."

His eyes widened and for a moment I saw some compassion that was not common among our kind. He almost whispered to me, "Aye, but Lass, I could tell ye it is completely fruitless and futile to even think such a thing might please 'em. They are a wild breed and perhaps have been in this wilderness for forty thousand years, say some who study wild and native men. We cannae expect them to take on our ways on some whim of our own." He frowned heavily, "Aye, I certainly dinnae agree with those who claim they are not 'human' at all, nor that they're too dumb to learn. …"

His face lost its normal flutter of friendliness as he stared blankly at the table top and went on with some consternation. "Oh my Lord! I tell ye it was outrageous what we did to them at first! We cut our main street and built the first buildings on the very meeting place of the Cimy Walubarra clan, or as we call 'em in our own tongue, "the Four Mile People". All the while they sat under the trees wondering what we were about! Then that ruffian lot led by Abbott smashed their camp and drove 'em off!" He shook his head. "'Twas not a wonder that they took to throwing their spears at anyone they found alone and picking off the cedar loggers up near The Rocks. And then would ye know it; there was not a man here that didnae shoot any found nearby whether they be up to mischief or nae. I thought, right then 'n there, that crimes were being done in front of our very eyes—and the Lord who made 'em, alike just as we. And no one stood to prevent it. Aye, when I saw it, and not a man would listen to those of us that protested, me heart started to fear what would become of all the rest." He sighed forlornly, "Aye, seems our numbers increase and theirs seem set to fade away."

Shyness crossed his face as he had looked at me and spoke of the afflicted natives who had once lived peaceably on the land we now occupied. A pause held us as the story of what had been done silenced us both and then finally, he shook the moment aside with a toss of his thinning, gray hair as though he could not bear to think on it in such a piteous manner and lowered his head. I would almost have desired to reach out and touch his hand in sympathy while I tried not to imagine such a thing happening to my own aborigine camped at the mouth of the river under the shadow of Walsh's Pyramid.

Suddenly, he looked up at me and his eyes sparkled with some inner fire as he went on in a hushed tone and his teeth clenched and it seemed to me that every quiet word was delivered with as much force as any man could do by crying, "injustice" at the top of his lungs. "Lass, if I could say what cruelty it is for me to see them that remain sneak into the town at dusk and go through the pig buckets …" he looked up with wide eyes as though he might speak to the entire town. "I did see two, with not more'n a dozen words they'd learned, begging for any kind of food and clearly willin' to do some task for it. Me heart just burns hot with anger and then is silenced with me shame. If only there was some other way—but none of us cannae turn back the clock and leave them be."

He looked up, catching my eyes with his and I could see they almost pleaded with me, as though I should be the very one who would understand his feeling. I knew then that he could not be more sincere, and my loneliness seemed somewhat eased to know it.

"Aye Lass, it is me greatest fear that it shall not be stopped now that we are flooding in every day and the town is doubled and doubled and the land taken up in all directions. I cannae think on it, but we may see the rainforest aboriginals disappear completely." He shook his head, "and if any remain, they need be turned into a sorry and dejected lot like these Cimy Walubarra. Indeed, Lass, it could be they will have no future as true men—and aye, men they are, I say!" A stern expression crossed his face, "But 'tis true enough, they be without a decent purpose as all men must have or they soon fall into trouble and that be the death of most, be they native or our own folk."

I heard his words and immediately my mind's eye found itself looking on at the people I had come to know so well. I could barely stand the vision of them being struck and scattered into the high forest in the mountains behind their summer camp, unable to hunt and roam freely in the wide reaches of their territory and for a moment, I drifted into a trance as though I were still with them.

Mr. McKenzie continued and I jumped a little as I returned to the reality of where I sat.

"Oh how I would love to rattle their heads and make some see sense!" He lifted his hands up and strangled some imaginary ghost representative of the men now settling all along this wild coast, seemingly without conscience or concern for the displacement of the people already here. He paused and took a deep breath and let it out slowly. "...but it does nae good to wish on that, for not a one would change his ways even if the sense could be beaten into 'im with a rod of iron and a will to match." His sad eyes showed me the matter grieved him, as though he had also known the people as I had, and could not bear their loss either.

"Is it surely to be as bad as this?" I replied, almost pleadingly as I had no wish to admit I also feared his ghastly thought and would wish to throw some doubt in the air between us.

"Lass, I've seen it before in the south when I first arrived. I was in Sydney then. In just a few short years, the aboriginals that belong to that southern breed were forced from their lands too. Those that couldnae find peace in becoming less than even servants or poor laborers were shot or driven off to the interior where no white man will go being it is wilder than the hills of hell in them parts!"

He laid his hand flat on the tabletop and wiped it across its width as though it followed the path of those first natives that were swept from their place to be replaced by horses and field animals considered far more valuable.

He looked up sharply and caught my eyes in a serious gaze. "It will be worse for them up here, aye, these aboriginals are not the same as those down there. Nae, not at all! Up here they're a rare breed and made special to the place. They may as well be as different as a German is to a

Scot!" He looked at me intently, "Lass, if these tropical rainforest types are gone they shan't be made again. Nae, and they cannae suit the desert places inland either."

I nodded, though I had not known or seen any aboriginals other than my own, and I did not know that others were different or had fared so badly elsewhere. A wave of fear began to creep through me as he went on.

"When I lived down in New South Wales, I took an interest and learned that those aboriginals have a whole other way of life and language. They are very much taller too and of longer bones, not like them here that are so small that some have named them 'pygmies'. Those southern breeds have foreheads with a prominent brow as though inherited from some man in eons past. Aye, and their hair falls in black and shiny locks, and in the rain, forms such perfect ringlets as to be the envy of any young lady that would do the same with hours of a blazing curling iron!"

I couldn't help but smile as his words conjured up the faces of the Mallanburra people I had known. They were certainly small, no bigger than myself, and I am a small woman. They had tight woolly hair and when worn long as the warriors liked it, seemed to mat together in rope-like locks. They did not at all fit the description he had given me of other aboriginals. Thinking of the River people brought a pang of sadness and a sense of longing enveloped me.

Mr. McKenzie noticed it. "Ah Lass, I see you feel the same as I. 'Tis a bad business that is all the more dreadful when some of us would wish to hold back the tide, yet know that it will still roll on in and cover everything."

"It is a hard thing to accept indeed," I whispered. I looked up as though he might still have some answer for me that would thwart that moon-dragged wave if I had some reason that would compel it to go back. "I confide sir, that my dealings with them are somewhat closer than they here in town could know.... And it is for this reason that I fear as you do because our civilized life is not well suited to them. They are truly men and women just as we, though sensibly removed of attire in this climate and embellished with a wisdom of courtesy, kindness and order that we seldom have such knowledge of. I cannot convey to you how precious and endearing they are to me, and to think of their loss wounds me with utter despair..."

I closed my eyes partly so he would not see a tear forming without my permission and partly so he should not guess that I felt more than Christian sorrow for a people I would easily call my own.

"Ah—I should think as much. You have a good soul, Lass, and sure enough, a more true understanding of them thanks to your close proximity." He stared at the tabletop and said wistfully, "Aye …being nae more'n bullies, we've pressed these ones here off their land and taken their very lives along with it. You may well be the last eyewitness to the times of the rainforest aboriginals still complete in their ways. Few will ever get the chance to see it in the future, if me prophesy be true."

He fell silent and so did I, not knowing what anyone could say to this, as the moments ticked by.

"Och, Lass! I have an idea that no doubt be heaven sent!" He seemed to jolt as it came to him and then he stood up quickly and threaded his way through the crowded space toward the counter.

"I've just the thing and I would bet me last Queensland pound, this will be put to good use by ye." He bent down low beneath the counter, and then reappeared. Between his hands, one above and one below, he held a book. He looked up and smiled with an odd expression. "It'd be me guess that ye have quite a story to tell, aye… so as your recollections come back to ye, write them down for those of us that dinnea know your River people like ye do." He walked around the counter and paused for a moment beside the grinding mill and looked toward the bright entrance facing the street. The green of the distant mountains beyond glowed like a sunlit emerald in his eyes and he spoke softly, as though he might have been talking to himself alone.

"Aye, 'tis true, we've procured this place at such an unholy cost and we will be the poorer for the loss of our Yidinji neighbors up and down this coast." He turned back to look at me, sitting still as a porcelain doll in the shadows. "Best you make a record of 'em just as ye saw it." He stepped forward, his eyes sparkling as he placed the book on the table, "Aye, perhaps there be some special thing about them that only ye might know. I cannae think of another soul who should write it better for posterity than ye." He looked at me intently and said somewhat sadly, as he pushed the book across the table, "Lass, better they be in this here book, than be forgotten altogether…"

I picked it up and saw that it was a bound journal of blank pages that I might write in it all I knew. I slid my hand over its fine leather cover and struggled to contain myself at the contemplating of such a task. "Dear sir, I fear whether I shall do the subject justice…"

"When the heart is full and has stored it all where nae can steal or change its truth, justice to the subject is always done." He said with certainty as he sat down.

I turned the empty volume over in my hands and opened its crisp new pages. It would become the vault for all that I had known and dared not say. At that very moment, I knew my joy and my misery would be hidden in the words I would write along with the lost times and lives of the River people who had been so dear to me and with them, all the truth about myself.

I thanked Mr. McKenzie sincerely for the journal and the tea, and stood up politely to say farewell. I left the store with a strange sense of portent as I stepped out into the heat and sounds of the day.

As I walked back along the road, I determined to tuck away in every clean, white sheath those precious, light-filled memories of my life with the Mallanburra. Walking steadfastly back to Mrs. Steadman's address, I dared to imagine that upon opening the diary in some time to come, unknowing eyes might look upon my words and see the sight of those dark-skinned beings as they were. Dwelling in peace among the bright green foliage of their home, filled with a multitude of wondrous animals, and the sound of exquisite birds, just as it has truly been.

I shall strive to form some way of speech that would have that world materialize, even after both they and I, have gone. Perhaps I shall do well enough to create its reality again, if only to live on in my narrative as though a memory you had almost forgotten, yet spring to life at the mention of a single word.

I will begin from the beginning, leaving nothing out, even those things that should be credited to my shame. And as purely and as naturally as are the lives of the Yidinji people whose secret world it is, so too, shall I tell it.

"The tide is at four o'clock, Margaret, are you completely ready?" My husband Edward had chided me gently as I somewhat looked for any new excuse to extend the moments before we would leave our home in London.

"I am sir. I have done everything as I should and I have said good-bye to everyone." I tried to summon a smile, nervous, as I was to be leaving the familiarity of my life for the unknown.

Edward's pocket watch was silver, it read two-twenty in the early morn, and I suspected he was not really listening to me but had his mind elsewhere.

"Oh… very good. Let us go then, my dear."

He came across to me, leaned down, and picked up the small bag standing beside my brown linen skirts that were ironed so well on this special day, that the smooth folds looked like the dark sea we would soon depart upon.

The rest of our luggage had already gone to the docks and been loaded the day before. All that remained was my small bag and the small figure of myself standing beside it.

"It is so odd to be going. I have hardly begun to be your wife and now we are off to the other side of the world."

"Yes madam, it is no doubt a little perplexing for you, but I can assure you that you will love this great southern land we are going to. And fear not… I shall be with you."

Rising, he kissed my forehead, and I could see him take a deep breath of the rose water scent that came from my newly bathed skin.

"Queensland is all that we could wish for, my dear, for any man wanting to make his fortune, and there we will certainly make ours—and not the least of it will be healthy sons and daughters that will keep you in comfort in your old age."

I grinned and turned away from him and the veiled passion those words implied. I could feel his keen interest in my femininity as his eyes flirted over my bodice, and I spun away shyly toward the door. My skirts brushed the wooden floor like a gentle broom that signaled my respectability even now, as his lawful wife.

"Yes, I'm sure you are quite right, sir ...quite right." I whispered with my back to him before he stepped around me, opened the door and strode through it. I took a last look at our empty lodgings and stepped through myself, shutting the door behind us with a gentle click of the brass lock.

As we descended the wooden stairs, worn smooth in the center, our leather boots clattered on the treads down the narrow stairwell and echoed far more loudly than was convenient at such an hour. Edward's long legs, contained in pressed woolen trousers, strode off each rise before me and I followed each step with my eyes firmly fixed on the spot where my floating skirts met the last of each of my husband's. I thought how strange it was, that just a month ago, I had been dressing hats in the little shop of Miss Preston's Millinery in Langley Street. Then, as though the chime of a clock had struck to announce that the hour had come, I had been introduced to this tall gentleman, whom I hardly believed would take any interest in me. He was older than I, twenty-six and I, barely seventeen but he was capable and by all accounts, a hard worker. I was mystified as to the turn of providence in my direction.

Now he was my husband, and just as suddenly, was taking me off to a land I had scarcely heard about before our meeting.

Queensland. It would be our new beginning in Australia and I could hardly imagine it.

Edward had shown me a battered picture of the mystery country he had described as "down under" and had spoken of it as being so vast that it might well have been never ending. The evidence of his confidence, complete with sketched figures of blacks under trees and soldiers in red coats lined up against the distant hills, lit his face like a beacon in the fog as he had looked upon it. He had assured me it was awash with new and boundless fortunes to be made and was indeed, a great "land of opportunity."

I confess, the thought had so filled my belly with excitement that it almost matched our happy wedding day and I had a sure hope of a bright and fortunate future.

I had not then known, that Edward's description could not disguise the hardships of such a venture. Certainly, for those that pose as wealthy gentry, claiming vast holdings to add to their estates, it 'twas indeed such a place. But for the many disaffected immigrants that came to these shores on a fare of two pounds and six pence, they might well have told a different tale. Bravely, they learned the meaning of fortitude to survive its harsh climate and unknown ways.

Nor did I know of the multitude of convicts that had free passage at Her Majesty's pleasure. They paid for their meagre crimes in toil and sweat for long years and after so discharged, barely made way at all. Many a poor soul was buried far from home, their names lost in the sea of time for all their hard labor in our new land of opportunity.

But Edward had painted an alluring picture to my young, naive and hopeful heart. I could hardly fathom his stories as he had courted me, my body vibrating with his nearness and awaiting the moment that all girls dream of, his proposal to make me his own and whisk me away on such a romantic adventure. I had listened as he told of strange animals and he described the birds as being "of such astounding colors as to defy creation." With his hands spread wide, he had painted the air before me and spoken with great passion of the huge boiling green cauldrons of rainforest waiting to be felled, the land ploughed and planted in fields of tall sugar cane. I barely realized the life this man's dream would bring me—nor the cost, such was my eagerness to embrace my future with him.

So, in the haste of my hopeful heart, I found myself setting off to discover what 'time and chance' had in store for me. Leaving all behind, I stepped out into the darkness of the streets of London in the early morn behind him to embrace it fearlessly.

It seemed the minute's juggled time into a fast-moving stream as the moments fled and we set off. We waved frantically to the well-wishers who were stamping their feet in the cold and I watched them slip behind us as our carriage pulled away. They seemed like the last dying embers of my old life, glowing beneath the lone street lantern of our address. I watched with a crystal tear in my eye as they faded into the darkness and with them, all I would remember of my last moments of my home disappearing behind us.

The journey had begun. I sat transfixed in the rocking vehicle as the carriage lantern swayed like a drunken firefly above the cobbled streets passing by. The smell of fresh bread came warmly in through the open window, pausing on us as it snaked its way from night-time ovens somewhere in a back street. In the hollow shroud of morning, the crisp, clear sound of a distant voice called out for coal and reminded us we were not alone in this London town so early on the fourteenth day of Our Lord, May 1876.

I pressed myself back in my seat and Edward leaned over and grasped my gloved hand. I looked up to his angular features in the fleeting bursts of light that came and went from his nose and cheeks. I could not help but smile, for he was a handsome man and he had chosen me.

"Adventure is far better than a cup of tea and scones is it not?" He whispered gently, perhaps thinking my silence meant I mourned the loss of my simple life already.

"I cannot say sir. This is my first adventure," I squeezed his hand, "that is, if you do not count our being wed." He did not reply but looked intently forward, past the carriage horse's black mane bouncing against its neck, to where the struggling dawn began to show dark shadows of people filling the streets with activity.

"Are we on time?" I leaned over in the dark, grasping his arm at the elbow rather more tightly than I needed to.

"Yes madam, indeed we are exactly on time. Are you warm enough?" He said as he gathered up the carriage rug and adjusted it across me and I caught its edge and tucked it in.

"I am indeed sir," I said, and perhaps to convince myself of my surety, added somewhat wistfully, "...I know you shall always warm me and I shall be completely safe at your side."

I remember, he was so attentive to my physical needs in those times, almost unreasonably so. No doubt due, in no small part, to burying two wives already in his beloved Australia. I, his third, had filled him again with the hope of building the family he so desired. For this reason he seemed to keep my health and wellbeing almost above all else in those early days of promise and with youthful trust, I felt sure such care would never cease to comfort me.

He turned his head to gaze at me and whispered, "You are unusually quiet my dear." I lifted my gloved finger and tapped his nose playfully, "I am beset with excitement sir! We shall soon be in your land 'down under' where our hair might well stand on end and have to be clipped in some new fashion for fear of looking a sorry sight!" I leaned slightly into his shoulder as he laughed with amusement at my jest and then lifted his hand to rest it on my knee and indeed, the act settled my pensive heart.

It was some thirty-five minutes, rolling through the streets toward the docks, before we could smell the distinct scent of fish and salt and oily ropes. The sound of creaking timber, bustling movements and quite loud voices began to reach us from ahead. Through the lightening morning air, I could make out a row of glowing lanterns, losing their grip on the night as the early dawn harried away the receding darkness. Tall, swaying timber masts rose above the low roofs of the buildings on the street our carriage jolted down.

Finally, with an unceremonious lurch, we turned the corner to haul up and stop amidst a melee of other carriages and people all about us. A multitude of barrels and a large pallet of unknown cargo, wrapped in thick canvas and tied with ropes, sat unattended beside our carriage in the confusion of so many other items waiting to be loaded. Passengers and onlookers threaded through it all, finding their way to whatever ship they belonged to. We were pressed together, hemmed in between the dockside and the town by the wooden side of long warehouse buildings that lay adjacent to the river. The windows shimmered with their melted faults in the light of the lanterns hanging from iron pillars along the dockside and they looked like strangely leering caricatures watching the parade beneath them.

"We are here at last, madam!" Edward said with some exuberance before climbing from the carriage before holding up his arms for me.

I slid across the leather of the seat, my skirts trailing off the edge to bounce at my ankles like a hanged man, and dropped into his arms. We strode through bundles and crates of various items strewn about and came upon a clear space among the clutter. A pen of goats bleated from the side of the fray and a man cursed loudly at his horse who labored to haul a cart piled high with wicker baskets crammed to overflowing with hens and ducks.

"S'cuse me ma'am!" a man jostled past and then lifted a wooden barrel lid beside us to reveal a seething mass of black eels, all bent on escape. He picked out a dead one and threw it to the ground where it skidded unceremoniously amidst the many feet of the throng.

The space was quickly being filled with long benches of fish being cleaned and staked ready for the early sales. Scales and guts flicked about and were soon trampled underfoot and I could not help but exclaim, "Edward, such a dreadful smell! I fear I shall be ill 'fore we even get to sea!" I lifted my gloved hand to my nose to stem the barrage assaulting me at every turn. He did not reply but instead, searched for a path through the maelstrom to reach the dockside berths.

Suddenly, the name of our ship stood out clearly before us, its gold painted letters reflecting the new rays of dawn on her stern.

"There she is!" Edward exclaimed.

The *Clara*, tall and worn, rose sweetly above the noise below. Huge ropes held her fast to the dock and a boarding ramp, fixed solidly to the wharf posts, came into focus. Edward led me toward her with haste.

All along the dockside, huge bollards held heavily swaying tethers on the mighty craft moored there in a row. The ropes sagged in perfect arcs, dipping in the river below, then rose up the sides of the great ships resting and waiting for the tide.

Suddenly, a man, who had been shadowing us from behind, yelled loudly from behind me, "What's that you say, ma'am? Did I hear ye say, you don't like the 'dreadful smell? 'Tis naught more than the perfume of the sea comin' ashore to visit them that don't know 'er charms!" I gasped in surprise at his sudden appearance and turned as Edward smiled broadly toward him. "Master Jack, good of you to meet us."

The sailor smiled back and yellow teeth appeared from the somewhat darkened skin of his lips that seemed to be covered by a layer of soot and oil permanently tattooed there. He tugged at his collar that barely showed where the fabric began, and the skin of his neck disappeared below it and then tipped his hat to us both.

"My pleasure to be sure sir, madam. 'Tis a good day to be sailin'." He walked beside us and led us to the gangplank. I paused and looked up a little pensively at our ship and he leaned in and whispered with whiskey-laden breath, "You'll soon love the sea, ma'am, and naught desire to forget her perfume once you know 'er true." Then he stepped aside and swept his arm low to usher me to the rail, saying in a loud voice, "Nay, even if you be planted 'midst a hundred roses ever after, she be creeping into your dreams at the first whiff of a bucket of cockles or a sprat from the fish market. Aye, you'll soon be just as we that be wedded to 'er." Edward nodded knowingly toward me as he led me to the gangway and the sailor continued with great gusto. "I'd bet a sovereign from a month's wages that you'll curse the scent of a rose at a hundred paces 'specially after eighty days aboard!" I sported a fleeting smile and replied, "I am afraid I doubt you sir, I shall be obliged to have a very large garden of flowers simply to drown out the memory of such... perfumes. He waved a half-bare forearm, sporting dark hair and murky, green tattoos, out over the ship toward the great unknown. "Well ma'am, best we get ye aboard right quick and out to sea where there be fresh air for ye."

I gathered my skirts and found the handrail, then reached up to grasp Edward's hand.

He leaned back and made sure I took the small incline carefully. At the top he stepped aside for me so that I could take the significant step onto the deck of the little brigantine Clara to find myself at last on her decks.

"Well, Margaret, this shall be our home for some 12 weeks or so. She looks like a fine vessel, does she not?"

"Oh yes, I do believe she will be very fine, I'm sure." Though I confess, I was not entirely convinced as I scanned the small decks that rose forward and back to the stern. Hidden behind the rows of ropes and tackle streaming up to the masts above, I could just see her bow peering seaward and I thought, "Is this small boat fit for Open Ocean?" But I concealed the thought and asked politely, "A fine ship is she, master?" my doubts hidden by my courteous smile.

"Yes ma'am, she is just as sweet as the niece to the queen. Perhaps not quite as rich mind, but more 'n twice so, in 'er seaward manners.' He walked ahead of us and stepped around a perfect circle of coiled ropes and indicated I should do the same. "Watch how you go ma'am. I 'spect you'll soon get to grips with the measure of all things here aboard. But p'raps you best be like the ladies in mid quarters who stay mostly below, for fear of losing one oft the side in a good blow!"

The thought of storms in such a small ship, and the vision of a bell skirted lady being caught up in the wind and tossed overboard to float like a paper cup lost at sea, made me gasp and reach for Edward's arm. Neither he, nor Master Jack seemed to notice, nor be even slightly moved by whatever perils we might face as they walked me the few feet toward the rear bulkhead door. Master Jack opened it, then stood by the small opening that led down to the heart of the passenger quarters and a wide grin spread across his face. "Watch your head, sir and ma'am, it's just a bit of a duck down them stairs for you."

I looked around the frame that was now clearly visible in the dawning light and scanned down into the darkness. It held a little promise, with a slight warm glow beckoning up to us from somewhere in its depths. Narrow steps greeted my feet as I held onto the smooth handrail and Edward's shoulder until we reached the bottom.

"Oh it's quite snug, isn't it Edward?"

"Yes. They waste no space, I'd wager, on halls and such."

"I hope they have wasted a little space on our cabin."

"I imagine we will have just enough for our purpose," he laughingly replied.

"Just up ahead, if you please sir. Just up to your right, you will see your door. It has a mark to it. ...Do you see, sir? The boson's anchor."

The hall had led to a dead end. To the left, right, and ahead small doors were shut fast, each marked with different insignia.

"Do you have the key master?" Edward turned back and I could see his cheeks shone slightly moist and flushed in the light of the lantern.

"Here now, I think I do have it sir." Master Jack jostled in his pockets and then thrust his arm past my shoulder and my face to my husband's outstretched hand. I could smell the warmth of the sailor's skin as it passed by holding the key firmly in his gnarled finger tips. It smelt of liquor and tobacco smoke mixed with the sweat of a dozen days on shore without recourse to a bath and the faint scent of mackerel, that distinct perfume he so loved.

Edward placed the figure-eight key into the lock and it clicked as it turned over. The brass door handle slipped in this hand a little but his grasp was firm and it opened to us with a loud squeak. "There now Margaret, these are our quarters."

"Well sir, I see that they have remained as frugal with the space in here as they have elsewhere!" I exclaimed as Master Jack pressed in behind us and lit the lamp fixed on the wall inside the door.

"Ah well, it is enough is it not? Look we have a storage locker upon that side..." Edward took less than three steps to the bunk bed no wider than a single cot. "This bed seems suitably firm don't you think?" He patted it and I stepped forward to look at it, at a loss to where we should both fit.

The master peered through the opening behind us and said, "Sir, ma'am, I shall see you topside when you are ready. We will cast off in a little under 'alf an hour." He tipped his cap before he turned away from the doorframe, without closing the door. It swung gently one-way, then the other, unable to decide whether to be open or shut.

I turned quietly, closed the door and heard the lock click. The tiny cabin suddenly closed in around us and I felt as though we had been trapped in a bottle. We could hear the muffled sounds of movements elsewhere on the ship and even our own breathing.

"How many passengers is there Edward? Are we going to have company?"

"I believe there will be three families and some eight children this trip in mid class, so the master told me. And I suppose a number of others will have purchased the cheaper fare and be housed in the steerage quarters below us, the first class cabins are aft and I should think we shall have little to do with them." he said as he sat on the bunk.

I pulled off my gloves and then took out the pin from my bonnet and undid the ribbon beneath my chin and put it on the bed end. I was not so far away that Edward could not lean forward and reach my waist and he stretched out and caught me.

"Ah, Mrs. Bermingham! We are at last beginning. I cannot wait to be on the wharf in Australia, but for now there must be a little patience, a little biding of the time." He smiled sweetly. "Do you think you might want to try this bed out for size, since we have some time to spare even in this present moment?" He grinned a little wider with a mischievous expression as he pulled me to him and buried his face in the bodice of my dress. I was warm and the linen was clean and smelt of the iron that had pressed it just the night before and he murmured into it. "Mmm... wife."

"Mr. Bermingham, how inconvenient! Sir, I beg you to remember that we are not alone on this... this... fine ship."

He dropped his hands to my hips, full with skirt and puffed with gathers, and I grabbed his hands in my own and covered them, locking them under my cold fingers.

"There will be none of that sir! Just let me get on with some kind of order for our things, and then we must be above board to say farewell to England for this is a day we best not forget."

My voice caught a little. A pause seemed to hang on the air and he looked up from my bosom to my face rimmed with gentle curls.

I spoke before his lips could form a word. "I'm not afraid you know. ..." I looked down, and a slight tremble on my lips gave the truth away.

"You have no need to be, my dear. I will do my best to make sure you have what you need." He looked past me for a second. "Mind, there will be a little toughness while we build our home and get things started, but our allotment is a good one. I paid my three years as is the law 'fore I could get a land grant and I have chosen a damn good parcel for that hellish labor." Looking back and catching me with his hazel eyes, he said, "One day you can walk through all the gardens of flowers you want. You can have a healthy milking cow and a swing for the children." He smiled and all my fears seemed to flee with it.

"Well, I suppose I can ask for nothing more than a swing and a milking cow!" I touched his nose with my finger and looked up to the bare, wooden walls. "There are no windows, we are going to be very tight and warm in here, I think." I turned my head to look at the door which had a slatted vent covered with tight gauze in its base section and seemed the only ventilation. "I hope we shall not suffocate."

"Of course not! You will get used to the confinement my dear. This is indeed more comfortable than those berths below." He grinned. "If you feel a little breathless you shall have to breathe 'small' breaths." He shifted his hands and raised one to cup my bosom. "...And I am sure I shall know how to make you do that my dear wife!"

"Edward!" I exclaimed somewhat taken aback by his candor.

He looped his arms around me and squeezed me to himself and I wrapped my arms around his head affectionately. A warm glow filled me and for a moment, all thought of trials and troubles, disappeared along with the world outside.

Finally, he pulled himself back, and with the tender moment over, dropped his hands from me and stood up. Pressing himself gently around me, and kissing me on the forehead, he headed for the door.

"I shall go up. Will I get the steward to fix a cup of tea for you my dear?"

"No, please don't trouble him. I think I will just put away a few of these things and then come up to watch with you."

"As you please." He nodded, and with that, opened the door, ducked a little to go through, then closed it and disappeared.

I could hear the echoing thuds of his shoes as he walked the length of the corridor and I followed the sound with my mind's eye as though I could not leave him and clung as a ghostly apparition to his shoulders, my presence only dissolving when he reached the light above and I could hear him no more.

Alone in the cabin, I surveyed its Spartan closeness. I unlocked a case that was up against the bulkhead, unfolded the bedclothes that were on top and set aside a good woolen blanket threaded with green and red that I had had in my dowry since I was nine. In the bottom of the case was a small tin tobacco box that was my father's and I left it there wrapped in a handkerchief of my mother's. It seemed too small a reminder of them and I swallowed hard as I looked at it, remembering their passing, a mere four years apart, my mother a mere two years before my wedding. For a moment, it was as though I still stood amidst the daffodils of the cemetery. I could still remember the white lilies I had laid on each of the caskets in turn, as they glistened with dewy tears in the spring morning as I said my final goodbye.

Chasing my sorrow at the memory away with the task at hand, I turned and put our things in the drawers of the wardrobe, where a small mirror hung on the door. It was patchy from the salt air that had eaten away a mosaic of missing silver at the back. Fixed to the dark, oiled wood with solid corners, it watched me with its blighted eye as I busied myself being a dutiful new wife.

All the while, I thought about the ship and settled in my mind that this was now home and that I should think on it fondly. I brushed off the front of my skirt, put on my bonnet and gloves, and left the cabin, tracing my way along the small corridor that my husband had traversed and headed for the light.

A door ahead opened quite unexpectedly and an ample woman appeared from behind it. Her head was cupped in a black bonnet trimmed with white ruffles around her full face, and she smiled and pushed her black skirts through the small opening into the corridor.

"Oh my, I do declare this is an alleyway for nothing bigger than a stray cat!"

She turned and saw me behind her. "Do you think they make the sailors a size smaller than the men of the mainland?" she asked.

I smiled, not feeling the smallness for myself as badly as this lady was.

"I think they are indeed very frugal with their space, but I suppose we shall be used to it by the end of this journey."

"Yes indeed, I 'spect you are right my dear—if we survive!" Taking a few steps forward she turned her head and said, "Oh, I quite forgot, my name is

Mrs. Crompton—Bessie, as my friends so call me. And I should think that you shall indeed be a friend of mine by the end of this ordeal, so please be so kind as to call me Bessie, too!"

"Certainly, if you will most amiably agree to call me Margaret." She nodded slightly and cocked her head politely as did I.

"I shall indeed, and to whom are you familiar?"

"Oh, my husband is Mr. Edward Bermingham, who is already waiting for me on deck, as I think we must be very soon casting off."

"Yes indeed, let us get up there, right quick, and wave to merry old England and all who bid us good-bye." She smiled a warm smile that revealed her true nature, and I felt immediately that the ship and the long journey ahead would be far more agreeable.

With this, we two rounded the staircase and one by one, hauled ourselves up the steep ladder-like rungs.

As dear Bessie reached the top, the sight of brightening skies and gray-smudged cloud of the opening moments of the new day disappeared as her ample rear fully filled the doorway. Then suddenly, she was out like a cork and puffing loudly as she stood on the deck surveying the activity. I pulled myself up behind her a little more easily and I too came up onto the gently swaying craft beneath us both.

The breeze now lifted quite strongly and all the sounds of the dock seemed clearer with the coming light. The tide was lapping up the sides of the wharf poles driven deep into the bedded mud deep below the keels of the ships loaded and awaiting their release.

A gull screeched overhead and a sharp flap of canvas signaled that crew were beginning to unfurl tightly rolled sail and others were finding the barge ropes before we could be towed out from the dock. We could feel our little Clara straining at the bow tether, desiring to go as much as we.

We women walked carefully to the side and grasped the polished rail between halyards and cleats where both our husbands and several others had gathered.

Edward grabbed my hand and pulled me to his side as I felt the ship begin to move.

The Captain arrived from the stern and bowed politely to us all.

"I trust you have all stowed away as you like. We shall be casting off. I must indeed welcome you to the Clara and hope that you are comfortable and fare well once we are at sea."

Some nodded pleasantly and several of the men thanked him. Then he bid his farewell from us with a courteous "Ladies" and a nod, and strode off with matters of the ship's sailing on his mind.

I leaned over the side and watched the harbor men shifting ropes and the many various merchants, laborers and seamen moving and working along the length of the dock that spread out a long way in both directions from our present mooring.

"Cast off bow lines, mister." A voice yelled from mid-ship. "…And away the stern line, if you please."

"Aye, aye… Cast off bow lines." A voice echoed back.

"Oh, isn't this exciting Edward! We shall soon be off."

He squeezed my hand and I looked up to him, then to the shore and whispered. "So, it seems I must, at last, farewell England!" I waved my hand to the many onlookers on the dock who had gathered to wish farewell and safe journey to the ship. "Good bye to you all!" I called along with many others, "Farewell, we shall not forget you." I called out over the widening gap as the Clara began to separate from the wharf side. Suddenly, I felt the distance between the past and future grow with every moment and I realized we were truly leaving and my voice became small and I whispered, 'Good bye ma and da, I shall not forget you."

The gray-green of the muddy water slapped haphazardly against our sides, and the entourage along the dockside waved and cheered frantically as we began to pull away. On board, the children had rallied round and were enthusiastically waving and laughing, adding their small cheers to those of the crowd below.

In a matter of ten minutes, Clara had pulled free from the grip of the docks of London, England, and embarked on her journey, like a plump goose being led out into the Thames to ride the outgoing tide toward the open sea.

Sails began to unfurl in the light breeze, the towropes released from the towing barges and very gently, she pulled away into the waterway on her own and began to sail freely down the channel.

Almost two and a half hours passed and with bells and great action, the vessel came through the heads of the wide river mouth. Little by little, she began to rise and fall with the greater waves of the open sea slapping on her bow.

Many of we onlookers, stood fixed to the side of the ship watching the busy sailors and listening to the shouted commands ringing from stem to stern. We watched the gray of the dawn landscape slide along beside us, and the muddy water beneath us foam and froth along our sides.

Many other ships passed and small craft busied themselves distantly as the Clara heeled gently in the breeze and sailed fast toward her escape.

"It's beautiful, isn't it"? I said to Edward standing close beside me.

"When you see the light and beauty of Queensland, Margaret, you'll see that you have been living in the shadows all your life." Edward's voice drifted off as he willed the land of England into the past and gazed out to the open sea where lay our future and some mysterious call in him, that I could as yet, not fathom.

"I am sure you are right, dear Edward. Indeed, I do so desire it with all my heart." I smiled, but my confidence could not cover a strange sense of trepidation that welled up in me as the land slipped away behind us. I swallowed hard and with every breath, I had to exercise a will of iron to contain that ominous feeling so that it did not spill onto the deck screaming, "For pity's sake, take her back!"

Yes, I remember that day, save one, more clearly than almost any other. I was sad and excited all at once. My stomach was churning along with the waves and I remember thinking that there, I left my poor mother in the ground and my father there beside her. I would not again put flowers by them, nor talk with the woman in the bakery shop, or laugh with my friend Sally who worked right beside me at the milliner's. I still remember the gray of the sky painted with cloud, soft as the cream that froths on fresh milk, and those humble buildings lighted with orange lamps in the dawn, and the distant sound of the familiar clatter of my life.

I can still see the great buildings of Parliament and the towers of the square standing over all the smaller buildings as the Great Lady, London, slipped away behind us. The green of farmland beside the river, dotted by muddy sheep still sleeping there and the gulls rising on the drafts by the rocks of the headland, still fill my mind.

Above them all, the North Star shone its beacon over my home before the day drove it away, and I thought that as long as I could see that star, I was just a little way away from my mother and my father, resting under it. I can remember fixing my gaze on it that first morning, and feeling quite a bit better for its tiny light for I was sure I would always have that sight to comfort me. So I said goodbye to my home, and I made sure that Edward could not see me cry.

By ten o'clock, we were well at sea. The channel had opened her arms to us and a strong swell raised the ship up and down in yawning dives as she rode the ocean current away from England and to the south.

By this time, many were not feeling at all well, and several of the children had already succumbed to its rolling, finding that an early breakfast of porridge had been of no use to them.

A small boy hung on to the rail with one hand and a wooden bucket with the other. His father held onto his collar at the back and patted him at odd intervals while staring out to sea, trying to deny the illness he himself was feeling.

"Do you think it will be like this all the way, for I don't think I shall at all get used to it, even if I had a year to do so," I asked Edward.

"No, my dear, we are sailing south and the Captain has assured me that when we turn to the west, we'll sail against the wind and the ship will be steady on her side."

"Thank God for small mercies!" I looked up at the great sails now filled with a stiff breeze. "But for all the discomfort of this rolling, it is quite wonderful isn't it?"

"Indeed it is but I have no doubt that the poor Stevensons won't thank you for observing that. I believe they have four of six children ill, and the mother also."

"I don't feel yet ill myself, however, I would thank the Captain to provide cushions for every place so that I am not black and blue by the day's end."

"I am sure he might do such a thing for you, my dear, as you are quite the loveliest woman on board. I shall have to guard you most carefully from the eyes of the crew."

I blushed a little as he said it, since I didn't think of myself as very pretty.

"Are you hungry at all? I can find the galley and bribe the steward to open up the pantry for a light brunch for us if you would like."

"Yes, I would like something. Perhaps a little bread and cheese or something of such that they have and can be put together easily and that will stick to my ribs for all this shaking."

"Will you stay here or come with me below?"

"I think I shall stay here if you please. I would like to feel the wind and the sea air for a bit while I may. I see they have chased the steerage passengers below already. It is too lovely to abandon my first hours at sea just yet—for that… 'ample' cabin down below."

He smiled. "I shall call you when the meal is ready. Take care you hold onto the rail very tightly—don't let go at all, my dear, I couldn't bear for you to fall over on the first day!" He placed his hand over mine and I confess, he did not need to tell me to hold the rail tightly. I was hardly willing to let go even for an instant, being pulled left and right with the heavy sway. He lifted his hand from the side and swayed himself as he turned and staggered across the deck to the opening of the stairwell below.

Alone, my eyes searched the skyline. We were far enough from land now that the coast could no longer be seen, though we were following it distantly and would soon come up to the French coast hidden in the midst of a storm that could be clearly seen there.

I watched as a sea bird rose over us in even flight, as though the rules of gravity did not apply to it. Its wings twitched and held the bird aloft as cleanly as a floating leaf upon a slow river in summertime, riding the waves of air above us and watching below as we sailed away.

Evening that first day soon came, and when we arrived at our cabin after dinner in the steward's parlor, the glimmer of a lantern showed the way.

Inside, I folded my shawl and placed it in the wardrobe, slightly swinging on the door as the ship heeled to port.

The vented door panel displayed its pattern at our knees and I realized that the light from our lantern on the wall would make us visible from the outside through the netting of the vent. The lack of propriety made me feel somewhat uncomfortable as our persons settled in for the night.

Edward began to undo his jacket and shirt and dropped them on the cot. I turned and picked them up, folded them carefully, and placed them in the wardrobe, hanging the jacket on the wooden coat hanger that clanged with every movement of the Clara.

He began to undo the buttons of his trousers and I scolded him in a whispered tone, "Edward, turn off the lamp! I cannot imagine how it will be if any sailor might come down here and look on us!" I pointed to the vent of the door.

He laughed lightly and I frowned as I went on quite earnestly, "I for one will not be undressing until that lamp is off, sir!"

"Margaret, dearest, they would have to lie on their bellies to see through that slat, if they could at all. And even then, they would have to defy the Captain's orders and risk being thrown in the brig if they come anywhere near the passengers' quarters."

"Still, I shall not be undressing with that lamp lit!"

Edward turned quickly and blew it out to oblige me and I heard the cot creak as he sat upon it in front of me.

With the comforting darkness around us, I unbuttoned my bodice and layer-by-layer disrobed, feeling through the small space for where I would put them. I gathered up my nightdress and as I did, I was aware of Edward moving to lie on the bunk.

For a moment, I felt a slight feeling of excitement at the nearness of my husband, as he waited for me to lie down in his arms as though there were no more natural place in the world to be. My experience as a young wife was still new to me, but his duty to me was as gentle as I could have hoped and so it was with pleasure that I desired him. I paused, my nightdress in my hand, and as I stood naked in the darkness before him on that uncommon night, it seemed that all my life had ended and a new one had just begun.

The moment seemed to defy the tightness of the cabin and I all but lay down beside him naked, as though the common rules of propriety had been left with the world behind us. But instead, I slipped the garment over my head, lifted the covers on the side of the cot and slid myself in. Edward was comfortingly warm and I found myself lying in the crook of his arm. We lay there quietly and unmoving for some minutes, being rocked with the ship as it gently sang its creaking, yawning song around us.

Then, on some equal beginning and unspoken understanding, our hands slid to each other and our lips found themselves meeting in the dark. Edward rose around me and sank his body onto mine like a great ship into the awesome deep and I gave way to his thighs weighing heavily on my own.

Quietly and with stealth, we became one as man and wife, and the rise and fall of the ship added to our passion on the small bed.

That first night at sea was as moving as it was marvelous. The ship rocked us to sleep and we were so tired we never noticed how small the bunk was. Nor did we suffer any cold, locked so tightly together and buried deep in the womb of the little brigantine, Clara.

For the first full week, Bess and her family were sick and we barely saw anything of them, but one morning we saw them seated like ghosts up on the deck and the smallest child played happily, quite recovered from his ordeal of the week before.

On the weeks that followed, we sailed down the coast of Africa, though we could barely see it, and every day it seemed that the temperature rose and the color of the sea became increasingly green like the color of my own eyes that gazed on it in awe.

The crew, from time to time, caught great fishes that they hauled up with large hooks and the children's curiosity animated their faces at the sight. The cook made good work out of it for us all. The fish was served in a bland but suitable white sauce, and provided respite from the various stews, pies, and dry cabin biscuits, which seemed to be his only repertoire of meals for us, served strictly at seven. Breakfast was served at six thirty, and not a minute later, or one should find oneself certainly going without and not even a bribe would have sway.

Most days I spied the boys learning how to make various knots and the girls busied themselves with drawing or the cross-stitches that they had brought with them and some of them could draw quite well and were pleased to show us.

Day-by-day, we sailed down toward the equator. At times, we saw strange sights or unfamiliar birds but many days, we women simply sat beneath our parasols in the breeze that thankfully never abated, and talked of our lives that had been and our hopes for the new life we would have in Queensland.

Night by night, Edward and I would find the North Star on those evenings when cloud did not prevent us, and each time we saw it, we watched it hang ever lower as our journey took us further and further south.

One evening, we could see it no longer. We had crossed over the equator and the Captain broke out extra rum for the crew and we danced a jig on the decks. That was a beautiful night indeed, and we retired with satisfaction, knowing that our journey was in fact making progress even though the sea dragged on endlessly and the creak and sway had become our new way of life and we now walked and moved with it automatically.

As we left the familiarity of the Northern Hemisphere behind and began our descent toward Cape Town, we came upon a calm for some days, and could do little more than sit in the torpid heat, sweltering in our clothing and waiting for the wind to carry us on.

At last a breeze sprung up and we sailed on, finding Cape Town almost a week later. The Clara tied up at the docks while fresh supplies were gathered for our journey. We were all pleased to see live chickens loaded, bread and nuts, and a case filled with such things that could be eaten in the weeks that followed—cheese, bacon and the like, and a goodly supply of fresh eggs, flour and raisins.

Cape Town was indeed a bustling and modern settlement and we very much liked it. Carriages with white-clad passengers rolled through dry streets, and covered canopies lined the new buildings that filled it with charm. Round about the main habitations were green farms spread out on gentle hills and some of the young men of our number made up their minds to disembark, thinking their futures were best served by starting there.

We were sad that they should leave us, but after the fifth day, the Captain called upon us to be ready to set sail again. We left that great harbor on a fine day in June and waved our farewell to the people there and to our former fellows.

The winds were fair and a petrel followed us for some time, to the children's delight.

The first mate said it bode well for us, and we all hoped that we would not suffer as we set our compass for the Cape of Good Hope. We had heard that many a ship had been lost in that place, and it was with some trepidation that I stood on the deck with Edward and looked past the bow to the islands and rocks of that formidable place.

I said a prayer for all those who had lost their lives in that deep trough and for the ships that must-need pass it on their way. I prayed also for us as I watched the land rise in great cliffs in places. The rocks looked very fierce indeed with the southern breakers powering themselves angrily upon them.

We saw seals flying through the waves and on two occasions porpoises rose at our bows, which made the crew very happy indeed. We had clear fine days and good winds, and although the swell rose very large and at times it felt that we were climbing small mountains, the gulls stayed with us and we sailed through quite easily. Several of our company were sick again, but Edward and I fared quite well, intrigued by all we saw.

At midday on the third day past the Cape, we sighted another ship to the west, a steamer. I could not help but wonder about its journey, alike as our own, carrying passengers, or cargo around the bottom of that great dark continent of Africa. Though the oceans were vast, it seemed to me that an endless stream of ships now transported our goods and our ways to every corner of the world. As I watched the steamer, having no sail, but blowing out her smoke into the good winds we claimed as our own, I thought how our world was shrinking to our mastery of it and was all but tamed. I wondered what would become of our Empire's hunger for discovery when all had been found and conquered. Soon the fleeting sight of the ship and the wonder she stirred disappeared, and again we were alone with the sea.

We traveled on and by the week's end we had passed the island called Madagascar and turned our heading to the east to cross the wide expanse of the Indian Ocean, some 6,500 nautical miles to traverse, in a wide arc and as we began, it was as though the land had entirely disappeared and we were alone on a great planet of deep blue water.

As a sailing ship, we were fast enough, but our passage was a lesser fare than the steamships that were now going by the shorter route through the Suez Canal. However, they were half our speed in a good wind and had many more passengers even though they were rather more comfortably housed, I'm told, than we. Still, Master Jack had been right and I liked our good ship with her sails billowing and her hull heeling to the power of the ocean. For me there could be nothing better than the salt spray and the clean air and I fancied we were still holding to those days of adventure disappearing in our wake.

The Captain ordered all sail up, as we had fine winds as we crossed the Indian Ocean and our passage was very fast indeed. Upon the third day across, the ship's crew sighted a great whale and we all rushed to the side to watch it breaching in the clear cobalt seas. For some hours it played, its huge black, back rising from the deep and its spout blasting like a train high in the air above it. Finally, it took its leave from us, and I listened to the sailors telling tales of the whaling ships and the profits to be had hunting the great beasts, albeit at the hunter's peril.

After a long and tedious journey of a seemingly never-ending ocean, the lookout from the main mast crow's nest called aloud with great excitement that he could see the dull smudge of the first cape of Australia.

It was but a haze of purple on the horizon and we sailed another day and a half before a finger of bold rock and white waves cresting on the shore, showed the wild coastline. We altered our course several times in the wind changes and followed the straight coastal line northeast.

We watched as the white breaker line and frosted reefs became an ever-present sight of wonder to our starboard side. The heat cloistered all around us but the running of the wind through our sails above deck kept it at bay. But at night our cabins steamed us half to death and I would have wished to be like the crew who simply slept on the bare boards' topside to escape it. As I washed my skin each night each night to cool myself with a little water in a small enamel bowl, I spared a thought for the steerage passengers who had almost spent the entire journey below decks. I never ceased to thank my Lord that Edward had the means to pay for our better berth.

Along the way, sea birds fleetingly staged their flight through our gaze, riding the ocean of currents above us and we saw great pelicans, floating like huge reed baskets on the tops of waves. They came and went from our view as we sailed close and in the lee of the land across the top of the great island continent.

In due course, we landed at the place called Darwin. This was our first landfall in Australia. It was little more than a muddy camp, and Edward pointed out the blacks seated under the wide umbrella trees on the hill at the end of the bay watching our Clara as she arrived.

This was the first time I had seen people such as these. They were naked except for a thin rope around their waists with raffia strings forming a small fringe to cover them. Many had, it seemed, no need for coverings at all, and the women nearby were bare breasted, many with children resting or nursing in their laps.

Their darkness amazed me. Until then, I had not seen a black man so naturally in his own garb and in his own way. I could barely make out the features of their faces, though many had feathers and such tied around their heads and wooden pegs piercing their noses. If they had not occasionally moved, I would have thought of them as part of Edward's sketch or a picture from some fanciful imagination, not realizing them to be very much like ourselves at all. With their black skin, shiny and clean on their thin arms and legs, and with no shoes upon their feet, I wondered at how different we might be. With that notion, I was tempted to consider how great our ship was and how civilized we were aboard and I somewhat pitied them in their poverty of soul without a jot of possessions or even decent dwellings to call their own.

It was unbearably hot. I, myself, was damp to a dreadful degree and Bess took to her cabin with a faint. Despite my proper respectability, I confess, I almost would have wished to be as those natives were, clad so sparsely and so freely, and for all appearances quite cool. While we, trussed up like a Christmas goose in our heavy clothing, felt like we might melt.

I took my leave from the deck on the second day, finding a bucket and getting Edward to fetch some water to our cabin, where I locked the door, undressed and poured it most lavishly on my own nakedness, not even concerned by the went splashes that soaked into the floor boards. All the while, I could not get my mind away from those strange people that sat quietly watching our ship and the business going on with us. They seemed to me aliens of another world, quite at odds to the truth from our Lord, whom we are taught, had made them alike to ourselves, as to even be kindred. Even so, they were evidently not as we, and I wondered what they knew that we do not, that they could live so peacefully in this place that was alike to the Garden of Eden. It seemed as though we had left that blessed place and had ever after, journeyed about the world to re-find it. And while we troubled ourselves to be industrious, they had remained untroubled from the start, even right to the present day, nestled in the bosom of this garden without a care accept to wonder at our appearance and why we had come at all to cut down the trees and build our towns, and plant our fields—when they had done no such thing and remained well despite it.

By evening it had cooled somewhat, and the Captain, having refreshed our water supplies was urgent to get us to sea again. There had been some troubles here with the blacks we heard, so he was not at all inclined to neither be ashore, nor stay in the bay.

He passed out guns to arm the watch that night and was determined to catch the tide in the morning. Sure enough, though I had not awakened due to the heat of our cabin, the ship slid out and away from Darwin in the early morn.

At sea, it was again cool enough, and we sat on the decks while the children played knucklebones. Bess stayed quiet, swaying gently with the ship, accept to vow that her husband was "indeed, intent to surely kill me." She complained incessantly about the heat we endured daily, given respite only by the constant breeze pushing us across the sea and I wondered how she would fare once we put to shore in Cook Town.

Edward entertained himself by helping the carpenter, who had rebuilt a small chest of drawers and was set on installing them as we rounded Cape York and began the southward and final leg of our journey.

I had grown so accustomed to the coastline that I was somewhat bored with it but my interest was rekindled when the children's peals of joy drew my attention to the side. We all rushed over to see twenty or more navy-blue and silver flying fish leaping from the waves all around us in a scatter of shining slivers.

I thought right then, that we were being welcomed by these small blue bullets, defiant of their natural world and a feeling of happiness settled on me.

At that very moment, I felt as though they had awakened me to the reality of our most certain goal and we had at last arrived—though it would be some days before we actually took a step onto the jetty at Cook Town.

Still, at that very moment, those little blue flying fish told my soul that I was going to be someone else in this place, an Australian, and with only a little sadness, I realized I would never see my beloved England again.

Chapter 2

"SEE, WE COME through the gap now."
A sailor hauling a thin rope with a heavy weight attached to the
end and knots staged at even intervals offered his knowledgeable
narration of the ship's course.

"We got to get ourselves through the coral now, so you be best to stay
out of the way ma'am." He politely tipped his cap in my direction.

I swished myself off to the rail without replying and Edward appeared
from below, smiled and came alongside me.

"Look!" He pointed to the lightening ocean water that was now the color
of turquoise and seemed to be patchy off to the port side and quite distinct
from the darker channel where the Clara sailed.

The Captain called aloud to drop the sails and we slowed considerably.
The gentle Coral Sea breeze spilled over the decks and all watched as the coast
turned from a distant haze to a clear ribbon of high mountains climbing
away from the shore toward the inland landscape.

Green and lush, the mountains seemed to fold over each other. Pale on
dark, they receded into the peacock blue sky that had not a cloud in any
direction.

The ship slipped with ease through the coral maze and the coastline fringed with mangroves and ribbons of peach coral sand led south toward Port Douglas and south of that, to New Port at Trinity Bay.

The broad expanse of great mountain ridges spilled onto lowland flats that were densely thicketed with bush and snaked through with small creeks and streams.

At intervals, rivers met the sea and yellow water from recent rains poured into the ocean, turning the sea around them from clear to milky.

We saw waves breaking on volcanic boulders in places and they frothed along the sandy shore all the way to the entrance of the great Endeavour River. Finally, the last of the beaches passed on our starboard side and the headland loomed above us on our left.

The Captain appeared beside us to watch the second mate navigate the craft in the river mouth with considerable prowess.

"It has a long history, this notable place." He was standing next to Edward and I listened intently as he spoke.

"Captain Cook stayed here to repair his ship, The Endeavour, in 1770, not knowing, of course, it would one day become Cook Town. You see, the reefs had split her hull more easily than a knife through butter at Cape Tribulation, much south of here, and so Cook named the place for that event. They had never been so close to disaster in their entire voyage, even while circumnavigating the wild coasts of New Zealand or even sailing the entire length of the Great Barrier Reef.

"Strange to think that they were all but at the end of the great navigation, and as though waiting for their guard to drop, the cruel spikes of Anthozoa polyps colonies, ploughed their limestone mouths into her side. The Endeavour barely escaped becoming a wreck, as so many would later suffer, so history tells."

"Are you a naturalist and historian, sir?" Edward asked politely.

"I do, sir, have me interest, just as they did… but not now having the great adventure of discovery left to me."

"What are Anthozoa…?" I asked trying not to sound like one of those curious but silly women not well liked for their want of education.

"They are the animals that make the coral, ma'am. It is their dead lime cases that slowly build up to make these infernal reefs. If you are not sufficiently experienced or keep your wits about you, these little blighters can do deathly work to even a steel-hulled ship."

"Are we in any danger then, sir?" I asked the Captain but Edward replied for him.

"Our Captain has sailed many times to this place, madam, and I do know of a few wrecks in these parts—but none of them his." Edward frowned lightly at me and winked at the Captain.

The Captain laughed, "Indeed I should hope not!"

"Please sir, continue your history," I said, as I was indeed very interested.

"Well ma'am, Cook's crew jettisoned cannon, iron shot, and the spare anchor to lighten the ship's draft and they limped through the coral to beach her for repairs under that rock they named Grassy Hill." He pointed up to the huge, oddly sitting rock escarpment, bare of trees and covered with windswept grass, at the mouth of the entrance.

"Captured by their wounds, they stayed seven weeks, and from the top of the very rock that rested them, they could survey the whole landscape and search for a channel of escape through the reef." He pulled from his pocket a pipe and lit it before he went on.

"There is an interesting aboriginal explanation to explain the rock being there." He stared at the headland and my eyes also studied it as he went on. "They maintain a great snake offended the inland god somehow and had the rock thrown at him! The serpent had fled with great haste, cutting a swath through the land, and his trail has become this river now named Endeavour after the ship." He looked down at me and smiled. "Escaping into the sea, that absconding snake had no notion of the resting place he would afford Lieutenant James Cook and the HM bark some millennia later."

Several others joined our little impromptu lesson as he went on, rather pleased by everyone's interest.

"Now, on board were Joseph Banks and Swedish naturalist, Daniel Solander, who accompanied Cook on the expedition. They collected, preserved, and documented more than two hundred new species of plants during the enforced visit. The young artist Sydney Parkinson illustrated the specimens and painted the first renditions of aboriginal natives too. The crew busied themselves exploring and gathering food to stay alive, and encountered for themselves these first 'Australians.' They had not had occasion to meet any natives up until then, as Cook had been unable to pierce the reef along the eastern coast. So it was a great oddity for the crew to meet them while setting out to make repairs. They gave quite a few trinkets, which were received at the time, but later found discarded."

He paused and scanned the shores as though searching for some sight of those first natives who had no need of anything, it seems, that the newcomers might bring.

"Now, the aborigine kept their distance initially, considering whether the strange persons that had appeared were reincarnated spirits of their ancestors or ghosts, them being so white.

"After some weeks, Joseph Banks met and spoke with the local people and got along quite well by all accounts. He recorded about fifty Guugu Yimithirr, words and it was here that these first Englishmen learned the name for that intriguing animal called by the natives, gan gurru. Joseph transcribed it as kangaru, Cook spelt it kangooroo, and today we know it as 'kangaroo'.

"Oh!" I exclaimed, so desirous of seeing the famed animal. "Is it here they first found one?"

"Indeed ma'am." He sighed and a long trail of smoke left his lips and dissipated in the breeze. "However, this pleasant start was short lived. The Guugu Yimithirr people found some umbrage with the newcomers when the ship's crew hauled huge green turtles aboard as provisions. You see, the aborigine rightly considered the turtles belonged to them and, had they been asked, would have happily applied their 'sharing' rules."

I listened intently, as this part of his story seemed to suggest that they were amiable creatures and worthy of some respect.

"The colonial visitors, who not only had no concept of their hosts being 'owners' of anything on land or in the sea, had little on their minds but re-provisioning, as they were all but at the point of desperation. Then, at their taking of a cedar log for wood for repairs, the aborigine became aggressively indignant. This wood is prized, you know, and used to make the long hollowed canoes they use for fishing. Taking it was considered a serious offence and no less for want of discipline than if we should have had one of our fat hens stolen or our best row boat taken without a by-your-leave!"

"Oh dear, it seems such is always the case that men everywhere fail to regard one another," I exclaimed.

"If it be true that they are 'men' at all, madam." Edward retorted and I confess I was surprised. He was not, it seemed, as convinced of the crime as the Captain was.

"They speared two of the 'thieves,' but did not kill them, which is their traditional punishment for that crime, and ordinarily would have considered the matter wiped and forgotten.

"It was with complete surprise and shock, therefore, that they received a volley of shot from weapons they had never seen before, which killed some of their number outright. They could not fathom how these invisible projectiles created holes that exploded in their bodies.

"Now realizing their danger at the hands of these few but magical interlopers, they proceeded far more cautiously.

"Negotiations ensued with Cook and Banks, and with some manner of understanding not linked to linguistic power, the interlopers eventually gathered their provisions and left without further harm. And the aborigine were well told that theirs was now a new world."

"What an unfortunate tale, sir," I murmured.

"Indeed ma'am... and here you are arriving some ninety-six years later." He smiled as he tipped his hat in preparation for excusing himself. "It's good to know such troubles are as good as behind us now." He turned politely, tipped his head and said, "I bid you fare well, sirs, ladies. I trust you will have much success and fortune here, and never need the hospitality of the natives to see you through as Cook did." He left us awaiting our arrival, and I was reassured by his last remark and his warm farewell.

In truth, Captain Cook and his crew had been the herald of a people not unlike the strangler fig that grows here, climbing up its host then sending a multitude of air roots back to secure itself in the ground, thickening with every season until the host tree is completely destroyed within. So too, were the original inhabitants of this land, now barely recognizable as such, surrounded by the new European hybrid in the town we should soon call our own. We would step off the Clara with no greater conscience for the demise of our native hosts than those that had already arrived and built this new place. Instead of feeling some sadness about these events, my face beamed with curiosity and wonder as I leaned over the rail to see the new land and town spread waiting before us.

Suddenly, the channel neared the shore in a long arc, and the large rock headland that hid the wharf in its shadow gave way to reveal it.

"Look, there it is! I can see horses and a cart there—can you see?" One of the children thrust out his arm with vigor and all looked across to the upcoming destination.

Cook Town was indeed a bustling port of civilization, growing from the earth like a patch of mushrooms in the warm humidity that laid her blanket over all life here.

"Oh Edward, we are nearly there!" I grasped his hand with mine and he curled his fingers around my own small digits.

"Indeed madam, it appears much more established since I was here eighteen months ago." His smile seemed fixed a little sadly and his eyes glazed a bit as we both became quiet staring towards the dock.

The children chirped with all manner of observations, and the crew scurried across the deck as they prepared for entry to the landing platform.

A low row of wooden buildings stood where settlers had burnt the brush from the hillside, and yellow clay sprouted scaffolding around skeletal frames of new buildings with men working from precarious planks. The echoing smack of a distant hammer wafted over to where we held onto the ship rail and watched as the Captain now supervised the piloting of the Clara in toward the dock.

Several ships sat anchored in the river at intervals as we slid into position. A small dinghy rowed across to one, and a man waved out heartily to us, to which our whole number waved back.

In front of the bow, the wharf posts and timbers reared up out of the tidal swath, encrusted with weed and barnacles. The dock lay parallel to the shore, which was piled up with boulders and rocks propping up the edge of a roadway.

Many people seemed to be wandering back and forth carrying, fetching, and doing the tasks appointed to them as I watched.

"I thought it might be bigger, Edward." I scanned the fringe of muddy water meeting the grass verge of the town edge a little way from the wharf and working its way along the river inland. "Where are our lodgings? I cannot see any building that looks like it is an establishment of that sort." I frowned a little because I had envisioned a township at the least like Brighton or Cornwell.

"The port has been here barely two years hence, and has only this year been named a municipality at all, madam. Still, there are very decent lodgings. I have been fully assured it will be quite homely for us. I booked them with utter confidence that the town's folk are seeking new settlers and are quite ready for them with most reasonable conditions. Mr. Broughton wrote me of a very agreeable place, so I am sure you will be comfortable."

This news made me smile again as I watched the crew positioning the ship in such a way as to ensure the towropes found their way into the waiting arms of the barge crew that had come from the port side and were now stretching a line toward the wharf to haul the Clara in safely.

All sail was wrestled into its folds and lashed to the yards by sailors seemingly walking on air, as they stood in the rigging of the two masts solidly pointing toward heaven.

The crack of the master's voice interrupted a gull screeching at the stern and the calls of dock labor loading bales and pallets of some kind onto two carts stationed at the wharf end, filled the air with activity and excitement.

I watched as the busy scene counted down to the moment we would disembark.

Edward, close at my side, made me feel that things would be bound to work out all right for us, and I pushed aside a nagging sense of foreboding that had been carried with me all the way from England.

"Edward, where is our parcel of land from here? Can we see it from this vantage, or is it very far away from the town?"

"Can you see over there?" He stretched a woolen suited arm past my face so that for a second, I could smell the earthy fabric as it passed by.

"Along those mountains to the south there. It is where you can see smoke over the flat land, past the mangrove swamp. Do you see? It is between the river and up almost to the valley where the Black Mountains are. You can't actually see it from here, but it is mostly flat and we have a good stream and plenty of wood that we will clear. The soil is red and fertile, and the cane will grow very well—as well as in South America. He turned, to look down on my face that was beaming and for a moment his gaze paused on me and he smiled, and then he turned back to the wide vista and went on in a serious tone.

"As soon as we have disembarked and found our lodgings and so on, I'll set out to find the boundary markers… I'll have very many things to deal with, Margaret. I trust you will forgive me if I leave you to your own affairs."

His smile seemed to fade a little, and I noticed it.

"Yes," I said, "We shall find the next few months very busy indeed, but it shall all be worthwhile, won't it dearest?" Edward did not speak but stared into the distance. "I suppose I shall have to learn all manner of things so I can be helpful. I am sure I shall be fit for it so do not think to coddle me…" He didn't see fit to answer me so I went on further, prompting him for some reassurance to his sudden silence.

"…It is no matter that it is quite a way from the town… together we shall still do well indeed, shan't we?"

"Well, of course!" he replied sharply.

Smiling a little shakily at his retort, I looked up into his face with its wide, dark moustache sitting atop those full lips I so loved and his head silhouetted against the blue-sky background. I pulled his arm in tight but he did not move to respond to me. Instead, he looked away and held onto the rail. His knuckled whitened as he continued to stare, long and hard, at the distant mountains spreading south of the land that he had selected, marked, and registered a year and a half before.

Suddenly, it became clear to me why he had fallen into this strange mood with our arrival imminent at last.

This day had been a long time coming for him. I remembered him telling me how he had first fulfilled his citizenship and entitlement to take up the right to apply for an allotment selection. It had taken three years of bitter labor in the south at Rock Hampton town. He had worked with blood and sweat, planting and cropping the tall shafts of cane for his employers who were more fortunate than himself and who had taken up the cheap land and secured its tenure without ever once touching the handles of a plow or machete blade themselves.

I guessed, by his strange silence, that he was no doubt remembering those times. I wondered if he was thinking of his child bride Sarah, an Irish girl who had lasted little more than a year in the shanty home on his employer's property. She had succumbed to fever along with many others, and had been buried in the cemetery that grew as fast as the colonizing of those new settlements.

Then, barely a year later, he had married again. He had been working as a leading hand on a cane field in Townsville, further north, sweating alongside the Chinese immigrants, to gain his chance at ownership of a farm of his own.

This time, he married the daughter of a mining engineer. Amanda was older than he by a year and a half, and full of the wild life that came with the territory—so he had told me with an unguarded grin. He had described her as one "that could dance a gig and sing until the dawn birds rivaled her for attention and yet, still lose out to her!"

He had not needed to tell me that he had loved her and nearly died of grief himself when, on the birth of their first child, she had fallen ill with infection and died within three days. Then, sadly, the son he had named Edward died as well, at just thirty-one days old, in the arms of an Italian "mama" who lived in the camp and had cared for him after his mother's death.

In despair from the death of his second wife and his son, he traveled even further north and signed on to a beche-de-mer fishing boat that was sailing to Cook Town.

For six months, he drowned his sorrow in the daily sun and salt of the fisherman's life. He had told me how the catch of sea cucumber was dried in huge piles and smoked in tin sheds on the outer islands of the reef. They would go ashore and collect red mangrove wood, then smoke the sea cucumber over fires fueled, stoked and left for days to smolder. He had described how the smoke haze would fill the inlets of the islands with a heady perfume and numbing smog. It choked the camp for weeks at a time, stinging their eyes and shrouding everything in a still silence. I was sure he had hidden his heart within it and perhaps it still wandered like a ghost on those tiny coral islands, far from civilization, and even me.

When the catch was prepared and ready, they brought it in to Cook Town, to this very port, for sale to the large Chinese contingency here. Those resourceful Chinese businessmen shipped it back to Hong Kong and other Chinese cities, where it was sold as a delicacy, and so built their fortunes too, from the spoils of this new land.

Edward's said his days had drifted by until he came ashore one day and heard of new "selections" of land being made in the district. He hired a Chinese laborer and, ignoring his meager and dwindling resources, marked out one hundred and twenty acres, and registered his selection at the Cook Town courthouse on 27 May 1874. He determined yet again, to follow his dream of being a farmer on his own land.

It seemed luck was not with him. While celebrating at the West Coast Hotel, he had been drawn into an argument with a cattleman. By all accounts, they did not intend to remove their herd that had been roaming freely in those hills on Edwards land.

Edward was beaten severely, almost to his death, and would have met that fate had not a party of cedar loggers been in the town for supplies that evening and had gathered him up off the street.

At the new hospital building behind the makeshift town, the Sisters of Mercy cared for him and nursed him back to health, though they could do nothing for his pride, nor his broken heart.

To add insult to injury, and much to his indignation, the police ranger and his men, neither investigated nor charged anyone for the crime.

On his recovery, by his own admission, he was a broken man. He could barely think of anything more than getting his passage back to England, to safety, and the sympathy of his aunt, where he might try to remember happier times and forget the trials of this Great Southern Land.

Within three months he found his way home to England and was back in the gray and cold of London. Burying the loss of his wives and child in the calm malaise of his Aunt Amelia's home for some thirteen months more, he tried to escape his poor luck and the distant memories of that lush and violent land that haunted him.

His aunt though, whom I well liked, considered it her personal duty to find him yet another wife as quickly as she could, for fear his grief would be inconsolable and so she paraded many prospects before him, hoping he might choose one.

Strangely, for all her efforts, none suited him until, by some accident of fate, he happened to meet me. He had quietly come in to my employer's shop to collect a new hat for his aunt on that cold and blustery day in November and without a word, looked across at me and our eyes met.

Edward said he was quite taken with me almost from the start, though I can barely think why. I was certainly no great catch with naught but my youth and manner as my dowry. Nevertheless, our romance had blossomed quite naturally, and within six weeks he told me his tale and of the acreage he was allotted in the great continent of Australia. He had said I gave him a certain confidence and if I would but agree, he intended to return to the new settlement of Cook Town after all but as man and wife. As the excitement and acceptance in my green eyes ignited his silent hope of fortune and family, our future was set.

He could have told me it was deepest Africa or some such other disagreeable spot, for I was mesmerized by his handsome features and charming disposition. With my young heart hungry for freedom from the drudgery of life as a milliner's assistant, and not finding his plans unappealing,

I had gathered my courage and accepted his offer of marriage without a moment's thought for what would become of us.

Our union was much to everyone's delight and I daresay, relief. Since I am a friendly and healthy girl, his aunt felt sure I would "cure him" and for a time, that is how it seemed.

I remember dear Aunt Amelia cried profusely at our wedding and repeatedly declared to any who would listen, that "God's Love is indeed displayed in this very union, and who could want for better... than a marriage made in heaven!" Her romantic nature and joy at Edward's happy state made it no burden to bestow on her nephew a generous gift of some five hundred pounds. She told me plainly that it was her deepest desire that he follow his heart and return to his land to settle the matter in triumph and raise a sweet brood of Australian children that she might well come to visit, since the warm climate was bound to help her joints.

So with money enough to fund the venture, Edward and I, his new bride, had set off for Australia to forge the future he felt sure was his and had been denied for some five years by his misfortunes.

Though he had always been kind to me, I oftentimes wondered if I had truly gained entry to his heart. I despaired that he would ever forget his sweet Sarah and much-loved Amanda and child. For that reason, I sensed he didn't allow himself the closeness I should have desired and though I knew something of his past, I realized that our speedy marriage meant I barely knew him at all.

I did my best to console myself with the notion that he would forget the poor beginning he had with the two before me when we began to build our future together and my light spirit invaded his heart at last and all became well.

Now, as he held the rail and stared into the distance, I turned my mind away from what he might be thinking for fear that tears should show and would spoil this first moment in my new homeland.

I looked on the bright colors of the Cook Town scene, so different from the brown and gray of distant London and as I silently gathered it all in so that I might never forget it. As I stared at the scene before me, I noticed that he suddenly seemed to wake and was aware of me again. He looked down at my small arm looped on his and he took a deep breath in.

"My dear, I cannot say… how a man might feel on his return…" He whispered. Seeing his eyes warm as he looked down at me, I replied with a certain pleading for things unsaid.

"Edward… please don't leave me in the town too long…" My eyes fixed on his as though I might cross the divide between us but his expression changed in an instant and he broke from me and looked past me over the water. "…I mean, sir that I so want to see the land that is to be ours as soon as is possible and I cannot bear to think that we shall be apart." I shifted my free hand and placed it on his as gently as a feather. "Shall we find some horses in the town for hire and go there straight away together?" My tender voice seemed to do naught to change him but he looked down at my small white hand and replied stiffly.

"The land out there is very wild madam… but if that is your wish, I will see to it as soon as expedient. Meantime…" he wrested his hand from under mine and raised his arm and laid it around my shoulders less lovingly than I should have desired. "I think you should ready our personal luggage for the porters to take ashore. I doubt we will take more than twenty minutes to disembark—they are already setting the gangplanks down."

"Oh, so right!" I quickly returned to my own formality, "I would have quite forgotten my shawl in all this excitement!" I bid him my leave and went below to make sure nothing else was left behind. Shortly after I gathered my shawl that I had left folded on the bed, a porter carrying a last bag found me as I opened up our cabin door. "Oh ma'am, best you be hurrying now, they is all going ashore any minute. You don't want to be left on this here boat alone, we might sail off home and you not found till we be round the horn!" He winked mischievously, "Mind, you be a pretty stowaway no one would be pleased to put ashore." I smiled politely and he escorted me aloft but when I arrived on deck behind him, Edward was nowhere to be seen. The first mate spied me looking about and came over to help me down the gangway. As I disembarked the Clara, I had a strange feeling come over me, as though I already knew my husband was not going to be the man I had hoped for, that long, long time ago, in England.

I stepped ashore on my own and as my foot landed upon the dock, I realized there was nothing I could now do accept steel my heart for whatever may yet come.

Most of the cargo was craned ashore and left on the wharf within the hour. The mounting pile of all the passengers' belongings, along with various other items on the manifest, seemed to grow faster than the dockhands could load it on carts and remove it.

I found Edward already on the dock and quickly came up to him in the midst of the melee of activity. Several ladies' from the town were waiting there for unknown passengers. They had raised pretty Chinese painted parasols and others wore white hats to shade their pink faces that shone with a light bloom of perspiration. We looked dark and hot in our London garb among the summer colors of their attire and I dabbed my handkerchief upon my face to ward off the wetness that burst from my skin.

I could see Betsy was bustling and fussing as usual, gathering up the children, who kept drifting away like naughty kittens. Mr. Crompton saw us and whispered in her ear as he nodded in our direction and she grabbed a child in each hand and they came through the crowd to give Edward and me a fond good-bye. She embraced me tightly with her damp arms. Moist tendrils of hair had fallen from her bonnet and her face was as bright as a polished apple. She promised to see us very soon, perhaps in church, if she should survive a week or more of this "infernal humidity!"

Mr. Crompton shook Edward's hand vigorously, tipping his hat and warmly wishing him well with our venture. He rounded off his pleasantries with "Well, farewell, old chap! Best be off, the adventure awaits!" Betsy frowned but I could see her eyes were alight with the excitement her husband's words had inspired and for a moment, I felt it fill me also.

Finally, the Cromptons bundled themselves onto a large cart that was waiting and drove off.

Edward ushered me off to the side, and from my vantage point up against the weatherboards, in the shade of the storehouse, I watched the activity of the dockhands. Some of them were dark skinned and speaking to each other in a muddled sort of English that made little sense to me. Their white-striped trousers and caps looked oddly fitted, and I could see the flash of white teeth occasionally as they spoke. Dark brows shaded their coffee-colored eyes and I was fascinated to see them working so hard to clear the load while all others seemed to ignore them.

I moved out from the wall to peer past it toward the awaiting township. I could see the white façade of the closest buildings peeping from the roadway that sailed away from us. Red tin roofs contrasted so unnaturally with the wild and beautiful scenery behind them. The sight of their gaiety seemed to push aside the lush green background, announcing there should be no holding back our progress now we were here and soon many more would be added to their number.

A sensation quite akin to joy rose in my whole being, as I realized this new country would be my new beginning and the future was ours for the taking. All around me, the warm and heady landscape, with its wild scents and strange sounds, buffeted me with delight so that I said quite loudly, "I shall like it here very much... yes, I am sure I shall, very much indeed!" without realizing I had spoken. Amidst the activity, the land seemed to flaunt the promise of new freedoms in whatever direction one might look and it seemed to literally throb with Mr. Crompton's declaration of adventure. Anything seemed possible here and my heart wanted to burst with it like a budding rose at the first hint of spring.

"Madam, take a care, will you stand out of the sun!" Edward's sharp voice broke in on my happy disposition. "Please Margaret, stand aside in the shade. I must leave you for a moment to arrange transport for us."

"Please Edward, I do so want to see..."

"Madam, there will be time enough, but for now I must insist. The sun is very fierce Margaret. You could crack an egg and it would cook before you had even poured it out! So what chance have you under that little hat?"

I watched him as he strode away and I admit, I had need to dab my forehead under my bonnet to stop a drip from skiing down the slope of my cheek.

In no time, Edward had arranged transport for us for the short ride into the township, where we would lodge at a two-story boarding house and hotel erected just a year before.

It was already late afternoon when we climbed onto a wooden cart that was a little worse for wear, but serviceable, and we set off toward our lodgings down the dry clay-and-sand covered roadway which faded into mown grass verges on either side.

Cook Town was a haphazard array of wooden buildings barely distancing itself from its frontier beginnings. A stretch of land, cleared by burning and cutting, spread out behind the road from the dock and was punctuated at intervals by several dirt tracks going up a slight hill to disappear into a fringe of jungle on the far side of the peninsula. Charred stumps were scattered randomly across an open area behind the main street with only an occasional spared sapling being left behind from the clearing. These twigs waved pathetically in the onshore breeze and made the open area look more ravaged by their sad survival.

The empty space behind the first buildings announced that the townsfolk believed the town would certainly grow. However, for now, most of the inhabitants lived in less-than-permanent accommodations and came and went continually.

Occasionally, the air carried wafting breezes loaded with the smell of damp and fetid marshes somewhere beyond sight—or else, conversely, the light fragrance of frangipani trees that had been planted somewhere in the makeshift gardens of the townspeople who had begun to live here.

There were already twenty restaurants, thirty-two stores, six butchers, five bakers, and three tinsmiths, as well as chemists, fancy goods stores, watchmakers, boot makers, boat builders, and saddlers. Most notably, sixty-five publicans and The Cook Town Newspaper rounded off the assembly.

The township with its makeshift, tinder-dry buildings stretched out along the low peninsula headed by its rock that had missed the snake. The buildings had been added one after another in single file, all the way down to the first big bend in the river boundary, hidden just behind a line of trees that stretched off to meet the wild inland vegetation.

Behind this, shacks and tents housed secondary businesses and living quarters. A myriad of smoke tendrils floated off with the breeze across the slope from open fires to tell all that life was well in hand.

That year, a school, customs house, and several churches had been added, and the notion was sealed that Cook Town was indeed an established outpost. On 5 April 1876 it had been declared a municipality, with a population of 2,200 townspeople, though not so many showed themselves in the fierce tropical sun as we sat atop the rocking cart heading towards our destination.

We would later learn that outside the town, over 9,000 miners came and went from the Palmer Goldfield up beyond the range and also swelled the town, though not with such folk as a town might wish to have. The mine was opened just six months before when alluvial gold was found and the rush had begun.

That feverish activity accounted for much of the fast growth Edward now noticed since his last sight of it. The town now lived and had her being in the wake of the discovery, drawing all manner of prospectors, Chinese immigrants, and anyone set on seeking their fortune, including those like us, looking for farmland and a firm foothold in the far northern state.

We rounded the bumpy bend made by the ruts of successive rains to find ourselves in the center roadway of the town and at last I could see the gateway to my new future.

As we passed the small buildings, a bank, a station house, and general store, I could peer between them to grassy yards, clotheslines, and life going on behind. I saw, a gray-frocked woman bent over a basket of clothes, and two children sitting on a box playing with a can attached to a long string and a stick.

Swinging round on the cart seat, I saw the Clara distantly behind us. Now unloaded, she had been hauled out into the deep outer channel far off in the distance. The brigantine sat peacefully along with a few other ships already anchored there, their masts empty of sail, waiting for their next departures in sync with the tides.

I barely heard Edward speak to our driver, so utterly entranced was I, by everything I saw but he turned to me and said reassuringly, "The driver has assured me we will like our lodgings, my dear. I think they are just up ahead if I can see right." Edward had leaned out of the open frame of the cart and strained to see around the old man seated in front of us.

At that moment, a horse and rider trotted past us quite closely. A man dressed in a blue cotton plaid shirt, and his head adorned with a faded gray hat pulled low on his forehead, rode a large red gelding. He nodded to us politely as he raised a gnarled and tanned finger to his head and called out "G'dday mate".

I nodded back politely, and Edward waved casually in reply.

I could hear the slush of the horse's hooves on the street's coral sand and clay paving and hear the swish of its tail-flicking insects away as it passed.

Suddenly, a fly as large as a fingernail, buzzed drunkenly into the wake of the moving cart and flew into my face.

I swatted it away desperately with my gloved hand but it turned lazily in the air and returned as if interested in this new immigrant so seemingly keen to attract his attention.

"Edward! My goodness! This huge fly… won't leave me alone!"

He laughed loudly and batted it away for me.

"It's a March fly, my dear. They are slow and stupid in the heat you see. But I warn you, if they land on you they might give you a nasty bite." He finally corralled the insect and squashed it with his boot.

"There are just a few new things you'll need to be mindful about here." He said rather matter of factly.

"I suppose you mean snakes and the like… and now you say even the flies bite! For heaven's sake, shall I survive?" I replied a little tersely and I confess, the nasty fly had now alerted me to the looming dangers hidden ominously amidst the beauty around us.

"I 'spect you will be perfectly safe my dear, as long as you take a care with your person and do naught to put yourself in harm's way. Anyway, there are only a few really dangerous snakes…"

"My Lord!" I said quite taken aback by the thought.

"Madam, this isn't England you know but don't worry, you will most likely never see one, since they're far more afraid of you than you should be of them."

The driver interrupted Edward's education and said. "Here we are, my lady, sir, the Cook Town Regent Hotel, at your service." He leaned around and smiled broadly before I could comment on my feelings about 'the few really dangerous snakes' Edward had failed to mention in England. I looked up and followed the sight of the old man's outstretched arm as he announced what was plainly obvious by the large sign above the door.

Edward immediately jumped from the cart as the driver looped the reins of the horse on the cart brake. My husband dropped over the side to the ground without the usual decorum I had seen from him in London, lifted me down, and then turned and began unloading our baggage.

"You have your crates coming on later, sir?" The driver's rusty voice asked with friendly curiosity.

"Yes, thank you, we have them stored at the ship's cargo warehouse for now. I'll get them sent on once we have got everything ready." Edward ushered me to the steps of the building and turned back to the old driver, who continued his questioning.

"You going to settle then, sir?"

"Yes indeed, we are going to farm the land inland, south of here, with cane."

"Good luck, sir! That will be a great boon to you and your family. It might grow very well in them parts—soil's good 'nough for it, to be sure. If you can clear the land of the scrub and the trees and get the dirt ploughed up, you'll have a very fine farm." He smiled a toothy smile, framed in a gray-stubble face that showed the wear of the Queensland sun. "Shall I take these bags up for you and your lady, sir?"

"Yes, thank you." Edward turned into the street and looked up the length of it. "I must say the place has grown immeasurably since I was here."

"Well, that would be right, sir, it's the gold you know, up in the Palmer fields. The place has taken off like a wild boar under roasting orders. But I've heard tell of a new discovery of gold further south."

"I beg your pardon, sir... you say a new discovery?"

"That's right. I heard a rumor: gold been found down at Thorn Borough. Some government 'fficial is going to survey it. 'Spect there will be a new rush in no time."

"Did you hear that, Margaret? They have discovered gold!" He swung back to me and his face seemed to become more animated than I had ever seen before.

"Well gold is a good thing for some, Edward, but for others it is a disease," I chided him, frowning, as I did not like the idea of such sordid pursuits.

"Disease or not, Margaret, gold can be the making of a man. Gold can turn his luck around in a short shake of a lamb's tail," he retorted as he thrust his hands through the handles of two cases and marched up the steps and towards the wooden doorway of the hotel.

At the top, on the landing, a white-frocked woman appeared, wide-smiled and apron-bound, she rushed forward to greet us.

"So at last we see you," the woman cried. "We been waiting ever so long, I can tell ya. Welcome, welcome. Me name's Mrs. Carmichael but I be pleased if you call me Martha, We don't stand on our dignity here. 'Tis enough to be plain good folk." She smiled broadly. "I be the proprietress of this grand hotel... and some would say a slave to 'er too!" She grasped my hand and shook it soundly, then turned with a frown to the old driver and indicated that he should take the bags from Edward before bidding us come inside.

It was dark and cooler in the whitewashed building, which was clearly quite new and showed no damp shrinkage or warping in its planks. Even though it was a little more bearable out of the sun, our thick English clothing seemed even heavier in the humidity of the interior and I suddenly felt rather overwhelmed as I stood in the stillness of the lobby, waiting for her and Edward to conclude their dealings.

I blew a long breath out as though trying to shed that loathsome heat from my body and stepped toward the counter and grasped it by the corner to steady myself.

The woman called Martha smiled toward me, seemingly quite at ease in the heat and interrogated us enthusiastically for details of England, the journey, and any news of Her Majesty, Queen Victoria, still in her reign since 1837, some thirty-nine years. At home, all expected her to vacate her post any day and live as "Heaven's pauper," but as yet, she held on firmly and Martha seemed fascinated by all such news of "jolly old England," a place she had never seen but obviously still held a fond affection and attachment to.

Martha finished entering us in her ledger and took Edward's crisp pound note, turning it over several times. With a slap for good measure, she closed the book with a thump, and gathering up a key and a pitcher of water, she hurried ahead of us to ascend the stairs.

"Likely you'll be wanting a bath, eh?" I listened as Martha's Australian accent revealed her birth in the wild new world of what used to be called Van Diemen's Land by the first Dutch explorer in these southern waters. It had long since forged an identity all its own and could not now be mistaken as anything but Australia just like the woman who led us.

"It won't want to be a hot one, that's for sure." she chuckled. "The day's been a real scorcher, even for up here. You could fry an egg on me roof I'd bet!"

I looked at Edward at the mention of the egg and said, "Oh madam, the sound of a cool bath is music to my ears," I spoke for the first time with my equally heavy London accent and the thought of being free of my clothes brought back the memory of those cool, and watching, natives I had seen in Darwin.

Martha turned on the stair and said, "Oh, you sound so fancy, my lady. That lovely way you 'poms,' as we call ya here, say this 'n' that! That talk's not too often heard 'round here because fancy folk like it better in the south, where it is a bit more kind to the washer woman and them of a fair complexion." She winked before turning back, hurrying up the plain staircase with the ease of an alley cat.

"What is the meaning of 'poms' Miss Martha?" I asked with curiosity, struggling to haul myself up behind her.

"You is 'prisoners of mother England' so they say. But I say, if you made it safe an' still liv'n this far, you be as close to free down 'ere as a pom can be!" She giggled to herself as she clumped up the last few steps and onto the landing.

As we hauled ourselves up, I spied the final step was scratched and worn from the gravel that would have been caught in many a boot sole that scraped over it, and the heavy knob at the head of the balustrade was round and smooth from oily hands that had made their last grasp at the top.

"Now, your room is down here, and we are just a koo-ee away should you need something." She ushered us to a slightly ill-fitting door and swung it open for us as the board outside it creaked loudly, as though it wanted to add its own koo-ee to the conversation.

"Clean chamber pot under the bed. Nice bed, mind, t'was brought up from Melbourne on a beche-de-mer ship last year in the dry season, so it's as soft and clean as they come." She sounded very certain of that.

"Outside privy... down the stairs and out the back door past the linen closet. Your wash basin is down the hall that way ..." She pointed with a brown hand and wrist poking from a white blouse that concealed the rest of her more pale skin that had stayed hidden from that ever present sun.

"Old Henry, he's my man for odds and sods, and he lives in the shed out the back if you need something collected or fixed. He'll bring up the rest of your luggage..." she turned and shot a sharp look toward Edward, "...and I 'spect you will pass him something for his trouble, sir?"

"Thank you for your help and hospitality, I shall be happy to oblige the man." He replied and nodded back, and her smile returned.

"I serve a meal in the dining room downstairs at six sharp. Tonight is buffalo and sweet potatoes and a mango cake with the best homemade cream cheese." She paused again as if to ram home the point that she ran a "good" establishment.

"We serve a good clean beer, sir, and English tea for the lady, not that local rubbish them silly drongos is tryin' to grow and pass off as 'good' compared to the real stuff." She shook her head before continuing. "Tastes to me like black sawdust…" She cocked her head on its side and said firmly, "No, you get nothing but the best and is all for two shillings."

Edward smiled. She seemed every bit the businesswoman.

"Oh that does sounds marvelous, Miss Martha, we have missed good cooking on our voyage." I interjected a little breathlessly; "Though I am sure our ship's cook tried his best…" My words somewhat faded off as the heat from the board-lined tin roof above me was beginning to make me feel a bit odd indeed.

Martha laughed loudly and replied, "Well, that would be right, you might be lucky to get any kind of meal worth eating at sea, as I've heard. 'Tis a wonder you survived to tell!" She patted my forearm affectionately. "And now you are here, best we have a spot of tea one day together and I'll tell you a few of the things you need be a bit mindful of here too, so you don't end in a heap in the infirmary as like many do from stepping where they ought not or from eating some poorly made fare. Best I give you some good advice and you stick to it 'till you gets to grips with things."

"Thank you so much. I'll be so grateful for all you can tell me. I have already met a very unpleasant and bothersome fly," I added wistfully as my breath seemed to fail me.

Martha burst into laughter, and even Edward smiled broadly. "Them March flies be big enough to roast and make a meal of, if they don't make a meal of you first!" She stepped forward and swung her arm in a wide arc.

"But in here you, you see we spared no expense… no expense, I say, to see our guests are right comfortable." She nodded as though agreeing with herself and walked over to the small window that had panes showing their imperfections in the sunlight, and opened it. "And see here, we got a good strong screen on ya window so none of them big flies or mosquitos can get in and make a mess of your lovely white skin."

I looked about me at the hot room. It was small but seemed enormous after our accommodations on the Clara. A faded red silk scarf was hanging above the bed headboard. It stretched from the side table on the far side of the bed and looked Chinese, with a gold dragon embroidered over the center. The moistness of the air made it hang somewhat limply on the frame and the room's only other decoration was a tiny, framed picture: a lithograph of London's Whitechapel that somehow looked entirely out of place.

The bed Martha was so proud of seemed to me a little knocked about. It had chips revealing the white undercoat under the black paint of the ironwork, and its mattress sagged a little. Otherwise, it was clean as Martha had said, and the room smelled fresh even though it too, was permeated with the steaming heat and the ever-present smell of the mangrove mud flats spread out around the river.

Toward the ceiling, a wide canvas air mover hung lifelessly with its rope looped over a hook, dangling down beside the bed ready for use. The sight of it made me wish someone had already got it swinging to relieve us with even a small breeze.

The oval mirror on the wardrobe caught our image albeit with a little distortion. I noticed how shiny my face was with perspiration. My lips had gone almost white, and my eyes looked gray instead of green and bright as they usually were. As I walked over and opened the wardrobe door to see what space there was, a slight smell of camphor greeted me. For a moment, I felt a shadow of fear sweep over me as I looked into the darkness though I know not why. The skin on my arms prickled under their woolen sleeves and I felt a trickle of perspiration crawl uncomfortably down the crease in my back. The dark opening of the wardrobe suddenly began to spin.

"Oh dear..." I turned to face Edward and Martha, who were watching me intently.

The room began to fade and the sounds of life seemed to fade with it. A loud buzzing filled my ears and I felt alone in some surreal world all of my own.

Moments later, everything went black and I must have collapsed like a rag doll to the hard floor.

I don't know what time went by but it seemed like only moments later, the world began to steam back to me like a railway engine arriving at Paddington Station. The buzzing sound returned and grew louder and louder and then it began to recede and I could hear Edward's voice over the pounding in my ears.

"Oh Edward... I can hardly breathe..." The faint at last seemed to dissipate, and I returned to normality as his face appeared in front of mine.

"Margaret, my dear..." Edward was holding me up slightly from the floor with his arm looped around my shoulders and worry on his face.

Martha had dropped to the floor beside me and was patting my hand before she pressed her cheeks with both her hands exclaiming, "Oh dear, oh dear... what a thing to happen in your first hour!"

Edward pulled me forward and cradled me to his chest as Martha jumped up and rushed to the door. "Water... yes, water is what you need missy!" We could hear her frantically clattering about in the washroom at the end of the hall as she collected a cloth and a pitcher all the while calling loudly for Liz Beth, the housemaid.

Edward held me off the floor, at a loss as to what to do and his face clouded over with sincere concern that made me feel quite awash with guilt at troubling him so.

"I'm all right... I'm all right, Edward... No doubt I fainted because of this heat..." I began to breathe again and sucked in the air as though I needed it as much as the cool water Martha had brought in and placed on the side table at that very moment.

"Oh my dear girl... we need to cool you off a bit, right quick. Sir! Get her on to the bed!

Edward scooped me up and rested me on his knees, then caught me into his arms. He carried me to the bed as though I were a bundle of flowers and carefully laid me on the quilt, as though he feared my petals might bruise at the slightest touch.

Grabbing the second pillow, he pulled me forward gently to prop me up, and then wiped my brow with the wet cloth Martha handed him.

I took the cloth from his hands and pressed it to my eyes and face, breathing through it so the cooler, damp air would fill my lungs.

"...Oh I do feel much better... I'm so sorry Edward... I don't know what came over me. Perhaps the camphor smell, was just a little too much."

"It's not a wonder you collapsed in a heap young lady, you're trussed up in this heavy clothing, which might be well for the clime of London—but here, missy, you have to shed most of your wardrobe or be cooked through to your bones like a slow roasted lamb at the Church fete at Christmas!"

Martha undid my shoelaces and relieved my hot feet from their prison. She gently pulled my stockings off to reveal the pale flesh of small tortured toes that had molded to the shape of their boots and were stuck together. She said, "Oh my, they are surely the feet of a fairy!" before she moved up to the head of the bed and adjusted my pillows, "How you feeling now, lovey? Are you a little bit better?"

Edward replied for me. "I think she is feeling much better, the color has come back into her cheeks."

Martha turned to him with affectionate scolding. "Off you go, man, find the sherry down in the parlor and hurry that Liz Beth along and I will get the young lady ready for the bath."

He obeyed almost instantly to my surprise. Martha's natural ownership of all things female was no doubt daunting, and he left without any delay, preferring to find Liz Beth and the sherry than tarry against her wishes.

"You had a bit much heat and excitement I'd say..." She said gently to me before taking a step toward the door and yelling with a shrill voice down through the building, "Liz Beth... Liz Beth! Mr. Edward is coming down to fetch you! And best you not muck about or I shall be cross, young darkie cross like the devil, you can be sure!" I could just hear Edward's heavy boots echoing down the wooden boards as he sped up with the sound of her voice harrying him away as well.

Turning back she walked to my side and patted my hand tenderly. She looked at me a little curiously and said matter-of-factly, "Couldn't be you are in the family way, lovey? I've seen many a girlie hit the deck when they get to breeding."

I looked up a little sheepishly. "No. I am sure it is not that. I think it is just this heat... I feel so flustered." My voice was wispy, still laboring to get the words out. "It was quite bearable while we were at sea..."

"Then it is a cooling off you need and, if I might say, you'll also need to get some light clothing to help you stand it. It's the start of the wet season and it gets intolerably 'muggy,' even for us who been here for a long while. It passes but. And I'm betting it will rain soon, maybe even tonight, and that will cool it down. In a few months, the rain will stop and the dry season will make you think you could not live anywhere else. Oh, it's lovely then..." She was smiling reassuringly and had leaned me forward and re-fluffed the pillow behind me yet again.

Edward suddenly appeared at the door followed by a small, dark girl.

"Come on then Liz Beth! You is as slow as a wet week! Get me a bath drawn for this dear lady... and where's the sherry? You didn't bring the sherry!"

The aboriginal girl seemed not to hear her. Instead, she stepped forward, her eyes fixed on me, as she held a porcelain jug filled with drinking water and a mug adorned with green fern leaves painted on the side. I took the mug and she filled it. I drank gingerly, a sip at a time, until the mug was empty.

"There lady, you be feeling better with water in ya." Her gentle voice whirred like a hummingbird in the still space between us.

My hands were shaking as I held the mug up to be re-filled. She linked with it carefully and the water poured in. I noticed the girl's small, dark-chocolate hands, smooth and shiny like oiled paper, as they wrapped around the white of the jug. I caught a glimpse of her tiny palms, soft and pink, lined with light brown wrinkles, and her thin forearms rising to hide under her pinafore. She was as tiny as a cocoa flower and entirely perfect.

When she had finished filling my mug, Liz Beth placed the jug down on the small side table and her hands came together in a matched pair to rest on her white apron while she waited.

I looked at her intently; as she was the very first aboriginal I had ever seen at close quarters.

Dressed in familiar European clothing, Liz Beth was nevertheless not disguised enough to separate her from those first natives I had seen on our brief arrival in Darwin. Her face was so different to European contours that I couldn't keep my eyes from studying her as I drank the water that tasted faintly of clay.

Her face was round and had high cheekbones. Her eyes were deep brown, almost black, with just a hint of whites on either side, fringed with black lashes, wet and clinging together as though made up for the theatre. Her brow, a heavy forward-protruding ridge, had only the smallest lines of eyebrows that slid off to either side. Her forehead was narrow and rimmed with tight fuzzy curls that looked oiled; they sparkled in the sunlight as she stood near the window. A broad nose and wide nostrils fluttered with excitement and concern for my plight and her lips rolled in a perfect wave toward the soft embankment of her chin.

"You be all right, missus." She shot a glance at Martha, whom she could see was looking at her with a dark scowl creasing her forehead in warning. She went on in a whisper, "Boss 'ill have you right primm'd up and shape shipped, no never mind." Her voice crooned with a somewhat nasal sound from her aboriginal accent mixed in every word. "I be pleased as punching you here miss, and you be good as gould, better even afore, time Miss Martha sorts you out!" she said lyrically.

As her lips moved, I could see her rows of perfect white teeth, pink gums clasping onto them, as they darted behind the full chocolate lips, smiling even when their owner did not mean them to.

"Thank you, oh thank you… I certainly needed this water. And I'm sure I shall be well in no time."

"We'll have to get you in the bath and that will really help." Martha spoke as she turned and hurried Liz Beth from the room, patting her affectionately on the full skirt of her behind. "Once you've had a nice cool soak then if you can manage, we'll get Old Henry to take us to the hill on the other side of the town, where there is always a cool breeze, and you can sit in the shade there and watch the sea. Then it will be time to come back in and I'll have a nice supper for you. And I'll bet you sixpence it will be raining tonight before the clock strikes nine and it be almost reasonable, even for you London folk!"

Martha placed a hand on Edward's shoulder, as she could see the worry in his face. "She will be fine sir, just you wait and see.... Dear me, I can see I'll have to chase that girl with a switch to pour the bath this very hour or it won't get filled till next week Liz Beth, where are you now, girl? I can't hear you moving yourself, best you not be scooting off to hide from work again!" She turned and swept from the room like a startled kangaroo, and the floorboard at the door again groaned to declare her exit.

"Are you feeling better, dear?" Edward almost gingerly stroked my arm. "I don't know what I would do if anything happened to you."

"Truly, Edward dearest, I am fine. I just got a little too hot and excited I suppose." I looked up calmly. "Everything shall be well, I am certain of it."

"Yes, at last, we are here." He leaned over and kissed my forehead, which was still moist. "Still, for the next few days I want you to rest and just get used to the heat and the new place your body has found itself in. Is that clear, my little hat girl? Rest!" He smiled a little shakily.

Martha arrived back again at the door. "The bath is almost ready, lovey. Come along, sir. Help your wife, and we shall get her cooled off good and proper."

Edward followed Martha with his gaze as she came to my side, and then he stood up to his full height over the bed. "Will you walk, my dear, or shall I carry you?" He asked as I looked up at him towering above me.

"I will walk. Will you just hold me—I don't want to fall on that floor again. I think I have a bruise right here..." I grimaced a little as I fingered the back of my head through my hair wrapped in its tight bun.

I swung my feet off the side of the bed and they landed softly on the smooth wooden boards. The wood was cooler than the air around us, and for a moment I sat there, catching my breath and holding off a little dizziness. Finally, I rose a little unsteadily and allowed Edward's arm to link around me. He held me at my waist, his other hand seeking out my left hand, and I walked carefully with him out of the room, down the stairs, and along the hall toward the bathroom at the back of the hotel.

Together, we negotiated the small door of the room, and Martha reached out to receive me.

"Right, now, off with you, sir! Liz Beth and I shall attend to her from here."

Liz Beth was holding a bucket filled with cloudy water, and poured it hastily into the enamel bathtub as Edward said his farewells and left.

Martha closed the door quietly behind him, and the three of us were alone in the room.

In typical fashion, Martha took control. She helped me from my bodice and skirts and folded them over the chair that sat in the corner.

Clothed only in chemise and drawers, I held onto Liz Beth's tiny hand with one of mine while Martha clutched my other; I stepped over the rim of the tub, and sank down into the water.

Though it was not cold, it was cool and I felt immediate relief. My cotton undergarments floated around my skin and I felt soothed in the milky water.

"I shall see to that sherry now." Martha smiled and her voice slightly echoed in the room. "It would not do you any harm to get some of that into you, I reckon." She chuckled and mumbled under her breath, "Wouldn't do me any harm neither, I can tell you."

She opened the door and closed it quietly behind her, leaving Liz Beth to mind me as I bathed.

I felt very small, lying in the bath. I gently swished the water over me and listened to Liz Beth as she shuffled around to the head of the tub to sit behind me.

"Been a big day for you, eh lady?" Liz Beth whispered as she unwound my tightly bound hair and let it fall over the edge of the bath. "Sit 'em up lady, I gonna wash yer hair…" Liz Beth's voice trailed off as she focused on the locks of my light brown hair in her fingers.

She separated the strands until it spread across my back. My hair was smooth and fine, yet warped and curled from the daily ritual of being tied in various tight hairstyles common in London. As it flowed through her small fingers, she said, "Yer hair is just like the dilly bag weave grass, all gouldy-like." Then added, "…not scratchy, but."

I leaned forward a little and Liz Beth filled a small jug and began to pour the water through my hair and around my neck.

"Now, feel better, eh lady?"

"Oh yes, thank you, that feels wonderful." I listened to the water trickling down through my white cotton chemise and into the water while Liz Beth mimicked several times, "Woon-ner-ful, woon-ner-ful, ..." trying to mimic my accent.

My drawers had become translucent in the water and I watched them ebb and flow around my knees. My white calves, so white as to rival the faded enamel, lay still in the bottom of the bath, my small feet reviving in the water, and I let out a long sigh.

Liz Beth's hand, holding the jug, appeared from behind me and soon its contents poured on my arms, neck, and chest.

I marveled at the perfection of her thin chocolate arms graced with her tiny hands as Liz Beth went about her business, dunking the jug and pouring it over me.

"You is gonna need ta get some sun on ya, that's for sure." Liz Beth's whispering voice broke into my thoughts. "You as white as a cockatoo... an' that sis white 'nough to even scare the moon away in night-time!" She giggled the sort of giggle that the young make when they perceive the humor of their own joke.

"Perhaps so," I smiled back. "Where I come from, 'getting the sun', is not so very convenient." I smiled and looked around into the innocent dark face. "But I suppose everything is going to be different for me here. Shall I ever get used to it?"

Liz Beth nodded and added a little raised eyebrow for effect, to let me know that she had understood how odd I must have been feeling.

She handed me the pouring jug and lifted herself from the floor. She swung round to my clothes laid on the chair a little distance away and curiously touched them. "You have nice dress, but we get cotton ones eh? An' I cut out the lining, eh, so it feels nice'n windy, 'cause I's don't really like cov'rin' up all's over like Miss Martha says we gots too." She smiled again as she looked back at me in the milky bath water. "My missus, she gets the China men to make her dresses, and mine too. She got one chinesy bloke who gives us fullas a good price, cause of my missus, you know that?" The white-toothed grin flashed under the dark eyes hidden beneath her aboriginal brow. "She be 'right proper' in this here town... that's what they all says. Yep, she don't do none of that 'perspirin' like them common fullas. Miss Martha says they got "no manners" an' get all scruffy an' all stinky just like a dead possum what been stuck in the piss barrel all week 'fore they collects it for the tannery!" She furtively glanced towards the door and whispered, "But you knows, me uncle Gurrabah an' me uvva peoples, they don't wear nuffink like me an' missus and all them uvva proper fullas round here. They cool long time an' never got's wet under them's arms! Noooo... they's not showin' up like them common buggers eh? Even though they gots no chinesy fullas ta make nuffink for 'em ...not never!" She frowned slightly, "I gots no idea why my missus say'd they still smell like a pole cat..."

Just then, the sound of shoes in the wooden hall echoed distantly. The steps came closer, and then the knob of the bathroom door rattled slightly and turned. Before it had time to release the door from its frame and reveal Martha again, Liz Beth quickly whispered, "...But I not 'lowed talking about them fullas, eh? They is walking like 'savages'... an' I ain't s'pose to 'member no savaging!" She shook her head. "You's a nice lady, you's not gonna say nuffink, eh? 'Member lady... I not s'pose to 'member no savaging..."

Martha pulled herself in and leaned back on the door to close it. She held out a tray with two small glasses, one of which, was already half empty, and a bottle of sherry with it's cork sitting beside it.

"Now this is what you need, my girl. Nothing much else I know, can cure the ailing of any woman, no matter how poor or fancy she be."

Martha immediately placed the tray on the empty chair. She picked up the bottle and filled the empty glass, then filled the other to the top.

"Well, this is certainly like being treated as a queen." I smiled as I sat up in the bath and took the small glass Martha offered me.

"Well, I dare say we rarely feel like queens out here, lovey, so if a little nip helps us feel like royalty for an hour or so, I say it be a good thing!"

She grinned, slugged back the drink, and let out a satisfied hiss of sherry-flavored air.

"Have you always lived here in Cook Town?" I asked as I sipped on my glass cautiously because I was not in the least, used to strong drink.

"I came up from Melbourne, did I, from the tenements where no queen would likely ever go. Even so, it was a shock and a half to end up here, I can tell ya. I was like you today, when I got here. All at sea!" Martha refilled her glass.

"I was a girl with no eye for nothin' but me husband Bill, who I'd say had no idea what a girl he had in me!" She paused for another hefty sip and refill before going on.

"Well, up we came, him seeking his fortune and me thinking I would make a nice shop for me self and sell wares to the gold miners' wives and daughters—you know, nice things."

She shook her head and a damp strand of hair fell forward. "When we got here, there was nothing here!" She threw up her free hand and the hand holding the glass of sherry correspondingly rose and fell as though rising over a wave. "Well, Bill soon headed out into the Palmer field and I got left to wonder what I was going to do. So I took me savings, the money me mum left me, and I got the Chinamen to build me the downstairs of this lodge so I could get on without him and have a decent roof over me head.

Oh, that first season was something! The rain fell and when it hit the iron roof you couldn't hear a man shouting inside. And I daresay if the powder house down there at the base of the grassy hill had blown up in the lightning, you wouldn't have heard that either!"

She pulled the chair forward and sat on the front edge as she told her story. "Then sure 'nough, no sooner had I got this thing under way than Bill gets blown up in an accident at the Palmer and I get word back, about a week later, that he had lost a leg." She paused and a little less dramatically said, "...and then went an' died of the gang green."

She hung her head between her shoulders. "Oh it was a terrible thing that day they brung the wagon down through the packers' track and it had been raining the whole way. There were four to be buried on that wagon. Someone said they should have been buried up there in the mountains, 'cept they all had family here in Cook Town. So they come down, them dead ones and two sick with malaria, one with madness from the alcohol and heat sickness." She paused. "The whole town was in an uproar...'cause the smell was so bad. Undertaker earned his money that day! We buried them in the cemetery down the end of Charlotte Street." She had faded off, drifting back to the day and the tears she must have cried. She swigged again at the sherry, which somewhat revived her mood, and she went on.

"So... I buried me ol' Bill in a nice plot looking out on the mangroves and set about making this hotel the best in the town. Some say I've got me wish!" She smiled broadly.

"This last year, I built on the top floor here with Bill's gold and got three extra rooms and the washroom at the end of the hall, you know, for decent folks' convenience. I had them line the roof with them boards so we are all comfy now, and it can rain good and proper and you can still hear yourself talking... long as you speak loud, mind you."

She smiled and patted me on my arm that I had rested on the edge of the bath.

Liz Beth rolled her eyes, no doubt having heard the story many times before. I could not help but take the opportunity to ask, "And how is it that you have Liz Beth?"

"Ah, Liz Beth is quite a tale. I rescued her from them white ghosts that call themselves 'Sisters of Mercy'. For what I could see them nuns were doing to poor Liz Beth, there was no mercy in it!"

I saw Liz Beth drop her head and quickly clasp her hands together.

"She was taken from her mama to be taught..."

Liz Beth interrupted. "To teach me 'decent' whitey ways and..."

"Shush, I'm telling your story Liz Beth... She was taken because her mama kept running back to the bush and the girl was set to grow up a wild animal. So the priest got a hold of her when she was maybe four years old and they put her in the school for orphans. Problem was..." Martha waggled a disapproving finger in Liz Beth's direction, "she was as wild as her mama, and kept being found out in the street or down at the river." Martha shook her head in remembered horror.

"'Twas a wonder them crocs didn't get her, a nice little morsel she would have been!" She frowned at Liz Beth, and the girl smiled mischievously, itching to say something but not quite willing to incur Martha's wrath.

"I was visiting a friend one day and I happened to mention that I was looking for some help in the house, and she put me onto the sisters, who had this child tied to a chair in the daytime and at night tied to her bunk by her feet. So when they said which girl did I want, and I said, 'that one!' Martha pointed straight at Liz Beth and grinned, "they were over the moon to give her to me, because she was a good deal of trouble for them. She frowned with sincere indignation and said sternly, "You know, she had enough welts on her back as to rival The Lord on the Cross!" She leaned forward and I could smell the sweet sherry on her lips. "Any road, she is quite safe now, tame as tame. Not like some of them out there..."

"Them not tame... no savaging 'llowed!" Liz Beth finally spoke up, very matter-of-factly.

"So she is from this area? Our Captain told us quite a tale..."

"Yes indeed, Liz Beth is from the very tribe that used to live right where Cook Town is now, the Guugu Yimithirr."

"That meaning, 'saltwater people'."

"Thank you, Liz Beth, I know that... You see they used to be in 'nations.' Each in his own all over, divided up you see, with a boundary. Each place in the nation has a different 'tribe' like Guugu Yimithirr, here, and down Port Douglas way, the Kuku Yalanji, And the next lot is the... I can't remember..."

"Djabuganjdji... an' after that Yidinji, then Mabaram, Djirbalngan, Wargamaygan!"

"All right, all right, Liz Beth!" The names of the tribal nations had rolled off her tongue so fast, I confess she sounded like a waterfall, but with a peg on her nose, as that strange nasal quality of speech the aboriginals have, came out from her.

Martha frowned sternly. "I'm sure she doesn't really need to know that tribal rubbish! Liz Beth, you know you is all Christian folk now. Well now…" she went on, "for each tribe, you have 'clans.' That is the family and hangers-on that has an area of the tribal lands to live off.

"Thing is, they are so stubborn that if they get run off their own bit of land, they can't go into another tribe's land or cross into another nation's territory, so they just cause trouble in their old land, and there's nothing to be done but let the church civilize them on some land they give for a mission."

"So are they safe to have around us now?"

"Oh, dear me, the lot 'round here are well sorted out, and the mounted police deal right fast with any troublemakers." She looked at Liz Beth, and the smile faded from her face. "The mission has done a good job, I should say. They aren't allowed to speak that gibberish language they used to, and they make them wear their clothes all the time—which is no mean feat, because they take them off at every turn, sometimes even in public, would you please, and no one wants to see that! 'Tis bad 'nough that they insist on wearing those bones in their noses and feathers and such stuck in their hair!"

Liz Beth shrugged her tiny shoulders, and I watched her as she fidgeted somewhat. I propped myself up a bit and swept my hands up to collect my hair and wring it out.

"Well, I see you are a good deal better, lovey, but you drink your sherry and Liz Beth and I will leave you to your peace." She grabbed Liz Beth by the hand and pushed her toward the door. "I think it will rain soon, a nice shower, like it do most afternoons or nights in the wet season." She rubbed her elbow to relieve some ache there. "I always feel it coming in me bones!"

"Boss's bones be talking!" Liz Beth grinned.

Martha picked up the tray and set off toward the door with Liz Beth in hot pursuit, one hand holding a piece of Martha's skirt as though she were a following elephant, holding onto the tail in front.

She broke off at the door and skipped back to me as Martha disappeared. Leaning down she whispered with cupped hands to my ear, "Missus' bones don't know nuffin'. Not just no 'shower' comin'. Big, big wind an' rain comin' a week more! Soon gonna have ta batten down me hatch an' tie down me head!" Then she added somewhat shyly, "My's people call it a mighty big Wirra Wirra an' they got no hatch and no nails too, so they just shoot inland outta the way of that bad ol' devil 'cause he gonna blow the whole town off this land!" Her expression dropped. "And I's hope he blow them nasty nuns away too… they got no place in dreamtime like us goodie peoples!"

I distantly heard Martha yell from somewhere up the hall, "Liz Beth!" The small girl, up and disappeared like a flash, leaving my ear hot from her hurried message.

As soon I was left alone listening to the muffled sounds of the hotel, I began to think of the brown-skinned natives Martha had spoken. They had been transformed like dancing dolls, taken away from their former dwellings in the savannah and the jungle to reappear as people like Liz Beth, in the employ of the invaders and perhaps a good deal better for it.

Settling in my mind that the area was indeed safe for us, my mind's eye skimmed the wide-open country robed in green set waiting for Edward and me to conquer. We would build fences and a home, roping her into passivity and in due course, our children would come and know this land as their only home.

Feeling much better, I roused myself from the tub and decided that after dinner I would write my first letters to send back to England, to Aunt Amelia and to Eliza and Sally at the milliner's.

As I stepped out of the bath, a drumming sound began to hum all around me, vibrating down from Martha's new, lined tin roof. It had started to rain, just as Martha had said. As I thought about it, I frowned slightly and wondered if Liz Beth's prediction of the big "Wirra Wirra" would also come true and we would find ourselves blown out to sea… sent back from whence we had come, having no claim but our own foreign laws to anchor us to the rocks of this great southern land and no right to even strike a fist at that old devil that only Liz Beth and her people understood or could hear his distant coming.

Chapter 3

MARTHA DID INDEED take it upon herself to see to our needs, and within a few days, arranged for a Chinese tailor named Mr. Wong to make new skirts and bodices for me and linen trousers and light shirts for Edward.

Everyone's clothing in the town was light in color or white. Apart from shoes and boots; all were dressed this way to avoid attracting the sun. It was as though we were images of reflecting angels moving about with the lush green landscape beyond us. The contrast against the dreariness of London and its preponderance of dark clothing was a delight to me, and I soon became familiar and at ease with my new home even though I most certainly felt the ever present heat even in our lighter clothing.

It was a busy little town.

The men tied handkerchiefs around their necks and rolled up their sleeves for almost any task. All had very tanned forearms and faces and many wore a soft hat, usually pulled low over their forehead, or a wide-brimmed Stetson to guard them from the brilliance of the Queensland sky.

The streets were always filled with cattle, horses, and carts laden with supplies, building materials, or trunks being carried about. The hotels were always filled with men cooling their thirst with brewed beer brought up from the south on merchant ships that regularly serviced the area.

Our little town was the main supply route for the goldfields so a continual throng of men and materials flowed through it, along with the beer.

Martha took it upon herself to show me around town, which was not so much a town as we think of it but a vast array of white canvas tents and makeshift sheds strewn about on the cleared land up behind the main roadway of Charlotte Street.

The sounds of dogs and horses and rogue cattle not tethered in any area, it seemed, greeted you if you ventured through the tracks that passed as streets, and there was always a friendly smile and someone waving out to say g'dday.

There was often the common sound of some Chinese worker being admonished by his employer, and the familiar smell of charcoal from their cooking fires somewhere in the vicinity.

Though most of the Chinese could speak little or no English, they were in good numbers and were hard working. They always seemed keen to take on almost any business and were not particularly troublesome, preferring to keep to their own kind and having a strict code of behavior that only they seemed to understand.

I thought they were very polite really, always nodding and bowing and smiling when you had occasion to meet one of them. Martha had no comment to make about them, so I took that to mean that she must have approved of their presence.

Gold miners were, of course, everywhere. They came into town in a never-ending stream, taking a break from the fields. They endured very hard living inland, so when they came to town, they came to sell their gold locally for a better price than the brokers at the goldfield shanty towns, then purchase a bath, some good food, and other comforts.

They came and went like endless copies of each other, dirty and thin, and one quickly became accustomed to their coarse language and the places they frequented.

There were those parts of the street where women sat smoking, quite without shame, on the porches above so-called boarding or public houses. Though they said little, their demeanor advertised their craft, and they were never seen in church.

The rough men often lounged about inside drinking, or they lolled about outside with their forearms hooked over the rail of the walkways, smoking raw tobacco and spitting frequently onto the grassy fringes of the street while they seemed mesmerized by the women's enchantments above. And the women seemed delighted to tease the wayward men below, no doubt hoping for some later engagement and reward of coin. It seemed to me to be an appalling state for men and women to sink to in a new world with so many opportunities. But such are people everywhere, London or my new homeland. As dear Mrs. Steadman would say, "Whatever is in us, goes with us."

Martha was a broad-minded person and claimed the local title of "Aussie battler" which was a description they had coined for themselves to embody an attitude of perseverance against any odds. And certainly, many knew well the hard conditions that surrounded them that, by the very trial, gave them title to their country. However, for all her quintessential character, she considered such behavior as far from decent and bad for the town so she would hurry us along and we always pass by quickly.

Still, whatever our opinions might be, they seemed negated by the large quantity of these bordellos, as well as a number of opium dens that had been established in full view on Charlotte Street and in the alleys behind it.

There was a constant flow of beche-de-mer fishing boats also coming and going, along with all manner of other craft, including steamers frequenting the port. They brought wares from the south, Brisbane or even New South Wales, and took away timber, pallets of smoked sea cucumber, or magnificent pearls and mother-of-pearl shell that were harvested all along the reef.

The wharf we had landed on was continually busy. I walked up to watch the activity on occasion, just to pass the time and marvel at the new batches of immigrants arriving. I knew the fine hats and black skirts dragging heavily at the women's waists would feel dreadful. They would gather their things and enter the town just as we had, but very soon after, they'd all be dressed in white cotton, propping up the trade of the Chinese tailors and seamstresses.

New guests arrived at the hotel and then left to their various adventures. This stirred Edward to much frustration, as he wanted to leave as soon as he could for our own property, but my uncertain acclimatization prevented him from leaving me.

A family arrived from Sydney—two children with them who always seemed to have more energy in the heat than should be normal. They ran everywhere in the hotel to the restrained admonishments of Martha.

Another couple stayed while the shop they were building became ready, as well as a Mr. Johnson, who was a watchmaker. He was very cordial and we struck up quite a friendship until he took his leave and went somewhere southeast to plant some new tree he had procured from India called 'Mango' with which, he was very enthusiastic.

The room beside ours had a very strange woman come to stay named Amelia O'Brien. She barely spoke, and when she did, it was with a voice so high and so squeaky that she might have been mistaken for a mouse that had transformed into a woman.

Liz Beth was adamant she was the reincarnation of a tree kangaroo whose spirit had somehow become lost and been born as this woman, who had no tribe or totem to cling to. It was lucky Liz Beth had not said this in Martha's hearing, for she would have caught the sharp side of her mistress's hand for the aboriginal superstition.

Even I couldn't fathom this woman's odd demeanor. She clasped her hands together wherever she went, and her hair was bound and oiled tightly on her head. We never saw her without her lips pursed together as though continually kissing the air. She maintained she had travelled from Plymouth to take up a position at the new school on Hadley Street. I was not sure what a woman such as she would teach, but Edward attempted to be cordial. However, she rebuffed his attempts resoundingly with her tight lips and her silence, so he gave up.

Another visitor was a young man, Jonathan Stanford, who had come from a good family, I would say, in Lancashire. He was tall and very handsome, and he had in mind to find land and graze cattle. He had such an eloquent way with his words, and his mind was so filled with enthusiastic dreams, that I fully believed he would somehow attain them. I oftentimes passed pleasant conversation with him as Edward champed at the bit to get on and get away to our land and seemed constantly busy with some errand or other to do with it.

In addition to the new visitors, aboriginals floated about all of us as though merely viewing the parade. Their stringent territorial laws prevented them from going anywhere beyond their own land, so despite what seemed to us colonials as vast distances of uninhabited wilderness to which they could move away to, they hovered around us and their now-unrecognizable old home.

I quickly became used to their strange looks and the muddled, nasal sounds of their language. The men were almost pitch black, very small, and they often had feathers tied in their fuzzy hair or bands of raffia adorned with shells or other decorations tied around their heads.

Many on the fringe of town remained almost naked, except for small plaited-raffia aprons or strips of waste material covering their private parts. A lady could do little but look away if they were seen in the open, and Martha tended to treat them like bothersome March flies.

Fortunately, the menfolk usually drove them away, and they were forced to live outside the town. They were quite fierce-looking to me, with ritual scars of manhood stretched across their upper arms, chest, or stomach. Sometimes they would paint themselves with mud of various colors, and I once saw one disappearing into the trees at the end of the last street, carrying a wallaby over his shoulder. He carried a long spear in one hand and an oval shield made of rainforest cedar hardwood that was painted with zigzags, swirls, dots, and stripes in the other.

In the main, most of the aboriginals stayed at the mission just outside town. They came in to get supplies, chaperoned by lay ministers, and were quiet and shy, seemingly very compliant. On those occasions, they wore clothes properly and spoke a kind of half-English that we called 'pigeon,' though I could not for the life of me work out what connection there was with pigeons. They were forbidden to speak their own tongue, nor follow any of their customs, and the children received a good slap if they lapsed.

There were those that were not so "tamed" but had separated from their wild contemporaries and from the mission. They wore cast-off clothing and made do with odd jobs, skulking about, searching for some opportunity. They had a great liking for whiskey and we were told never to give them any because their "poor savage nature" could not manage it and they would soon be lolling about so drunk they would fall asleep even in the ditches.

These aboriginals were a distrusted minority by both their own kind and ours. They clung to the ragged dog of civilization like a flea not desiring to jump clear to preserve itself.

"They are caught," Martha said, "between a rock and a 'mad' place."

The town's folk did their best to ignore them or sweep them away from their shop fronts whenever they could. But like the shadows cast in the Queensland sun at three o'clock, they returned to drink or sleep under the corners of our European world.

The only aboriginal I came to know well was Liz Beth. It was from her, that I soon realized that her people were not at all ignorant or dull, as some said, but rather they were endowed with a gentle cunning and an astute curiosity. They were, in the main, a generous and amenable people, moved to do whatever was asked of them, and they loved to laugh and to please.

Some, like Liz Beth, were enlisted as home help and lived with their white families as servants, washerwomen, or animal handlers. They were also forced into the rituals of Christian faith that we are so endeared to, but I believe they simply mimicked the people whom they followed and I was not sure at all, that they understood our Lord's offer of salvation nor the earning of such marvels.

It seemed to me that they had two lives. The real one, which belonged out in the bush with their wild kinsmen, and the one they led us to believe they had accepted. In reality, whether by choice or nay, they were swallowed alive by our culture and spat out and eventually deposited in one of the rows of graves in the separate cemetery. Their passing was marked with only a simple Christian name, if they had been baptized, or a wooden plaque that read "Native," if not, the marker rotting and disappearing by year's end.

Aboriginal elders looked on with innocent surprise as their young men and women became disconnected from the land and the customs that they had enjoyed for a time so long that it could only be described as "dreaming"—and we looked on, pleased with the progress we had wrought in the name of civilization.

On Sundays, we would all go to the church on the hill behind the West Coast Hotel.

It was a wooden building, painted white and raised with a high roof of red iron. A small room had been built in the compound beside it where the children learned their lessons on Sunday, and during the week, the aboriginals learned theirs.

Polished seats of wood lined the chapel where families sat in their rows and the minister presented the holy sacraments in some fashion that displayed the goodness and patience of the Lord.

It was a strange affair. Women fanned themselves and clean-shaven men, who at other times of the week were unrecognizable, stood in rows singing hymns to an organ that sounded slightly out of tune. Not really having command of the language, the aboriginals sang the hymns in a strange staccato that rose and fell a little later than the rest of those singing.

The mission aboriginals in their new white garb sat bolt upright, as did some of the men, who could only be described as halfway converted, clad in striped trousers and shirts that did not fit.

The wilder ones persisted in wearing wooden spikes through their noses and feathers in their hair, despite the continual admonitions of the priests and lay ministers who did all they could to train them otherwise. But it seemed the loss of such adornment was an affront to their manhood, so they persisted with it as the last bastion of defiance toward this God they were told they should fear. Though it is true that to some extent they did tread carefully, perhaps this was because they had cause to fear the ones who had brought Him to them. It seemed to me that the Lord's "grace" was somewhat denied them by their teachers in favor of their religious duties and rule. Still, I wondered if, in some deep way, they already knew it in a manner we had not recognized.

Though one could see they tried hard to emulate us, they danced out of step and their natural rhythm "tripped" them at every turn—even in our house of God.

Even as a newcomer, I could see that eventually the existence and way of life of the first real Australians would be swept away. The wilderness, the strange animals, and the aboriginal people would be poor and depleted, only a remnant of its former glory, and I knew it had begun in that small church on the side of the hill in Cook Town and all the other places our kind had been. Surely our civilized ways dictated they "Conform to us," even if their own ways were well and good to them and I fancied I could almost hear the mountains reply solemnly, "You will come to learn that it is you who will conform to us in this place—or likewise be swept away—for we shall outlast you all."

Those first few weeks in my new Australia were daunting yet fascinating to me. I soaked up the life of the new settler and waited for the day when we would begin our new home for ourselves out in that land that stretched away as far as the eye could see, seemingly untouched and empty.

Edward had bought a horse and hired a Chinese laborer called Mr. LeeTong and an aboriginal tracker named Wongoree who had horses of their own. They planned to set off to search the boundaries of our parcel that he had marked out nearly eighteen months before. He would now consider the lay of the land and get ready to begin building lodgings for us. Although he warned me they would be somewhat rudimentary, I too was in a hurry to begin. So, I agreed to wait patiently at the hotel since I was still not faring well some days, while he went off in the direction of the western horizon to begin all we had dreamed.

He left on a Tuesday and waved me good-bye as happily as I was sad to let him go. Martha held onto my elbow, as she must have thought I would be "all at sea" to be left so soon after arriving and being such a young and new wife. She firmly said, "Take care, Mr. Edward," as though he was merely going to take a leisurely ride while Liz Beth sniffled and undid Martha's stoic posture at his leaving with her dramatic portrayal of tragedy and woe. Martha tutted and shook her head at Liz Beth, who had taken to singing some kind of aboriginal dirge behind us on the porch.

As soon as Edward had pulled away on his big gelding, Martha let go of me and waggled her finger toward Liz Beth, declaring, "He's to be gone for just three weeks. You would think we should never see him again with that nonsense."

Liz Beth rebounded sharply: "Missus! Your heart 'tis cold as fish water!" having no experience with ice as she should have said, but just as well declaring her opinion of her mistress's heart with her judgment by 'fish water'.

"Fiddlesticks!" Martha grabbed the girl by the arm and marched her inside, saying, "Is just your lazy bones that'll take any good opportunity to avoid your chores!"

I listened as the banter died away, with Liz Beth tweeting like a sparrow, "I know me bones is always rattlin' boss! They is just tooooo busy long time!"

And Martha was cackling like a frantic hen behind her, "I'll be rattlin' your bones alright, with a switch on your behind, my girl!"

They left me to the silence of the porch as I watched Edward and his crew disappear down Charlotte Street leaving me forlorn to wonder at the adventure that lay ahead.

In the days after they had gone, I busied myself learning the ways of the settler's life, collecting water and learning to cook. Living in the hotel with Martha, Liz Beth, Old Henry, two Chinese cooks and two cleaners that lived nearby and came in every day. They brought with them the gossip and news of the town and I listened with fascination to every word.

The first week went quickly and I barely had time to miss my husband. I began to become quite confident, and one evening I set out for the headland, where I knew I should find a quiet spot and a cool sea wind. Oddly, the usual light breeze seemed to have disappeared that afternoon from the town, so I sought it out at my favorite place at the mouth of the river. Even when I faced the sea, the familiar breeze did not come in as it usually. Only a small current of air lazily snaked its way over the mangroves along the coast from the north adjacent to the beach but was hardly enough to blow out a child's birthday candle.

I sat on a large boulder, wondering about Edward and his men who would sleep under the night sky that would soon appear. I watched the bright Southern Star rise in the fading light as it was eaten away by the turn of the earth and was painted with apricot and mauve like the colors of exotic water lilies. Looking deep into the oncoming blackness, I imagined I could almost see into the place where God must reside on the other side, and was quite at peace.

The burning heat of the day had left and the warm pungent evening air enveloped me in its steaming embrace and as I sat there alone, and I began to hear faint, distant chanting carried on the wind. Far north of me, aboriginals were singing and it was accompanied by the strange sounds of hollow wind instruments that Martha had called the "duga-ree-oo."

Liz Beth had quietly corrected her pronunciation, whispering to me that the long painted wooden tube, revered by the aboriginals, was the didgeridoo.

I could hear the rhythmic clicks of many sticks beating out their magical pattern, and I strained to hear the voices.

A warm glow seemed to rise up from some distant point, where I imagined the singers would be seated in a ring around their fire or stamping their feet in ancient dance.

I listened until the evening grew still and dark and all good folk but me were probably on their way to sleep. The distant evidence of truly wild aboriginals had made me wonder what such people would be like, by comparison to little Liz Beth in her white linen and aprons or the ones who did not belong to either the wilderness, or to us, that that hovered around the town.

The haunting sounds continued long after darkness had fallen and as my mind flew out to greet their music, a mixture of fear and curiosity filled me. As the night laid herself quietly over the land and blacked out all but the mass of crystal stars painted across the southern hemisphere's sky in wide arcs of scattered jewels, in some strange way, I wished I could find my way to those people and sit down beside the fire and listen with them.

I knew such musings were the dreams of silly people, for I had been well told. Up against the mountains and on the landward side of the dividing range, small bands of those wild aboriginals had been known to attack unprotected settlers. All said, they were "punishing" the white interlopers with "pay-back" for stealing their food and their resources and for squatting on their land. Their action didn't end these matters as they should have thought, but rather, cruel reprisals and bitter bloodshed were exacted against men and women. And the children, were often dragged screaming to be dumped at the mission. Those men that escaped, no doubt felt compelled to reply with vengeance at every opportunity, and the cycle continued in fits so that it was not safe to travel far from our established places without a good gun or an escort.

Old Bill had assured me that though they raided far on the fringes of the district, the parcel of land Edward had set his heart on was very safe. Still, I was pleased to know and it eased my worry for him that he was not out there alone as I sat and listened to the oddly imbued wind.

It was getting very late, so I picked up my skirts and began down the small grass slope, walking briskly past the powder shed without a care for my safety in the dark. I strode along the grass verge and on past the dock at the top end of the street toward my temporary home.

Within ten minutes, I had walked the length of the road and came up on the path in front of the hotel.

Lanterns blazed happily at either end of the upper porch and a mass of flying insects gathered there to worship and give up their lives.

I quickly skipped down the path beside the building and found my way around the back to the entrance I always used.

Slipping through the kitchen, I said goodnight quickly to the Chinese woman who was cleaning and who nodded without reply.

As I skipped through the foyer, I met Martha carrying a large tray with seven or eight empty beer mugs.

"Goodnight then, my lovely. It's hot tonight, isn't it?"

"Oh yes it is, and no better out there." I paused, "You will never guess Martha. I heard natives singing."

"Well that's a treat then—wind must be swinging 'round." She swept past the foyer counter and out to the kitchen, and as she went, she called back to me. "See to it you lock that window tight tonight my love. It's a full moon and the weather is too hot, so I'd look to a good storm coming up."

"I shall do that, Martha. Goodnight then."

Up in my room the window was still open from the afternoon and it was unbearably hot in the small space, so against Martha's instructions, I left it open.

I donned my nightwear, folding my clothes neatly over the chair and untying my hair to let the locks fall around my shoulders. My scalp ached a little as they changed direction to fall free after the long day of restraint and I rubbed my fingers through it to relieve my discomfort.

Then picking up my shell inlaid hairbrush my father had given me, and counting as I went, I brushed it twenty times on each side, laid the brush down, and climbed into bed.

As I lay there in the heat, I could hear the sounds of evening drinkers in the front parlor bar of the hotel downstairs. Every night Martha served the town's menfolk who came to eat and drink. She considered them "of a better type, you know" for frequenting her establishment and laughed her way through the work of keeping the rowdy lot from disturbing her other guests.

Tonight they were particularly noisy, perhaps because the heat was suffocating all, and the beer flowed faster than it should to cool their desperate thirsts.

I could hear the sounds of chairs scraping and the raucous laughter of deep-throated men echoing through the timbers of the building.

A voice barked out from along the outside wall of the building below. "Jake, better get moving… storm's coming." A muffled reply came from somewhere at the front of the hotel, coupled with the crash of something hitting a distant wall and a series of curses echoing through the alley. The light of the moon came and went through the window opening as I listened to the sounds of a stiff breeze howling around the corner of the building only to fade back into silence. I turned my head toward the window and wondered what was happening.

Suddenly, I heard the clumping sound of heavy boots rising up through the stairwell, echoing through the walls of my room.

I wondered where they would go, and for a moment my curiosity overrode a feeling of uneasiness made by the sounds outside.

As I listened, I realized the steps were coming down the hall, and as they came up to my doorway, the board in front of the door creaked loudly.

I was suddenly gripped with fear, as I could not remember locking the door.

My heart stopped. I gripped the sheets around me and froze, breathing so shallowly as though by doing so I could make myself fade from that room and not exist at all.

The tin doorknob turned with its customary scraping noise and I could see, even in the dark, the panels of its shape open and a dark specter fill most of the opening.

I could not bring myself to move or say a word, and for a few moments the figure stood there like a dark statue.

Ice cold, and still as the dead, I readied myself to spring up and scream until my lungs might burst. The breathless heat filled the space between the intruder and me. The man also stood still, deciding it seemed, while I lay as a corpse, hiding in my silence with not even an eyelid flickering.

Suddenly, a new gust of wind broke the spell, which seemed to have lasted for hours instead of the brief time it was. The window slipped its iron slider and swung out sharply as the wind caught it, tearing through the fine mesh and slamming hard on the wall outside. Then a sudden flash of lightning lit up the room.

The menacing figure quickly ducked back out into the hall when the light hit him, and then turned and fled. I could hear his heavy boots striding off down the hall and pounding hurriedly down the stairs.

I immediately jumped from the bed, bounded across the polished boards in my bare feet to grab the door, and swung it hard on its hinges until it slammed shut.

I dropped to my knees and frantically turned the key in the lock until the bolt clicked and announced safety.

In a crumpled heap, I hung from the door handle with both hands, breathing as though I had run a mile. Tears filled my eyes and I shivered as though I was deathly cold when in truth, perspiration beaded on my brow and my hands slipped around the doorknob.

"Oh Edward, Edward," I whispered, "why couldn't you have taken me with you?" I cried, quite against any logical reasoning that might have drowned out that question in the light of day.

Loud voices called from below and interrupted my despair. I heard the wind catch something heavy in the street and throw it against the wall of a building.

Then the open window, now waving loose from its catch, began to slam hard against the outer wall with the sudden onset of the gale. I could feel slight licks of rain carried on the wind that buffeted the opening. I got up and hurried to the window to try to close it, but I could not gather up the rod dangling from the frame outside the mesh it had torn through.

Too afraid to go downstairs to fetch Martha, I tried to pull away the mesh from the window frame but to no avail. With every gust, I could feel the building yawing and swaying as the storm pressed onto us so suddenly.

The noises outside and the bustle from inside the building grew louder and louder.

Lightning blazed repeatedly and then almost immediately crashing peals of thunder boomed overhead. I realized the storm was all but on us and I knew this was Liz Beth's "old devil," arrived at last, just as she had predicted.

The wind began to howl around the building corners and through the alley as though the fury was looking for any way inside.

I heard the locked doorknob rattling again. For a moment, I froze but Martha's voice called loudly from the other side.

"Margaret, lovey, are you all right?"

"I'm here, Martha. Oh my Lord, what is happening?" I ran to the door and unlocked it.

She stood in the hall, a lantern hanging from her hand and her face glowing with perspiration. A look of uncertainty that I had never seen in the usually immovable woman, showed on her face.

"She's going to be a good one all right! You had better dress my dear and come downstairs, 'cause it ain't guaranteed to be safe up here in a good blow …"

She turned to the sound of the children crying in the hall as their mother pushed them forward toward the stairs.

"She's set to be a real doozey this time. You children do just exactly what your mother tells you," Martha called out. Then realizing how afraid they were, she called back, "'Tis all right children, we are safe as houses down in the parlor and 'twill be blown out by morning."

She grabbed me by my hand while she swung the lantern about, searching for the chair with my clothes laid on it. "Wouldn't like to say aloud to them, lovey, but last year, I nearly lost the whole building! The roof was torn right off… 'Course we didn't have it lined as it is now." She threw a hand up above the lantern to indicate the painted boards she was so proud of having installed, which now seemed in some jeopardy. "No lovey, 'fraid it's still not totally safe here. You must come downstairs with us all, and we shall wait and see what will come of this storm."

A peal of thunder boomed above us again and rain began to slam heavily onto the iron roof above the boards. The noise rose so much that we could have been inside a drum, and I hurried to dress and obey her.

I grabbed my clothes and pulled my bodice and skirt over my nightdress, with Martha tugging and helping, quickly pulling together my buttons at the back. Then she grabbed the flickering lantern from the side table and my hand and we rushed from the room.

The door slammed shut as Martha pulled it behind her and we hurried along the hall and flew down the stairs with Martha muttering "Oh dear, oh dear!" as we went. Her voice bobbed up and down with the hasty steps until we rounded the bottom of the stairs and she ushered me into the drawing room behind the front lounge.

It was a little calmer in the central room, and the howling gale that pushed at the building, making it creak and groan, seemed all but held at bay.

"Liz Beth, have you got that billy on? Come on, girl, we will all need a hot cup of tea." Martha growled, "… and bring another lantern in here."

Liz Beth's eyes were wide as saucers as she hurried off to comply with Martha's instructions.

Martha rushed about, flitting like a sunbird from one guest to another, patting shoulders and smiling, muttering calming sentiments to all between thunderous peals and flashes of violent lightning from above.

The walls vibrated and the wind howled louder and faster by the moment. At odd intervals, the crashing sounds of things being thrown about by the tantrum of the storm made us all jump in our seats. Guests huddled together, trying to console each other by talking reassuringly. But the violence of the tempest made all afraid for their lives inside the wooden building barely holding together in the cyclone.

Jonathan Stanford had been helping Martha and Old Henry shift a heavy sideboard over the door that opened from the room into the entrance foyer. He sat heavily down beside me when they were finished.

"Well, this is a turn up for the worst, is it not?" He spoke loudly over the din.

I spoke back as clearly as I could, trying to disguise my dread.

"Well sir, I am sure it will take more than even this storm can dish out to deal to our Martha." I added a shaky smile. Just as I said this, a flash of lightning jammed its blazing spikes into the almost completely enclosed room. Even through the boarded window and barred doors, the flash clearly lit us all from some apertures unseen. Shortly, the ominous smell of char found its way to our noses.

In the dull light of the lantern, I saw Jonathan's handsome features, young and fearless. His eyes were wide with excitement, his moustache curled over a slight smile as he looked around to see where the burning scent was coming from. A draft swept over me and shredded timber fell like confetti to the floor behind our group. I felt a drip fall into my hair and I let out a loud, "Oh my dear Lord…"

A roaring peal of thunder shook the room directly overhead with tremendous force and several of the women cried out.

One of the children began to cry loudly, and his mother folded over him like a protective cloak. No sooner had she done this, than her second child began to pull at her and cry too so she spread her arms 'round them both, looking as terrified as they in the dull light of the now flickering lanterns.

Drops of water began sparkling in the light as the ceiling above us patched wet in places. And then these tiny mirrors formed and fell on all our company. We shifted our chairs to miss the worst of it but they splashed up, catching in the light of the lanterns, and wet our skirts.

Even so, Martha poured out cups of hot tea amidst all this and all received it with shaking hands as a distraction from the howling sounds, shaking building, and the water now splashing to the floor.

All that long night, the rain and wind was hurled savagely at the town, but by about half past three in the morning, the noise eased, and we could clearly perceive that the storm was passing.

The thunder drifted further and further away until all that remained was a distant flash in the sky to mark the storm's path as it tracked south, grazing the coast with its fury.

"Well, it seems the worst is over. Thank the Lord for that!" Martha whispered, as some of the guests had succumbed to dozing in the corner, and both children had slipped into sleep on their mother's lap.

Liz Beth lay curled up under the table, sound asleep, and had not roused throughout the whole ordeal.

"Jonathan, do you think we shall let ourselves out and search the house?" Martha had got up and turned to begin to push at the sideboard up against the door.

Jonathan stood and helped her move the heavy piece of furniture away. Martha had to force the door a little to open it, as it had swelled tightly in its frame.

She peeped around the corner and Jonathan peered into the darkness beyond the door behind her. Then the two, gingerly walked into the foyer, stepping over some timber that had fallen from above. I took up the rear.

A few of the other guests were also waking, and a couple bravely followed, eager to get out of the warm damp of the central room and see what had happened.

The stairwell was dripping from the top floor and a strong breeze greeted us as we walked around and up the first few steps. Jonathan took the lead. We climbed the stairs up to the floor above very slowly and carefully. The doors of all the rooms along the hall were swung open at different angles and puddles of water lay on the boards of the hall in odd places. Most of the incoming rainwater had already seeped through the cracks to the floor below, but the boards shining in out lamp light and smelled of wet timber as we walked down the hall to survey the damage.

"Mrs. Peterson, your room is all well." James called down the stairs toward the woman who had made up the rear of the train. "I'm afraid yours is not so good, Miss O'Brien, nor yours Margaret… roof's missing and the boards too."

"Oh no!" Martha's voice shuddered a little, and she pushed her way past him to survey the gaping hole in the ceiling. An iron sheet was rolled up into the dark night sky, which was still covered with clouds hurriedly passing overhead as if trying to catch up to their master. "Oh my dear… I don't know what to say!" She shook her head. "Where are me boards?"

I came up behind them as Miss O'Brien tentatively peered into her room, barely lit by the light of the lantern.

"Oh dear, looks like I shall be sleeping in the pantry!" I said, and smiled, trying to sound flippant.

"No, you shall most certainly not have to do that. You shall have my room, lovey, behind the kitchen. I'll bunk in with Liz Beth, and we shall get the carpenters onto this first thing in the morning. I 'spect our roof will be spread all over town tomorrow. We shall have to send Old Henry out and look for us, won't we, Mr. Stanford?"

"Indeed madam, I think ours won't be the only roof that has taken a tour of the township."

"True, Mr. Stanford." She nodded with certainty before her thoughts sped off to other matters as she surveyed the remnants of the room. "Where's Liz Beth? We're going to have such a pile of washing tomorrow by the looks of this."

Martha had stepped into my room. The bed linen hung from the remains of the bed, which was now covered in leaves and debris. They trailed off the edge and sat in a pool of water along with half the mattress, which was equally sodden. The breeze could still be felt pouring over the remainder of the roof, and a light mist of rain fell through the opening. The droplets glittered in the light of the lantern as Martha picked up a corner of wet sheet.

"Where is that girl? We should get this linen off the floor and over a line." She leaned forward and began scooping up the wet sheet, wringing it in her hands. The water twinkled in the light and disappeared into the floorboards, some of it splashing on Martha's cotton skirt. "Seems the mattress will be ruined, and that me good one, brought all the way from Melbourne …" she trailed off and sighed.

I patted her on the shoulder. "Surely it can be saved. We could dry it in the sun."

"I s'pose we could try, if we turned it a good many times. But it will smell like an ox has slept on it for a long while after I 'spect." She shook her head.

"What a night it has been," she said, speaking more to herself than anyone else. Then she looked up. "I think you should all head off to bed to sleep a few hours after all this excitement. What a terrible fracas!"

She turned her head, and in the light of the lantern, she seemed smaller with the open sky above her and the wet walls behind her. At that moment, Liz Beth appeared from behind all the others and forced herself between us to peer at her mistress.

"Looks like Rainbow Snake don't like your top floor again. He's pulled it right to pieces, eh missus, just like afore?" Her eyes and her white teeth smiled in the light, though the rest of her face could barely be seen, so that she appeared as the Cheshire cat might amidst our skirts. "I say'd all along, is sure unnatural to be livin' up here like a possum, eh Boss, didn't I tell ya that ...?"

"Where have you been Liz Beth? Where's Old Henry? We need to string up a line in the kitchen and get this linen over it until morning 'fore we can wash it. I need to see to a bed for Miss Margaret and Miss Amelia. Come on girl, Pick up these wet things! You and I shall have to put up a cot in the pantry, so we best get on."

She grabbed up the last of the dripping fabric while Liz Beth dutifully obeyed her and pulled a sodden pillow from under a timber on the edge of the bed. Suddenly Martha looked up and saw us all watching in a daze. "Well my ladies and sirs, no mucking about now, you should be off to bed! I shall see you in the morning. Then we can all go and look at the damage to the town. I would bet it looks a real fright after that. I'd say that storm was twice the size of last year!" She shook her head. "So, come on then, off to your beds. I shall bid you goodnight!"

Her stiff frame demanded obedience, so we all eased ourselves back from the door and down the hall, and those who still had rooms intact retired. Only Liz Beth, Martha, and Henry stayed up to make beds for the teacher and myself and clean up the wet linen.

With the type of exhaustion that comes from fear, all went gratefully to the world of slumber. The children had already succumbed to sleep in their parents' arms and were placed in their sheets without waking. Within the hour, the house was in deep sleep and the hotel finally fell into silence, except for the drip, drip, drip overhead.

Chapter 4

MORNING BROKE AROUND half past five. I could feel that the clear air was damp and clean and I heard the birds resume their singing just as they did every morning.

Martha and Liz Beth were up a little later than usual, and it was already light when they appeared in the garden at the back of the hotel, fussing with boiling water and washing linen.

I walked around the damp stairwell gingerly and stared up toward the top. Apart from uncommon light and a slight breeze hinting at the opening there, things looked quiet and normal.

Jonathan Stanford startled me by suddenly appearing from behind.

"Well, I see we are all still in one piece and the sky has not completely fallen in."

"Quite right, Mr. Jonathan. I see Martha is already under way with the cleanup. I'm certain she is not really a woman at all but something descended from the titans with the amount of work she manages. She'll have everything back and shipshape in no time, I'll be bound."

Suddenly we heard Martha's voice: "Henry! Where are you, Henry?"

"Here boss, right here …"

"Hitch up the cart—we are going to take a look at the town shortly."

"Yes ma'am, will do." He lumbered off to see to it, and Jonathan called out to her, "May we come too, madam?"

"Indeed, Mr. Jonathan… as you like."

I nodded to Jonathan and headed off to wash and get ready so I might see what had befallen the town along with them.

By the time I appeared, Jonathan and Martha were waiting at the front step with Old Henry pulling up the horse and cart before them.

The horse looked a little frisky in the morning air and its eyes were rolling sharply forward and back, so that a hint of whites could be seen. The storm had upset it, and Old Henry held it by its halter firmly as it stepped back and forth.

The cart sank back and forward a little unsteadily as Martha and I climbed up with assistance from Jonathan. We sat along the seats on each side and swayed in time with the horse's nervousness.

Old Henry climbed up to the driver's seat, and in the crisp light of ten past six we headed off down the main street to see how others had fared in the storm.

It was not a pretty sight. The town had taken the brunt of the fierce winds, and it no longer looked like the bustling hub of adventure it had the day before.

Along what pathways could be seen, branches lay torn and stacked up against the sides of buildings and the roadway was covered in leaves.

As we came up to the general store, we could see the whole front porch and part of the upper roof had been torn off.

A huge tree that just the day before had been spreading its shade over the workers building the new auction house next to the West Coast Hotel, now lay full length across the road, having been unceremoniously torn from the ground. The clay hole where its roots had been included a large bite of the roadway, and the branches spread themselves like a huge broom over the road's surface.

I marveled at those branches, imagining what interesting birds and other creatures had just yesterday called them home. And just as I thought about this, I saw a boy of about seven sitting a little distance from the tree. His trousers were wet to the knees, and in his hands he held a bright green reptile.

Jonathan jumped down from the cart and offered up his hand. "Shall we look at the carnage?"

Martha from her vantage point on the cart muttered, "Oh dear, oh dear... poor Mrs. Frankton... She only had that porch put on last August."

I stepped off the back of the cart into the waiting arms of Jonathan, who lowered me by my waist to the ground with ease. I took his hand and we stepped around the great branches that lay before us to the edge of the building.

"Damn shame," Jonathan spoke to a man standing there, also looking intently at the damage.

I walked across to the boy seated on the edge of the walkway of the shop beside the alleyway between the two.

"That is a nice lizard." I said kindly to him.

"Yep, it's a gecko. I have been wanting one for ages!"

"Did you find him in the tree branches?"

"No, the dog got him first and I saved him."

"So what shall become of him now?" I asked as I bravely put out my finger to gently touch the bright emerald green back of the six-inch lizard.

"I'm gonna, keep him and... I'm gonna call him ...um ..."

"Sebastian?"

"Greeny! Cause he's green, eh lady."

"Well that is quite right. I think Greeny will be a fine and suitable name for him indeed."

The boy looked up and smiled. Two of his front teeth were missing and a smudge of clay was painted across his cheek.

"You want me to find another one, for you?"

"Oh thank you, but I wouldn't know how to look after one like you, so I suppose I shall have to do without." I smiled as the boy stroked Greeny and unhitched its little legs from his left-hand fingers to re-attach them to his right hand.

"Shall we move on, Margaret?" Jonathan's voice interrupted. I said my farewell to the young man and his lizard and moved back to the cart.

"Made a new friend there, I see," Jonathan chuckled as he spoke.

"Indeed, I have been introduced to a gecko called Greeny, and I am much amazed by its beauty. I don't think I've ever seen anything as green as that and with little gold spots down his side and huge eyes."

"And a great deal of fun for a small boy I'd wager."

Old Henry leaned back toward Martha and said we should have to go around by the way of Walker Street. With a little cursing at the horse and negotiation of the cart, he managed to back up, turn around, and head up the gravel of the alternate street.

Huge ruts the size of small canyons showed in the gravel and clay of Walker Street, as the torrents of rain had gouged them out during the night. The cartwheels bumped and forded the rivulets and finally reached the top before going down the length of the next block.

Eventually the track, as it now was, came out again on Charlotte Street, far on the other side of the fallen tree.

The Chinese merchandiser on the corner of Hogg Street had not suffered too much, but busy Chinese workers were already sweeping and washing the front shop walkway and were splashing buckets of water across its length to sluice away the thousands of leaves that had been deposited there. A pile of debris had been cleared to one side and contained window frames, wooden shingles from roofs, and tree branches.

By the time we had traversed the whole length of Charlotte Street, past Howard and Boundary streets, and turned up to go over the slight hill where the tent city was, we had seen a myriad of various damages.

The trees beside the mangrove swamp were stripped bare of their leaves, as though a giant had come along in the night and run his hand up each trunk and torn off everything to the stems, and then cast them free in the air, to blow where they would.

The tent city should more accurately have been called the city of sheets, as not one seemed to be standing.

A brindled dog hovered near an upturned box, and men who had obviously fared badly during the night were walking around looking for belongings or rounding up horses or mules from the trees that edged the camp.

The blackened steps of the land burned and cleared for the new areas of settlement stood out starkly in the new morning, wet and strewn with debris, while the red gravel and clay looked scoured and flattened from the massive pelting.

Small creeks seemed to have sprung up at the base of the undulating area. Yellow streams ran away toward the lower land on the other side of the peninsula, down to the sea of the bay.

Even the March flies were nowhere to be seen this morning, and only the distant sound of birds could be heard to declare that yet another warm, albeit wet, day would be had in Cook Town while repairs and cleanup began.

"No sign of our roof, Henry?" Martha had been scouring the landscape, hoping to find some of the sheets torn free from upper floor.

"Nothin' to be seen here. I'll go a-walking and talk to them that is about later. You never know, perhaps they will turn up. I 'spect I should be getting Fredrickson to get the roof fixed straightaway if we can't find them sheets anywhere. What do you say, Miss Martha?"

"Yes indeed, as soon as you take us back. We cannot have that roof open for another night. Mr. Fredrickson will have to board it up as fast as he can or we'll be drowned if there be more rain."

Martha looked up at the sky, but the wisps of cloud didn't show any hint of more rain.

"Sky looks set to clear, madam. I think you shall have more than enough time to fix the roof," Jonathan said encouragingly.

"Looks fine now, sir, but everything here happens quickly, I can say. It rains and blows like the devil is whipping his horse... Then it is gone. But when all seems calm, it comes again—just as sudden! And if you thought the last time was the worst, that devil will surprise you with an even bigger whipping! Must always be prepared, sir. Always prepared ..." She trailed off.

By the time we had returned to the hotel, Martha had found her normal calm and industry and got busy again, relentlessly organizing labor and the usual affairs of the hotel.

Just a few hours later, Jonathan pitched in to help the Fredrickson builders, who had been all but "press-ganged" into the fixing of the hotel's roof by Martha. She had insisted her repairs were of "the highest priority" in light of her guests being "good and important people, who cannot be expected to sleep day in day out in the pantry!"

No one dared deny her; so that very day, new iron sheets from the mercantile yard were hauled screeching up to the second story to close in the open roof and were battened down by the resounding clang of hammers.

I settled myself in the parlor, which was closed to the public for the day, and made use of the time to think about the events of the week and write to loved ones in England of the terrifying yet exciting drama we had encountered.

The steam master at the docks had told Old Henry that several small craft had been wrecked and that he had heard of a frigate going aground on the reef toward Cape York. No one knew what had become of the crew, and we all prayed that they had not drowned or been eaten by sharks but had rather found some friendly natives ashore.

No one seemed to know what state the natives were in, in those parts, and the opportunity afforded by the lost seamen started rumors circulating that the aboriginals are fond of that abominable habit of cannibalism.

Liz Beth told me that she knew of no such thing among her people and that most were already converted and would not ever do such a thing. She seemed to me, however, a little unsure as she spoke about it, and she admitted that she was not from that tribe that lived up in the far north.

I came to know much later that it was not a common practice at all, as some had been fond and even delighted in saying, but at that time, the town was abuzz with the idea.

It was strange, those few busy days after the storm, that I did not worry once for my dear Edward, as I suppose would have been natural for me.

Instead, I seemed content to help where I could and see to it that some comfort was given to our odd little schoolteacher, who did not recover from her fright. She did not, it seems, find the interruption of such wild weather conducive to her peaceful relocation, and it was not long before she abandoned us, leaving by ship to go south to Melbourne, where the weather was much cooler and more stable.

Jonathan was my happy companion for the next few days and I admit, it was a relief to sit or walk with him and partake of such good conversation. He was educated and was of my own understanding in many things, and such company was welcome being as he was a fine young Englishman and full of inspiration and common sense. He was a pleasant respite from the new settlement life and the hardy people I had been thrown amongst in Cook Town, and he distracted me with his humor for many of the days and evenings that followed.

However, it was not long before he, too, gathered his supplies and left to search for suitable land for his endeavors. We all bade him a hearty farewell and even Martha commented as he went, "…Shall miss that one."

I found myself feeling alone, and for the first time felt miserably homesick, so I kept myself busy at the hotel helping out, visiting with Martha, and reading. Day by day, two weeks went by. With the absence of Jonathan's cordial distraction and the emptiness of my bed at night, I counted down the days and looked forward to seeing my Edward again.

Chapter 5

THURSDAY MORNING, MARTHA came rushing through the hall and appeared in the parlor, where several guests and I were seated resting, reading, or chatting about the plans some had for the day.

She flew up to me, Liz Beth following, and sat in the opposite chair, her hands firmly grasping the arms of the worn leather arms. Liz Beth stood behind with a stoic and serious look on her face. Martha whispered a little breathlessly that Old Henry had heard from the carpentry merchant that the body of a cattleman had been found up in the valley past the Black Mountains.

"Oh my Lord, that is where our selection is ..." I had whispered breathlessly back.

"He was killed by natives, by all accounts... dammed savages! Lovey, I don't know, do you think we should call the rangers? Not that they could get up there in anywise time enough to help poor Mr. Edward if he has come upon some trouble."

My stomach turned as though I would be sick, and I stared into Martha's eyes. They held a certain horror I could not fathom. A moment passed, and then for some reason I felt I should console her, even if it was my own dear husband that was the subject of such worry.

"Martha, he'll be all right. He has two experienced men with him, one an aboriginal himself, so I think not that he will come to any harm. And… he has his good gun."

"Oh, true my dear. So true. So then we have nothing to be concerned about."

"That's quite right—there's nothing at all to worry about," I said.

Liz Beth mimicked my words in the best "London" accent she could manage: "… Quite right! Nuttin' ta worry 'bout!" and followed Martha as she got up and left me to my thoughts and my book. I listened as they disappeared down the hall, Liz Beth scolding Martha ingeniously: "You is nuffink but one of them worry wots, wot worries! Missus 'tis quite right you know boss, quite right!"

"Warts, you silly girl… Wart, that worries!"

They faded from my hearing with Martha saying, "And do stop that foolish mimicry, girl! You don't sound anything like you're English!"

I tried to focus on the pages I was reading but the words seemed to wander off like lost sheep and I could not round them up to obey me. I began to contemplate what I should do and what would become of me if my husband met an ill-fated day. The prospect shook me to my soul. I imagined what such a life alone might be like, and the picture of Martha filling up her days at the hotel came to view. I wouldn't want to be so busy as she and supposed therefore that I could use my only skill as a milliner's assistant to start a small enterprise. I would have to hope hats became a fashion in Cook Town. My heart sank as I realized I could not bear the thought of Edward being gone, and no amount of hats would make up for his loss.

I had not long to concern myself, because half an hour later the sound of Liz Beth shouting "Miss Margaret, Miss Margaret!" with her usual lack of decorum came through to the parlor. We saw her through the window, running as fast as she could down the side alley past the window to disappear around the back of the hotel toward the kitchen entrance as she was not allowed to come in through the front door, and I stood to go meet her there.

Liz Beth's shoes made a clumping sound on the worn path, as they were a little too large for her, and the sound echoed on the top steps and porch in front of the kitchen door as she tumbled in. Even from the reception desk, I could hear the Chinese cook exclaim loudly, not happy at the invasion of her territory and the irreverent manner in which Liz Beth came running through the room. We met in the hall as I caught the flying girl like a bouquet of wild flowers cast away by a happy bride.

"Mr. Edward's back... He coming! He coming!" She panted.

"Liz Beth, please!" Martha was ahead of me in the passageway, and she did not approve of Liz Beth's rushing through like a small tsunami either.

"Quick as quick, boss... Tell Miss Margaret, Mr. Edward, he back. I see'd him downtown past the dresses shop." She paused a little to catch her breath. "He with the China fellow but ..."

She was about to say she had not seen Wongoree when I said, "Oh wonderful!" I'm sure my face lit up as I grasped her hands in my relief and Martha also smiled broadly.

"How far away is he, Liz Beth?" Martha asked before her skirts spun around her in a perfect fan and she headed off for the front porch to see if she could see him.

"Just down street... down street. I see'd him true."

"Well I'll be bound!" Martha had led the way as Liz Beth and I followed out onto the front porch and stood peering in the direction of the dress shop some dozen doors down.

I stood between the two of them and my heart raced.

"That was a quick trip ..." Martha cocked her head to one side curiously.

"Perhaps the storm brought them back, or they heard of that trouble." I did not really care why. It was all I could do to restrain my excitement.

I held onto the porch railing and peered along the street past horses and carts that were about their own business.

Suddenly, there they were. Distantly, I could make out Edward sitting high on his horse and the Chinaman slightly behind, leading the third horse and the laden mule.

The Chinaman stopped for a moment, and Edward could be seen swinging his horse around to speak to him. Then the man passed Edward and the big brown horse and peeled off with the mule, through the gap in the shops, toward the tent city. I stood transfixed on the progress of my husband up the mud-and-sand thoroughfare. I could see he was a little thinner and the sun shone brightly off the perspiration on his face.

Finally, he appeared within hailing distance, and I cried out quite without restraint, with Liz Beth in chorus behind me.

"Edward, Edward!" I broke free of the railing and sped down the steps onto the roadway.

Liz Beth followed me and stood with both hands firmly wrapped around my elbow, while Martha stayed at the top of the steps smiling widely.

The man I knew, who now looked more like a bushman than a gentleman, dismounted as Liz Beth moved forward to the head of the horse and held its bridle. It snorted loudly with his master's descent and the second horse backed away slightly.

Edward turned his mount to the rail to tie the gelding there. Then he gathered up the tether of the dark brown mare walking behind and hitched it beside the other.

He turned and walked between the horses, ignoring Liz Beth, who backed away from in front of him, whispering as she went, "Good you back, Mr. Edward… Good you back."

I had waited for just a moment before throwing myself into his arms. He smelt of salt and perspiration, horse and mud. He seemed not to return my affection, but I thought his stiff response to my embrace was to avoid ruining my clothing—or perhaps he didn't want a show of affection in public.

"Are you all right, dearest?" I leaned away from him and noticed the dark stain on his forearm. "Oh my, are you hurt!"

"No madam… not really."

"Oh, I imagine that storm made it very difficult." I looked up into his face with concern.

"Margaret… Yes, it was tough out there. Still, we… ah, we found our way back."

"Mr. Edward, will you come inside sir, and we shall see to a cup of tea for you straight away?" Martha volunteered the usual pleasantries.

"Thank you, madam, but no. I think I would just as sooner get out of these clothes and into a bath if you don't mind."

"Of course, of course!" She had already signaled to Liz Beth to stop mucking around with the horse and get up the steps. "Liz Beth, get some water boiling for the master, and start fetching for the bath …'

Liz Beth shrugged her shoulders, pursing her lips in her usual rebellion, but was not quite brave enough to complain of her servitude. She disappeared in the dark opening of the front door and we could hear her telling all loudly, "Mr. Edward is back… and alive, too!"

Old Henry appeared from the alleyway between the hotel and its neighbor.

"Shall I pasture these out with our mare in the back paddock after I've cleaned them up, boss?" He was looking at the dry mud that clung all the way up the horse's shanks. With an experienced hand, he smoothed his palm down the big gelding's muscles just as a March fly landed, and the horse's hide shuddered the insect away before it could bite.

"You been in a mess of mud, Mr. Edward, a mess of mud." He grinned with his blackening teeth showing from beneath tanned, leather-like lips, and his head half hidden under the wide-brimmed hat that was never off his head.

"Yes, my good man, there was a bit of it about."

"This is the tracker's mare, ain't it?

"True it was… we made a deal for it and he has gone off hunting, I believe."

"They is an odd people. Up and leave a good horse to chase kangaroo." Old Henry shook his head and gathered up the horse by its bridle to take it round the back.

Martha nodded and skipped up the step quickly after Liz Beth, leaving me to follow on my husband's arm.

"Oh dear Edward, you must tell me what you saw of our land. Did you get that far before the storm hit?" I was excited and was already prying the information I most wanted to hear from Edward.

"Margaret! Please! I have only just arrived. Surely you can let me have some peace before you begin your infernal conversation!"

I reeled at such a response and let go of his arm.

He turned from me, refusing to meet my gaze, and I suddenly felt a gap of some vast cold glacier slide between us.

"Oh, I am so sorry, Edward ..." I recovered my poise and followed him up the stairs almost as though I had become a dog on a lead trailing its indifferent owner, instead of a young wife reunited with her husband.

He strode in the front reception area and, without a word of explanation, stormed up the stairs toward the upper washroom.

Martha frowned slightly and I held onto the bottom of the banister, looking up to his tall frame ascending. His boots had left telltale prints of clay and sand on the wooden risers, as he had neglected to brush them off at the door in his haste.

I turned and, somewhat sheepishly, apologized to Martha, who was transfixed at the center of the reception area, watching the occasion with noticeable concern and curiosity.

"Oh dear. I'm so sorry, Martha, about your floors. I don't know what has got into him. I cannot say I have ever seen him so out of sorts. He must be quite worn out from the adventure. I'm sure we shall hear how it went later, when he has recovered."

"Oh, I am sure you're right, lovey. 'Tis a fair way out there and back, and that weather would have been very disappointing for them... Not to worry, I shall get Liz Beth onto the floors—we shall have them cleaned up in a jiffy." She was looking down at the floor, surveying the prints as though they held some clue to Edward's change in demeanor.

She cast a final smile to me and with that turned and headed off to the kitchen. "Perhaps you had best go up and attend to him, lovey,..." she said in a sympathetic tone. Then with her next breath, she yelled loudly, "Liz Beth, I hope you have that water ready!"

I turned my attention away from the footprints and followed Edward up the stairs. Rounding the top step, I looked down the hall where the washroom door was partially open. Edward was standing over the basin washing his hands. I could see the side of his face and I realized something was troubling him.

He stared for some moments into the mirror hanging from its chain, studying his reflection.

Very slowly, he lifted a wet hand up to his chin and rubbed the heavy stubble that had grown there in the time since he had last shaved. I quietly watched him and thought how he looked wild and unknown to me.

Without interrupting his inspection of himself, I turned very quietly and walked the length of the hall to our room at the far corner of the hotel.

Letting myself in the room, I scanned to look for anything amiss, and then crossed to the dresser. I pulled the solid drawer out and extracting clean underclothes for him and a white shirt with pale blue stripes, I placed them on the bed. Laying the clothing out properly, I smoothed the linen sleeves with my hand, and then returned to the large dresser to find trousers and a waistcoat, and set them out on the bed as well.

Edward appeared at the door. He walked without speaking to the window and stared out of the screened opening to the alleyway and the roof of the nearest building beside the hotel.

"Margaret, I have to go down to the courthouse straight away. Can you see to that bath?"

"Of course, dear." I tried to sound friendly and unconcerned, but inside I realized something was very wrong. "I'll go and fetch Liz Beth and hurry her along. Would you like some tea brought to you while you are waiting?"

"No, thank you."

"Is there something wrong, Edward?"

"No." He turned and looked at me for the first time since he arrived and forced a smile. "I'm sorry, my dear. No, there is nothing the matter." His gaze was fleeting, and he quickly turned to sit down on the chair. He placed his forearms over his knees and hung his head for a moment between his shoulders.

Suddenly, I noticed the raw wound in his forearm just at the edge of his pulled-up sleeve.

"Edward, you are hurt!" I rushed over and bent to hold the forearm and look at it. "How did this happen? This will have to be cleaned and dressed."

Immediately, I stood up and spun around in a flurry of skirts to fetch water and bandages.

My attention to the wound made Edward lift up the arm to study it. It had already begun to crust at the edges but was weeping from a large open wound in the center, and the sleeve that had been covering it had a deep brown stain on the underside. "Oh this …" he dreamily faded off. "I… fell, and speared myself on an upturned branch." He pulled at the shirt to open the area for a closer inspection.

"I shall be back in no time to tend to that, my dear. Just don't move!" I lost no time and before he could make any further comment, disappeared out of the wooden doorway and hurried down the hall with my leather shoes clacking down the stairs.

I reappeared at the bedroom door a few minutes later, this time with Martha and a bowl of steaming water, bandages, and an ominous brown bottle with a large label that read Iodine.

"Oh Mr. Edward, what have you done to yourself? No wonder you were so dizzy coming in… I quite forgive you!" Martha immediately pulled over the small side table and placed the large enamel bowl on it.

I began to pull the stained shirt from Edward's shoulder and arm. He grimaced as I lifted the wounded limb and pulled the whole shirt away from his shoulders to reveal his white torso and the arm, which was quite red and hot.

Bruises that had already turned blue with tinges of yellow also became visible, and I frowned slightly as I fingered them gently, tracing where each had been made.

"Oh Edward, you have had quite a fall. There must have been rocks. You have bruises all over your side and back." He did not reply.

"We had better rub some witch hazel into those." Martha was also examining the patient with diligent care.

"This wound has gone right through your forearm sir. Right through!" Martha was frowning with real concern. "This is a strange accident… such a round hole on the one side." She was washing the arm carefully yet Edward's discomfort showed on his face as she pressed the cloth gently onto the matted blood and debris. "Had you not have said otherwise, it looks quite like a gunshot wound, save for all your bruises."

I broke in on Martha's comment quite innocently as she opened the bottle of iodine and poured some on a dressing ready to douse the wound. "Never mind my dear husband, we shall soon have you cleaned up and hopefully it won't fester... Oh I hope it doesn't fester! It should have been cleaned as soon as you did it."

"It will have to be opened and cleaned again every day." Martha added her valuable experience, as all locals were inclined to have. "If it goes bad even slightly we shall take him to the Hospital and let the doctor there tend it... but best we pray it heals. You were lucky not to have broken it."

Martha dried off the arm and I immediately stepped in to dress it. "This may be a little painful, ..." I said.

I placed a towel under his arm while Martha fussed and dabbed the iodine on the small, clean hole, which had already closed and dried like a dark plug on the entry side and did seem such a small wound as to quite confound the notion of a stick. Then we laid his arm over a little and poured the iodine into the open area on the underside. The branch must have taken flesh away with it when it was removed and it was torn and as soon as it was washed it began to bleed.

Edward stiffened instantly and his fist curled to resist the stinging pain of the iodine on the open flesh. The towel stained brown and orange as the powerful antiseptic dripped from his arm, and he muffled a groan in his throat. With Martha's help, I dabbed it dry and we dressed it, tying it tightly.

"Thank God for that!" he exclaimed; now the pain and prodding was over. He lifted up his arm to inspect the clean bandage and tested whether he could turn his forearm, first left then right.

"Let's hope there be naught to worry about 'cept cleaning." Martha picked up the debris on the tray and looked down at him sternly. "We will have to look at that tomorrow... Have to be very careful here in the tropics. Even a little cut can be dangerous." She prodded the excess rags and gathered up the bowl. "We'll need to get that shirt in the soak, as well."

Immediately, Edward thrust out his hand to scoop up the shirt with his good arm, even before Martha or I could turn to collect it.

"I think this is one shirt I shall not have washed… or mended." He laughed casually to disguise his obvious retrieval of it. "Thank you ladies, I believe I shall have my bath, and that will complete my return to civilization."

He walked to the doorway and stood in it patiently, indicating that our medical service was now concluded.

Martha looked at the bowl filled with the brown and bloody water. "Yes, a good hot bath will get you right," she said as she frowned slightly and turned to leave us. "Is an odd thing the way a man finds himself in trouble and no telling what that may be, but sure as sure… it is a woman who will like as not clean it up!" She smiled wryly at him and then swept from the room.

I confess, I had neither inkling nor desire to know but was just pleased to have him back and safe.

An hour later, Edward was clean and shaven, had had tea and a thick slice of bread fresh from the oven that morning, along with bright yellow cheese and chutney. It seemed to me that he was feeling considerably better and a brief smile touched his lips when I looked across at him.

By midday, he had gathered the record of the land selection he had made from the bottom of his suitcase and was about to set off for the courthouse, when I stopped him.

"Edward, I feel sure I should come too. After all, I am a good witness to your right affairs, and they can hardly find fault with two of us."

"Well …" He seemed to pause, not really willing to allow me, as this was by no means women's business. "Perhaps so." He paused, deciding. "I suppose it is as well you come, and they shall be fully aware we mean to raise a cane farm and a family in these parts and will have a mind to clarify the matter forthwith."

"Clarify the matter?" I asked with a frown.

"Don't trouble yourself, madam… but if you insist, come along."

His tone prevented me from pressing him, but my curiosity was now searing my mind with a hundred or more questions.

The folded receipt reassuringly clamped in his hand, he kissed me on the cheek and told me that all was well and we would be back shortly with no further worries so I obeyed and put it from my mind.

When we arrived at the courthouse, the sun was beating hard on the stone and mortar steps. It was the first solid and permanent building to be erected in the settlement town. The pillars at the front were designed to give the impression that this was a building that represented age-old foundations, underpinning the law in all Christendom and that, even here.

Its solid appearance, however, was a façade hiding a wooden building raised on pole foundations to encourage air circulation and covered by a red iron roof.

Edward opened the heavy front door, which swung wide on its hinges, and as he did, hot air pushed out from within, spilling around us. It seemed no cooler inside than in the direct sunlight outside, and he paused, blowing out a long breath as he steeled himself to enter the heat inside. I, likewise, needed fortitude to press into that bath of humid air and followed him.

In the front reception hall with its wide-planked polished floors, clay footprint stains showed where other patrons had visited sometime earlier in the morning. The owners of these would have come to register claims and do various other business that the courthouse accommodated.

Edward smiled as he approached the man attending the counter, and I held close to his elbow.

"Good day, sir …" Edward pulled himself up to the iron grate that somewhat protected the occupant while demanding that persons behave civilly in this place.

"G'dday, sir, ma'am." The Australian accent rebounded in the echoing cavity of the reception area with its high ceiling and open stairway leading off to the left. "What can I do for you?"

"Well sir," Edward pulled the folded receipt from his waistcoat under his jacket. "I seem to have come upon a dispute over the entitlement for occupation of land some thirty miles southeast of here. You, no doubt, do not remember me. I registered this selection some twenty-two months ago, before I had occasion to be badly mauled, and I returned to England for my convalescence."

Edward took a deep breath and went on, without so much as a glance in my direction.

"I have since returned to find that the pegs have been removed and cattle are grazing in the valley between the range and the Black Mountains. I want assurance that I can in fact run these beasts off and prepare my lodgings and fields there as planned."

The clerk looked blankly at Edward, and a few seconds ticked by as though he were considering what had been said to him. His black waistcoat, covering a white linen shirt, seemed to continue breathing of its own accord, although the man sat entirely still. Then, having paused for a moment too long, he coughed a little and replied, "Well sir, perhaps I had better see that receipt."

Edward paused as he opened the folded paper and prepared to slide it over to the clerk. "You should no doubt have a copy of this." He looked up at the man who held out his hand to receive it and as it came into his fingers, began to speak in a voice that sounded almost apologetic long before he really needed to be.

"Well, sir, I cannot recall any settlement selections in the area you speak of, though I do know of the valley you have described. There is not much arable land there as I recall, prior to the open table land beyond, and this whole area is not generally considered appropriate land for agricultural use." He looked over his spectacles at the paper but Edward and I could see he wasn't really seeing anything on the page.

"Well, this valley is in fact, a prime location and most suitable for what I intend."

"Maybe so… but there is the matter of your holding the said selection." He dropped his gaze to the paper again, pretending to read it. "I suppose, we shall first need to see if this is a genuine receipt of registration …"

"Genuine receipt?" Edward replied with consternation. "What can you mean, sir?"

"One moment, sir. I shall need to consult our records and my colleagues."

Edward stood still as he watched the small man dismount from his chair. The clerk hurriedly opened a door in the back of the reception room and closed it just as quickly against our gaze.

"What does all this mean, Edward?" I was puzzled by the whole affair, which Edward had said naught about.

Edward wore an odd expression and his face seemed to turn pale. He hung tightly to the polished wooden shelf that framed the opening of the counter and his fingers rubbed the wood nervously. He was so unusually disturbed that a cold sensation began to fill my stomach and a sweat broke out on my face along with the dawning possibility that something had gone terribly wrong.

"Edward, dear, it will be all right, I'm sure, ..." I said confidently. But I had no sense of certainty in my mind, as this was indeed a place so far from sensible rule that I guessed anything might happen and none would have true right of law to stop it.

The moments dragged on and it was all I could do to resist the urge to run headlong out into the street to be in a "cooler" climate.

Finally, the clerk reappeared, accompanied by another man dressed in a similar waistcoat but carrying, by his manner, considerably more authority and he came up to the other side of the bars that separated us.

"Well sir, ma'am, seems we have some confusion here. Perhaps you would like to go through that door at the end and follow me and we will have a chat."

Over to one side, a door suddenly opened and the clerk cordially stood aside for us to go in. Once we were inside the office, he offered me a seat at a wide green leather-topped desk made of dark polished wood while he dragged a second chair from the wall for Edward.

On the desk top an ornately cast silver penholder and ink well sat to one side, and a number of papers were placed perfectly squarely, beside it.

The man introduced himself as Mr. Peters; he was the registrar for the county, he informed Edward with an air of pomp. He sat, rested his elbows on the arms of his curved wooden chair, and interlocked his fingers. A heavy gold signet ring on his right hand shone conspicuously.

"Well, it seems firstly, we don't have the corresponding record of this receipt of yours." He paused and the room fell deathly silent. "This may be because, last year, there was a fire at this courthouse, and the original building was burnt to the ground." In fact, it had. I recalled Martha had mentioned the event.

"My God ..." Edward uttered under his breath.

"This, of course, means that you may have made the selection you desired and registered... nevertheless... you were not physically in occupation of the land, a further entitlement has been made in your absence, and it has since been reallocated, albeit unknowingly, and henceforth... surveyed quite legally... and title given by the Queensland government to... another party." He spluttered disconcertingly as he delivered each morsel of information.

Edward and I sat somewhat dumfounded.

"Unfortunately, at this juncture, we are at a loss as to what anyone can do about it... other than offer you our heartfelt commiserations and hope that you can make another selection."

"Sir! I find this intolerable!" Edward slammed his good hand down on the chair arm and the slap echoed around the room. Mr. Peters jumped and unclasped his fingers as though preparing to eject himself out of Edward's way should he fly over the desk.

"I paid five pound, seven shillings, and sixpence and registered this particular valley because it was suitable for my exact purpose ..."

"Well that may be, sir, but circumstances have somewhat altered your course. Might I suggest that, if suitable land can be found, we simply transfer your payment to a registration on another parcel?" He leaned back slightly and his chair creaked. "Let me call the registrar clerk and see what land has not been surveyed or selected as yet ..." He rose and scurried around the huge desk, heading for the door while Edward continued his objection.

"Sir, I find it utterly unacceptable that such a thing could happen to me. I am well aware of the land available in these parts and there will be little here that will either interest me, be within reasonable travel, and suitable... I believe sir, I shall be entitled surely to some compensation!"

The man stopped reluctantly at the door. "I do understand sir, but the Queensland government has no provision for such an event as this, and might I remind you, you were neither occupying the land nor even in the country." He felt a little surer of his ground as he enlarged on this aspect. "Why, if everybody could just make a selection of some such section of new territory and then go back to his life prior, then take it up again at his convenience, some years later, the whole of Australia would have been claimed and still be vacant! No sir, only Her Majesty can make those sort of claims and insist on her rights." He smiled, obviously pleased with the strength of his argument.

Edward sat and held his head in his hands as the man shut the door behind him. I felt desperately for him and gently rubbed my hand across his shoulder. "Well, there is nothing for it but to choose again …"

"Margaret, you do not understand!" He spoke with a voice of utter defeat, as the prospect of the dream dissolving loomed large and cold, no doubt in the forefront of his mind and I closed my eyes and secretly said a prayer for him.

Some moments later, Mr. Peters returned with a new clerk who carried a large, roll of papers. They took up positions either side of Edward and myself. Between them, they laid out huge sheets of maps, carefully bound with a wooden beam and clasped at the top with brass clips. It landed with a thud on the desktop. "We have here a title plan of the whole area from Darwin through Arnam Land, Cape York, and all the way down to Townsville." The paper smelt of ink, must, and a hint of smoke. Edward leaned forward and surveyed the thin black lines and dark green ink lines that showed rivers and creeks named for those that discovered them, or dubbed for more obscure reasons with names like, Surprise Creek, Danger Valley, or some such other, equally creative title. Dotted lines showed territory boundary marks for areas labeled "Native Land," "Station," and "Catchment." And I marveled that such an apparent wilderness was already seemingly fully known down to the inch.

"Well sir, as you can see, much of this area has been selected and subsequently surveyed and a title issued. To the north here," his finger pointed beyond the general area of Cook Town to the areas still uninhabited to any extent, "… there is still plenty of land for development. However, this is most efficiently suitable for cattle, I believe, but there is a nice parcel here, about five miles north."

A sudden wave of concern tingled in my stomach as I thought about the news of the cattleman's death and remembered the strange music of the wild aboriginals I had heard from the river mouth before the storm. It did not please me to think we should be even more isolated.

"I suggest," Mr. Peters, said, somewhat dismissively, that you and your lovely young wife think on it and come back in the morning. We can resolve this unfortunate mishap then. I shall instruct young Daley here to help you go over these maps and set you out a new selection of your choosing.

"I suppose, sir, there is nothing else for it," Edward said sharply. The older man glared at him as if he did not thank Edward for ignoring the favor he may have thought was being done.

"We should speak with Martha and Old Henry," I said. "They know this district …" Edward frowned as I spoke, not wanting my suggestion.

"Well, sir?" Mr. Peters said. It was clear our interview was at an end.

"Tomorrow then." Edward replied, and stood and offered me his hand so that I should rise beside him. "Good day to you." He said stiffly.

"Indeed to you too, sir, ma'am. Daley will see you out."

As we went to leave the building, the younger man we now knew as Mr. Daley pulled Edward aside and I was left standing close to the door looking out the small panes of glass to the street.

The clerk seemed to scrape and bow as he chatted with Edward, and finally, I turned to see Edward pat the young man on the shoulder and bid him farewell.

We returned to our lodgings despondently. I barely registered the hours going by and later in the afternoon, Edward excused himself. He said he should be a short while at the West Coast Hotel to meet with Mr. Daley, who had offered to have a drink with him to console him on his disappointment at losing the pretty valley we thought we'd come all this way to settle.

I thought nothing of it then, but when he had not returned by late evening, I became somewhat concerned for fear the troubles of the last few weeks and his wound may have led him to some unfortunate event.

I decided to go to the West Coast Hotel to bring Edward home, but did not inform Martha, who was busy with her night duties, as she would most certainly have stopped me. Instead, I slipped out into the street.

The warm night air was pleasant and the street was all but clear, other than one lone dog that was taking the opportunity to sniff out some possible morsel. I walked a good way before the night silence was displaced by the noise of the hotel famed for a pie made from kangaroo meat and a fast-flowing set of beer taps.

Most of the patrons had already left, as closing hour was not far off. I saw a man stagger from the door and I ducked into the shadows, for I knew it was quite unseemly for me to be there and, no doubt, a mite unsafe. I sidled up the steps and walked quietly along the front veranda, taking care that my shoes made no sound. When I reached the end I was concealed in shadow and peered from my vantage point through the window open to the cool breeze. Three empty tables in, Edward sat side on with Mr. Daley, and I could just hear the two as they laughed from time to time. I could make out quite clearly Mr. Daley's slightly higher pitched voice.

He was recounting his miserable existence as a junior clerk: "Not a jot of a chance of advancement." Then he pressed his fist on the table and leaned forward to speak more seriously: "I just do not agree it is favorable at all to block out every acre expressly for the purpose of running cattle alone, but they are set on it in these parts."

Edward seemed very intent, lowering his head, and nodding a little furtively as though discussing such a matter in public might be far from wise. Mr. Daley went on quite loudly, blissfully unaware of the need for prudence. "But my man, you have an opportunity like no other! You shall be far better off to look one hundred and sixty miles south, as now that land is free and close by to the new goldfield!" I suddenly had an inkling where the tone and turn of the conversation was leading.

"Ah, what I would give to stake a claim myself!" Daley went on, sounding somewhat tipsy and slurring his words, "But I have not a pound to rub together to make the move… 'twould only be me fitness and me ardor that I could bring to such a venture should I find a man so endowed to take me."

Edward had lowered his drink and rubbed his chin as though deep in thought.

Suddenly, I heard below and behind me a shuffling sound. I ducked low and sped along the deck rail and down the steps, and then ran to the end on the road side, darting into the safety of the shadows again just as a gruff voice yelled "Oi!"

My heart was pounding and I kept running more or less the whole length of the street.

When I came up behind our hotel, I paused in the grass at the back, rested both my hands on my knees, and panted until I had a grip on calmness once more. I let myself in and passed through the dark kitchen until I found my way up the stairs to the washroom. I washed my face and hands and quickly made my way to our room. There I brushed out my hair to hide the straggling strands that had worked loose during my fitful run and put myself to bed.

A short time later I heard Edward return, and I lay on the fresh mattress Old Henry had dragged up the stairs after the storm, pretending I was asleep. Edward undressed and crept into the bed and was soon soundly snoring. The smell of alcohol that surrounded him like a cloud seemed to escape from his breath and his pores and fill the room. I could not sleep at all but waited with concern for the morning, wondering what direction our future might take and dreading what answer Edward might have given to Mr. Daley.

Chapter 6

FORTUNATELY, EDWARD DID not rouse until late, and I along with him. The room was hot already and I got up feeling as though I had been slow cooked and every part of my flesh was tender.

By the time we had made ourselves respectable and had something to eat, it was well into late morning. Edward hurried me along and said, "Come on, madam, we should have been there well before now." His scolding did not please me, as he was as tardy as I. We asked Old Henry to take us by cart down to the courthouse and he obliged without question.

Mr. Daley greeted Edward as fresh and as spritely as a young lamb, and when he greeted me, I held my distrust at bay and said, "Good morning to you, sir, I see you are quite well." He looked at me rather oddly, and I observed he had what appeared to be a good "egg" sitting near his temple, blushing with a blue bruise.

We were ushered into the same room as before, and sat in our same chairs while Mr. Daley unfurled the same maps. Then we waited for Mr. Peters to attend.

When he arrived, he seemed more pleased than the day before. Sitting in his customary, self-satisfied way in the big chair opposite, he said, "So sir, ma'am—it shall be good to get this matter dealt to."

"Indeed," I smiled politely.

Edward ignored him and instead scanned the sheet maps to the south where there was no occupied territory. Mr. Daley hovered eagerly with him over this undeveloped area. The handwritten label New Port showed on the coastline south of Port Douglas. The map also had a faded-ink name marked along the southern stretch: TRINITY BAY it read along the slightly curved outline of the coast.

I watched as Edward slid his finger down the letters of the name. I remembered he knew this landfall. It was the beche-de-mer fishing coastline where he had labored for some six months, catching and drying the sea cucumber on the outer reef at Green Island and Franklin Island. He had told me how they periodically came ashore at the Trinity Inlet to collect the red mangrove wood that was used to smoke the delicacy. His memory of it was of a wild and beautiful landscape, but far from habitation and any civilization.

"So what is this?" He pointed to the marking of New Port, and the older man looked up at Daley and raised his eyebrows.

"Oh sir, that is perhaps well worth considering. Dalrimple completed suitability surveys some two years ago, and this is marked out as the site for a new port that can service the Atherton tablelands and north to The Palmer. The government surveyor is due to map out a new town that will compete with Port Douglas. Won't it, Mr. Daley?"

Daley nodded smugly. The man of authority grinned and his small moustache curled upward along with his purple lips. "I believe… is it Thorn Borough goldfield, Daley, that the townsfolk are abuzz with? Isn't that the latest discovery… down there?"

He nodded over his glasses to the young clerk, who was holding his palm down on the sheet.

"That's right, sir. They have only just declared it a strike. Just this week, the field has been advertised in the Gazette. The rush will be on, I should say… In fact, I was speaking with Mason, and he said it will be at least as big as The Palmer."

"Really, Mr. Daley, is that so?" The older man raised his eyebrows quizzically.

"So I believe, sir."

Edward's face was alight with the idea of new gold in yet another location in Queensland. His eyes slid over the Bellenden Ker Range in the south to the Great Dividing Range in the north. He scanned down through the thin lines of creeks and rivers as though actually flying over the terrain in one of those hot air balloons we had seen at the Crystal Palace.

"Plenty of flat land here," he whispered under his breath. He pointed to the area inland from the inlet that threaded back from the end of the Trinity Bay into the basin between the Little Mulgrave River and the Lamb Range standing sentry at the southern edge of the tablelands.

"I remember there are towering crags, and the rainforest acts as a barrier to the much higher plateau of the tablelands inland. They say it's very fertile up there, could grow anything."

"Oh Edward, surely not!" I spoke without thinking. "Surely we shall stay here." He ignored me entirely, as did the two other men now. They realized they might settle this quickly with Edward and did not care where he chose; just that he might make his choice.

"The climate is increasingly dryer the further inland one ventures, until eventually nothing but red desert and sparse scrub covers thousands upon thousands of acres, I heard." Edward was letting his finger slide inland past the tablelands. "That land is good for little but scattered cattle and kangaroo, but the tablelands has a strong hope for fruit and pasture, I believe."

"Too true, sir, too true. Might you try your hand at that?" The registrar inquired encouragingly.

"No sir, the real jewel is the basin below the ranges." Edward brought his finger back to it. "It is 'cocooned' under the mountains all the way to the coastal beaches. I know that coast—it is very lush with flats and fertile plains spread out, ready to be cleared, and perfect for cane, I'd wager."

"But there is no civilized settlement there, is there?" My voice pried into the men's exclusion.

"Well, no ma'am. But it takes no time to change that, and the gold rush will have that land soon taken up and a settlement under way."

Edward scanned the area, but his eyes continued to flick back to the small place named Thorn Borough, some way inland. The small camp settlement named Mareeba was on the supply route to Thorn Borough, above the Kuranda Range. It clutched to the Barron River and had already found its way onto the map, ready to serve the new venture. Beside it, someone had written in red Mining town.

As I watched Edward, I realized he was fixated on the place. Young Daley interrupted his thoughts by moving around to the seat beside Edward, and he too was staring at the spot.

The older man was becoming clearly bored. He was looking into Edward's face, leaning on his elbow with his fist sunk into his cheek, the gold signet ring strategically shining toward us.

"Sir, if you would like to make a selection down there, we will most certainly guarantee its registration. And provided you can assure that it is occupied in a continuous fashion until title is awarded, I should imagine that you and your family will have a good start." He turned his head and smiled wryly at Daley.

"Well, I suppose… I have very little choice."

"Edward… please!" I had not a single moment to think how to appeal to him before the older man interrupted me.

"At least, sir, your choice is entirely first on this map, so I would suggest you make the best use of the opportunity."

I sat there with my hand pressed to my lips as the matter went on without me.

Edward let his finger rest on the area south of the inlet under the Lamb Range, where a peak showed the name Walsh's Pyramid. "I know that place …" He lifted his finger away. "All right, sir, I take it that this is providence. I shall select one hundred and twenty acres through this area here." He slid his finger over the land, river, and stream that encompassed the flat triangle all the way to the inlet swamps.

"I suggest you spend some time with Mr. Daley and map out that new selection. Then we'll finalize it for you. After that, there remains only setting out the boundary markers—and, of course, occupying the land. How does that sound, sir?"

"I suppose this is the best alternative I have." Edward continued to stare at the map, and the registrar sighed and leaned back in his chair, satisfied. "Well Mr. Daley, perhaps if you would make the necessary documentation and prepare a plan—latitude, longitude, in principle… and a receipt for the gentleman, if you please."

Mr. Daley nodded and smiled at Edward knowingly, and the other nodded his farewell courteously, happy to exit the room as quickly as he could.

As soon as he had left the room, another clerk knocked and walked directly toward Mr. Daley, obviously dispatched by the exiting senior registrar. As soon as Mr. Daley had instructed him, he left through the side door for the records room, where cabinets sat in the corner. He left the door open and I watched as he pulled a rolled document from a row of pigeon holes marked "Selections; Cook Town Shire, R S T," which must have been carefully re-packed and re-installed after the fire.

A waft of musty air and smoke somehow made its way to where I was sitting. The fire last year that had supposedly "left nothing" had obviously spared the contents of the cabinet. As he unrolled it, I could see it was marked in large blue letters 'Bermingham, E, L. I watched him as he held up the receipt Edward had given the registrar yesterday, examined its stamp, and slipped it into the roll that quietly tried to hide itself by rolling up between his hands just as it had been before.

In my full view, he shook his head, and without a moment's thought, twisted it soundly as though wringing its poor neck.

I gasped as I saw it, and the man looked at me without a shadow of concern at being caught out. He carried the smoky pieces to the bin marked 'Burn' on the far wall and dropped it in. He turned and faced me and smiled sourly, and then walked a step and closed the door. With that, my life, and Edward's, took an entirely different course.

"Edward... please, that man just ..."

"Margaret, I beg you to be silent!" Edward looked up at me, and a blazing fire in his eye told me I should be still and let fate have its way.

So be it. I suddenly felt a sense of anger and the need to get away from this uncomfortable and disagreeable occasion.

"I think, sir, I should take my leave. It is well and good that this is men's business, and I have many other things of importance to occupy me."

"Yes madam, I think that will be well." Edward said offhandedly.

"Shall I arrange a carriage, Mrs. Bermingham?" Daley asked.

"No sir," I replied, with a distinct tinge of distaste for the man in my retort. "I think I should like to walk, as I am entirely happy on my own."

"Mmm... as you please." Edward was barely interested. "I shall return after this is managed."

I left and made my way back along Charlotte Street to tell Martha the grim news.

When I arrived, she was in the kitchen and had just lifted the kettle from the stove, holding the handle with a tea cloth.

"Ah, there you are, lovey. Shall I pour you some tea?"

"Thank you, yes. I need such fortitude."

"Oh? What troubles you, lovey?"

"Well... as you know Edward has been quite odd since his return yesterday... and as it turned out, our selection has been lost!"

"Lost? Oh my goodness... what shall you do?"

"It has been fully decided without me, Martha." A tear came to my eyes, more for the sadness that my husband seemed so estranged in his decision and had no thought for me in making it, than for what the decision was.

"Now, now... Here get this into you and tell me all about it."

"Oh, my dear Martha... I am to be settled in some empty wilderness at a place called New Port because it does not as yet even have a name!"

"Down there? No!"

"Yes! I'm sure Edward has been seduced by that man Daley and has chosen one hundred and twenty acres of pure wilderness only because it is near the new goldfields. How shall I manage, Martha?"

"As you always do, my dear girl. You are indeed the bravest and most spirited young woman I have yet met. And though I shall miss you, I know you will whip that place into a fine home—and we can stay in touch from time to time by letter if and when they have a post and riders for the service." She said the words boldly, but I could see a look of desolation pass over her face.

"Thank you, dear Martha. I hope you're well right. I know I shall have to find the stomach for it, and I'm sure Edward has a good head for such things... After all, he knows something of that area."

Martha frowned with due concern but stayed silent, knowing full well to meddle in a man's decisions by counseling his wife was neither becoming nor wise.

She patted my hand and whispered encouragingly, "Who knows what good will come from this? The Lord knows, and he says just this, lovey, 'I know the plans I have for you, plans for good, not for evil, to give you a future and a hope'." Martha sang the quote in a lilting tone and lifted herself from the table to place her cup on the bench. Standing facing the cupboards, she chimed. "At any rate, these towns spring up just as fast as spring grass, and before you know it, there are the likes of nice people like you coming from all over, marrying and having families and filling the churches with good souls. So don't worry, it will work out exactly as He wants it to."

"I'm sure you are right," I replied, but I was not in the least convinced in my heart. Still, her words very much cheered me. I smiled and left her for the parlor to consider the turn of events.

By very late in the afternoon Edward returned to the hotel accompanied by Mr. Daley, and sought me out in the parlor with renewed excitement. He told me very proudly and with a good deal of hope in his voice, that they had completed the land selection. Mr. Daley had prepared, from Edward's general idea of the land area, boundaries, a plan, and registration, and after they had finished, the two had set off down the road to our hotel.

Edward said he was very obliged to Mr. Daley, and the young man smiled knowingly. My husband patted my hand affectionately and said that as Daley had accompanied him down the road, they had talked "with a good measure of interest" about the new field a mere fifty miles west of the new port. Edward's voice told me he was clearly very impressed by this fact, and he said this could be "nothing but favorable to us."

It seemed that the previous troubles had now been forgotten, and I noted that Edward had found new vigor in the company of the young man but in my heart I felt no kindness about the association and would have wished he had never met him.

I listened with indifference as Edward told me he had agreed to meet Daley that evening at the "West" to enjoy celebratory drinks and further discussion. He did not ask me if I should miss his company, and I began to wonder what strange power the young man had to steal my husband away from me.

Edward ordered tea for himself and Daley and asked, "Will you have one, dear?" He was quite the pleasant gentleman again in Mr. Daley's presence, and I said with as much displeasure as I could display without losing my manners that I thought not, "It will soon be time for supper." I hoped Mr. Daley would take my hint and excuse himself, but neither he nor Edward caught my inference, and they carried on in enthusiastic talk as they sipped tea. I sat for a good while without saying a word, which neither man seemed to notice.

Mr. Daley, by his animated discourse, clearly relished the idea of fresh and exciting adventures—the ultimate being the making of one's fortune overnight by finding gold. My ears pricked up when he said that he would leave immediately for the field and "stake the claim." I could not help but wonder why he said "the claim" and not "my claim," and I wondered if Edward had lent him money, as Mr. Daley had said he "had not a pound" just the evening before.

He spoke without seeming to take a breath about the ease with which men could make their fortune. He made it sound without peril and far easier than could be the truth. Martha had said how many only just survived these northern fields, fraught as they were with deprivation, snakes, dangers and ever-present disease.

Edward sat nodding and smiling, not in the least bit giving away whether the possibility was enticing for him also.

I felt sure the idea might fester in him, because I guessed our resources, including Aunt Amelia's one thousand pounds must be dwindling and would soon be exhausted. However, with still more settlement costs required, I was convinced that these might only be covered with diligent hard work and success of our venture. I hoped that Mr. Daley's enthusiasm did not lead Edward to be tempted to think this new gold discovery might be a deceptive miracle to solve any shortfall and was an easier path to new wealth.

When Mr. Daley said his farewell with a view to meeting Edward later, I followed Edward upstairs and questioned him on it.

"Edward, please… I beg you be truthful to me, as I know you to be. Has that uncertain man gained an attachment to you? I am sure he has not a penny, yet now seems to be off to this infernal gold venture. Have we money enough that he has convinced you to support him? I feel sure we will need all our funds for ourselves and our farm, not for chasing gold …"

Edward suddenly lost his pleasant demeanor of the last hour and turned on me fiercely.

"What think ye, that you should have any business to ask anything about such things? I'll thank you not to meddle, girl!" He gathered up his coat and shook his finger at me. "I warn you not to question me on my affairs. You shall have your farm… and your needs met, and that is all that is pertinent for you to be concerned about …"

With this, he stormed from the room and headed out for the West Coast Hotel to meet Mr. Daley.

Left alone, I began to wonder where my attentive, kind, and polite husband had gone. I sat with trepidation and felt so unnerved that I could not muster even a single step to go down for supper. Instead, I swallowed back my sobs and waited for his return.

When at last he did come back to me, it was well after eleven. He entered quietly and found me sitting in our bed by the light of the lamp, reading to distract myself of the time.

He was oddly calm and much to my surprise, seemingly, had not been drinking. He sat upon the bed with his hands on his knees and his head held low. I could smell the fresh scent of Martha's soap, and his hair was combed and wet from having bathed prior to coming up to me. I thought it somewhat strange and rather at odds to how he had left some hours before.

"Madam, I owe you an apology." I sighed with relief at his return to the man I felt I best knew. "But lest you forget, that it is for your good that I do what I have, and much easier it will go if you don't resist me." He paused and looked around to me sitting quietly and still against my pillows.

"On the morn, you are to get ready immediately, for I am set in my mind to leave tomorrow."

"What! Sir, are you entirely mad?"

"Madam! I will have none of that. I shall arrange transport at dawn and gather supplies we shall not find at the new port. We will leave on the tide."

"But I had thought that we would be here at least some weeks …"

"Margaret… I will not let you speak thus again! We go tomorrow and that is the end of the matter. You will get your things, get supplies to manage for a good month or more, and have it done by the tide!"

Not wanting to anger him further, I replied, "As you wish." I closed my book and set it under the lamp, turned the flame down very low, and settled down into the sheets. "I shall get Martha to help me. She will be surprised, but I am sure she will see to it that I put together what we shall need for this… adventure."

He seemed very much relieved by my acceptance, and put himself to bed. As I turned on my side and shut down the lamp, I felt his arm rest across my waist.

As I lay there still but awake, I wondered what had so upset him that he had entirely changed from the man whom I thought I had married and now desired to abandon Cook Town so hastily. I wondered how depleted our financial reserves really were, and whether the lure of Mr. Daley's enthusiasm for gold had hastened Edward's desire to reach those southern parts before the rush took up all the best claims and the opportunity was gone.

I lay in the dark wondering what it should be like if I must accept living in a mining camp instead of farming cane, now that everything had changed and our new selection was taking us far away from the beloved friends I had made, and safety.

Chapter 7

BY EARLY MORNING, Edward had secured a fishing vessel to take us down the coast to the new port, past Port Douglas. It was a very old Beche-de-mer working vessel that had seen better days. It had unloaded its cargo of smoked sea cucumber the night before and was happy to take a back load of our luggage and ourselves.

Edward had come down to make sure our crates came out of the warehouse shed and had brought me, too, so I could see the extent of the space allotted to us.

I held my hand up to my nose as I surveyed the craft that had been hauled into the dock ready for loading. I was very concerned and said to Edward, "Is there not another way we can go, perhaps by cart and horse?"

He turned from the ship, walked back over the dock planks and explained quite civilly, "The only way down there is the Bloomfield track that hugs the coast all the way. It passes through the Daintree wilderness and on past Port Douglas. The distance from here to the new port is one hundred and sixty miles, Margaret. Even if we had time enough to waste, all the will in the world could not make such a journey possible as it's utterly impassable in the wet season." He slapped his thigh and shot a glance at me. "This is the only way at this time of year …"

I wanted to shout out Then why can't we wait!' but I held my tongue. Edward had rarely looked so determined and his face was set like flint.

He tossed a look at the craft. "It is seaworthy, I'd wager, and the Captain knows the reefs about these parts… it's a relatively short trip, so don't trouble yourself."

I swallowed hard as the smoke and rancid smell of the previous cargo turned my stomach, even though we were a good many paces away. "We had best get on with our preparations then." I said with as much sincerity as I could muster, happy to use the excuse to find fresh air elsewhere.

We went back to the hotel and I busied myself packing a list of cooking essentials that Martha had given me into boxes and baskets as Henry and Edward fetched the larger items from the general store.

The flour and wheat, corn, sugar, tea, and a little coffee, maize, lard, and butter all came packaged in barrels or wrapped in brown paper sealed with wax. Bacon, wrapped and pressed in a wooden box, and eggs neatly wrapped and shut up in a basket, all found their way to the cart ready to load in the waiting holds of the Fern Leigh, so named after the town the Captain had come from in Ireland.

Martha found more and more items that "you simply cannot do without."

She made sure that everything we might need was ticked off, loaded, then taken up to the dock and packed aboard.

"And you simply must have more soap than you think you will need!" She had grinned broadly as she handed me yet another cake to add to the basketful I already had. "And also candles! You can never have too many candles!"

Martha had taken on a strange air of sensitivity. I could feel her sadness and trepidation on behalf of myself, such a young woman, embarking on this uncertain adventure. She kept bringing forward this or that, from some cupboard or other, declaring that, "I have no need for it at all," and "Best it go to some use with you than sit here for the silverfish to eat away!"

A live nanny goat was procured from the Chinese market garden, and Martha made sure the animal was pregnant so that we would have milk in due season.

Seven plump red hens and a fine rooster, which was unrepentantly feisty when we attempted to catch him, found themselves stuffed into waiting wooden cages before they were taken to the docks along with everything else.

I was more than thankful as the day rolled on. It seemed like a never-ending Christmas, and I was barely aware that with the rising tide our last moments in Cook Town approached.

By half past three, we had brought our horses up to the dock from the grazing paddock behind the hotel. The crates we had brought from London, a cartload of supplies bought from the general merchant, and our luggage were all being loaded, with Edward helping the fishing crew to stow everything away.

A block and tackle was used off the dock to pull the crates of tools and materials, sheets of iron, and even a parcel of timber to the deck of the boat. All was transferred from the comfortable stability of the solid wharf into the yawning maw of the boat's hold.

Every now and then, shifting in the slight current, the craft would hit the bumpers attached to the dock and then away, the ropes straining, sending out a kind of music made up of creaks and squeaks as the boat moved in the river tide.

Though Edward was kept busy, I noticed he never stopped watching the water for something. It occurred to me that perhaps the famed crocodiles of these parts might be attracted to the animals, so I dismissed it as simply his diligence.

The horses had been well watered and fed and were led up the gangplanks and corralled in a makeshift stall at the aft of the boat, topside.

At four fifteen, when all was aboard, Martha, Liz Beth, and Old Henry came up to the dock to wait with me and to say our farewells.

I stood arm in arm with Martha, and Liz Beth clung at my elbow on the other side as the moments counted down and the Captain and crew made ready to embark with the late tide to get away to sea again.

"That Wongoree's mare, Miss Margaret. My's people not seen 'im come back to town at all." Liz Beth pointed to the smaller mare nudging her flank against the big gelding.

"Mr. Edward said he has gone off hunting Liz Beth. And Mr. Edward needed another horse so he bought it from him for a good price."

"Oh." Liz Beth stared at the mare and continued to hold my arm tightly, as though doing so could prevent us from leaving.

A kookaburra barked out its long cook, cook, cook, ck, ck, ck from the grassy hill, and no sooner had it done so than the ship's mate yelled from the dock, "All aboard, if you please… All aboard!"

"Well, the time is here, lovey… I shall miss you so." Martha gathered my hands together and smiled widely as she looked into my eyes. "I feel sure we shall see each other again, and you can write to me, to let me know how it's going, eh?" She paused and searched my face almost pleadingly. "You will write… won't you, dearest?"

"Oh yes, dear Martha. I would not think of abandoning my first friend in Australia." I squeezed her hands and patted her shoulder affectionately.

"Me too, me too!" Liz Beth tearfully chirped.

"Of course you too, my darling Liz Beth!" I leaned in and hugged the tiny girl and I felt her hands cling like 'Greeny' the gecko to my back.

"It's going to be a cruel trip for you, lovey, on that thing, and heaven knows what kind of food you shall be getting. So we have made you some sandwiches and some shortbread and a little cheese for you both. And look, Henry found this bottle of wine that really is in need of being drunk on the first night after you arrive."

"Oh, that is simply marvelous. I do not know what we would have done without you. Oh, I shall so miss you. It will be hard not having our little chats. What shall I do?"

"I suppose you shall be too busy to even think of such things. And if worse comes to worse, you shall have to make do with the nanny! They always give more milk if you talk to them!"

"Nothing shall be as much comfort as you have been."

Martha shook her head a little and turned away to hide an unfamiliar tear that moistened her eye. "Oh dear, none of that... Let's get on, or you will miss the boat."

Liz Beth gave me another hug that threatened to stretch on indefinitely, until Martha wrested her tiny arms from me, saying, "Come on my little girl, you must let her go ..."

I waved good-bye as I turned and hurried, somewhat blind with tears, across to the gangway. Edward reached out to catch me and help me aboard. We moved to the rail, which felt sticky to my touch. With all the gusto I could manage, I waved to the three on the dock.

Behind them, the trees at the base of the hill were shimmering in the afternoon sun and reflected light sparkled off the water and danced like silver coins in our eyes.

Seabirds had already begun to arrive in the new breezes lifting from the Coral Sea to observe the activity of the craft beneath us. The picture was all but perfect, and I determined to commit to memory the beauty, hope, and tenderness of those last moments in Cook Town.

Martha was holding Liz Beth by her shoulders, and from time to time she looked across at me. I could see Liz Beth looking up at Martha and adding her observations and narrative minute by minute and Old Bill stood stoically beside them looking on as though he might have wished he could renew his youth and come too.

The tide was high up against the wharf and the current was running out to sea as the old boat pulled slowly away from the dock and Liz Beth's voice faded, "Love you Miss Margaret. Miss you long, long time ..."

"We shall be out to the ocean in a short while," Edward said. He seemed as nervous as the horses, still searching the waters beside the wharf as though the devil might suddenly come up from the deep and take us all away.

"What is it, Edward?"

He looked up at the afternoon light now filling the air and turning the water into a sea of molten gold all around us. "I shall be pleased to tarry no longer and be about our own business at last," he said quietly.

"Are the horses all right?" I asked with genuine concern.

"They will settle down. The sea is looking very calm and I imagine once they get used to the general feel of it they will rest easy."

Edward held me tightly as the ship began to move more rapidly away from the shore, and I was pleased to have his closeness once more. The crew moved purposefully around us, stowing ropes and making sure we were ready for the coastal journey. Then the wind caught the main sail and the Captain yelled instructions fore and aft. The sheet billowed out and the ship jolted forward and began to slice her way through the water running out to the Great Barrier Reef.

I held onto the sticky rail and watched as we moved through the more troubled waters of the opening in the reef and sailed out into the turquoise sea laced with the cloudy residue of river waters.

The triangular canvas of the huge sail, struck by the gentle afternoon breeze, shaded me from the western sun still working its way across the sky up above the mast, and I marveled at the beautiful form of it hauling our craft along the surface of the water.

Time seemed to slip away as smoothly as the ship did from the land, and the sails took up the fuel of the wind and pulled us south. The brilliant cornflower blue sky stood out against the distant hills, and the land became a rolling carpet of emerald piled up high against the horizon.

We sailed steadily south on the outside of the reef, and as we did, the distant mountains curved nearer to the shore. Before long I could see wild buttresses towering over a narrow strip of green coastline punctuated here and there by sharp rocky points and golden peach-colored sandy beaches.

The Coral Sea lay deep and blue-green beneath us, and our little fishing craft skipped through the spray with abandon.

The afternoon soon became early evening and the light changed. I had never seen anything as lovely as that long line of coastline peeling out in front of us with the red dusk forming in the lower atmosphere. Every mile that passed became a mile closer to my new home and our new adventure.

At half past five, we ate Martha's packed "lunch," and Edward showed me down the creaking and oily stairs of the fishing craft to the only cabin aboard.

The scene below was not at all as tolerable as the Clara had been. The pungent smell of putrid fish and fetid water sloshing in the bowels of this working vessel assaulted my nostrils, and I found it almost unbearable to be down there.

I battled to use the chamber pot, and the close, dank air made me feel seasick. I held my nose while my face became glossy in the heat, and held onto the thought that this trip would be over in just two days.

Above deck, wherever I moved the men of the fishing crew leered at me with thoughts I could only imagine with disgust and trepidation, and I longed to be back on the land.

By early evening, we changed our course to follow the channel through the outer reef and sailed for some half an hour until we were in sight of Port Douglas.

We set down the anchor just inside the reef where the water was calm for the night and the Captain saw to providing a brew of quite good tea when all was at rest. After we had finished we stood on the deck together listening to the crew laughing and humming unknown tunes as we watched the distant lights flickering in the few tall buildings of the town that lay in the lee of the headland and sparkled like a gathering of fireflies.

Edward held me gently but remained silent. He was evasive to any question I made and I wondered if this new man was just a temporary state or the revelation of the husband he was always destined to be. By comparison to the charming and optimistic man I had been courted by in London, he was in no way recognizable, and it troubled me greatly for I did not think the turn of events so justified the change in him.

Still, he was warm against me, and I reassured myself that when we arrived at the new port and settled into our new life, he would again find himself. But for now, a severity seemed to have settled around him and a secretive coldness kept me at a distance.

The sleep I had that night was no remedy.

The Captain had vacated his cabin for us, as we were his "paying customers," but the bunk was less than clean and the room little more than a cupboard with a small desk at one end opposite the door, and the bed in between.

We had slept uncomfortably, our backs against each other, and I had my hands pressed up against the inner hull all night, my face just inches from the damp and oily wood.

My dreams were wild and angry, and I woke more than once, cramped and hot.

Edward did not fare well either, and rose at about three to go up on the deck. I felt him leave but pretended to be asleep. In truth, as soon as he had quietly let himself out of the cabin, I rolled onto my back with relief and was asleep at last before I even realized I was drifting off.

At first light I woke. I heard the sound of muffled calls and we had turned with the tide and the boat creaked strangely against the pull of it. I dressed and went above and as I came into the clean air, my lungs filled and so did my soul. It was breathtakingly beautiful. The sun warmed the Coral Sea and hews of gold and pink crept into every place. Seabirds sailed aloft and against the dark green vegetation, white herons stalked for prey. I drank in the scene with awe and from my vantage point at the rail; I surveyed the town waking to the new day.

Port Douglas was similar to Cook Town, nestled in the wilderness that spread inland. Hidden waterways created a wide area of marsh and large estuarine crocodiles, I was told, abounded here. I had heard a loud splash just before midnight and wondered about its origin, but there was no sign of the giants now in the stillness of the sea, nor lying up on some muddy bank to catch the warmth growing with the hour.

The dock, wharf, and township straddled a wide spit that led over to a long, golden-sand beach on the far side, which began a stretch of pretty beaches, rocky points, and rainforest to the edge of the water all the way to Trinity Bay.

Coconut palms had been planted along the first beach and huge fig trees fringed the high hill that looked down on the sheltered township.

The familiar range of mountains rose across the dusky skyline as they had done all the way from Cook Town. The flat land that spread out from that distant point looked undisturbed, dark, and uninhabited, while the port bustled with the activity of being the only supply line for the inland gold miners.

Nigh on six, I was called for breakfast and Edward nodded politely as he sat on a crate with his tinplate in hand and ate a little away from me. I looked on with some dread at fried, salted fish, laid on crusty bread, with not a jot of butter, facing me. A chunk of cheese sat beside it that at best, was long past fresh. A crewman handed me an enamel cup filled with tea that was far better than one might have expected by the rather common fare otherwise presented so I picked meagerly at the food, but drank the tea with relish.

Shortly after the meal was finished, the ship's crew began to ready the boat to move on with the tide and Edward bid me well but seemed well pleased to ignore me with the excuse of helping with the tasks aboard. When well at sea and on our way, I watched him as the crew settled into the rest that comes with open water and the boat sailing rightly.

I could see Edward was more in his element than I had ever realized. He was leaning on the gunwales and holding on to the lines that swung off the full sail as he talked to the Captain. The Captain was smoking, as was his usual habit, and the two laughed periodically.

He looked at ease and I was tempted to join them then decided not to disturb Edward but wait with the hopes he might feel a mite sorry for me. Holding on to the rail as I stared across to the shoreline slipping away behind us, along with Port Douglas, I did my best to look like the forlorn girl in Longfellow's, Wreak of the Hespress, my bonnet barely keeping the tendrils of my hair from streaming out in the breeze.

When Edward saw me standing alone, he paused and then excused himself from the Captain. The older man slapped Edward on the back and walked up forward to the bow where he checked a seaman and tightened a line on a cleat before disappearing behind the curve of the sail.

"Ah, here you are… We shall pass Double Island soon—see over there—and then after that, we shall come in to Trinity Bay."

"I can see a huge headland way down there on the horizon. Is that it?" I said, happy to have his attention at last.

"Yes that is the southern end. Beside it is the inlet that goes all the way inland through the flat basin. It used to be a lake, they say. When Cook was here, he thought it was a river, but it's not." Edward patted my hand as I rested it on the scarred wood. "The land I've selected is a little south from that waterway, but we will still be able to get our crops to sea easily by shipping them down through the tributaries and along to the landing at the mouth of the inlet."

I did not reply as I was staring hard into the wind, waiting, wishing us to our destination, and watching for some sign of civilization I hoped would greet me.

"See there, that is Double Island."

He pointed to two small-mounded islands showing against the shoreline as pebbles thrust out in the sparkling waters. "That is where the rainbow serpent, that the natives say made all this land, finally came to rest and is sleeping to this day."

"Well, I am not sure about that, Edward. Seems to me that the idea of a huge snake curled up between two islands is, thankfully, farfetched. If he were real, what if he should be awakened? I have absolutely no desire to meet such a creature!"

"I am sure you shall not meet him." Edward scanned the distant coastline, which he no doubt remembered well from his days fishing along this coast, and we stood together in silence.

On one occasion, we saw natives slipping along in their cedar canoe and a party of three disappearing into the undergrowth that fanned out along the shore.

I gasped and lifted my arm to point, and Edward nodded, without, it seemed the slightest concern. But I noticed he clamped his hand tightly on the wood of the rail and his knuckles whitened.

"Soon be there, Margaret. We shall soon be there …" He muttered more to himself than to me.

Within the hour, the sails had been set to carry us toward the land, but the tide was against us. "We shall have to wait for the tide to turn and an offshore wind." The Captain yelled out to Edward.

"It'll be too late to go ashore tonight by row boat to take a look then?" Edward replied.

"Aye, that's right. Best to sail up the inlet in the morning and take a boat ashore at high tide if ye have need to see the settlement."

"Edward, where is the town? …I cannot see any sign of habitation." I had hold of the rail with both hands and was leaning hard into it, looking up and down the sandy beach that spread out north in a perfect golden ribbon under the green foreshore scrub.

"The town has only just been surveyed. The main part is behind that sandy bar." He looked across but didn't let his gaze settle there. "I wouldn't trouble yourself about the town… we're not going to be very near to it. Our land is back that way, toward that mountain in the distance."

He lifted an arm and pointed to the perfectly triangular Walsh's Pyramid, sitting forlornly between the Headland Mountains and the inland range spanning the full length of the bay and beyond.

"We've got one hundred and twenty acres of flat, fertile, soil. I don't think we shall have any time for the town."

"Oh Edward… I didn't realize it would be so… so wild." I touched his arm, "Will we be safe?"

"Of course we will." His voice sounded shallow, as though he had said something he was not sure of. "This is the adventure we have been waiting for." He said as he led me to a place to sit while we waited for the evening meal.

We sat on two crates as the day gave way to the new night. I could smell fish frying again and the sound of crewmen's voices which seemed to get lost in the vast open space and the evening stillness. We were handed a dish of food each and a mug of tea. Edward's nearness made me desire to unburden myself of my rising fears.

"Edward, I'm not sure… perhaps I should have stayed in Cook Town until you were ready. I mean, I am not a frontier woman. I don't know if I can manage way out there in the wilderness in this strange land."

"Enough of this!" He slammed his plate down and the sound of the crew up on the forward deck temporarily stopped.

"I do not need to hear any moaning nor complaining from you! This is the chance we have, madam. Moreover, might I remind you, you were more than happy to be saved from that hat shop and whisked away to 'this strange land.' I might point out that women equally as 'fine' as you worked and died without a whimper in conditions twice as difficult as this." He swept his hand angrily over the scene. "So I don't want to hear another word about it. Do you understand me, madam?"

I winced at his angry tone and the sudden eruption then I gathered my wits and replied with careful duty, "Certainly sir."

I spoke very quietly to avoid the crewmen's curiosity and my embarrassment. "I am sure… if, 'God be with us, then who shall be against us?'" With this, I placed my plate carefully beside me and stood up as silently as I could. "I will take my leave, sir, if you do not mind. I am a little tired and I want all my strength for the 'adventure' you speak of. I presume we will start tomorrow rather early."

I nodded politely and turned away from him, heading for the cupboard below and hoping he would see fit not to require sleep himself, until well after I had left the conscious world.

As I lay down for the second night in the oily-smelling cabin, I began to feel the despair of my predicament.

Lonely and confused, I did not stop the tears from falling, wetting the unpleasant pillow, and soon was wracked with sobs. For a long while I wept unrestrained, until emptied of all my sorrow and homesickness.

When worry came upon me that Edward would find me in such unseemly despair, I checked my emotions and tucked them away in my soul like a tidy mistress. I consoled myself that I was far stronger than many. Indeed, before long the sea air and the boat's gentle rocking did its magic and I was overcome with the drowsiness that only the ocean can bring, and fell into a deep sleep.

Edward, for his part, did not come below at all and must have found a place on the deck with the crew. In the warm night the constant gentle breeze would have blown across the sleeping men and none would have need of a blanket so I did not concern myself for Edward's comfort. A quiet lapping at the hull and the squeak of the anchor rope stretching rhythmically lent peace to the night, and we were all left to our dreams and fears, separately.

The day broke with a flush of pink and gold rising from the turquoise sea out past the great shadow of the headland.

The crew roused early and smoked their pipes as they chatted quietly to themselves, leaning on the rigging, looking out at the picturesque skyline.

I woke early too. I rose and made my way topside to find Edward washing his face in a bucket of water.

"Good morning, sir." He looked up at me as I greeted him and smiled as he dried his bristled face in a rough towel.

"Good morning, my dear." He seemed in much better spirits today, and I smiled gratefully.

"What time will the tide be right for us?" I looked across to the expanse of trees and mangroves, noticing that several curling pillars of smoke rose up from the landscape, showing that we were not entirely alone in this place.

"About nine. We are going to start in and the tide will rise with us. By the time we get most of the way in, we should be at full tide and able to land the horses and set planks ashore and begin unloading. They are going to stop first at the town's landing point. I want to see if I can arrange some labor."

"Oh? Is there labor here?"

"Should be Kanakas and China folk, according to the Captain."

I walked past him toward the aft deck, "I'm going to see that the chickens are all right."

"Yes, that is a good idea, my dear. I haven't seen to them yet."

He carried on and ignored me, as I swept along the deck boards in my swaying skirts.

Soon the ship was on the move. Two deck hands hauled up the anchor by turning the winch and the water swirled with mud as it unloaded its debris closer to the surface. Within a half hour, the ship had slid through the mouth of the inlet into the deep channel that ran all the way from the ocean to the inland plain where the ancient lake had been but had broken out to the sea.

I could see things in much more detail now and smell the dank, salty freshness that comes from the new tide washing around the mud gathered under the trees.

The New Port town was exactly that: a proposed new port, not yet built.

Cairns was one of the names suggested for it, to commemorate Governor Cairns. Such things were just musings scribbled on the map as yet, and a hand drawn map at that. The coastline was uninhabited, apart from natives, a few settlers to the north in the district of Smithfield, and cedar loggers who had drifted down from Port Douglas.

I had thought we were coming to some kind of village, at the least. Instead, I looked out on nothing but a small scratch on the least part of the body of the land.

We slid gently around the bend until I could clearly see where the new settlers and prospective townsfolk had begun to clear sections of scrub a little back from the coastal marsh. With relief, I realized that the place was not as desolate as it had first appeared. I could see a few people. Men appeared, attending unknown work.

The open framework of a building under construction, with men crawling under and over it, showed where progress was being made in the young port. The men had materials in hand, and the encouraging thud and smack of an echoing hammer traveled across the water to us as we sailed by.

The Captain edged his craft closer and came up near a roughly laid, planked area that was intended to be the rudiments of a landing dock.

There were two hundred men already in the small area; the Captain was quick to reassure us. "A Queensland government official surveyor has already completed a survey and plan of the future town," he said. "Most of the men on the shore there have put in two hundred pounds each to erect a full-size wharf."

As the boat hauled up to the makeshift dock, the crew swung our gangplanks over the side, and a landing party was soon preparing to leave to collect supplies, Edward among them.

I wanted go ashore also, but Edward forbade me. As soon as he had taken leave, however, my curiosity could bear it no more. With a little care, I negotiated the springing planks and stepped down to solid ground.

The heat ashore was bearable, and I headed for a crate under the eaves of the first shack at the end of the so-called jetty. Before long, however, I could not resist venturing a little further, stepping around the wet ruts and puddles to explore the area that I hoped would one day be a real town.

All around me, cleared scrub was smoldering, and mud covered the wheels of various carts standing laden or moving along the track. A team of horses stood in the shade of a lone tree nearby. Their legs and underbellies were covered in mud and sand and they seemed more dirt than alive as they held their heads low, resting from whatever heavy work they had already done.

The screech of a big cockatoo broke my inspection of the ground, and as I looked up I caught site of it in flight. Yellow under feathers fanned out over its pristinely white flight feathers as it glided overhead. It seemed to be surveying the unusual activities below, which had never been seen before in the millennia of the land's history. The bird's screech seemed almost a cry of exclamation. I wondered what the beautiful creature thought as I watched it sail away.

As I walked on, I began to smell early morning baking and hear the sound of chattering Chinese.

Several small wooden shacks with iron roofs had already been thrown up upon what seemed like the rudiments of street corners. In the center of them stood a larger wooden building, square and unpainted, and hanging from a string, a small painted sign read General Store.

Out on the veranda I could see buckets, picks, shovels, and all manner of equipment and necessary implements.

I mused as I walked up to it, Seems someone is always quick to get business going, no matter how uncivilized things should be. And I thought of my dear Martha who must have likewise, begun so humbly.

As I watched, I saw Edward coming out the door. He turned to shake hands with a man, and then strode across the street to disappear between a square tent erected beside the roadway and a tree that still had its roots firmly placed in the way of progress.

He hadn't seen me, and I didn't follow him for fear his newfound anger would erupt again because I had disobeyed him. I decided to head back before I should be discovered. But I took with me the slightest inkling of hope, and I felt a good deal better.

Just before seven o'clock Edward arrived back and greeted the Captain who had appeared a moment before with a box marked Turkey under his arm.

Edward had two men with him. One was a Kanaka, from some south sea Island, and the other a somewhat thin and dejected looking Chinese boy of about eighteen or nineteen years of age.

Edward didn't bother to introduce them but showed them to the aft area and indicated a place to sit near the horses. Then he returned to me.

"Well, we have some labor at least. And the Captain has finished getting his supplies, so I imagine we'll set off for the last time."

"I have been sitting here looking at the town… it is going to be very nice in a few years, I dare say."

"Oh, yes there is a goodly amount of flat land here, all the way back to the mountains, so I imagine there is room to grow and to have excellent farms round about." He looked down at me quite warmly. "Perhaps one of them will be yours, madam."

I smiled and shyly looked at my small white hands, still locked together on my lap.

"If you say so, sir. I am sure I shall muster up the fortitude and courage to be a completely satisfactory cane farmer."

I was inwardly wondering how such a thing could ever happen when I had barely even studied a plant in a pot, let alone a field, or any form of livestock.

At almost exactly seven-thirty, we pulled away from the landing and out into the channel.

The sheets slid up the mast again, and with a nice breeze, we sailed down the center of the inlet, where the width allowed a good speed.

In just an hour, the channel had narrowed and the sides of the inlet had pulled in to resemble a wide river. As it continued to taper, Edward and I watched as the so-called river narrowed enough that we could see the banks on either side.

The huge pyramid-shaped mountain became clearer in the distance, and an occasional tributary showed where streams dumped their flow into the inlet in odd places.

"Look, Edward!" I thrust out my arm from under my cream-colored parasol and pointed to a beautiful white egret taking flight from the background of green foliage. It lifted on the breeze and sailed off inland, away from our view.

"We are so lucky to see this land as it is now." I looked up at his strong angular jaw and the dark stubble growing in patches on his cheeks. "I fear one day all this will be gone …we will have tamed it all and in doing so lost the sight of such things." He shook his head as if to wonder how such a thought would ever come to mind and I realized in an instant that we were as far from "one" as called for from our Lord, as any two could be.

Finally, the "river" became more of a muddy creek and the boat was as far inland as it could safely go, so the Captain called a halt.

The sails were dropped, and the boat slowed until it was barely moving. I began to truly feel the humid heat for the first time amidst the damp cloister of trees.

"That's it, mate," the Captain grinned as he called across to Edward.

"Yes, I would say we have done our dash …"

"Drop the anchor, Jones. That'll do, I'd say." The Captain barked his orders and the anchor rattled off down through the hull and splashed heavily in the high water still running into every cranny it could reach.

"We'll have to hurry, sir. The tide'll be on the turn soon and we'll not want to beach 'er here. No sir, I don't fancy being stuck in the mud for a night on her side in a croc-infested creek—not to mention the heathens 'round about these parts!"

"Crocodiles, Edward? …Are there crocodiles here, too?"

"Yes dear, there are. In the winter, when it's cooler, you will see one or more as they come out onto the banks to sun themselves and get warm, when the water is lower." Then he added, "And sometimes in the wet season too, around November to March, when they breed. The big old males will defend their territory, so we have to be careful then."

He was already striding away to help the crew, the Kanaka, and Chinese boy as they slid the gangplanks out onto the muddy bank between the trees. "Don't worry, Margaret, our land has two nice rocky streams, and crocs don't go up into those." He was puffing a little as he helped lever the big planks over the side and lock them into place.

"No missus, you won't find nothing to scare you where you're going 'cept the odd native and maybe a python or two," the Captain grinned, while supervising the construction of our entryway to the shore. It looked hazardous, to say the least.

"That's comforting." I replied as I watched the activity from the side and tried not to get in the way.

Soon the men were hacking at small scrub trees and making a way up the muddy incline to drier ground.

"Looks like this will have to do for now. There's just nowhere good to land up here." The Captain was scanning the tidemark and wanting to cut short the work ashore. "Just mud and mangroves the whole way… But this will shorten your journey a bit. The long way round would add a week, I'd say."

Edward nodded and surveyed the task at hand. Unloading our cargo would not be easy. "Certainly, I am very grateful sir, for your trouble in bringing us in this far." Edward smiled and nodded toward the Captain, who stood with one foot jammed up against a tree.

"Well, best we get you unloaded 'fore that tide makes a run for it." Edward nodded in agreement.

I stood leaning against the rigging and watched the men begin to unload, following the rudimentary track they had made up onto dry land.

Edward seemed quite the intrepid explorer striding back down the track with his hatchet in his hand, his sleeves rolled up, and his wide-brimmed hat pulled down low. From under the latter only his nose, mouth, and chin could be seen.

"Shall I come ashore, Edward?" I waved out to him, quite at a loss as to what I should do.

"No madam. I think it best if you simply stay out of the way. We have some heavy lifting and unloading to get done, so stay where you are."

"Well, if you please." I shook my head, disappointed a little, and decided to press him a little more. "Are you sure there is nothing I can do?"

"Well, all right, you can see to those chickens."

"Ah my, little chickens… I certainly will."

I spun around and headed to the stern. Our "chooks," as they were called here, were stacked up in their wicker cages. I held each of them up carefully and gently explained the somewhat rigorous ordeal they must undergo until we could be in our new home. I apologized to them for what I was making them go through, but the little dears simply stared back, likely terrified of my small face peering gleefully through the wicker.

I carried the first basket to the side and passed it to the dark-skinned Kanaka, who grinned a huge yellow-toothed smile toward me. I politely flicked a smile back as the broad-shouldered islander uttered in a deep voice in something resembling, "'Siz good chicken, lady mama."

"Thank you sir, I'm sure," I fleetingly replied.

The gangway swayed as crewmen struggled with barrels and boxes, and then Edward called to me from the bank.

"Margaret, for Heaven's sake! Get out of the way before you end up in the water!"

"Oh dear!" I thrust the last cage out to the young Chinese man, who had hurried up to take the last basket from me.

"I think I shall just pop ashore, Edward, if you don't mind terribly, and see to them, out of the way up there." I pointed to the incline and didn't wait for him to agree or not

I stepped eagerly onto the boards and gingerly shuffled down the slightly curving walkway until I could jump clear up onto the bank.

My feet sank a little in the mud and my skirts skimmed the surface, gathering a new layer of gray over the top of the dirt I had already collected in the new port.

I climbed the incline and found myself in the clearing, looking across at boxes, barrels, sheets of iron, timber, and all manner of materials piling up in the center.

I stood in a pool of sunlight that beamed down and I could feel real heat was already brewing, even this early in the day. The dappled light shivered around the base of the sparse scrub trees, and the thin grass, green and fresh, wavered in the light breeze from the distant sea, evident even here.

Behind me, I could hear the men grunting and puffing, straining their backs, lifting, and manhandling heavy items up into the clearing.

In front of me, the wild landscape seemed to beckon me toward it, as though welcoming and challenging me at the same time and as my eyes looked into it, I realized no mans' foot had walked away in ot it and we were more than likely, the first.

"Well, it is as far from a London as I can get. There is nothing for it but to 'gird me loins' and trust the Lord!" I whispered to myself.

I turned from the moment and rested my eyes on "my" chickens where they sat beneath the trees making worried little book, book, book sounds.

I determined to find some new water for them as their bowls had tipped over and it was very hot, even in the shade.

By the time I had found a gap in the unloading parade and climbed back aboard to get a pitcher of fresh water, the gangway was completely blocked with six men hauling a large dray, a foot at a time, complete with chassis and huge wooden-spoked wheels towards the shore.

The rails were tied inside it, along with other parts and the outline of a yet-to-be-assembled plough could be seen.

"Oh Edward, this is wonderful to see all our wares come ashore!" I looked at the item of transport and had been very pleased indeed when they had rolled it aboard at Cook Town. And seeing it as it was manhandled up the slope made me imagine far more civilized times. "We shall be well set with the dray. I shall be able to go off to town to church whenever I want, won't I?"

The men burst into laughter. Edward turned and glared at them disapprovingly, the laughter died away to be replaced with knowing looks and grins.

"Margaret, I think you had better stand well clear… Perhaps that nanny should be brought ashore after this… Go and get a rope round her, and I'll help you as soon as we are finished with this here …"

Edward did not even look up to see if I had gone as he had bidden, but continued with the men hauling the dray ashore and up the muddy incline with the aid of ropes looped around the bigger trees at the top.

I stared over the side and considered why the men had laughed so heartily and then it suddenly occurred to me that there would be no roadway to the town. At that moment, the wildness all about me, suddenly seemed so vast and overpowering and I shuddered as though I might be chilled with some ghostly premonition instead of steeping in the tropical heat.

Deciding not to worry myself about it, I headed aft, where the nanny was happily eating hay in a small crate-like stall with a lid tied on top.

The animal, which Liz Beth had called Gangoo, welcomed my hand when I passed it through the slats and stroked her nose. The small goat's pink lips rolled up immediately as she tried to "taste" my thin white fingers.

"I think we might find this quite an ordeal, little Gangoo. Looks like we could be each other's only female company—apart from the chickens. And I don't think they are going to be much good at conversation."

I took a deep breath, as though steeling myself for the reality of my situation. "Oh well, the empire has been built on females such as we…"

The nanny bleated quietly and looked about for more hay while I scanned the deck for a rope to tie around her neck.

When I found one, I untied and opened the lid of her crate and tied the rope around her neck, making sure it was not too tight. Then, happy that I had done as Edward had asked, I stood beside the corner of the crate with rope in hand and waited.

A little while later, the young Chinese boy appeared. He bowed and repeatedly thanked me as he took the rope from me.

"Jackie takes now, mam... Jackie takes?"

"Oh, thank you Jackie, I shall bring the water for the chickens."

Jackie leaned into the crate and wrapped his arms fully around the four legs of the small nanny.

He lifted her from the crate, dumping her on the deck beside us, and she looked around with fearless curiosity.

"You come... goat! You come." He pulled hard on the rope but in total defiance, Gangoo refused, pulling equally in reverse.

"Mam, you push behind... She come."

He looked up at me and nodded to the rear of the goat, which was solidly determined not to move an inch in his direction. "You push... Goat, she come?"

His smattering of English was just enough to make himself understood, but I thought he should do much better so I smiled and held my face squarely in his view. I paused and pointed to my lips, correcting him kindly, "You say it like this: If you wouldn't mind getting behind the goat and pushing her, she will come!" I spoke the sentence very clearly for him to learn, fully assuming he could manage it.

He shook his head and giggled. "Very quick, quick, mam... many word!" Then he pointed again to the goat. "You push goat, she come!"

I sighed and realized it would be quite a task to improve his English, so I shuffled around to the back of the goat, put my fingertips gingerly onto her back, and then with a little grimace leaned my knees beneath my skirts into the rear of the goat as Jackie pulled.

With a little teamwork, we soon had her moving forward and made our way to the opening in the side of the craft.

I lifted my hands and rubbed them together with satisfaction at our accomplishment but then took a quick sniff of them and screwed up my nose because Gangoo had indeed, an unpleasant smell about her. "You need a bath, Gangoo... and a good deal of Martha's soap!" I said to her and then called out to Edward, who was walking down the now, slippery incline toward the boat. He was puffing, and the crew behind him was breathing hard likewise.

"Edward, I have got the goat." I declared with delight.

"Well done, my dear. We're almost finished. Just the horses and a few crates."

The horses were hastily bridled and led from their stalls at the aft section of the craft. They were brought to the gangway, and the mare obediently negotiated the slight lip and staggered down the bouncing wooden planks with the crossbars that provided traction. Her hooves slid to each small rail, preventing her from slipping down its length, and step-by-step, she made it to shore and up the bank.

The big gelding, however, was not so compliant and less adept. He looked from side to side at the water and his ears flattened. Huge draws of breath showed he was more than uncertain of the journey, and he kept reversing back up the incline. Then gravity would get the better of him, and he would slide forward again.

Edward held the horse's head and another man stood aside the the hind quarters and nudged him with a slap to be obedient.

Suddenly, the big dark horse took a flying leap as though trying to avoid stepping on the strange moving slope altogether. He missed the bottom entirely and his right fore and hind legs slid down the side of the ramp. As both hung off the side, he slashed them wildly in the water and men howled, "Whoa!" and jumped back on the bank.

He thrashed there on his stomach for some moments as men erupted in frantic yells but the horse finally rolled awkwardly off the gangway and plunged into the deep water between the boat and the bank.

Edward had kept hold of the bridle rope and a second man grabbed the end behind him. They hauled on the head of the horse to give the rope no slack in case it tangled as he thrashed about, his eyes bulging in panic. The gelding kicked and struggled in the water, occasionally hitting a hoof on the slippery mud sides of the bank but never getting a foothold.

My heart was pounding, the situation looked desperate.

Edward and the other man, amidst loud instructions from the boat and the shore, finally hauled the horse by his head along the gap and clear of the ship at the stern.

Once past it, they looped the rope around a tree and four of them hauled the horse up the bank. With a last struggle, the gelding clambered up on his knees, still kicking in the water with his hind legs. Finally, he stepped up and dug his hooves in the mud until he could climb to solid ground.

They pulled him up into the trees, and standing there with head down, the horse breathed hard from his ordeal, shaking from head to tail.

Edward quickly ran his hands over the horse's forelegs. There was deep bruising along the inside of the front left fetlock where it had slipped from the side of the gangway, but fortunately there was no gash or broken bones. Except for a triangular surface cut on his rear right gaskin, the gelding was unharmed, though severely shocked.

Edward took a deep breath. The loss of the gelding would have been a heavy blow. However, he seemed all right, so Edward left him standing in the shade of the trees and walked back along the bank toward the gangway.

"That be a narrow escape." The Captain smiled and shook his head. "He'll be a bit sore, I 'spect, for a day or so."

"Mmm," Edward agreed, and looked up to where I stood, no doubt white-faced and nigh on as shocked as the horse. I stood stock still, still holding the goat by her rope as she chewed her hay, oblivious of the drama.

"Best we get you ashore now, Margaret… Now be careful, madam, we don't want you thrashing about over the side too."

I passed the rope to the young man and at the bottom of the gangway, held out my arms as Edward reached for me. With his help I made it to the top of the bank, the Chinese boy bringing up the rear with the goat in his arms.

The bank was now almost completely trodden into a muddy sluice, and suddenly the Chinese boy lost his footing. He slipped headlong onto his face, and the goat sprang from his arms excitedly, trotting to the top with ease. She let out a large bleat of disgust as she looked back at him.

He looked up from his landing place, his face covered in dark gray mud, to see the goat's face, her ears dangling beside her head and her large yellow eyes with their vertical pupils fixed on him in perplexed wonderment.

The crew erupted with uproarious laughter from the top of the bank.

"Well, I seen it all!" the Captain yelled from the side of the boat, "a yellow man made black!"

He shook his head, and then returned his focus to the water now lazily turning its head back to remember whence it had come.

"Now come on, you louts! …'Nough mucking about and playin' around. We need to get this ship back to her draft and on her way back to sea! We got some fishing to do to make up for all this malarkey!"

The crew shuffled down the slope, still grinning and giggling, and Edward came with them to check for any last items left aboard.

He called back to me. "Do you have everything, my dear? …It's now or never."

"I've already checked twice below and on deck… the nanny was the last." I called back as The Chinese boy clambered up to the top beside me and picked up Gangoo's rope.

Edward swung himself aboard for the last time. I could see him slapping the Captain on the shoulder and the Captain doing the same in reply. Then Edward pulled his purse from his waistcoat pocket and unfolded large pound notes.

The Captain turned his back slightly on the crew, and between them, they counted out the rate and nodded and thanked each other accordingly.

Edward then trotted down the planks and helped the last of the crew slide the heavy timber up until it was level. Then they pushed hard to slide the planks on board.

Edward found a length of tree branch on the ground, and with as much effort as he and the Kanaka could muster, they pushed the craft off the bank until it began to drift clear.

The dinghy was sent astern and two men rowed hard until they had pulled the boat around in the channel.

After a few tense moments, she pulled free of her near entrapment and began to ride the ebbing tide back toward the sea, drawing away quietly into the dark, muddy open water.

Edward and I stood on the edge of the bank, our goods behind us, and watched as she pulled away to disappear beyond the mangrove fringe.

A distant yell echoed through to us over the water and through the trees: "Good luck mate!... Good luck!" Then they were gone.

Together, we walked up the newly hacked track and came upon young, muddy Jackie and the Kanaka, who's name was Billy, sitting in the grass amongst the boxes piled up in the clearing.

Edward stood, his legs apart and his knuckles firmly planted on his hips, surveying the load and catching his breath.

"Well, it seems, madam, we are at last about our business." He looked at the pile wistfully. "... But I confess, I doubt that I have a jot left of energy to do much more at all 'til we eat."

Suddenly, I realized the enormity of making sense of the huge pile for even the necessities of the moment.

"Well, I suppose if you can make me a fire, I shall find the tea and... the egg basket and make something for us all."

I looked about to see if I could find anything familiar for the task. "Has anyone seen the pot and the frying pan?"

With that, Jackie swung into action, and while Edward strode off to see to the shocked horse, with Billy following dutifully behind, I found what was needed to get a rudimentary camp under way for a late midday meal.

"Can you water my poor hens?" I grinned up at my helper, who had found firewood, bundled it up, and lit it for me. "They will expire I am sure, if they don't have water."

Jackie frowned. "X-pie?" The young man practiced the sound of it cooperatively, not having any idea what it meant.

"Ex-pire... It means to die." I was trying hard to teach him.

He looked at me quizzically. "Why you not say die?" He turned to pick up the pitcher I had filled with water and shook his head. I could see English and its various components made little sense to him, but he seemed kind and willing.

"You brave woman... Must be brave, brave, come out here. Jackie help if Jackie know what mam say."

"Well, I can teach you if you like," I smiled at the young man who was only a little younger than myself.

"S'alright, Jackie already learn big time," He frowned and sucked in a breath dramatically, "Oh... very hard, poor Jackie... Very hard.'

I turned and looked up at him, smiling. "It's very good for Jackie to learn properly... I, teach, I insist! We are in Australia sir, and you must learn to speak English, properly!"

Jackie, it seemed, realized I had given him little choice, so he nodded politely and carried on with his task.

I busied myself with the creation of a somewhat unimaginative meal, but in doing so, I felt strangely contented and satisfied. Perhaps this was not to be so daunting as I had first thought. I determined that I would think of it as a "rough picnic," and with that, I called the men and we all ate under the shade of the bush that surrounded us.

After the meal, we assembled the dray and stacked the crates and the plough on it.

When we had everything packed, the mare was hitched to the new vehicle. Though the load had not been planned for her, Edward was unwilling to strain the gelding that day.

The goat was hitched behind it on a tether and the chickens in their baskets were strung over the side of the dray.

By the time we were ready to move, the gelding had calmed himself somewhat, but Edward did not saddle him. Instead he led him through the brush at a gentle pace to where he had decided to make camp further from the water. He and Billy had cleared a track about fifty yards to the south ahead of us.

By early evening, we stopped and unloaded a more sensible camp than we had arrived with.

Edward set his map and compass out carefully, and began to trace where we would go tomorrow.

The journey through the wild landscape was roughly thirty miles, but for most of that distance we would have to cut our way through as we skirted the base of the mountains toward the pyramid, keeping the dense rainforest-covered range to our right.

To our left, the marshy upper reaches of the inlet confined us to the flat middle passageway of scattered bush that led to the mountain and the land we would settle.

I stared into the fire as I thought about the journey still ahead.

"How long will this take, Edward, before we get there?" I was seated on a box of nails in the mouth of the new white tent he had erected. The fire crackled softly and Billy sat just outside the range of the heat, some distance from us all. Jackie, who lounged in the grass on a blanket, shielded his eyes with his forearm and lay dozing so Edward and I spoke quietly and might well have been alone.

"Well, it depends on our progress through the bush. If it isn't too bad, we might make about five miles a day, maybe a little more."

"So we will be there in six days?"

"Could be more like eight or nine days."

"How far is it from the town?" I began to feel ill at ease again, and sat up slightly on my box.

"Not that far, Margaret. It's more about the time it takes to make a track for the dray."

He looked up at me seated in the glow of the fire. "It might be better than we think, if we find someone else's track."

"Someone else's track? Oh I do hope so, if not for my sake, for my poor, innocent, chickens'!"

He grinned and shook his head.

I sat there thinking quietly as the fire flickered in my eyes and I became mesmerized by it.

"I suppose... when we get there, our land will be like this too. We shall have to clear it before we can start?"

He looked up, then back to the fire. "Yes, my dear, that is right. Good things never come except by hard work, I believe you said in Cook town... backbreaking work would be more accurate, I'd wager. Still, we shall have our farm, and you shall be the great lady that rules it." He smiled.

I could see his handsome face shining in the firelight and his eyes reflecting the sparkling flames. For a moment, I remembered this was the man I loved and I wouldn't want to be anywhere else in the world.

"Edward, I think I will turn in. Are you tired?"

"That I am, my dear. I am not sure if I could be more tired." He hung his head down between his shoulders and sighed. "What I would do for a hot bath... but it will be some time before that luxury is available, I suppose."

"Edward, come to bed now. We need to sleep. It will be another big day tomorrow, taming the great outdoors of Queensland!"

"Yes... I suppose it will be." He rolled on to his haunches and stood full height over the light of the fire. "Goodnight, Billy... It is Billy, isn't it?"

"Yeah boss, me Billy. I going make sleep now." The dark figure rolled over and wrapped the edge of the blanket over his back until he could hardly be seen at all.

Jackie had already succumbed and did not reply to Edward's goodnight, and then Edward bent his tall frame and entered the tent, and followed me in.

I pulled myself out of my dress and underclothes with difficulty and held them tightly to me. For a moment I saw Edward stop, quietly watching my white shoulders until I found my nightdress and quickly pulled it over my head. I lay down patiently on the thin mattress that had been unrolled onto the tent floor over the grass pushing up here and there from underneath. Even so, I was quite comfortable.

I watched Edward undress and fold his shirt and trousers at the end of the bedding. His wide back made a shadow against the sides of the canvas tent lit by the firelight outside, and I reached out to slide my hand over it.

It was oily and damp from the day's heavy work, but I didn't mind and rolled my fingers over to stroke down his spine with the back of my hand.

He seemed to sit there motionless for a moment, enjoying the sensation, then in a low whisper he said, "Margaret… we really must get to sleep."

I dropped my hand and brought it back to my chest. With a deep sigh, I whispered back, "Goodnight, Edward."

He lay down beside me and very quietly, he whispered through the still blackness, "Goodnight, little hat girl."

In the morning, we found ourselves alone in a maze of bush with nothing for company but the heat and humidity.

Each day after that it seemed to rain for some part of the day. We had to cut our way painfully, mile by mile. Sometimes we walked through the rainforest trees, wet to the skin, which at least cooled us. Then we continued in the steam that followed, until we were dry again.

When evening came, we would look for a grassy clearing in the trees to rest. Each night we had to rebuild a camp and find water while Edward shot wallaby for our meat. He also shot fat Torres Island pigeons, which I became good at cooking, with a little help from Jackie, who turned out to be an excellent chef.

When darkness fell I would thank my Lord for his providence toward us and each morning I would thank him again that a snake had not found its way into our tent in the night.

Fortunately, we had the horses, Jackie, and Billy, but what we thought might take us a little over a week actually took nearly three.

We suffered from a myriad of insect bites and lived in constant discomfort and every mile was fought for. There was not one day of that trip that I did not look into my husband's face and wonder why he had married me and brought me to this wilderness.

He had become quite the stranger to me. In such a little time I had gone from a young and excited wife to a "camp hand" whom he hardly spoke to, let alone offer any comfort, nor even the touch of his hand.

Nonetheless, leading my little goat behind me as we cut our track through the wilderness, I felt stronger.

This land was becoming our home by the investment of our suffering and our struggle. The sweat we bled and the pains we felt had purchased for us our citizenship, and day, by day, we began to be infused with the notion that this was our land.

I began to embrace the idea that we were now truly "Australians." and that whatever the hardship, it would be worth it, because one day we could say we belonged.

One fine day in May, Edward called a halt as he went on ahead to check his bearings. We could see ahead the pyramid mountain clearly now and from up ahead, could hear the sound of distant water. The cool afternoon air was filtering down from the ranges to greet us for yet another evening and I sat on a crate that Jackie had put on the ground for me. I was hot and dejected. My hair hung in wet threads over my forehead and my dress was damp, dusty, and muddy up to my knees.

My hands seemed like the legs of a spider, thin and bitten with red splotches all over them.

Under my boots, red blisters remained covered but nonetheless, had made the walk of the day torturous. Though I would have given up my manners in front of the hired men to tear them off and have my feet naked in the grass for all to see propriety forbade such luxury.

Still, I sat looking around at the clearing and decided that it was quite possibly the most beautiful spot on earth.

A bright purple emperor butterfly sailed across the breeze, alighting on a leaf here and there, then fluttered away through the trees and the sound of the rainbow lorikeets sprinkled the air with their playful chatter.

I watched as Jackie made a drink for us.

Billy was seated under the trees dozing until "the boss" demanded work from him.

The dappled sunlight that filtered down through the twisted boughs of the trees and the gentle shuffle of leaves made me feel sleepy too, as I rested from the grueling day.

From the edge of the clearing, Edward appeared in a rush. "At last! I think we have found the eastern corner."

"Oh Edward, thank the Lord!" I called out with excitement, and my head flopped forward with the last of my energy, seemingly dripping from me with the words.

Edward saw me sitting on the crate looking more like a street waif than a lady from Langley Street and he paused.

"I suppose we should make camp for the night and go across in the morning. There is a nice stream just over that group of trees, and that is the boundary on this side. Margaret, do you think you might want a wash? I can help you to it if you like." Edward had walked across the clearing and offered his hand.

I looked up. My face must have looked very pale, and his demeanor changed, a pang of fear showing in his eyes. He lifted me gently up in his arms.

I welcomed the affection and grasped him.

"Come, my dear. A nice cool wash and a meal and you'll feel much better."

"I'll get food going, Mr. B. You want stew?" Jackie asked.

"Again Jackie? Yes, that will be all right. Can we have some of those good oven bread things you make as well?" Edward smiled at the Chinese boy who had become such a great asset to us. "And you, Billy, get the tent up for Mrs. B, so she can rest when she gets back."

"Yes, Boss. I'll do." The Kanaka seemed to move slowly, not really interested in doing much more for the day but unable to ignore the command.

Edward carried me over to the big basket that held things we needed to use each day and I alighted on the ground. I scooped out a cake of soap, a towel, and a cloth, and Edward put his arm around my waist and helped me walk down the small incline that led to the stream.

"Thank you Edward... I admit, I have run out of strength... a wash should revive me."

He led me down through the trees as I limped beside him. The thicket became denser as we left the higher, drier ground. As we neared the stream, green leafy plants that soaked up the deep water grew with abundance and he forced them aside for me.

Within a moment or two, he had led me down the incline to a ravine that revealed a stony riverbed with larger boulders strewn about between narrow sandy beaches.

The water looked cool and clear, and the sound of it trickling through the gully was delightful.

"There is a nice pool just up this way a little. Can you manage?" He led me by the hand with care as I hobbled over the stones in my boots.

When we arrived at the pool, it took my breath away. Green and shady, the water lazily spilled into the deep chasm under a small precipice from above. Fronds draped their shawl like leaves around its edge and champagne bubbles frothed where the stream dropped into it. I leaned on a large boulder and balanced on the rocks embedded in the sand at my feet.

"Shall I leave you?"

"Edward… I'm not sure… shall I be safe here?"

I was scanning around the stream wondering when a crocodile or some equally fearful creature might appear.

"There is nothing here to hurt you."

"What about snakes, Edward?"

"If a snake is here, it will have long since slithered off at the sound of us arriving. They have no ears and can't hear anything, but they can feel our coming. They're more afraid of us than you might think, so don't worry about them." He looked into the cool pool and the light reflected on his skin. It looked inviting.

"I tell you what… I will come in with you, how should that be?" He smiled and with unusual humor and said, "I can scare off any fish that might be in there!"

"Shall I ever find a place in this country where there is naught that need be 'frightened off' so I might enjoy the place in peace?"

He shook his head and smiled. Grabbing my free hand, he helped me negotiate another large boulder and I followed him over the stones and rocks of the riverbed toward the pool.

"It's beautiful, Edward …" I stared into the green water as though ethereal spirits had mesmerized me from its depths.

Crickets and the familiar cicadas droned in the background, and a green parrot let out a squawk high above before he abandoned his private world to the interlopers below him.

I sat on a rock that dipped its base in the water and, putting one of my stifling boots on the opposite knee, began to undo it.

"Let me …" Edward came over and gently grasped my ankle in his hand. He lifted my white stockinet leg from my skirts and rested it across his thigh. "I do little enough for you, my dear and I'm sorry for it…"

I watched him as he crouched before me with my thin leg dangling off his wide thigh. As the cool air and the silent place enveloped me, I began to feel relaxed, and I rested my palms on the rock behind me and leaned back.

He carefully pulled my heated foot from its leather cage, and I winced at the soreness of my heel.

The boot set aside, he lifted my skirt and felt for the top of the stocking around my thigh. Gently and slowly, he pulled it from me. It peeled off like the skin from an imaginary snake, and when my foot was free, he swung the stocking through the air like a winter scarf. It sailed from his hand and landed over the rock behind him and he laughed.

I took my foot from his thigh and rested it on the wet stones at my feet. The shock of cool water made me sigh with delight, and the clear, cold movement across my instep eased my discomfort.

He grasped my other foot, lifted it to his knee, and began to unlace my boot.

I could see him swallow hard as he peeled off the second stocking, and I wondered if he would take me right there.

He did not, but collected the boots in one hand and carefully placed them up higher on the bank.

"I shall turn away as you undress …" he said politely, and I was a little glad for this, for the area was so strange and unfamiliar for me that I felt shy in his presence.

He took off his shirt, hung it on a tree, and stood with his hands on his hips and his head down waiting for my word to turn and face me.

I undid my dress and undergarments and folded them roughly, placing them on my rock.

A little unsteadily, I stepped into the water like an unsteady nymph.

Step by step, my bright pink feet tentatively found their footing on the stones as I edged into deeper water, and then slid into pool. The water enveloped me and I felt the cool rush as it lapped over my body.

It was blissful. I called out as I floated and swayed in the center. "I'm in, Edward… It's heavenly!"

He hurriedly removed his boots and his trousers and without care for his nakedness, stepped into the pool while I looked away and waited for him to be covered by the water. He walked in up to his thighs, then dived in to come up near to me.

"Ahhh!" He raised his hands and swept the hair from his forehead, then wiped the water from his face. "This is the life!" He smiled, and with renewed energy, swam over until he could reach me. Grasping my hands in the water and pulling me to him, he said, "You are beautiful, Margaret."

"I thought you had all but forgotten me."

He looked past my shoulder as though someone on the other side of the pool required an answer for why he had done this thing to such a young wife.

"It is not that I do not desire you, my dear …" He looked down at my breasts floating discreetly beneath the water. "It is just… this is a dangerous place for a woman." He stared into my face. "Not dangerous from the wildlife, nor the natives, but dangerous for a 'woman'… because of her husband… and nature itself, concerning her… functions."

I realized what he was saying. "Are you afraid for me if I become with child?" I frowned a little.

"I have lost a wife already… I don't even like to think of her… because you are my life now. But I would never forgive myself…"

"Oh Edward, silly man! Nature has designed me for the very act. You have nothing to fear. The women in my family have been good with childbirth."

"Perhaps so Margaret, but have they had to give birth miles from another woman or help? And we have such a lot of work to do before you'll have even a modest place to live." He smiled and touched my nose playfully.

"Perhaps you are right. I hadn't considered that."

He pushed himself away from me, and I let him go. He began to swim with long strokes over to where the pool was much deeper and the waterfall created a current. Floating in the deep water and looking up at the fronds cascading off the hillside, he said, "It is my duty to think of things for you."

I frowned as I replied to the back of his head. "Well, I understand now, but perhaps you could have told me before, so I didn't think that you no longer loved me." I began to make a few pretend strokes in the water in his direction as I spoke, then as I finished speaking; I dived forward and began to swim after him.

He swam away from me playfully, and then let me catch him. As soon as I caught up, I splashed him, and he returned the game with sparkling fistfuls of crystal water.

"When we are established, I shall enjoy making you a mother."

"And I, … I shall enjoy being a good mother, so you will be welcome, sir!"

"Ahhh…" He rested his head back in the water and let it run through his hair. "Where is that soap, Margaret? A good soaping is just what I need. That will scare the eels away."

"Eels!" I spun round in the water and headed for the bank.

Edward burst out laughing while I rushed from the water like a frightened, white-skinned waif to find the soap for myself.

Hovering in the deep water, he watched me without moving. I could feel his eyes flow over my form, svelte and wet, and for a moment, I wondered how he would keep his hands from me. I did not at that moment think I cared for such restraint regardless of his sensible concern.

As I turned back with my nakedness forgotten and the soap in hand, I could see his hand had casually begun to handle his member beneath the water, and his desire rose and changed the expression of his face.

"Oh dear, I see I have been less than modest…" I whispered, and swallowed. I smiled shyly and waded back into the water with the cloth held in front of me. "Take this soap, sir… I shall not come out there for obvious reasons."

"Is it me or the eels you are afraid of, madam?"

"Both, sir… and mind yourself! I shall not suffer at the hands of either of you!"

He laughed with unabashed abandon and seemed to let the ardor he felt wash away with the cool current flowing past, but as I came close to him with the soap held out in my hand, he reached out and pulled me to him.

Within moments, his arms had encircled me; his lips found mine, and his grip tightened around me. I could feel his muscles shivering and when he stopped and looked into my face, his breath escaped quickly.

"Touch Me, …" he whispered shakily and pushed my hand down his chest to his engorged maleness.

I felt shy and unsure but slid my hand over his stomach to the shock of hard muscle that had grown with my nearness. The arousal ignited my own, as I pulled in tight to his body.

Quickly, he began to rub himself between my thighs, and I felt the flush of my own desire with the water splashing between us and abandon soon over took me, but he refused to enter me. Instead he pounded the space between my thighs and a wave of water compressed against my stomach with each thrust as I clasped my free arm around his neck and held the soap with the other, still not letting it slip from my hand.

He held me tightly around my waist and flashed a glance at my breasts bobbing in the water before sliding one hand over them roughly and nuzzling the wet of my neck.

With a sudden jerk and a low groan, he stiffened, and I realized he had released himself.

For a moment, he held me tightly with his eyes closed, and then he slowly let me go to drift away in the current. Then without another word, he turned away from me, and looked back to the shore.

"Forgive me …" He struggled to speak and I realized the shame he was feeling.

"Edward," I called kindly to him, and he turned to look at me.

"I have soap," I said, "I'm not afraid of the eels anymore."

Somewhat relieved by my disposition, he laughed a little uncomfortably and came back to me. He let me soap his back and neck with the cloth, and he did the same for me, and before long, the water was white with foaming suds that collected around rocks as the stream dragged them away.

We bathed together for some time after that and came up out of the water like new people.

I felt alive again. I tied my hair back in a tight knot, the drips trickling down my neck to wet my bodice, and though I would have wished to abandon my boots, convention demanded they be returned to my feet and we set off back to the others.

By the time we got to the camp, a meal was waiting for us.

Jackie and Billy were seated with mugs of tea and were trying to have a conversation, each in English that was so poor it was debatable that anything had been understood by either of them.

I smiled and suggested they dish up the food just as the sunset began to disappear behind the mountains.

Jackie had made a stew from wallaby that had been caught the day before. He had also prepared dough, seasoned it with a little dry herbs and salt, and cooked it in the embers in a large camp oven made of cast iron. The blackened crust belied the soft, bread-like interior, and the smell was wonderful.

I ate, drank, and felt entirely exhausted, excusing myself early to disappear into the tent.

By the time Edward also retired, I was so deep in sleep I did not feel him lay down beside me.

I woke to the new day to find myself nestled in the crook of his arm as the birds sang in the softness of dawn. He whispered to me that he had been laying in the dark before I woke, listening to the sounds of the bush and the trickling water in the distance and watching me sleep. My warmth beside him and the fresh smell of soap had been intoxicating but he had restrained himself. He had determined that until he had a decent home for me, and enough money to sustain it, he would maintain a kind of courtesy that a husband need not usually concern himself about. Edward vowed he would not lose another wife on his account, so he had lain still and frustrated beside me.

I didn't want to say that I, too, felt frustration and had no thought for my safety nor concern for it either. As the new daylight spilled over the landscape and bathed the trees where our camp lay, I reached for him, sliding my hand over his chest and kissing the skin of his shoulder. I felt him shudder but he stopped my hand and roughly turned me away.

"Margaret! What think you? This is neither the time nor the place …"

He rose, covering himself and quickly grabbed his trousers and thrust them on and then rose and left to wash. His sudden return to the stranger I had come to know left me saddened and I sighed heavily. I too rose to dress, struggling as always, to put on my clothing in the confines of the small tent, but for all that, today was indeed different. Though I was already getting hot and the fabric clung wherever it touched, I sat, in a bloom of skirts all around me, with a sense of utter joy in my heart. I dragged on my stockings cross-legged and laced up my boots amongst the billowing fabric, like an excited child on Christmas day, urgent to get out and greet the surprises that awaited.

At last dressed, I poked my head out of the tent to take in a huge lungful of the new morning air.

Standing up fully, I stretched and with one hand, smoothed my hair above my ears as I marveled at the pretty scene around us.

Jackie had already made tea and something akin to toast from the oven bread, which was laid out in a tin plate sitting on a rock. Bacon was sizzling, and the smell drifted everywhere, sufficient to rouse even the herbivorous wildlife that lived here, with its mouth-watering promise.

Soon Jackie had broken eggs into the splattering fat, and before long we were all eating a good breakfast.

"Well, today is the day!" Edward announced, knowing the final few yards to our selection was imminent on the other side of the stream. "Billy and I will scout down the stream and find a crossing, and then we shall start looking for a likely spot for a permanent camp on the other side. After that, the first job is to lay out the boundary markers. Jackie and Mrs. B. will stay at the camp; Billy and I will survey the land." He seemed so sure and in control, as I watched him muster his troops for the tasks. "Looks like this will be the last time we have to pack up. On the other side, we will be 'home'," he said confidently.

When breakfast was finished, I helped Jackie clean up, and we carried the utensils and the plates in the pan to the stream I had swum in the night before.

It was as lovely as it had been, though the colors had changed. It was darker and more foreboding. The pool was not lit with the green light of the afternoon sun but was now a dark, bottle green in the shadows of the overhanging trees.

Jackie knelt down to wash the bacon fat from the pan with the use of some leaves and sand from the river's edge.

I watched him as the crumbs of bread and left over egg yolk washed out into the water and the fat twisted in apparitions on the surface before slowly floating into the general melee of the stream.

Suddenly he jumped back. "Gai se wooong lee!" His voice sprang out in all directions and returned to him in an echo.

"What's there?" I also sprang back from the water's edge, dropping the knives on the stones with a clatter. "What is it?" I squealed as terror gripped me.

Jackie had recovered from his initial shock and was now peering closely, pointing into the water. "See madam... is fish!" He was following it with his arm as I, with morbid curiosity, hovered around his elbow looking into the shaded water.

"See... see!"

Finally, I caught sight of it. It was an eel, black with fine gray spots from nose to tail. It was snaking through the rocks, looking for the source of the inviting scent in the water.

"We catch, missus... we catch! Make good lunch!"

Before I could do anything to stop him he had spun round, hurled himself up the bank, and disappeared, so I was left alone to watch the eel as it continued its search among the rocks, oblivious of my attention.

Within a few minutes, Jackie was back, this time with twine and a hook in one hand and a piece of bacon rind in the other.

"How are you going to get it, Jackie?" I asked as he focused on threading the bacon onto the hook.

"You watch, missus. You watch!"

Carefully, he laid the bacon down in the water in a place where the rocks opened up and a deeper hole could be seen. He swished the hook and its bait through the water and waited expectantly.

Sure enough, suddenly something tugged on the line, but he waited a little longer until he was sure. It was tugged again, with greater force, and he knew he had it.

"I got it… I got it!" he yelled, and I squealed with delight.

With a few pulls and a little maneuvering around the rocks, he had the eel out of the water and on the shore. It thrashed away wildly and twisted over the twine trying to escape, wrapping and coiling with a thick slime.

Jackie pulled out a hunting knife and dragged the eel up onto a piece of sandy shore. He held it by the twine that disappeared into its mouth and started stamping hard on its tail.

"What are you doing?" I could not understand the wild jumping about on the eel's tail.

"First, knock out, when hit tail!" He grinned at his secret knowledge, and continued very seriously, "Then kill."

The eel had slowed the instant Jackie had struck the tail and he now took the chance to dispatch it by stabbing it through its head until it was clearly dead.

Holding up the limp, sand-encrusted carcass with some effort because it was heavy, Jackie grinned broadly at me. "Good lunch… I cook!"

I came up gingerly to the dead eel, hanging with its tail dragging on the ground as Jackie held it slightly aloft, and inspected it.

It was quite a size, not small like the black eels I had seen in the marketplace in London, but thick as a man's arm and about four feet long.

"I gut, then skin!" Jackie showed me how to open it and clean it, then we took the washed body up the bank and back the hundred yards or so to the camp.

Edward had arrived back to help pack up.

"Look Edward… we've caught your eel!"

"Ahhh… I see you have. Well, that just goes to show …"

"What, that there was an eel in that pool?"

"No Margaret, there is always an eel in every pool… No, it shows that eels don't come near when there is a lot of soap in the water!" He smiled, and in a slightly more gentle tone, said, "You see, my dear, you were quite safe."

Jackie selected a convenient branch of a tree and tied the eel to it securely using a piece of twine threaded through its head. Then he cut a small incision around the skin of its head, and with the aid of a sock, he grasped the slimy edge. When he had a good hold of it with the woolen footwear, he pulled down hard, peeling the skin from the fish. The pink flesh showed like perfect salmon underneath, and when he got to the tail, he cut the skin away and it dropped to the ground like a spotted tie. The pile of skin shrank quickly to a mere shadow of the size it had been when covering the body and lay in the grass slippery and wet.

He rubbed the flesh with salt from top to tail and left it to hang in the shade.

"We had better be off." Edward came over and kissed me on the forehead before turning to the Kanaka, indicating that they should go.

"We will be back when we have found a good crossing point for the dray and the horses." With that, he lifted his arm up with his gun balanced firmly in his fist and waved goodbye.

I watched him disappear through the trees with the big, dark man following behind. It seemed I saw more of his back than anything else and I longed for a time when we would not need to move.

I chided myself. That time was coming. On the other side of the "eel" pool, our land lay waiting, and it heralded our new beginning.

With that thought, I dismissed the desire for my husband and set about tending my chickens, which needed food and water and their baskets mucking out. I had become quite close to them over the weeks we had been traveling, and now they recognized me as I came up to them, clucking and seeking a way out—to no avail. Strangely, they seemed to forget their lack of freedom entirely as soon as I had poured in some handfuls of wheat.

It was not long before Edward was back without the Kanaka. He had left him with a shovel, digging out the bank down to the crossing point in the stream. They had found a wide and shallow stretch where the stones were small and closely packed together. The water spread across the whole distance so that it was barely a stream at all but a fiord. A deeper channel formed on one side where the water could escape, so they cut branches and filled it with logs and debris, and then began to dig out the bank so that a track formed down to the water in a gentle slope. They would do the same on the other side.

"All right, chaps," Edward grinned, looking directly at me as though I was one of his troops, "get ready to move for the last time. Let's be on our way. Jackie, you come with me. We will get the horses loaded while Billy is seeing to clearing the way. Margaret, get your chickens."

In no time, we were on our way. The big horse hauled the dray with the chickens mounted on his back, huddled and squatting on their feet in their swaying baskets, making no sound as they set off for the last leg of their journey. The nanny and I walked behind, and Jackie ran ahead.

I thought to myself as I watched my hens bobbing and swaying, that there would be nobody more pleased to get there than they as I caught up beside the horses, my goat keeping up faithfully.

We threaded our way through the trees and finally took on the incline Billy had already dug away to cross the stream.

Edward took the big gelding's head and pulled it gently while Billy and Jackie held onto the dray at the rear to act like a brake. With a little sliding and puffing, they pushed and pulled the dray down to the rocky streambed.

It quite easily hobbled across as though the stream were just a cobbled road. The sound of the wheels creaking and clacking over the stones and the water sluicing between the spokes filled the air and I led my goat a little haphazardly behind them. She struggled, not liking the water at all, but I dragged her over the whole distance. When we finally got about six feet from the opposite bank, she bleated loudly and ran, springing onto the bank and pulling me with her.

The men needed only to knock off a little of the soil bank, which was knitted together with roots and ferns, to make the natural incline passable, albeit a little steeper than the other side.

The big gelding began to have trouble hauling the load up the slope, so they harnessed the mare and linked her to the dray ahead of him, and both pulled, led by Edward who spoke encouragement to them as they strained their muscles to obey him.

Jackie stood on one side of the dray and added his weight, making sure the wheels could not turn out of the track, and he struck the gelding on his haunches with a small stick to move him along. The Kanaka leaned into the far side to stabilize it.

With a final effort, the two horses pulled the load up the slope, and we were again up on flat land with trees spread out before us, a soft grass carpeting the ground under us.

We all took a moment to catch our breath, and then Edward broke the silence.

"Well, Margaret… Say hello to our selection. We are here!"

I looked about me. The cicadas rasped loudly in the mid-morning sun and the trees barred my view so I could see less than ten yards ahead. It looked much the same as the land we had been traveling through. I smiled and said in a clear voice, "I shall call it Notre Maison!"

"Hear, hear!" Edward replied, and Jackie lifted his hat and howled out at the top of his lungs, "Not a rai-son! Not a rai-son!"

Even Billy let out a peal of whoops and catcalls, and we all walked about as though we had newly discovered the moon while the horses flattened their ears at the ruckus and the nanny ignored all instead making good use of the ample grass.

"Let's find a suitable camp. As far as I can tell from the map, there should be a second stream, a tributary off the Little Mulgrave, which comes out of those mountains and comes past here on its way to the sea." He pointed up to the dark green mountain valley that swooped down to the plain just before the foot of the pyramid.

"… And that stream is the junction of the lower part of our selection. I think we should go that way and set up camp between the two streams. What do you think, Margaret?"

I had walked over to Edward, who had unfurled the map on the back of the cart and was studying it carefully as he spoke.

"We're here …" His mud-stained finger prodded the loose sheet of map.

I slid my much smaller finger alongside his to trace along the boundary where the two streams met, and pointed to the area in the center of the corner. "If we put the house here, then all the fields could fan out facing the east and the morning sun, and we'd have the water in front of us. That will make a pretty sight for the children and I."

Edward smiled. "Yes, my dear, you are quite right." He considered it for a moment. "All right, let's make tracks and head that way. If we're lucky we shall make it by nightfall and spend our first night right where we shall reside." He smiled. I could see excitement and relief in his face as though a corner had finally been turned in his life.

I quickly gathered up my nanny, who happily trundled along following my lead.

The horses were rested, and Edward gathered them up and began to walk with Jackie and Billy, who were slashing and making a way for the cart through the trees.

The day drew on, but by afternoon, we had worked our way down to the first stream to find ourselves at the place I had pinpointed. Below us, a gentle slope and a mass of scrub hid the two streams where they met. We could hear the sound of a small fall and the music of the water tumbling into a pool at the junction.

It was a clear and beautiful day, and I felt a lightness enter my spirit. For a distinct moment, I realized this was indeed, my home.

That first time I saw our land, the place where the first cabin was built, it was as though a great hole in my heart had been filled.

The streams were beautiful, clear and running over rocks, and the bigger one, the tributary off the Little Mulgrave River, had a fall where we could go for a swim or picnic under the shade of the big fig tree there.

There was a sandy bank and the light filled that lovely spot all day. It was the place I liked best in the world.

The beginning of Notre Maison farm was a modest affair. We spent weeks cutting and burning. I thought I would never see the end of smoke and the fragrant scent of charred eucalyptus trunks that were stacked up to the west where we dragged them with the horses. Their stumps smoldered on, even after rain, and it began to look more like a battlefield than the beginning of the beautiful cane farm that we hoped it would be.

Still, there was nothing I liked better than to see the trees felled and the lay of the land appear from beneath them. It took us less than a few weeks to clear a good-sized paddock all the way to the stream, and then we began to build the cabin that Edward assured me would be "just the beginning."

Chapter 8

AFTER JUST TWO months Edward and Billy had built a solid dwelling I would call home. They also made a shed for the horses that also stored the implements, and beside it, a chicken coop. Jackie and I had ploughed and planted the house garden and planted something like a sweet potato that is a native here and grows fast and well. We also planted the first crop of tomatoes that we had grown from seed that Martha had given us. The long fields for the new cane had been cleared, but no ground had been broken but I could already imagine the day when it stood tall and green across our land.

Though we had only been working for three months, I started to notice Edward was becoming surly again, and one morning I saw him in the front of the stable with both Jackie and Billy, whispering and pointing in various directions as though he was giving them detailed instructions. When he came up the steps of the cabin, I questioned him.

"Are you planning a trip into town, Edward? I would so desire to go too."

"No madam… No trip to town can be managed in the dray. The track we cut will most certainly be overgrown already.

"Then what were you telling Jackie and Billy?"

"I have a mind to seek out Mr. Daley and see if we can improve our fortunes."

"No! Surely you would not leave me here?"

"Margaret, you know our land must be 'occupied' continually. I should have no choice …"

"You shall do no such thing, sir! We have only just begun, and I cannot imagine any husband would abandon his wife to the wilderness …"

"Madam, you are hardly abandoned with Jackie and Billy as help!"

I tried to continue, but Edward ignored me entirely and strode off the steps and away to the southern field. I stood at the rail of the porch and watched him walk away, and my whole body shook and my mouth had gone dry.

That evening he barely spoke to me but ate his meal quickly and went to the shed to do something unknown to me. A full week followed while his demeanor continued its downward descent.

On the morning of the first of the month, he told me plainly that he would be leaving that very moment.

"Edward, no!" I had hold of the fabric of his shirt as I pleaded with him.

"Let go, woman!" He snatched his arm from my grip.

"I cannot manage here alone… you cannot leave me!"

"I have told you once already, I am going. I must go. I will be back as soon as I can, perhaps just a month."

He swung round and took a few steps to the door. "I am not going to talk to you any more about this, nor will I suffer your hysterical behavior. I have told you… we need the money and I must go and get it."

"But Edward… If you love me at all, please!"

"God damn it, woman… I am all but bankrupt! I cannot afford even the cane cuttings… now stop your incessant whining!"

He stood by the door and stared at me perched in my skirts on the side of the bed. His voice dropped a little as though he could not manage the guilt and now grasped at reassurances.

"You have Jackie and the Kanaka with you... you will be perfectly well here. You can tend the new garden and so on. They can continue to clear the fields and till them, ready for planting."

He seemed sure of himself, standing with the light of the day streaming in across the porch and around his arms and legs, as he stood motionless in the doorway.

"I have given you their wages for the month. See to it you don't give it to them 'til it's due... and make sure I get my money's worth."

"Edward... I don't want to be without you... I don't care about the money or the cane. We can make do somehow ..."

He did not wait to reply but turned and walked off the porch in a few steps, eager to get on his way.

I jumped off the bed and ran after him. Seeing Jackie and Billy look up, I controlled myself and slowed to walk with composure down the steps toward the gelding which was already saddled, his head held at the halter by Billy.

Edward spoke to the man as he came up to the horse to mount it.

"See to it you do as I say, Billy. I shall be back in a month, and I want that field ready to plant. And mind you take care of Mrs. B. She can tell you what she wants, and you see to it you do it."

Billy nodded sheepishly, even without understanding fully. He glanced at me and I knew he could see I was upset, but he was astute enough to know his master had fire in his belly and not a single word should be said.

Edward swung himself up on his horse, which was laden with a pick, shovel, and sieve, and he looked down at me standing small in the grass in front of our makeshift home.

"I shall be back soon. It will be all right, Margaret. You have my shotgun, so get one of them to shoot some game for you and keep yourself busy. The time will go quickly. When I get back, we can see to the cane cuttings and start the new season planting just in time. You make sure these two get those fields ready." He tried to force a smile.

I gathered my strength, since there was little else I could do. "Of course sir, we shall do everything we must." My tone was formal, and Jackie shot a glance at the Kanaka, who raised his eyebrows in reply.

"We be all right, boss. We get it all done for sure," Billy reassured him.

"Yes Mr. B. We look after Mrs. B., and you come back soon. Be all right, I tell you." Jackie nodded reassuringly as he spoke up to the big man on his horse.

I watched as Edward turned the gelding without looking at me again and rode down the track. I watched him until he disappeared in the trees, where he would cross the stream and head back toward the new town of Cairns.

I didn't say anything to Jackie or Billy, but simply turned back toward the cabin. I was at a loss at Edward's determination to leave me alone, even if all our financial reserves were almost gone and for a moment my beautiful imagined future looked dark and burnt to the ground like the empty fields all around me.

That night, I lay in the dark on our bed made from eucalyptus logs and slats covered by a mattress of hay and goose down.

I didn't even bother to pull the sheet over me. It was hot and suffocating and I stared into the darkness listening to the sounds of the night, feeling lonelier than I had ever been in my life.

My mind kept sailing back to the shores of England, and I pined for a cold day, a gray sky, and the comforting sounds of busy streets. How I longed for polite conversation, a cup of tea, and the sight of people all around me.

I could hardly understand how Edward's manner had been so different to what I had expected. And now abandoning me to manage the Chinese boy and the lazy Kanaka whom I was not certain I could handle.

With my mind exhausted and confused, the night took me into a deep sleep. When I awoke, the day seemed the same as yesterday but my husband was absent and the shock of my position dawned like a creeping cold, frosting the edges of my heart and freezing me into its fear.

Sitting on the side of the bed, I propped myself up on my hands on either side of me and looked toward the one small glass window the cabin had. The glass was warped and the light filtering in had a strange, surreal quality. I shook my head to clear it of my troubles. There was nothing I wanted to do, but I realized I must do something, so I pulled myself together and went outside to find water to wash.

Jackie was already out in the garden, raking the rich red soil after the plough had done its work. There were still some big stumps scattered across it and the plough furrows bent around each of them. As I looked at them, I had in mind to get them out using the mare and a fulcrum later in the day.

"Jackie, where is Billy?"

"He down at stream, Mrs. B.," Jackie called out as he worked.

"Can you go and get him?"

"Yes Mrs. B. I go." He walked across the open ground and propped his hoe up against the tree they had left near the shed and continued on to walk down to the stream.

When he got back, he was without Billy.

"Was he there?"

"No missus, he not there. I dunno, maybe he go fishing."

All that day, I watched for Billy, but there was no sign. I fed my chickens, that now lived in quite a reasonable hen house with a long wire netting run and because Gangoo was stretching on her tether to reach forage, I shifted her to a new patch of pasture under the trees.

By evening, there was still no sign of Billy, and as I made Jackie and myself a meal, I wondered why he would leave without his wages.

Suddenly, I felt a cold feeling fill me, dropped my knife and fork on the small wooden table, and rushed up the steps of the cabin to go inside.

Jackie watched me go, and picked up his plate to put some more of the beans and sausage I had made on his plate, since Billy had not arrived.

When I got inside, I looked about for the small purse that we had hidden behind the door in the framework of the cabin, where a shelf held various personal items.

I felt behind the small vase that sat there and at last found the purse. I took a deep breath and sighed with relief.

Carefully I unclipped the twisted catch and opened it. To my horror, all the money that Edward had given me the day before was gone.

"Oh my Lord!" I cried out and rushed through the door onto the porch. "Jackie, Jackie... he's taken all the money!"

"Oh Mrs. B. What you say?"

"Billy, he has taken all the money! He must have come in during the night... I never heard anything. I was so upset I must have forgotten to bar the door. How would he know where I put it?"

"Through the window, Mrs. B. He hanging 'round there yesterday after Mr. B. go."

"What am I going to do?" I looked at Jackie, realizing that I had no wages for him."Jackie, I am so sorry, I can't pay you now until Mr. Edward gets back." I looked at him pitifully, "You are free to go if you like... I will understand. Oh my Lord! What will I do ..?"

"No, Jackie not go. Mr. B., he not be long. We be all right, eh?"

"Oh, thank you, Jackie! I am sure you will be right. I suppose I will just have to pull myself together and get on with it."

"Pull together... where be your bits? Jackie not see you in bits!"

I laughed a little shakily. I knew this was his attempt at humor, and I was grateful for it.

That evening, I retired to the cabin and Jackie put up the tent close by.

As I stopped on the porch to go inside, Jackie said he would take a last look around. I waited for him. He skirted the clearing and stared into the darkness. There seemed nothing there, just the rustling of the trees and the warm air smoothly settling on the night landscape, so he nodded to me, climbed into the tent, and closed himself in.

In the morning, we continued to work the garden that would be the household vegetable supply.

By mid-afternoon, we had created neat rows, and I pressed holes in the soil and planted maize in three perfect lines.

Jackie planted the next batch of the tiny tomato seedlings so we might have a continuous yield. Finally, we planted three long rows of sweet potato, which had all sprouted in the basket along the way from Cook Town and needed to be planted beside the others.

By the end, we were exhausted but satisfied, and we settled down to a well-earned meal.

All the following week we worked on the little burgeoning farm. Jackie was not only a hard worker but also a cheerful companion. I began to calm, and I realized the month would go quickly if we stayed busy and did all we were able to.

Each day, we would carry water from the stream and trickle it over the little seedlings, and on the morning of the nineteenth day, the maize speared up through the soil and showed that we had the beginning of a good crop.

"Jackie, look, look!" I was more excited than a small child, and Jackie was captured by my excitement, too. We danced around at the sight of the new seedlings growing from the rich soil and together surveyed the reward for our hard work.

"Thank you, dear Jackie …The Lord sent you to help me."

"He not help one, without help-ing other, Mrs. B.… He like all us, equal-ly."

"Well done, Jackie! Your English is so much better. Let's be quick and get the bucket to water them before the sun goes. I want these to be the best maize Mr. Edward shall ever see."

"Sure thing, Mrs. B.!" He sped off and headed for the stream.

The moment he was gone, I realized I should get a second bucketful for the chickens. He was already out of sight, so I gathered another bucket and followed the well-worn path to the stream.

When I got to the incline, I could see him below.

He was sitting on his haunches with his knees to the side as the Chinese do when they squat down to do anything near the ground. The water was flowing clear and beautiful as ever. He tipped the tin bucket into a deep pool and it tinged as it hit the stones and then filled quickly.

I was just about to call out to him when suddenly he and I both heard a sound, though neither of us could have said what it was.

It made him look up and so did I, frozen to a spot a little hidden by the trees. I half expected to see the Kanaka standing on the bank of the stream.

Instead, there stood three aboriginals.

They stood silently, and their naked bodies gleamed in the shade, their spears held at their sides. The black skinned men also carried tall shields covered in white and red ochre patterns of the totems of their tribe. Their faces had white lines drawn on them, and their hair glistened with oil and decorations of feathers and shells.

Jackie stopped dead.

I ducked back in the trees not sure if I had been seen. Jackie was hardly breathing as they stood watching him, and I think I had stopped breathing entirely. These were wild natives, not the "halfway converted type" of Cook Town.

The bucket filled, and Jackie pulled it up slowly and quietly.

As he moved, I heard the natives mumbling in the nasal language that I would come to know as that of the Yidinji.

I could see Jackie wasn't sure what he should do. He started slowly backing up the track, and as he did, they stepped out from the shadow and crossed the stream, separating slightly as though stalking a kangaroo they had surprised at a water hole.

Jackie saw the move and I suppose he thought he was in danger.

One aboriginal spoke to the others without taking his eyes off the small Chinese man.

This was the moment that Jackie became filled with utter terror and he dropped the bucket, turned, and fled up the incline.

Immediately, the three started running and jumping over the stones to catch him.

He ran with all his might through the trees and the flight sparked the youngest of the aborigine to raise his arm and throw his spear, full force, toward him in an effort to stop him. The spear flew with perfect accuracy and hit Jackie clean through his back. He fell without a sound to the carpet of grass, dead.

I saw it happening in slow motion and thrust my fist in my mouth instinctively to halt even a gasp from escaping.

The taller aborigine spoke loudly and seemed to admonish the younger man. He slapped him on his shoulder angrily as they came up to the body.

The young one did not reply but placed his foot on poor Jackie's back and pulled the spear from him. The body sighed as he did.

The three looked down, perhaps trying to decide what to do with Jackie's body.

I pressed myself deeper into the bush and slowly dropped to my haunches, hiding in terror, while they remained preoccupied.

Finally, two of them picked up the small man and hauled him over their shoulders in unison to carry him back down the path and away.

The taller aboriginal turned as the two others disappeared down the track. He looked back in the direction of the smoke from my cabin, which was no doubt what brought them to us. He seemed to ponder the scene as though he could feel the disturbance the new farm had caused to the land. He stared into the remaining brush that obscured the flat area where the cabin had been built, but he did not see me hidden there. He shook his head as though amazed at the destruction we had wrought, and turned and walked silently down the track to disappear into the trees with the others.

When I could not hear them anymore, I ran with my heart beating a hundredfold, to the place where Jackie had lain. As I approached the spot I slowed to a walk, as though what had happened might prove not to be there, if I refused it. As I stepped through the grass, I wiped the sweat from my hands on my skirts hoping it was all a dream.

But there it was. A flattened section, near the path. And in its center, I could see a poolsof dark of red blood seeping through the grass into the ground.

My breath caught and I turned and looked back to where they had been. I don't know what curiosity compelled me, but I turned and crept back down the track to the water. Cautiously, I stepped down the incline, scanning the far bank. Somehow, I knew that they were already far away but even so, my eyes darted about for their dark figures in the bush.

When I reached the stream, I picked up the bucket, and as I did, fear swept through me. In the ground that had been cut for the dray to come up the incline, there were naked footprints. Several of them. The marks seemed to bring the visitors into reality.

"Oh my Lord!" I whispered to myself, and then put my hand to my mouth, realizing I should not have made a sound.

I stepped under the canopy of a tree and stared out over the stream to see if there was any movement or any sign.

There was nothing. Evening was beginning to fall, and the light changed to announce that soon darkness would wrap itself over this land and it would be pitch black for yet another turn of the earth.

I pulled myself out from the tree and carefully, step by step, crept back up the path.

Quickly heading back to the cabin, I made sure I kept close to the tree line. When I was ten yards from the building, I broke into a run that was nothing short of a sprint. I flew up the steps and into the cabin, where I turned and slammed the door shut, grabbed the shotgun, and sat on the bed staring at the door.

No one came.

I sat there all night in the darkness, listening to every sound outside until I drifted into sleep without meaning to.

I awoke in the morning with Edward's gun still across my stomach. Carefully, I moved to the door and peered out. There was no sign of anyone, so I slowly edged outside.

I kept the gun with me the whole day. I fed the chickens and shifted the goat with one eye scanning for the intruders and my hand clamped firmly to the gunstock.

When evening came, I looked over my little seedlings and realized I would have to go to the stream to fetch water for them.

With as much care as I could muster, and with the gun held out in the front of me, I went down the track and quickly got the water. My heart was racing, but I completed the task without mishap and went back to the field.

Nothing happened thereafter, and there was no sign of the aboriginals. I began to think that perhaps they had no interest in me or no knowledge that I remained.

The next three days passed uneventfully. The strange silence played on my mind and I began to imagine Jackie might return, that I had misinterpreted the blood and the footprints and that he might have escaped and would return to me. But he did not, and as the days passed, I began to accept that he was truly dead.

Day by day, I went about my business, and nothing but loneliness and my desperate need for Edward to return invaded my thoughts.

Thinking that he must surely soon come home because the month was over, I decided I would draw a real bath and wash away a dozen days or more of dirt and perspiration so I might at least be presentable upon his arrival. With enormous effort, I fetched water, set up my tin bath by nightfall on the floor in front of my bed and bathed. Afterwards, I dressed in a clean nightgown, placed the gun beside me on Edward's side of the bed, and slept as soundly, and as safely, as if the weapon were my beloved husband, to be replaced by the warmth of his true body at any moment.

However, he did not return as I expected. The days turned into weeks, and the weeks rolled by as though a dream.

Soon a second month came and went. I stopped counting and simply took each day as it came, hoping it would be the day that Edward returned.

He did not, however. In fact, the single month he had promised had already turned into three, and I began to think that if I did not starve, I would go mad with loneliness. A pervading fear gnawed away at me. Perhaps Edward was also dead and there was now no one to protect me from my torment or the spears of the aboriginals.

Chapter 9

ONE EVENING, HAVING completed the work for the day, I decided I was in need of a hot bath once more. Most days I bathed at the stream but because it was getting late, and the eels would be coming out of their holes, I decided I would have a proper bath.

I brought two buckets at a time up from the river, and carried them on a pole across my back, just the way Jackie used to do. After three trips, it was deep enough. I added two buckets of boiling water from the fire, closed the door and bolted it, and in the privacy of my small enclave, I undressed.

I settled into the bath with my knees pulled up tight inside the small tub and sat there soaking away the work of the day and the worry of what had become of Edward.

After a while, I lifted myself out and stood in the bathwater with my foot perched on the side and began to soap my body.

The foam felt smooth on my skin and I lathered it under my chin and over my stomach and thighs.

Suddenly, I felt, rather than heard, something near the window.

I pulled my hands over myself and dropped into the bath to hide under the level of the window. I watched like a breathless deer, the blood draining from my face and my heart pounding.

A shadow passed the pane and I jolted in the bath as I realized there was someone out there.

Slowly and carefully, I eased myself out of the bath and crouched down on the floor. I carefully grabbed for the towel hanging on the bed and clutched it to me.

I knew I could be seen in the light of the lantern, so I moved over to it slowly and pulled it down from its resting place on the chair that Jackie had made for me from the boughs of a eucalyptus tree. I blew it out and in the darkness, found Edward's gun, pulled it close to my breast and waited. Sitting on my haunches with the towel pulled around me, I listened for any sound.

The crickets continued to chirp and the night seemed unbroken, and I wondered if I had imagined it.

Slowly, I made my way to the bed and dressed myself quickly. Sitting on the covers with Edward's gun in my arms, I waited for what seemed like eternity, but nothing stirred.

Leaving the water where it was, I climbed up onto the bed and hours passed, and before I even realized that I had slept, I awoke and it was the next morning. The dawn had come and gone and the rooster had long since finished his crowing, though I had not heard him.

I left the cabin and walked around it, searching for some clue near the window, but there was nothing to show that anyone had been there. I told myself that I was becoming a silly woman with a nervous disposition as I waited for Edward so desperately and I consoled myself that the shadow must have been a bat flying by.

Even though the fearful moment seemed put to rest, my heart took the opportunity to break free of my control. As I walked aimlessly toward my hens and knelt beside their cage, I grasped a sprig of grass in my fist beside me, pulling it angrily from the soil as tears slid down my cheeks.

Surely, I thought, he must come home any day now.

Suddenly, a prayer escaped my lips as though it had a will of its own and desired to help me even if the world could not.

"Oh Lord, please bring back Edward… Do you not see that I need him? Dear Lord, I fear I shall not survive alone. I need the help only you can give… please, hear me …" It seemed a futile whisper, drowned out by the resounding silences only broken by the sounds of the chickens eagerly pecking up their grain.

I waited and when no answer came that I could discern, I finished feeding them and collected their eggs. For a little while, I sat beside them in the midst of my skirts and wept.

When my tears subsided, I decided I would let them out for the first time and give them the run of the yard as though their freedom might signal a day when I should have my own.

I rose up, brushed my hands on my skirt, and decided there was nothing for it but to stop my nonsense and get on with tending my little farm.

I leaned down and opened the coop and the rooster immediately approached. "Well sir …" I wagged a finger at him as he guarded his hens, "you shall have your freedom, but I wager you will not abandon your mistresses, as I have been. What manner of creatures are we that a humble rooster has more honor than a man?" He ignored me as if to say the answer was obvious since he lived in a cage made by such creatures.

Pulling at the door, I opened it wide, then stood back and waited for the chickens to make their way through it. The rooster did not hesitate and slowly led his girls out to the yard. They followed each other around until eventually, they began to get bolder and spread out over the open area.

I walked up to the nanny, who had had two kids, that I named, Molly and Pansy.

"Good morning my little friend… it seems you are doing better than me. I should hardly know that I am a married woman. My husband is so far away as not to be my husband at all. I don't even know if he is alive, though I suppose he must be, for if he was dead, surely someone would come out to find me, if only to give me his clothes."

I stroked the animal and watched as her little ones bounced about. She was happy for the touch and lifted her lips to nuzzle my skirt.

"Silly goat… you are always happy to see me. I supposed you to ignore me now you have your kids. Will you mind giving me some of your milk too? I shall be able to make all kinds of things with it, I suppose, if I have a mind to."

I continued chatting to the goat for almost five minutes and the one-sided conversation calmed me and made me feel almost human again.

When I had finished, I walked down the slope past the house to the place that lay between the joining of the stream and the river.

I thought I would take a moment to look at the pool that lay at the junction. There the ferns fringed the mossy bank and the overhanging fichus trees formed a perfect backdrop for the scene.

"I should start drawing," I said to myself. But before I could finish that line of thought, I froze, even before I recognized what had paralyzed me with fear.

It was they.

The owners of the footprints at the stream, the shadow in the darkness, the murderers of my dear Jackie. I was so filled with fear, I could not think of a single thing to do so I stood frozen to the spot.

The three men walked across the stream and stood near the clearing.

One spoke to the other. I listened as the muddled sounds of their language darted back and forth between them.

They were completely without a shred of clothing, but I was unable to look away, even though everything in me cried out for flight even apart from the propriety toward such naked men demanded.

The tallest one walked toward me and I stood entirely still as he came near. My heart pounded and sweat was beginning to run down my spine.

I felt the blood drain from my face as the second one walked up with calculated steps, staring at me from the side, examining my dress, my hands, my hair.

Finally, the taller one-stepped into my view, face to face, within feet of me.

He stood looking into my eyes. As mine stared back a strange feeling stirred in me. At first, I couldn't fathom what I could see in the chocolate pools of his, but gradually I realized a strange moment of recognition. The kind of recognition that comes from two spirits knowing each other in the language of souls.

It shocked me. It seemed as if an electric jolt coursed through me, and the awakening made me ignore the fear I had felt and respond by thrusting out my hand.

"How do you do!"

The three men looked at each other and immediately burst out laughing. One shook his head.

The taller one replied in his tongue, which I was unable to understand. I stared blankly at him with my hand stiffly hanging in the air.

I must have looked like a tin soldier without a sword. He blinked, and then responded in kind, thrusting out his hand. He didn't know to grasp it in the embrace of greeting, so his hovered in the air beside mine.

I realized his dilemma, so I smiled shakily, moved my hand over to his, and gently squeezed it.

His hand felt warm and smooth and I shook it a little. Then I let go, and as I did, I think he was distressed that I had broken our touch. He thrust out his other hand, which held a short, carved, wooden stick, and placed it in my hand.

I could not understand the motif or the meaning of it, and I suddenly wished Liz Beth had been there to help.

Not sure what I should do with it, I accepted it gingerly. "Oh, thank you… I say, thank you. It's a pretty stick, it's very nice!" I mouthed the words as though speaking to a deaf person. My somewhat strange speech made the others begin to mutter to each other.

I had become acutely aware of the nearness of the naked men, and now I wanted to look away. Glancing downward instinctively, I found myself confronted and I blushed, quickly returning my gaze to his eyes. They connected with mine again and the unsettling feeling returned. I wondered what the man behind those eyes was thinking as he looked at me.

He was taller and older than the others, who giggled with some private joke I could not fathom. As I stood there with his stick in my hand, he smiled broadly. Perfect white teeth show a good deal relieved by it.

So here they were and I, alone with them. I smiled at the seemingly congenial men who had been dear Jackie's murderers. My heart had slowed a little, but I still couldn't decide what I should do, and it occurred to me that I might still be in some danger.

The older, taller man now seemed to stare at every part of my body, and there were three of them, clearly men. Their inspection made me feel very alone and uncomfortable knowing I had no protection if they should desire to do something untoward.

The older warrior began to walk around me and reached out his hand to touch the fabric of my skirts. The feel of them surprised him and he withdrew his hand as though he had touched something hot, only to be tempted again by the soft, smooth feel beneath his fingertips.

I stood still, watching them move about me as they investigated my clothing. Then the first man came back to face me and gently took my hand, lifting it with the stick still clasped tightly in my fist.

I let him hold it without knowing what else I should do, and as he looked into my eyes, he began to speak to me.

His strange tongue nasally spoke a string of words that I had no way to interpret, but when he had finished I tried to reply.

"I... my name is Margaret." I lifted my hand and pointed to myself, and said it again. "Mar-ga-ret."

He recognized what I was doing and replied by pointing to himself. "Mullegadajawara, Mullegadajawara."

"Mulla... wara?"

He grinned at my feeble attempt to form the strange syllables in my mouth.

"Ah... shall you come for some tea?" I said as I looked up to the cabin, longing to be nearer to where I had left the gun propped up by the door. I pointed in its direction hoping they would let me move that way.

Mullegadajawara kept his eyes firmly on mine and continued to hold my small white hand until he turned toward his companions. In doing so, he let go of my hand as he pointed to the cabin and then to the mountains far away. I was relieved he had released me. The touch of his fingers, so black against my own, was too intimate for me. I would not have held the hand of my own menfolk without wearing gloves, nor for such a time.

Suddenly, the two other men turned and left. I wondered why this one was staying while his companions disappeared over the stream the way they had come. Still, I felt happier that only one remained, so I smiled a little tentatively and said, "I shall make you tea and... perhaps... Oh dear, I suppose you have not a jot of understanding of what I say." I turned slightly and began to walk slowly up the incline to the cabin with the aboriginal following me at a little distance.

When I reached the building, I walked up the steps, and he watched me from the ground in front of my small dwelling. I turned on the porch and waved him up to sit at the small table with its two seats.

He declined by pointing his spear into the ground, indicating I should come down to him.

"Oh! All right then, as you wish sir." I said, and I suppose I was glad of it but I glanced at my door knowing well that Edward's gun sat just out of reach behind it.

Walking down, I sat on the bottom of the cabin steps and watched him as he grazed the tip of the spear in the fine dust there, almost a little pensively.

Immediately, it occurred to me that the dry ground made an excellent drawing board so I jumped up. I hastened to the outer fringe of grass around the cabin clearing and picked up a small stick of my own to write with.

I knew he was watching me as my skirts bounced over the ground, and he was no doubt wondering what had ignited me to such action.

When I returned, I sat down on the step again and began to trace out the boundary of our selection in the dust.

I drew the two streams and a box for the cabin, and then pointing my stick in the center of it, I said, "Cabin here," while I slapped my palm on the boards of the porch behind me and repeated the word. "Ca-bin."

He smiled and copied me quite well. "Car-bine."

"Yes, ca-bin!" I smiled broadly. Then I undid the small buttons at my wrist and pulled up the sleeve to display my thin white arm.

Pointing to it, I said, "English."

I pointed again to myself, "Margaret... English."

He must have understood, because he pointed to his own arm and said, "Malanbarra Bama... Mullegadajawara, Malanbarra Yidi."

He pointed to his naked chest marked with the scars of long-completed initiation rites and repeated his name, "Mullegadajawara," several times, and I tried to repeat it as best I could. Sweeping his spear across the sky and pointing in the direction of the mountains he said, "Malanbarra Bama!"

Feeling sure that communication was possible, and understanding he was indicating the land of the Malanbarra people, I moved on with my stick and deepened the lines that showed the boundaries of the farm.

I looked up at him. "Notre Maison farm... English. Well, Australia, really... But I mean, our land. Yes? Do you understand?"

I could see he had lost me almost immediately, and I realized it would be a slow and painful process. However, the aboriginal was quick witted, and he caught the word English, so he knew that I was trying to show our place on this land, our farm and our ownership.

He walked forward and very slowly; he placed the tip of his spear under my stick and lifted it off the ground.

He stepped back two paces and began to press the spear into the ground, pulling it along so a small furrow appeared.

I watched him as he traced the spear in the dust and disappeared around the side of the cabin.

I stood on the step and wondered what he was doing. Then he reappeared from around the outside of the shed and the chicken coop, still pulling his spear through the dry ground and came back toward me.

Finally, he dragged his spear to the place where he had begun and stood with the spear-point upright in the ground, exactly where he had started.

With a strong stab, he speared it in the ground at the point and left the thin weapon waving in the air, upright.

He stepped inside the huge circle that encompassed the buildings that my husband and I, with the help of the Kanaka and Jackie had built, and then walked up closer to me.

He looked up into my eyes and caught them in a link with his own. Then, very carefully, so that I would not miss the point, he waved his arm over the whole area encompassed by his spear furrow and said, "Malanbarra Yidi."

Then he stepped over to the spear and pulled it from the ground, walked over to my drawing of the farm boundaries and scratched them out with the tip of the spear.

He turned back to me.

I suddenly saw him standing as the dark sentinel and warrior he was, and I realized what he had shown me.

"Malanbarra Yidi …" I repeated in a whisper as my eyes stayed locked on his.

I finally broke with his gaze and sat down again on the step, thinking about the matter. He could see I was troubled and he waited for me.

I shook my head and said to myself. "Well, I know what I would do if I were dealing with anyone else with whom I had some need and no other course but mercy." I immediately stood up and stepped down to him.

I knew he could smell my rose water perfume as I stood near, and I noticed he did not step back but instead he took a deep breath in and held it, and then let it out very slowly.

Liz Beth had told me it is not the custom for aborigine men to be near women too closely, so I was reassured that this man was accepting of my presence and to some extent, I did not mind, as I somehow knew he was not as fierce as one would imagine.

I held out my hand with the message stick and he took it. However, as soon as he withdrew it to himself, I held out my hand again and said, "Please, please!"

He must have thought me strange to begin with, realizing that I wanted it back with this hissing word, but he handed it to me again and I could see the puzzlement on his face.

I looked into his eyes and tried to make him understand what I wanted him to see.

"Now... Mulley... wara." I motioned with my hands that he should ask me for it again, using the word I had.

So he tried: "Pliss ..."

I smiled, corrected him, and offered the stick to him again. "Please... that's right, please!" I smiled and held my hand out for the stick.

"Plesse!" he asked, quite happy with the sound of the word in his mouth. And I handed him the stick.

As soon as he had it, I asked for it again, using the magic word.

Very soon, we were saying please repeatedly together, with much humor.

He would hand it to me and then I, to him. Quicker and quicker, we played the game, passing the message stick back and forth.

It seemed I had taught him the word please, and he understood it.

I could see he was satisfied with himself as he whispered the word over and over, swapping the stick from one hand to the other.

I walked back to the step and sat down.

He stopped repeating the word for a moment, watching me, wondering what I now had in mind to do.

With my skirts piled up around me, I picked up my drawing stick again.

He watched me as I retraced the little map of Notre Maison farm in the dust of the ground. I picked up a small stone out of the dust and pointed to myself, showing it to Mullegadajawara, then placed it inside the rendition of the square dwelling.

When I was finished, I poked my stick into the box indicating the cabin with myself in it, and then looked up at him.

I caught him with my eyes and said, very slowly, very carefully, with a tone of voice that could not be misunderstood or misread, "Please! ..."

He understood exactly what I was requesting, and he stood still, held in the grip of my green eyes.

Without a word, he picked up his spear, walked over to the post where he had leaned his shield and walked toward me. My stick was still resting in the dust and he lifted his spear and moved it over to it, resting it under mine.

Time stopped, my stick and his spear touching.

Very gently, he pulled the spear tip away and left my stick still where it was, and then turned without a word, and walked steadfastly to the edge of the trees.

Stopping for a brief moment, he turned and looked back to where I had stood up on the step in surprise at his sudden departure.

He raised his spear into the air in a gesture of farewell, and turned and trotted off into the bush beside the stream, disappearing from my view.

I sighed with a huge breath of air, releasing the tension that had been held in like a racehorse ready to break free of the gates, since the aboriginals had arrived.

"Oh Lord, I hope I did not offend him or break protocol or something… What on earth is going to happen now?"

I stared into the bush-lined area, half-hoping the strange naked man would reappear; as my loneliness had momentarily evaporated in the time we played our game.

I turned and walked up the steps and stepped inside my rough-sawn cabin, gathered up the gun by its barrel, and shut the door firmly behind me.

Whatever was to happen, I determined I would use my wit to contend with it. Knowing full well that, this was my only true defense and no gun alone would make a way for me.

I crawled into the comfort of my bed and soon fell into a deathly sleep brought on by the strange events of the day. In the depths of that quiet rest, I think my heart had already begun to ask that I might see again, the strange naked man who had spoken to me with his eyes and said, You are not alone, white woman, I mean you no harm.

Chapter 10

A ROUND SIX THE next morning it started raining and I awoke lazily to the sound of it beating on the tin of my roof.

I had barely roused, for the air was cooler, the birds quiet, and the darkness welcome to my tired and undernourished body.

When I did, my thoughts immediately turned to the encounter with the aboriginal the day before. I could not fathom why I felt a little expectant, a little happier, for the first time since Edward had left.

I greeted the day by opening my front door and walking out onto the porch.

Sheets of rain were now falling, and the corrugated iron of the porch roof was leaking as the heavy downpour battered it from the sky. The water had wet most of the deck boards but I didn't mind. It was wonderful to hear it and watch it falling in cascades from the edge of the iron. It had already dug a deep trench along the front of the cabin where it had hit the ground and rivulets speed away down the incline.

I walked to the handrail, which was wet with spray and leaned into the damp air, breathing in the cool, fresh, beauty of it.

Suddenly, peering through the mass of water falling from the sky, I realized the ground was beginning to disappear at the base of the clearing, replaced by a yellow sludge that had risen up from the conjoining waterways and was now creeping up the slope toward me.

"So, we are going to have a flood!" I whispered to myself.

I knew the cabin was a long way from the bottom area it looked down on so I was not worried but rather curious. Still, I thought, in due time, I would make sure there was nothing left out that might float away around the vegetable garden.

With the decision made, I turned from the deck, wiped my wet hands on my skirt, and went inside to find something for breakfast.

By ten o'clock, the rain had not eased at all. I had to feed my precious chickens, so I tucked myself under my parasol and ran to the coop. I became soaked to the skin, even so, as I threw the grain in for them. They all looked somewhat bedraggled but still ventured out to peck up what I had for them.

The horse had turned in her stall to keep her head dry and her tail gently blew in the draft from the falling rain. She was eating hay since I had not pastured her and as I went in to check on her, a pungent smell locked in by the heavy rain greeted me at the opening. The nanny beside her was, as usual, not worried by anything inside or out but focused on her desire to eat. Molly and Pansy bustled about, jumping up on anything they could find, but now and then, one or other would sneak a quick suckle from their mother who could not escape them.

They were well but the water had continued to rise, and I watched it as though it were a yellow tide coming in.

Ahead of it, a swarm of insects never seen in the normal course of events clambered over themselves and up sticks and blades of taller grass, to get out of the way of the rising water. All animosity between them seemed suspended as they clung to each other and the bending stalks to escape the rising flood. I watched as spiders, crickets, and all manner of creeping things fled before the water and crawled like a wave of their own ahead of it. I hoped upon hope that they wouldn't get to my cabin and use it as a comfortable island of safety.

By midday, I realized that the water must now be twenty feet deep at the river, as it had risen to encompass all the land of the bottom field. My new maize plants were now submerged, with only their uppermost tips gasping for air above the water.

I began to worry that the flood would reach the shed and chicken coop, so I braved the downpour yet again to rescue the mare, nanny goat and kids, and the chickens.

I took the basket cages from the shed and looked in at the hens huddled in the back of the coop. The wet, smelly floor was a pungent concoction of mud and manure.

Looking around at the sheets of rain still falling, I took off my skirts, looped my wet outer linen over the fence rail and let the rain have its way, bending low into the coop to save my chickens in my undergarments alone. The white cotton became translucent almost immediately and stuck to my limbs and my "ladies" were all huddled in the corner, just as wet and glossy as I. They looked at me somewhat beseechingly from their sea of mud and I whispered to them, "It's all right… I shall save you."

I carefully gathered up each one in my hands. They felt heavier than I remembered, and they squawked a little as I bundled them into their cages.

I piled their baskets under the eaves of the cabin's porch and then collected the mare and the goats from the shed and walked them in turn through the knee-high water behind the cabin to the area under the big fichus tree higher on the hill where there was a little shelter.

I left them tethered together under the big tree as they looked on with some confusion as I walked back down the hill like a barely clad nymph leaving them behind.

Wading through the deepening water I found my way back to the steps of the cabin, which now rose up from the depths of a nine-inch sea. As I stood on the porch and dried myself, I wondered when it would stop rising.

Little by little, the water climbed up the bottom step, carrying a floating cargo of twigs, leaves, crickets, spiders, and grasshoppers.

I used my broom to brush the insects off into the waves and watched them desperately turn-about like slow spinning tops, floating on the skin of the muddy flood water and crawling over one another to try to save themselves.

To my relief, by early afternoon, the rain eased and the tide began to fall somewhat. The second step bore a faint high-water mark where the flood had found its highest point before beginning to fall back. Within a few hours, the power of the river flowing fast through the gully had drawn the water from the land and towed it toward the sea, where it would dump the fresh sediment in the tide.

By evening, the water had left altogether, and in its place was combed grass pointing in the direction of the stream and a line of debris showing where the water had reached beyond the cabin almost to the foot of the big tree.

I wandered about, surveying the effects of the monsoon downpour. My precious maize plants had strained at their roots and fallen over. The tomato plants straggled on the ground. All the leaves of the sweet potato were painted with brown sediment. I frowned as I looked at the bedraggled plants, but I knew that I could stake them up and the deluge of water would make them grow quickly in the next few days.

I returned the damp chickens to their coop, where they shook themselves off and immediately began pecking up the odd insect that had been left behind in the sludge.

"Well, I guess I should clean up and hang out the washing!"

By nightfall, I had eaten a meager meal, cleaned up the drips, and hung out my skirts to dry. A brilliant red dusk fell, burning the sky behind the ranges. I decided I'd sort out my garden tomorrow, blew out my lamp, and went to bed and fell into a deep and restful sleep.

The following day arrived with a bright chorus of bird song and golden hues that speared through the cool clear air. The rain was finished, and the crisp new shoots of grass began to miraculously appear from whatever clear ground would let their heads rise.

I roused at the break of day to the soft but persistent sounds of thumping on the front porch. The sound made me rise quickly and quietly, pick up

Edward's gun, and sneak from the bed. Creeping to the door in my nightdress, I listened for a moment. I could hear muffled snorts and the thud, thud, of something moving.

Very carefully, I opened the bolt but as soon as the door creaked and I peered around it, the noisemakers bounded in full flight from the wooden planks out into the surrounding area to scatter in all directions. I watched the wallabies as they hopped with ease between the trees, then stopped dead to look back at the cabin. Bolt upright, they stared with their ears pricked forward, paws held neatly in front of their chests, and their wide rumps propping them up on sinuous tails spread out behind them.

"What have you been up to? Shoo!" I waved my arms and the sudden movement, made them turn again and flee with all speed, away into the bush.

I looked around on the porch and noticed a strange smell and a somewhat white, sticky ooze coming from the bottom of the barrel that housed the remainder of the flour. I could see where tongues had licked away at it, and white footprints spread out around it.

"Oh no, what now?"

I opened the lid and it "shushed" with a gasp of escaping air. A powerful smell like whiskey and kerosene greeted me, and I could see what seemed like a million seething worms of some kind moving in a slush of fermenting flour, wet from rainwater.

"Oh my Lord!" I grimaced and replaced the lid.

With my hands tightly over the end of the barrel, I tipped it and rolled it on its base with the weight of my body behind it. It was a struggle, but I reached the end of the porch, where I lifted the lid again, tipped the barrel over the side and emptied it, pouring the horrible mass onto the wet ground.

As it landed, I saw there was a little dry flour in one section and it piled in a heap with the wet slush around it.

I ran inside and collected a bowl and a large ladle, and returned to the mass. Crouched low, I carefully scooped as much of the dry flour out as I could from the mess. The dry flour was filled with the unknown worms too, rolling and twisting and coated with the powdery substance.

Taking the bowl inside, I laid out some brown paper from the bacon box and tipped out the contents. For at least half an hour, I picked the small creatures out of the flour and dropped them into the tin mug.

By the time I had finished, the mug was half full of the wriggling grubs and I had cleared the precious flour that remained so that it was still usable.

Rolling up the paper, I poured the flour into a jar and sealed it, looking wistfully at the small amount and wondering what I would do when it was gone.

I let out my chickens from their coop and led them to the mess. The chickens scrambled to peck up the larvae and feast on the wet mush.

"Oh you like that, don't you, my ladies?" Watching them, I thought how I should like to have such an ignorant palate so that I could eat almost anything as well, for I knew that my supplies were now all but finished.

"I suppose I shall have really good eggs tomorrow!" I forced a smile.

As the hens feasted, I decided to fix up my garden and think on better times, which must surely come.

When I arrived at the beds, an involuntary screech escaped me.

"Oh my God... what have I done to deserve this?"

I threw up my hands and held my cheeks as though in doing so I could evoke sympathy from some invisible force that could turn back the clock against the sight before me.

The green spears of the maize shoots had all but been eaten back to the roots and the sweet potato and tomatoes too were nibbled away or trampled. A single surviving soldier lay on his side, clawing at the footing he had lost from the flood.

"Those damn wallabies!"

Knowing I was in real danger if I couldn't grow something to eat I wished I had taken a shot at one of the wallabies with Edward's gun. A wave of terror flooded over me and would have pushed me onto the ground had I let it.

"No!" I yelled to the surrounding silence. "No! I will not die... but live, to declare the praises of the Lord in... this... the land of the living!" I shook my head as I quoted the text I could only partially remember, but knew in doing so I had made a declaration that would have evoked Martha to say Amen!

"All right, you demons… you shall not get into my garden again!"

With that, as the sun began its climb into the blue sky, spotted with white cloud, I stormed off to the edge of the clearing. There I found a long bough of eucalyptus wood and dragged it back to the garden. Finding the saw, the hammer, and twine in the shed, I got to work.

By the end of the day, the beginnings of a makeshift fence made from the twisted branches of eucalyptus had been created. Rails of heavier wood were nailed to trunk posts, and at even intervals I had tied uprights so that a barrier was made against the invasion of the herbivorous marsupials that appeared and disappeared like ghosts.

That night I could barely command my eyelids to close. I was hungry, and the thought of a slow death in this wilderness held my thoughts prisoner. I was no hunter. In fact, I had never fired the gun, nor could I think of anything that could be eaten in the forests around me. I wondered if the wallabies could be tempted back and if so, I could try to shoot one, supposing that they might agree to stand still for me. As I thought about this, I knew it was futile. The first shot would have to be my best and I wasn't sure I could manage it even if I had ten tries.

I said a short prayer, too tired and befuddled to manage anything eloquent, and when sleep finally came, it was filled with twisted visions.

I found myself dreaming that I stood in violent wind and rain, battering me almost to death. But in the midst of the storm, a calm place emerged that was still and cool. In an instant, my spirit eased as I felt it there. From its center, I could see the aboriginal. He stood quietly. His warm eyes smiled into the depth of my soul as he waited for me to walk forward. I could feel his sanity, and a peaceful cloud of safety encased him… and I felt no fear. Instead, I closed my eyes and walked into the peaceful eddy around him, and he held out his arms to me and he spoke a single word, Please …

Within the welcome refuge, my mind silenced itself, and I slept on without dreaming again.

At about three o'clock I was woken with a start.

The chickens were clucking loudly and I could hear panic in their cries.

I grabbed the gun, lit the lantern, and still muddled from sleep, opened the door and peered cautiously into the dark.

There was no moon, so I couldn't see anything. Even the wind was still. I walked slowly across the porch and gingerly down the steps.

Around the corner of the cabin, I thrust out the lantern before me.

"Who's there?... I know you are there. Come out and leave my chickens alone!"

No one replied to my demands and I waited for a moment while the chickens continued their frantic clucking and flapping.

Little by little, I crept into the sea of darkness, leaving the security of the wall behind me.

When I reached the coop, I let out a screech of terror as I saw what was disturbing the chickens.

A huge brush python, now disturbed by the interruption to his hunting, curled its head around toward me. In lithe swathes of coils, it unfurled itself and headed quickly back through the hole it had forced in the coop to get in.

I yelled as loud as I could manage before remembering that Edward had told me that snakes are deaf feeling only the vibrations in their body and smell scents in the air with their tongue. With that, I began to strike the ground heavily with a stick and jump up and down wildly. Grass flew up in the light of the lantern as the giant slithered off into the darkness, and I followed it until it reached the big tree.

As soon as the monster disappeared behind it into the darkness, I ran back to my chickens and found them huddled together still clucking in terror.

"Oh my poor ladies... Shhh!" I consoled them, but realized they could not now stay in the coop in case the hungry snake returned. I walked to the shed and, with real care looked around me fitfully for fear another snake should also lurk in the darkness there. I brought the wicker cages back and gathered each little hen off its perch, even as they clung desperately with yellow-clawed feet to resist me. Each one went into its basket with the rooster in one all his own, and I carried them up into the cabin and stacked them in the corner. They looked forlorn in the dim light of the lantern, but as I took one last look around the yard and closed the door against the night, I realized I would have to have the little group as my nightly companions or risk losing them to the hungry predator.

As I lay down, they too slowly settled and their muffled book, book, book sounds soon quieted. The little family, complete with me, their mistress, fell back asleep.

There were no eggs the next day, nor the next. I rationed out my remaining food supplies and wondered what I could do to ward off starvation.

I tried catching an eel in the stream but none took the bait. I thought perhaps they had been washed away in the flood and would take some time to return. Whatever the reason, fishing provided nothing.

The wallabies had not been back since I made the fence. The maize and sweet potato recovered from the slaughter of its first growth and from the center of their nubs, new leaves began to spring forth, but the remains of the tomatoes rotted in the ground. I realized it would be a long time before either crop, could be harvested, and I feared what would become of me.

The warmth and water in the soil made all the plant life around me grow quickly. It seemed like one could almost see them growing, but this didn't herald any quick relief from my deprivation. Each time I looked, the sweet potatoes did have new leaves and I planted more tomatoes that added to their height daily, but I knew their bounty would come too late.

I dreaded the thought that I would have to sacrifice one of the chickens.

Pale and gaunt, I spent the hot days tending the little plants and clearing the furrows of wild grass and weeds that were growing as fast as the crop. I chewed on thin grass sprigs, ate an egg or two when I could, and prayed the Lord would not forget me.

At nightfall, I would gather the hens and stack them in the corner of the cabin and go to sleep with the sense of dread that comes to a woman who is strangely alone and to whom there is no one to turn to for safety or comfort.

On a Sunday night in February at a little after three o'clock, I woke again to the sound of the hens flapping and clucking in terror.

Immediately I had the feeling that I knew what was causing the ruckus and went cold with panic. I grabbed the gun from beside me and thrust it out into the dark beyond my bed. Awkwardly, with the gun over my arm, I lit the lantern.

In horror, I saw a long diamond-patterned body hanging from the ceiling of the cabin. Its body was wrapped around a beam and it held its head parallel to the floor, pointing in the direction of the chickens in their cages.

"Lord!" I screamed, and as I did, the snake dropped to the floor with a heavy thud, its tongue licking the air in the direction of its prey.

"No you don't!" I yelled.

Standing shakily on the end of the bed, I brought the gun up to my shoulder and aimed directly at the snake's huge head.

With a resounding boom, the gun fired. The recoil threw me back on the bed and my shoulders crashed into the wall behind the pillows. I scrambled forward with my gun and peered over the end of the bed.

The body of the snake was twisting and contorting, writhing with the last of its life, and the head lay almost severed and fixed to the floor where the shot had smashed a ragged hole in it and the boards beneath. The coils thrashed and bumped into furniture, but little by little, the snake stopped moving. Even partly coiled, its corpse stretched across half the length of the little cabin like, a serpent to rival the one who had escaped the inland god in Cook Town.

The chickens were shocked into complete silence.

"Are you all right, my little ones?" I gingerly stepped across the body of the snake and peered into their cages to see if any had died of fright. They were all still alive but one had flopped its head back on its body and was panting, its gray lids half closed.

I stepped back across the body of the snake and tried to open the cabin door, but the creature was wedged hard up against it.

With great effort, I lifted a portion of the body clear. I could feel the sinews under my fingers moving slightly and I winced with the horror of it.

In the light of the lantern, I strained to drag the body onto the porch. The thought came that there was enough meat to keep me going for weeks if it could be preserved.

My mind raced with excitement. I would gut it and skin it just as Jackie had shown me when he had butchered the eel those long months ago.

When I had shifted the entirety of the fourteen-foot snake onto the deck, I washed my hands, put my Bible over the hole in the floor, and weighted it down with the water pitcher in case anything should find its way in through the opening. Then I said goodnight to my chickens and we all fell back to sleep.

In the morning, I woke lazily and with a headache. I lay watching a small chitchat lizard wriggle up the wall and out under the iron roof sheets.

Suddenly I realized I could see daylight from one corner and remembered the ordeal of the snake during the night. It had forced the nails up and slid in through the corrugation, then along the beam, to reach its prey.

I wondered what would have happened if the beam had been over the bed and it had dropped onto me. Immediately, the awareness of the enormity of what had happened filled me, and I rose quickly, creeping to the door in my nightgown.

I opened the door a little and peered out, half expecting it to have slithered off in the night, miraculously moving without the use of its head.

It had not. It lay in twisted sections. The curves were shining like polished pewter, crisscrossed with green, white, and gold patterns in the morning sun, and the belly was polished pearl. Flies had already begun to buzz around the smashed head, which was covered with dried blood that had turned almost black.

"So this will be breakfast, lunch, and dinner!" I dizzily shook my head and grimaced at the task of preparing it.

After I dressed and set the chickens free outside—all of whom stood without moving for some minutes—I considered how I would deal with the dead monster on my porch.

I found the chopping board, lay it under the beast, and, cut the body into foot long sections that I could carry.

Piece by piece, I took the snake out to the bench on the outside wall of the shed and carefully gutted and skinned it.

I cut the fillets off the spine and took one piece eagerly to the camp oven, which had lain unused for some time, to cook it.

Once the fire was lit and the fillet sliced into thin strips, I added some herbs and salt and fried it in a little bacon fat until it looked thoroughly cooked.

While it was still hot, my hungry fingers juggling it in the morning air, I ate until I could eat no more.

Sitting in the sun after my feast, my belly full and my lips shiny with oil, I decided that the snake was indeed edible. Although I could not imagine it would be served at any fine restaurant, it was most satisfying, and even more so in the face of my starvation.

Before the flies could spoil the rest, I skinned, cleaned, and filleted each of the remaining sections. Within a few hours, I had a pile of pink and red meat in buckets beside the bench. Half, I salted and pegged out on a line to dry. The other half I would smoke. I made a salt mixture with the last of the sweet molasses and rubbed the meat with it, and then packed it in buckets with cloves scattered throughout and sealed the lids so it could cure. I pressed clay from the river bank, all around the rims so the flies couldn't get in and spoil my plan.

When I had finished, I sat back on Jackie's chair and rested. My stomach twisted and turned from the new sensation of sustenance and gave me pain as it remembered how to digest solid food. The day's hours slid by and I surveyed my new world now with fearless satisfaction. I had fired the gun—and killed to eat.

The rustic fence now protected my crops, the hens might stop laying again for just a little while, but my pantry was full of meat, so hope had returned to Notre Maison farm and to me.

The broken night and my full belly made me drowsy, and it was not long before I dozed in my chair and drifted off to sleep in the warm afternoon.

I awoke gently. Rubbing my eyes and threading my fingers through my hair, I released the knot at the back so that it fell to my shoulders. I did not perceive that I was not alone.

Suddenly, my eyes focused and I realized that "Mulley", which was all I could pronounce of his name, was back.

Standing in front of the deck, he was as still as the shadow of a tree and equally as dark. He did not move a muscle but watched me as I sat looking down at him.

For a few moments, I did not move either, and we two seemed fixed in our places, staring into each other.

Finally, I pulled myself up from the chair and without fear, walked to the steps.

He turned slightly to watch me step down, my skirts flowing out from my feet as I did.

"Well, hello. I am glad to see you again." I said quietly. I smiled as I walked to him and looked up to his rounded shoulders glowing with the sunlight falling on them from behind. "It is nice that you should come back and visit me."

He did not make any sign that he had either heard or understood me but studied my face closely.

Finally, he looked away, and using the spear in his hand he pointed to the snake meat hanging from the line and nodded in the general direction of them drying in the hot sun.

"Oh yes! I had a visitor last night." I smiled. "He was an unwelcome one... so I shot him."

He nodded without understanding a word of my humor but raised his eyebrows in surprise at the kill I had managed and the way I had hung the meat out to dry, not dissimilar to the way the women of his clan might do.

"Shall we have tea?" I pointed to the deck and the cup that still sat on the table where I had left it.

He nodded, not knowing what he was agreeing to, but followed me up onto the porch.

I indicated where he should sit and, with caution and curiosity, he lowered himself to the chair. It must have seemed odd to him, as he had likely only ever sat on his haunches, the ground, or the trunk of a tree. The chair slightly creaked with his weight and he immediately jumped up. Then watching me, he gained assurance and slowly lowered himself to it again to sit at my table.

I boiled the tin kettle and very soon had made a pot of tea while he watched me complete the strange ritual.

I asked him if he would take sugar but he simply sat silently, watching intently.

I used a silver teaspoon to scrape the last of the sugar from a small tin into his cup, and put the hot drink down in front of him.

He watched me carefully, no doubt wondering what the protocol was for this strange custom. I picked up my own cup and blew on it gently, and then sipped a little, and he watched me as my lips gently touched the edge of the enamel cup.

Carefully, he fingered the side of the metal and the lifted the cup to his lips as I had done. Lacking experience, he blew a little too fiercely and the tea bubbled off the side and dripped to the tabletop.

"Oh dear... Look, blow on it just a little and it will cool. See?"

He tried again, but it was still too hot on his lips, so he thrust it to the table where it slopped, slightly and left a brown ring on the cloth embroidered with pansies. I continued to gently sip, and after a moment or two, he picked up the cup again and followed my lead, trying to politely master the strange ceremony.

Finally, he was able to drink the tea, and he nodded to me. The sweet, earthy liquid was pleasant to his taste.

Suddenly, he licked his finger, stuck it in the bottom of the small sugar tin, rubbed completely around until it had cleaned out the container, and then he returned it to his mouth.

"Mmm!" He nodded, and I smiled.

"Yes, sweet." I replied.

"Swit!" His attempt to mimic the word sounded foreign and childlike.

I grinned and repeated it correctly, and with a little trial and error, he got it almost right.

For the rest of the afternoon, we entertained ourselves with the game of "language" and he proved to be a fast learner. We started with the basics of animals and scenery, clothing, and other items I could point to and name. I found him to be near my age, perhaps nineteen or twenty, though his people did not commemorate it as we do. But for his age, he was by far, a more sound man than any of the young men I had known and might well have been thought of as much older. The hours seemed to pass quickly and as I taught him he repeated each word and practiced it diligently. He was an excellent pupil, far better than myself, who could barely master even his name.

Soon the light faded, and he finally rose from his seat and stared back toward the mountains and I knew we must bid farewell.

I walked him to the steps and we said good-bye, but before he descended, he turned and caught hold of my hand. My small white fingers curled around the larger dark ones as though nestled in a bed of velvet, and I suddenly remembered the feeling of the dream.

"Pless, Mullegadajawara, ...see... Margaru?" He seemed to ask to call on me again using words I had taught him that very afternoon.

I paused for a moment before I replied. "Yes," I whispered and gently pulled my fingers from his. "Margaru will teach you English... Mulley... come back here." I smiled sweetly to him and pointed from the mountains to the ground at my feet. "Come here and I will teach you."

He was a gentle man. I could see that, and the first fears I had had about these wild natives were all but washed away like the flood. All that was left was the clear dark world of his eyes and the warm touch of his hand. The afternoon had already cemented a firm friendship between us and we felt at ease in the other's company.

I pointed to the sky in the west, where the light was glowing with the moisture over the mountains and fading into the licorice color of their majestic mantle.

"Today... gone." I pointed to the dark horizon in the east where the sun would rise and said, "Tomorrow, Mulley come. Tomorrow."

He looked at me without any sign that he agreed. Instead he smiled, and I knew he had understood me.

He turned and jumped from the bottom step, picked up his shield and spear, and began to trot off into the growing darkness without a sound or a word. It appeared I would have to get used to his sudden appearances and his equally sudden departures.

"So Lord, you have heard me. I not only have meat... you have brought me a friend indeed."

The warm evening air whispered around the corners of the cabin, and I turned and gathered up the items off the table, took myself inside, and closed the door.

Chapter 10

IN THE WEEKS that followed, Mullegadajawara appeared every day and often brought me edible greens, bags of nuts, or meat in the form of a speared wallaby, bush turkey, or lizard.

I enjoyed his lessons, as he was an astute and willing student. For the four or five words I would learn of his language, he would devour thirty of mine, and he remembered most. Soon he was putting together quite intelligent sentences, could manage time and place, and could even express his feelings.

I realized this was a man who, had he been born in our world, would have been adept at education. His lack of such benefits did not prevent his mind from thinking and advancing himself in the wild terrain he lived in. He showed me traps he had devised and a number of innovations that seemed likely to make his and the life of his clansman more profitable.

The days seemed complete as we walked and talked and I learned more of him as a man than as a mere native as some would only presume him to be.

As our conversations became more detailed and more revealing, he explained that at our first meeting he and his companions had not seen a white woman before and had marveled at my appearance. They had said to each other, "What is this person, is she woman?" The one called Djingelagar had said with curiosity, "These are their females, but they are too ugly to mate with!"

I laughed as he translated the remarks of his companions.

Mullegadajawara said our first encounter had them perplexed, and they had asked each other, "What shape is it? They must have the behind of a male kangaroo inside that weaving!"

"No," Mullegadajawara had assured them, "There are lots of coverings to fatten her but she is shaped much the same as our women. She is longer perhaps, and she has pink nipples that you can see. They are the color of the fig blossom. She has a good full bosom too, but on the body of a girl." He told me they had questioned him, "How do you know this Mullegadajawara, you been watching the waterhole?" He maintained he did not reply nor tell them how he had been watching me often.

He confessed that he had come back to the cabin alone when "the night was dark, and there was no moon." It had been he standing at my window as I bathed.

He had walked silently, like a shadow through the landscape. He believed the trees had opened to him because he was meant to see me, and they pulled their boughs aside in homage as he passed between them and headed for my cabin.

He had listened to the night owl in the high trees and had walked steadfastly to the river where the crossing was shallow.

Most of the village would have long since curled themselves in their bark-covered huts, fast asleep, as he stalked up the incline, past where the Chinese boy had been speared. He said he could see my settler's cabin, "the shelter that cannot be moved," and from the window, he could see that I had lit a fire inside.

He told me he could not understand this, and said to himself as he crouched camouflaged in the night shadows, "These are a strange people. They roast themselves near the embers in their shelter and it will burn and begin a forest fire."

The light from my shelter inspired his curiosity. He wondered what manner of people we were that would leave our territory and "squat" on Yidinji land.

He told me he thought we seemed like people from the moon, white and strange. We spoke in voices that sounded like hissing water and crackling fire. We were as far from honorable human kind as he could imagine.

Still, he had walked up to the opening as silently as a spotted quoll hunting in the dark mountain peaks to where the light was spilling out into the darkness.

Tentatively, he had stood in the shadow beside it hoping to catch a glimpse inside.

He said he could see a kind of "skin of unmoving water" over the hole that was my window and his finger reached out and touched it. He said it felt cold, hard, and so strange to him that he withdrew his hand quickly in case the magic got inside him. He said he thought about it curiously, "They have made the water hard somehow, to keep the fire in." Marveling at it, he watched insects battering the glass, attracted to the only light across this land.

Without guilt or conscience, he said he looked through with wide eyes. The surface of the glass warped and swayed the image from within as he stared into the interior of my cabin, seeing my outline, a woman, but not like any woman he had ever seen.

He described me as having skin that was white like the milk from the fichus rubber tree; my limbs long and slender like the young, nubile girls of the village. Yet, he said I had feeding breasts like the pregnant women. He had told me this matter-of-factly. But as he told me, his words made me feel as naked as that night, and I felt strangely shy.

He had seen every part of me and said I was curved and thin-waisted instead of flat and straight like his women, and my rump was rounded and shining pink from the warm water. He wondered why I had not just washed in the stream, as his own women would do.

As he watched, mesmerized by my young female form, he said he had stared and been perplexed at how my pubic hair could be "seen" because my skin was white and he was amazed at how naked I appeared compared to his women, whose hair was black on their ebony-colored skin and cloaked them as though they were not naked at all.

Because I looked so different, he had wondered if all my parts were as his own women were and whether I birthed the same way. When I used my soap he became almost fearful as it began to slide all over my body, and he wondered what ritual this was. "Looked like animal fat," he said.

He told me I had conjured up foam that lined the shoreline after a big storm, and he could smell a hint of the oil of tree leaves and flowers.

A moth had flown past his shoulder and he felt the wind of its frantic wings before it hit the hard water barrier and clicked loudly on impact. He said the sound had made me stop and look up as a wallaby does when it is surprised. He could see I was very afraid, so he ducked back into the dark shadow where he could not be seen.

A few moments later, he said, the light disappeared and silence held us both, on either side of the wall, wondering what would happen next. We each held our breath, unknowingly poised on the future, and as he told me this, I knew what he meant.

After a few minutes, he said he shifted without a sound and stepped back carefully so that not even a grass stalk would declare he had been there.

A few days later he returned, but this time with his young warriors, and they stood before me.

He'd told me he was a trained "message man" as well as a warrior. He explained that the post fulfilled the diplomatic needs of the tribe and was the reason he had been the first to come to me.

As an ambassador, he ensured that meetings with other tribes or clans on various matters such as marriages, disputes, and sharing rights were observed with decorum and negotiated peacefully. He did not remark on the unfortunate events with Jackie and I did not interrupt his story to question him about it.

When he touched my skirt that first time, he said, "I thought it was soft like cockatoo feathers but looked very finely woven like our baskets. It was woven so small ..." he lifted my hand from my skirts and looked at my fingers, "that I thought your fingers must have magic weaving skills in them." I smiled and shook my head as I listened to him.

Mullegadajawara said that the other warriors had wanted him to keep making me speak because I sounded so odd and my voice made them want to laugh. As he said this to me, he smiled himself. "You speak like the waterfall... with pebbles in your mouth."

Mullegadajawara told me they had first interpreted my being on their land alone as a trap and had discussed what they should do. "I think she wants us to come up to her shelter, and when we go, her mate will spear us," they said.

"She has no mate... or if she does, he has gone on a long walkabout and the small slave we killed was her only companion. She is here alone," he had told them.

I felt a pang of sadness at the astute observation and thought of my husband and poor Jackie.

Mulley went on, not noticing my sadness. He told me they had been afraid and had not wanted to come near me. They said, "We do not like it. She is not normal." They had wanted Mullegadajawara to stay away too, and he told me they had been insistent: "She has been given the message stick, and she has received it... we should only come here with warriors hiding on the plain."

Mullegadajawara smiled at me gently and said, "But you are 'tame,' and I am not afraid of you."

Every day he spoke to me like this. His heart spilling out through his struggling words, and I delighted in the innocence and truthfulness of his company. And that, not all, I delighted in his very soul.

One morning he declared to me that I should be brought to his village and meet with his family and the elders, whose interest in me had been heightened by his tales of my lessons and my willingness to learn their ways also.

Regardless of the fears they first had of me, Mullegadajawara was determined so later that very morning, I rode on the mare with my new friend at its head. He led me through the plain until we reached the big river I knew as the Mulgrave, which spilled from the valley leading up to the gorge.

He had chosen this day because it coincided with the only two weeks of the year during which a particular delicacy was available, Torres Island Pigeon eggs. These were a seasonal delicacy. Like the sugar bag bees gathered later in the season. These additions to the aboriginal's diet marked the beginning of the annual seasonal produce of each year and had done so for time immemorial.

Collecting the eggs would also afford Mullegadajawara an opportunity to hone his young nephew's skill at harvesting them and allow him to introduce me to the women of his clan.

He told me I should stay with the women because protocol did not permit me to meet anyone else until I had spent time with and worked among them.

I was nervous and hoped they would accept me.

He said they would teach me to weave a dilly bag so I could learn to leach poisonous nuts in the stream so they could be eaten.

I did not care for the idea, as I felt shy, but I knew that knowing such things were essential for survival, and I realized it was a great privilege to be shown by his people who had no doubt never had occasion to include a stranger such as I, before.

When we arrived near the camp, we stopped and I let him tie the mare nearby so we could walk together into the clearing.

He stopped me just outside the ring of habitation and I stood obscured by trees, watching.

Mullegadajawara walked over to the women, who were seated as they wove. He stood a few steps away from the oldest in the group and waited.

They were singing as they worked with their raffia baskets, fronds flicking through their fingers and shining strands twisting as they went.

When he spoke to them in his language, they stopped and looked up then began to laugh.

He looked back to where I was standing a little behind the trees and pointed to me. The women did not rise but stared at me somewhat curiously.

They sat with their legs spread out, sprawled over the grass, bare breasted. Behind them, their burru shelters made from loya cane palm fronds and paper bark, curved like small igloos with dark openings that gave no glimpse of the interiors. The scene looked primeval, but these people were by no means simple. I would learn that a complex and well-ordered society was spread through these lands. But that day, I watched them as though looking back in time.

A young woman began to speak, but I could not understand her. Mullegadajawara told me later that she had suggested that not only his nephew should take lessons in collecting the eggs but his cousin, Weipaneigulu, too. He had grinned at me as he recounted the tale, the humor of the moment, crossing his mind and he said, "She always no-sey and never miss op...tun-ity to remind man of faults!"

"What did she say?" I asked and he looked at me with a mischievous smile. "She say, "You should take cousin Weipaneigulu with you an' nephew, Mullegadajawara... he need lesson in tree climbing too. His wife tell me, he always fall out of tree before he get to eggs!" As he retold me of their conversation, I could see the scene again with the rest of them laughing loudly at the double meaning, because the couple had had no children thus far. Mulley maintained this joke was also directed at him because he had no wife.

They had chided him playfully, "And you, what makes you think you can teach "second boy" how to gather eggs let alone Weipaneigulu? When are you going to get a wife and collect eggs of your own? Is no one good enough for you?"

The oldest woman of the group, with breasts that hung low and empty, grinned at him with perfect teeth. Then she looked across to where I stood and her smile had faded to a scowl and he saw it so he said back to her candidly.

"Menge, I'll get married when I can find a woman that does not gossip all day." He shook his head as he replied and she dropped her eyes away from me and looked up trying to conceal her grin at his retort. She feigned false innocence and said, "Well, I don't know of anyone of this bama that does that, so maybe you don't want to be a man at all! Standing here, like you are so pretty and bringing us a stranger so ugly that even the women of her own kind won't come near to gossip with her." One of the others who was giggling said, "Maybe, we should show him how to dress like a woman and he and the strange one can join us together and we'll teach them how to be proper women!" They were all laughing loudly then and from my vantage point in the trees, I could not contain a smile not knowing I was the brunt of their joke.

From the trees I caught the word for "pretty," as Mulley had taught me it, and I wondered if it was me that they spoke of. But when Mulley left them giggling together and returned to me, he told me what they had been saying and I realized I was not so welcome as he had said I would be.

The old one had looked up to Mullegadajawara standing with me and called out. "Are you and the ghost woman planning to help us, or are you just planning to stand there all day and watch?"

Mullegadajawara walked back to them and waved to me to come forward.

With some annoyance in his tone he said to the old one while I hid in his shadow shyly, "Where's second boy? I want to take him up to the mountains today, not tomorrow! I'm going to show him how to really collect eggs this time, and he is not going to eat most of them on the way back like he did last time."

I had understood some of what he said and smiled shakily as I came closer." He leaned around to me and pulled me forward by the hand. "You must stay here while I go." He said in English and the women all stopped their weaving and looked up at him with surprise.

He pushed me toward the women from behind and indicated I should sit down. I did so, a little gingerly, and tucked my skirts in under my knees.

There was no introduction, as the custom would have demanded among my own people. Instead, it was expected that I would simply include myself. I watched Mulley and clasped my hands together tightly on my lap, waiting. He scanned around the camp and said, "That boy is like his mother... happy to eat but not so happy to do the work to eat!"

He looked down at the older woman, now grinning broadly as her fingers returned to deftly threading the raffia and split cane in and out of a forming basket. Almost ignoring me completely, he carried on with his conversation. "We shall have a good load for you this time old woman don't you worry yourself. You can pickle some for me, and I'll let you have some for your trouble, if I shall ever get up the mountain and back in this day."

"We shall see. Last week, second boy was looking fat from his lesson with you and there was not a spare egg to be seen. And anyway, might be there is someone needing them more than me, eh?"

She lifted her hand and indicated toward some young women gathering wood for the new day fires while others were grinding roots and seeds between polished stones.

One of the girls looked up in the direction of all the laughing and smiled at Mullegadajawara as he turned his head in the direction of the old woman's outstretched arm. He looked away from her quickly and down to me seated in the grass waiting and wondering what was happening.

I was not sure if I should speak but my expression showed him that I wanted to know what the old woman had said. He lifted his eyes from me to the surrounding bush and said that they were always pressing him toward one woman or another because they liked an excuse to feast and he was past the age of marriage because he was already twenty.

He looked back fleetingly at the slim and well-featured young woman but did not offer anything that would encourage the old woman. Rather, he returned his gaze to beyond the scattering of camp dwellings to the trees. Suddenly, he saw the boy.

"Hey! Second boy, you coming with me today? We're going to get some more of the pigeon eggs," he yelled out as he saw the young boy loitering around a eucalyptus tree.

The boy was harassing a green tree frog he had found and had stuck it to the trunk. It was clinging with its sucker feet to the smooth bark trying to crawl up and away but the boy continued to keep it where he wanted it.

I thought how similar all boys were and remembered the child in Cook Town with his gecko Greeny, and a pang of longing suddenly filled me.

"Come on then… I want to get up there and back today, not after the moon has gone full."

I listened and understood most of what Mulley said, but before I could say a word to stop him to say, perhaps I should come back when he could remain in the camp and I would not feel so out of place, he stepped away from us and left. I watched Mullegadajawara gather the boy gently by the shoulders and they began to walk to the path that led out of the camp and up to the higher ground. I could see the tree where the boy had been and strangely, the frog had stayed right where he was, frozen to the spot, as the two strode away toward the mountains.

The taller man held his spear in one hand and the boy strode alongside. He was carrying a bark basket and clearly liked his uncle's attention.

Mulley had described his family to me when we had been on our way. And I knew that the young boy was his brother's son, and his name was 'Second Boy', because he was one of a twin. Such a birth was extremely rare, so the second child was not awarded a name as the others were.

The Yidinji children had names like 'Forest Lizard', or 'Fast River', or any one of the many descriptions intended to speak a 'blessing' over them or describe the character they should have. But this child would only be called Second Boy in case he was a ghost of the first. If the other died, the survivor would keep the proper name.

I saw Mullegadajawara point with the tip of his spear toward the high peaks as he paused with Second Boy. It seemed to me he was never without his spear, although he often did not carry his shield. Sometimes it was left at the camp but would be proudly taken to coroberee ceremonies or to meet newcomers. He had told me his shield was painted in the colors of the clan. The shield was crossed with zigzags of white and red ochre mixed with blood.

Its designs showed his totem, the god being that which had turned into an animal in the dreamtime and guided his family ever since.

That day, those spirits and I rested our gaze on the tall black back of Mullegadajawara shining in the morning sun. The warrior and message man strode away, he and the boy completely naked as was befitting for them. His people had long since lost any sense of nakedness in the tropical heat. His torso slid perfectly down to his waist, below which strong buttocks rested above muscular thighs. His only decorations were feathers and shells knotted in his hair, and the scars of his initiation, and a long necklace of rare shells showed he was the son of the head of the clan. But for all this, I knew his nature to be gentle, and it appeared all treated him with love, rather than fearing his authority.

As I watched him leave with his nephew, I thought how fortunate I was to have his attention and care. I had little to offer in return save teaching him our language. And though he learned eagerly, at times I wondered if he had some hidden purpose for my inclusion in his world. I thought of this as I sat in the circle without him.

Around me, the smooth-skinned women now sat very quietly. They wore raffia skirts of rope-like threads tied around their waists, which dangled between their legs when they walked or sat. Otherwise, their skin was their "clothing," and the chocolate-black was perfectly even over their entire bodies. Their heads were topped with thick black, wiry hair that glistened in the sunlight, and although they were naked, it now seemed perfectly reasonable to me.

Watching on as the women wove, I wondered if I should be accepted at all. Then, quite suddenly, one of the younger women got up and shifted her position to come alongside me. The old woman Menge said nothing, raising neither an eyelid nor a smile.

The young woman said to me in the Yidinji tongue, "Take!" and she thrust a handful of split cane toward me, which I accepted without knowing what I should do.

She began to fold the strands together in a ring, occasionally holding it up a little higher so I could see.

I attempted the task myself and as I faltered, she darted her brown fingers in to show me where I should thread next. I became quite confused and soon had something that looked like a square, loosely wound together. She took it from my lap and held it up.

The older women burst into laughter, and many of the other women slapped their thighs and covered their faces as they laughed until they cried.

I said in the best Yidinji tongue I could manage. "I have sick hand." Again, the group roared with laughter.

The commotion made the young women who were pounding roots a little distance away come running over, and they too joined in the amusement at the sight of my appalling first attempt of such a rudimentary task.

I could not help but laugh myself, and the cool reception that had come before dissolved with their bright white smiles and shiny bodies flocking around me.

Soon, I could feel them tugging at my bodice cords, and in no time they had disrobed me of my outer garments. Had I not called a halt determinedly, they would have had me as naked as themselves, but the old woman shooed them away. So I sat down in my undergarments and soon was trying again with my dilly basket and, I confess, quite pleased to be so un-attired.

When Mullegadajawara returned hours later, I had managed to make quite a good example of a basket, and I barely noticed him and Second Boy coming back down the track.

When I saw him, I quickly scrambled into my skirt but could not manage to cover my linen chemise, so I sat half-dressed in the circle while the others greeted him. I held one hand over my breast and the other clinging to my dilly bag as he came near, but he did not acknowledge me.

I could not make out what they had said to him as he arrived, so I asked him, "What say they, about me?"

"Ah," he smiled mischievously, "I plessed your 'sick hand' has healed!" He pointed to my finished dilly bag.

"Oh, that!" I giggled, and the younger girl beside me hid her own snicker under her hand.

"They also want to know why you wish to wrap yourself like a goanna in banana leaves ready to be cooked."

"Well, it is our custom, as you know."

They shook their heads and began muttering to themselves as he translated for them.

"They think your people strange and you white because you have been boiled too long."

"Oh I see. Tell them it is cold where I come from, colder than they can ever imagine, and we don't have this sun as they do, so we wear many clothes."

He nodded, probably not understanding how cold I meant, as they had never experienced anything less than perhaps sixty degrees. Somewhat matter-of-factly he said, "It not cold here, Margaru. You have bad custom—must lose."

He took eggs from his bark basket and some dry grass and placed them in my newly made dilly bag.

"Come, we go."

I got up and thanked the women but they just smiled, each setting off for their burrus to complete various tasks.

I put my bodice over my shoulders and then mounted the mare, and we began our journey back.

As we crossed back over the scrub and tussock land between the camp and my cabin, I asked him to tell me about his trip to where the pigeons were. I looked at the small collection of white eggs nestled in my dilly basket and thought about how they might have collected them.

"Me and Second Boy reach nest site midday, when sun stops to rest..."

He happily told me how he and his nephew had climbed the rainforest giants with a plaited sling of unbreakable raffia around their backs, walking up the huge tree trunks. Then they shimmied out on the long limbs until they could reach the nests of the birds though they were so high in the air a fall would be certain death.

They raided the bird nests of their eggs one by one, and the disturbed fowl cooed and fluttered among the branches, unable to do anything but object.

After they had filled their bags, they descended the tree again, with their slings around their backs.

Mullegadajawara helped Second Boy hunt a lizard that was hidden in the fallen trunk of a great tree, and they found fat grubs among the rotten timber and ate them alive.

I was shocked by this horrible thought, but he said they both enjoyed the sweet-tasting morsels as one after another slid down their throats. He said he would bring me some, but I declined, quickly saying, I would not wish to take a meal from them that they so clearly relished.

He told me he had watched the boy light a fire to cook the lizard. They wrapped it in large fragrant leaves with some of the eggs and cooked the green parcels in the embers. While they ate the meal they chatted about the various matters in the camp and then rested for a while under the forest canopy before beginning the return trip.

When they neared the camp, the boy had run ahead down the path calling loudly for his mama and his brother while he held the bark basket closely in his arms, the eggs packed tightly between forest leaves.

Mullegadajawara told me how it pleased him to see the boy so happy. He had seen him grinning broadly as the boy was greeted by his mother and several 'aunties' that had come out of their shelters to see what they had collected and take a share. It was the way of his people and I confess I envied his 'belonging'.

He fell silent for a few moments as we walked along.

I wondered what troubled him. "Is something the matter?" I asked.

For still more moments, he did not reply. Then he fumbled with a few words and began to tell me what was on his mind.

"Long time back, moon months past, when the plums were ripe." He struggled as he told me of the occasion when he had come home from hunting as usual. He had walked up to the men grouped and seated separately.

Placing his shield and spear down beside a tree, he came and sat down with them as was his right. He told me that the conversation had begun with the subject of Second Boy, as light-hearted as it ever was.

"Second boy is fit as they come. Perhaps he will get a name of his own. He always collects more food than we can carry, so we eat some just to get rid of it... He caught two fruit bats as well as the plumbs we collected today. If I keep giving him lessons I will get fat!" He looked ahead of us and said the boy was often the subject of interest in the camp, and it was easy to enter the conversation of the ring with the boy's adventures.

The men had responded equally light-heartedly, and the older men laughed, remembering their youth. The special gathering trip seemed a plausible excuse for having a feast in the mountains.

"That boy won't need to eat tonight. He is always eating enough for himself and his brother. Someone had better tell his mama."

I watched Mulley grin a little to himself as he remembered the day, then he continued to tell me the story with a somber expression.

The men had asked him, "So what of these strangers that invade us? They seem unable to be taught anything, Dujiewa was saying."

"This is true." Mulley said Wanburra had replied in a serious tone. "It is said that they are so dumb, they have no better thing to do than burn out of season and tear up the ground. They build places that cannot be shifted when the trees fruit and they let a big beast wander about eating the grass away and trampling mud into the water, making it hard for all the animals."

I felt a coldness come into my stomach as I heard the ungracious words spoken of myself and the other settlers carving out farms somewhere beyond our sight.

Mulley went on: "Wanburra said, 'I have seen the beast they sit on. I do not think you could dry all the meat on that animal, but they seem unwilling to eat that one, only the one with great horns.'"

Dujiewa had spoken up, 'But it can't taste very good because it stinks! Everything they do smells bad just like they do. Downwind, they smell like something has died.'

"'They are very impolite too, they do not ever ask permission to share. Gulgibarra has sent out messages, but they throw them away. They are so ignorant that they do not know how to ask for anything. They use up the canoe trees and kill so many pigeons in just one time that there is nothing left for their neighbor to catch at their turn... What kind of people are so rude and so stupid?... Yet they are so many in number.'" Mulley repeated his memory of the conversation, and I was not sure if he wanted me to answer Wanburra's question or not. But he carried on anyway.

Wanburra had said, "Gimuy Walubarra are fighting. Many have been run off or killed."

Mulley looked up at me and said, "I warned them that your people have a stick that when it points, it explodes the flesh, and there is nothing to do but run."

He said they knew of it and they had all nodded and murmured in agreement.

"Some said, 'Should we fight too, join the Mandigalpi?'" He said a few froze still at the suggestion, as though fearful of what the words might mean for their clan and rightly so.

Mulley shrugged his shoulders as he led the horse by its bridle. "They say to me, 'How does a man fight another when he can point a stick and kill before a spear can even be thrown or a sword even make a strike?'" Mulley seemed to drift into his memories of the meeting and then he went on.

"The circle thought about this," Mulley said. "Then I said, 'I carry the message stick, we must try to come to agreement with them.' But Dujiewa, he not like this idea." Mulley looked down in the grass. "He spoke angry to all as he does all time." Mulley shook his head and swatted a fly from his face then, carried on. "He say in a loud voice that scare the birds off the trees, 'They have no understanding of what we say, nor what we know! Sure as sure, they are unable to think sensibly at all! How can our messages do anything with such a people? They are deaf and dumb and think they are alone in this place, with no spirits guiding them, no animals walking with them, no trees sheltering them. Just them alone ...'

"'These are men who are nothing short of animals,'" Mulley said Gunija had added, and then shook his head as he had then while he waited for his turn to speak.

He paused for at least four steps of my horse, then he said, "Another man, Gulligungarra, say, 'We have this discussion many times! Time gone, long, long, time, you know if 'nother tribe came on our lands; we drive them off an' kill 'em if we find them? So why worry about their sticks? They sleep and eat some time, and they not know the forest or any of this land. We trap 'em; take one here, one there. They be gone, short, short, time!'" Mulley said Gulligungarra had nodded at his own observation and some of the others had nodded with him.

Mulley patted my horse's head as he led me through the trees. The path was invisible to me, but it led home and had welcome shade and I trusted my guide entirely.

He said gently, "I wait for the angry men to settle, then I say back to them, 'Should be also thought by you, that these men aren't like tribes warring us long time past. They are like sands in sea or mosquito in swamp... many we kill, more come, and they come angry. Avengin' even our own food gathering. One death we do, they kill ten of our people, or neighbor's tribe. They don't see our tribes, our clans, or our territories. Them see all is "theirs" and we are ones to drive off.'" He paused and frowned and I knew this recollection was coming to a point. "We must friend them and teach them right ways!' That's what I said to them."

Mulley said that Dujiewa had stood up and strode off angrily and others began to shift as though to follow him. He had shot out one last retort: "Good luck, if you can teach even one of them to know the time of the day... apart from being good!"

Mulley looked up again to me and I said, "I understand that young man's feeling."

Mulley nodded to himself because he had often scouted throughout their territory and had seen our lives displayed so dishonorably before him.

I felt an odd sense of shame for my kinsman.

Suddenly, he looked up and I saw the anguish on his face as he told me that he knew there was no future for his people if they adopted the ways of the Mandigalpi, who had been driven back to the foothills of the ranges trying to defend the area around the inlet.

He sucked in a great breath of air, and told me what he had said at the meeting, addressing his grandfather, who had not spoken at all before. He was sitting cross-legged among the flattened grass of the circle. 'Speak the spirit that is in you Mullegadajawara', he said.

"I will seek the people on our flat land that are planting their shelters. I convince to stay apart, not deal to each other 'cept friendly. We make room for them. Keep our bama from being taken from our place like others north of here." I listened to his tortured English and I began to realize how it was that he now led me through the trees toward my home.

Mulley said the men across from him had disputed the suggestion, but, the old leader settled them, and with the wisdom of his age, he had replied, "Time has been, now ended, has come. Way of wallaby much gone. Go, Mullegadajawara, tell that people we leave them to their madness. We make new tracks 'round them. We live as we are for a little while longer."

Mulley said some of the men had shaken their heads but all stayed silent.

"I stay very quiet …" Mulley smiled at me, pleased that he had been given this mandate to bring the message to the "white ghosts" now swarming across the land, claiming a nation for ourselves where one had never been.

He told me that with this in mind, he had picked up his spear and his shield and called for Gunija and Muninga to come with him that very first time.

Gunija had listened to the warrior and message man for the Malanbarra Bama as he told him that he would show his companion the way of negotiation, and if he was right the whole tribe would understand that this was the way to prevent great harm coming to their people, as it had to many of the other tribes.

He said the younger man had replied, "Mullegadajawara, I obey you and I will go with you to visit them, but I do not agree with you. These are not people that understand proper things."

Mulley had replied that perhaps he would agree when their tribe was left to their peace, when not one of the other Yidinji would be elsewhere if they fought with the whites.

"If you are right," he had answered Mulley, "it better that we just go to the 'dreaming place', and make no agreement with these people because what is a man if he survives without his people?" He had considered this line of thought before went on, very certainly, "And you cannot make settlement with a man unless you share his spit and his spirit! You share with this people, and you no longer are a people of your own… you a 'ghost' that has no dreaming."

Mulley said he was determined to try, so he declared that the three of them would set off in the direction of the land between their camp and the landing point of Gimuy where the new town now sat. They would stop at the site where they knew a new settler had already begun to make dwellings they could not move when the wet Gurrabana season ended and try to talk to us.

He said they had come across the trail cut by our very horses and dray, and they followed our journey, noisily scraped through the land as though we had been a forest fire that ran behind us where ever we went, all the way to the joining of the two streams.

By the time they came to the junction, they could see the smoke pouring up from the land and rising up to the heavens to show the sky spirits what we had done.

He looked up at me and said, "When we saw your signs, Muninga said, 'They are like children. They don' know when or how to burn the land. And look, they tear up seeds so grass will not grow again for the wallaby! They will go hungry next year.'" The man shook his head and rattled his spear in the air.

"The youngest, Gunija, said, 'They're idiots, better they die and are buried without ceremony.'" This was the greatest insult he could think to say about us. He had spat the words in disgust and Mulley said the leaves rattled as the wind passed by as though it understood his disrespect and agreed.

Mulley told me they walked quietly down to the stream where the wheels of the dray had left deep, ruts in the soil, and one said that the floods would tear all our work away because we left no roots to hold the bank. They had stood on the edge staring at the mess with astonishment.

Mulley pulled the mare's head around to take the path down to the stream and we stopped, looking out across the stones and the water. The raw clay of a huge hole in the bank had appeared after the flood, just as the men had predicted, and the dray could no longer cross the stream and climb up that side, even if I had the will to try.

Mulley pointed to the other side and said that they had suddenly heard the unfamiliar "chink" of something hard striking the rocks of the stream. Standing still and quiet so as not to disturb the animal, whatever it might be, they looked out and over the stream to see a man wrapped in strange woven grasses they had not seen before.

They had watched him for some minutes as they stood very still on the stones of the streambed.

Mulley turned to me, and I saw the sorrow and guilt in his eyes. He almost whispered as we stood looking over the now-empty space, "Something alerted the man. He looked up to us."

I remembered clearly the fear and shock filling Jackie's face as he saw the native warriors standing in the shade of the overhanging trees with their spears and shields.

"The man slowly stood, began backward over stones. I said, 'Don't frighten him' …"

Mullegadajawara dropped his voice reverently and spoke quietly as he went on. "I said, 'Walk out to greet him …'"

He told me that Gunija had stepped to the right, putting a little distance between himself and the taller aboriginal who led them.

Mulley went on, "The man drop his dogobil."

I looked to Mulley and realized they would not have recognized the metal bucket. Mulley used the word for the vessels they carried water in, which were made from bark and hollow lengths of tree trunk, sealed with beeswax. Mulley said the strange dogobil was shining like lightning and hit the stones with a loud clatter of musical thunder as the man had jumped up and ran.

They had been shocked by the strange sound and his sudden flight, and Muninga called out, "What people run if they are good Mullegadajawara?" And Gunija yelled back, "They are not good!" As they ran after Jackie up the bank and over the grass of the upper plateau, Gunija had raised his spear instinctively with the chase and before Mulley could say or do anything, he had thrown it into the air. It flew, sure and true, and hit Jackie cleanly through, and he fell headlong into the grass.

Mullegadajawara had run forward and raised his voice angrily at the young warrior. "This is not way to start introductions! And who are you to decide if a man is to live or not without it being settled at coroberee? If they find him, they will come looking for us and they will not kill you alone. They kill all!"

He said he had looked down at the dead man and decided they must remove him.

I remembered the sight as he recounted the story, and tears filled my eyes.

"I said, 'Take him up, you both. We carry him back.'" Mulley seemed to let the horse's neck hide him from me as he shifted to the other side of her head and I lost sight of him for a moment but I heard his words and a chill momentarily flooded over me.

"Gunija said we should throw him in the river. But I said, 'No, he is not criminal. We bury him in correct way. Maybe they see we are not against them but have respect.'

"Gunija said he did not believe your people could understand. He said, you are 'a people with no respect' for anything so how would you know it if you saw it and he yelled at me, 'Look how they do things!'

"I said, 'You misunderstand them… much the same as they misunderstand us. It is their way of doing things, though they do not know that it is not good.'"

He said they pulled out the spear from poor Jackie and he told them they were lucky he was small. With his body draped across their shoulders like a kangaroo, they had headed back to their camp and he was buried him near their own people in the mountains.

We crossed the stream and Mulley pulled the horse up as we neared the cabin. He looked at me as I sat high above him silently remembering.

"Is Yidinji way to make amends at coroberee, but you cannot go there, so I tell you now, Malanbarra Bama is sorry we take your slave and harm you this way."

I thought about it for a moment and said, "He was not my slave. He was my friend."

"Then Malanbarra Bama cut grief into their soul for you… and give you themselves as friend to make up for this evil …"

"Thank you. I should have liked to have had you both, but it is well that you have said this."

"Margaru, is true, when the tree cut, no one lift it back… but can only plant a new one."

"We are taught the way of our Lord, the great God of all, that 'forgiveness' is given freely Mulley, so we must do the same. Your people need not make amends."

"What is this for-givey-ness?"

"It is the letting go of a debt, what a man owes, because he has done wrong. And when we do wrong to one man, we do it to The Lord who made the man and is in him. So our wrong is really against The Lord himself. So we forgive because we want to be forgiven our own debts for the things we have done against the Lord since he has the right to payback, as your people know to do. Indeed, if he has to give out that justice, we should not survive."

"Ahhh. This is biggest dream time God."

"Yes… I think you already know Him."

"Only some of what you know. I not know this way. Is easier to payback than take this thing you call, for-givey-ness!" He went silent. "But if you know that way, then I am Margaru's friend for… no payback. I take, for-givey-ness, and I am your… friend… free."

"Free-ly …Then you are a friend indeed." I smiled and got down from my horse, for we had reached the cabin.

"And I am sorry to the big God who made you… He did good job! You not that ugly."

I smiled lightly and stepped away from the mare.

We said no more about it, and when he left, I sat alone on the porch and thought about the turn of events.

So much had already happened. I had survived the loss of Edward to his precious goldfields, lost the Kanaka and Jackie, been tested by the elements and even the inhabitants of the land, and then faced the very real prospect of starvation. Amidst all, I could do nothing more than pray and hope. It seems the Lord had not forgotten me, but his answer was far from the one I had expected.

He had given me two things to survive, a gun and my aboriginal friend, and I was grateful. As I thought about my plight, I realized it was the death of poor Jackie that had brought me much grief; it had also been the catalyst for my salvation.

I could almost hear Martha's voice echoing around me: "All things work together for good, lovey, for those that love the Lord and are called according to his purpose!"

It occurred to me now that this terrible event had been the very thing that had led me to this newfound friendship with the people of this land and the warrior who was my frequent companion.

Far from Mulley's being an understudy to my civilized ways, I now found myself in his debt. I was his student, and now that I had begun my lessons at the Yidinji camp, his purpose was materializing.

He had been teaching me what could be eaten or used in the rainforest, on the plains, and in the rivers, and now he was beginning to teach me the ways of his society and the peaceful life they lived. It was clear that he intended not that I should just survive but that I should help my fellow settlers understand the Yidinji.

I began to wonder if this was the intent of the Lord from the beginning and we had all played into the plan. I remembered Jackie saying, "He not help one without helping other... I knew it to be true, indeed, He favors equally.

As I sat on the chair that Jackie had made and watched the night form her cloak around me, the thing that most beautifully settled in my heart was the knowledge that Mulley was my friend and, in his words, freely. Somewhere deep down in my body a sensation filled me. I thought to myself, Time and chance happen to us all, but it seemed there was purpose in everything, and for the first time, I truly believed I had nothing to fear from the future.

Chapter 12

IT WAS SEVEN months since Mulley and I had met face to face for that first time at the junction of the twin streams. As though a cyclone had blown all my ideas about men away, I had to begin again with just the raw dust that we all come from.

His body was not his only nakedness. His soul, too, was open, frank, and visible. When we looked at each other it was in such a way that I knew we were seeing into each other. This was a private thing that I never shared with anyone else, before or since.

We were entirely different as far as race and type and knowledge, and all other things that are the so-called trappings of man. Such matters were almost the debasement of what he and I began to experience together as people. Our communion was the re-enactment of a long-lost play between man and woman right from the beginning, before we had become anything else, and I knew, almost from the first, that what would be between us would be uniquely our own and that no one would ever have that in me again. Even my long-distant husband had no claim on that private world where we knew each other so perfectly.

One afternoon, as we sat near the stream where the waterhole was, under the big tree where I would correct his English or introduced a new word to him, he began to tell me what this strange connection meant to him and show me his thoughts and the secret world of the Malanbarra Yidinji.

He said that after he had brought me back to my cabin the day he had introduced me to the women, he had walked the long way back to the camp. He had taken the route around the river basin and along the bank without crossing it because he wanted to think about the strange word forgiveness and about me.

He said his mind was full of me because he understood that he had seen my inner self in my sadness over the death of Jackie, and this inner view had been married to the image of my naked form behind the hard water opening, my glass window. He said something had happened to him as he had looked into my green eyes as we talked and learned together and he had declared me as his friend. He said I had spoken to him in "dreamtime language" and he understood that we had a special bond that happens in that place and is not made for normal men and women.

Such intimacy left me free to ask whatever I wished, even though I would never dare speak thus to any man of my own kind and I was curious about his true impressions of me. I asked a little shyly at first, "When you met me for that first time, how did you find me?"

He said he thought I must be clever, which in his opinion, compensated for my symmetrical "ugliness," but he reassured me that he, "didn't mind that now because I see you inside… and that is not ugly.".

It was odd to be thought of as unattractive. Most of the remarks I had ever heard about my appearance had been complimentary, and I usually performed the delicate task of deliberately denying this to maintain my humility.

Now however, I found that my looks were not the thing that attracted his interest in me, and I felt somewhat exposed. I could not say that I had ever been considered for my thoughts or personality beyond the courteous indifference afforded a young lady in polite society.

"What is ugly about me!" I rebuked him playfully.

He made me laugh when he described my face as flat and said that it looked like the images that stare back at you in a pool when there is no wind. My skin was a milky apparition, he said, and my eyes had "no shade" in them because I didn't have the heavy brow above them as theirs did.

He said my nose was like a mountain peak, not smooth and rounded like theirs, but sharp and cold. He wondered if it got in the way when I ate or tried to smell something. I assured him it did not.

My white skin was continually ablaze in the heat with the red flush of a "fresh born child," and he said I moved like a quoll on the hunt, always peering into hollow trunks looking for meat. I had yet to see the famed quoll and he promised to take me one day to where we would find one.

It was my courage he said he liked most. It seemed odd to him that I had stood firmly before them at our first meeting as though "equal like a man warrior." I had thrust out my hand at him, and had I had a spear, he said I would have pierced him all the way through. He added mischievously, "I made myself 'member, never give this woman, spear!"

I laughed at his remark, but what truly pleased me was that, without guile or concealment, he told me all he thought, and everything that happened in his world. This put me at ease, as I felt I was rightly honored and respected. I would happily have placed my very life in his hands because I could see the truth about him would never change.

"Tell me, your people what say they?" I asked with equal curiosity.

He looked at me quizzically and then opened his soul and began.

He said when he had finally returned to the camp that day, he knew I would be special to him, but to his people, he was not sure. The men had been seated in a circle as usual. They had eaten and were in the lazy phase when a full belly is doing its work. He had sat down where the circle was widest.

"So Mullegadajawara, the women tell us you have been bringing one of the strangers to visit."

"I have."

"They say she is well enough mannered, but what kind of beings do you say they are really?"

"The woman has the manner of being like Mandigalpi, like the warriors of that clan. She is not warlike but is strong enough to defend. She does not have a mate, as he has left her and gone on walkabout. There was only the slave who stayed behind, whom she called 'friend,' and he is the one we killed. So she has been alone, but has much courage."

"Oh... friend?" The men were immediately concerned for me, because to kill a friend is a great breach of their code and they knew recompense was owed. Knowing their mind on this he said matter-of-factly, "She forgoes recompense and accepts friendship,"

"What friendship can Malanbarra have with her? She is one of them."

"She has only asked us that we let her keep the land she is on, between the twins, and she has asked that this land be safe for her.'" He kept looking down away from my eyes while he repeated their conversation as though my hearing of their words might still offend.

"Nothing more?" I said, waiting with more than a little worry in my mind.

Mulley said they were surprised I had wanted nothing more than I had already asked, and he said he had thought about their question for a moment before he explained the nature of our connection because it was already drawing some interest in the village, "We are teaching each other a way of understanding. She is one who will listen to the right way, and I have learned their hissing tongue."

"We had heard you can talk with her,... but she is a woman?"

Mulley turned a little toward me as he related this and said; "I told them that you are too ugly to consider a "woman" in normal way. I said our lessons are good for Malanbarra and for the strangers."

He said they asked, "So what will you do when you have learned all?"

A sheepish look crossed his face, as though the purpose of telling me what he had been talking with the men about was about to turn into a request, then he said, "I answered them and I said, 'I will ask her to speak with her people at Gimuy, where they have built giant shelters and are gathering like flies over a dead turtle... and ask them to leave us to our own ways.'"

He stopped and waited for me to think about it. I could imagine him seated among the circle with his legs folded, his fawn soles lying on their sides and the dust coating his ankles and calves. The circle of men, already aware that many of their tribesmen in other clans had been driven off their land, would have been troubled and wondering how they might prevent it from happening to their own clan and now I saw Mulley's plan.

As I stared into the water below us, I wondered if anything I might say to my fellow settlers would have any effect at all. Then Mulley broke into my thoughts with the rest of what he had said to his people concerning me.

They ask me, "Do you really think she can be taught all our ways and learn to be peaceful? And who can imagine a woman doing the work of a message man!" Some of the others had muttered fiercely and his grandfather frowned too with the idea that I should be their white ambassador, carrying a message stick of my own, be it willing or nay.

Mulley knew he must say something quickly because their confusion and murmuring might attract a bad spirit and they could swallow it with their mouths open and then be angry every time they considered me as one of them.

Mulley looked up at me and said, "I told them, 'She is the female of this kind, but not like the tree stealers or the people that leave the big animals grazing the grass away. She is not like those men who have no conscience. She is more like the cassowary' …" Mulley's eyes twinkled and he grinned a little.

I stopped him, frowning. "What is a 'cassowary'?" He looked at me with utter amazement.

"It is the bird that stands as big as your grass eaters, and it has bone on its head." He put his two hands above his head like a prayer demonstrating the hard comb that crowned the creature. "He has blue skin on long neck, and he is easy to catch because he's not smart like other birds.' His hands slid down his own neck and rested over his initiation scars on his chest. "He not fly… He stalk about eating the grubs and grasshoppers."

"Oh …" I said, "Ugly and dumb! Are you sure this is the only way your people will accept me? I must see this cassowary, surely it is better than you say."

He stood up and with his knees bent outwards, he began to dance the aboriginal dance of the cassowary. His elbows were pulled tight into his sides and his head darted about, flicking left and right to look for morsels of food. His feet stamped the dust under the trees where we sat and I could almost hear the clicking of the stick instruments keeping time with his feet and the didgeridoo accompanying him.

I laughed and he stopped and returned to me and sat down and then he said, "Djingelagar said loudly, 'You speak the truth, Mullegadajawara!' because he had seen you have a behind the size of the cassowary and everyone believed me after that."

I raised my eyebrows and shook my head in feigned disgust. I knew my full skirts had deceived them, and I smiled as Mulley told me the men had roared with laughter at the ungracious interruption and the angry spirit was frightened away.

Mulley said several of the women, who were seated by the fire some distance away, had looked up with all the noise. The old woman Menge had called out indignantly, "Do you men do nothing but amuse yourselves? Go, if you have that much energy, and hunt for us!"

The younger men had scowled and muttered under their breath, not liking her rebuke. I remembered that she was indeed a formidable woman, and I, too, felt fear for her quick tongue and sharp looks.

The old man, Mully's grandfather, had still been smiling as he returned to the serious conversation. Mulley told me his verdict: "Well, son of my own body, you may be able to teach sense to this ugly woman, and perhaps she will survive on this land she wishes to camp on with us. She shall be accepted into this tribe, as the women have said should be done."

Mulley lowered his eyes as he delivered the words of his grandfather soberly, their intent finally visible. "And perhaps she will agree to talk with those of her kind still coming, and we might live in peace in this place with them all about us—in return for her claiming a place with the Mallanburra yidi and living at peace on our land as one of us."

Mulley looked at me as though I had been in the circle to hear this too and now was required to make an answer.

I imagined the scene of the old man as he looked to the group and pronounced his decision and I stared deep into Mulley's eyes. I was happy to know the women had not rejected me, but I was afraid of what he and his people asked of me.

A silence held us in the dappled light under the tree, and as I thought about returning to civilization to help them, I realized for the first time that those settlements were the last place I wanted to return to for any reason. Sitting in the cool of the trees alone with my companion, it also dawned on me that I no longer cared about what had happened to my husband and I wondered what kind of woman I had become.

Mulley could see my face was troubled with the dilemma in my soul. He whispered to me, "I tell them, Margaru, there is only small time before this season ends and we move to the Gulligungarra camp. And you not move with us... so I will stay with you."

He said the others had agreed and nodded their approval, but he knew that when he was gone, some would raise again, the subject of arming themselves. They would go looking for the interlopers that could not be "taught" and give them payback, as was their custom to those who had not negotiated sharing rights. Then any peaceful solution would be gone, not only for them, but for me as well.

I knew that if Mullegadajawara did not stand in their way, I would not be left alone on my farm. Nor would I be safe even from these who knew of me as a friend to the clan.

Much depended on my learning all I could from Mulley, being fully accepted and somehow standing in the way of my people just as he did for me.

As I watched him waiting for me to answer the clan's request, I felt a pang of sadness that my place among them was not due to the strange, beautiful, innocent, and magical connection Mulley and I had. It was caused by the urgent need to prevent violent heads from crashing in the darkness of each other's lack of understanding.

Still, for whatever reason we had come to know each other, I knew that his people, strong and wise and masters of their land, would need an ally. It was clear that I was less threatening to them than the males of my kind, so I determined that I would fulfill their hope in me.

So I said quietly and with as much conviction as I could muster, "I shall speak up for you. I promise ..."

The following day, Mulley took me again to the camp. I learned to prepare blue plums, drying them in the sun. Menge instructed the younger women to show me how to collect certain seeds and grind them between stones. In the coming days, they took me along the path that led to the Mulgrave and showed me where the big trees fell after successive floods and were rotting in the undergrowth. I learned how to pull away the strips of wood, caked in moss, to reveal hollow tubes with two or more fat, white grubs as thick as your thumb, lying in their opened tunnels.

The girls did not hesitate to delight in eating them. They held the shiny black heads of the grubs in their fingers and ate them as though they were morsels of cake at afternoon tea. When they offered me one of the wriggling creatures, I declined politely, which made them laugh. I shuddered at the thought and squeaked in horror, as they pressed them up towards my lips, urging me to eat, and they found my reaction and refusal very strange and hugely funny.

On the last day, after we had collected various items for the evening meal, we returned and I looked about for Mulley. He had been hunting for the afternoon, leaving me with the women, with whom I now felt quite at ease. I saw him at the far side of the camp beside his sleeping hut and started to walk over toward him.

Before he saw me, a woman yelled across to him and he turned and walked in her direction.

"We got goanna for meat. It's been roasted in the coals with some nettle. You want some?" she called out.

"Yes, I'll have some, I'm hungry. Tomorrow I'll hunt and bring you something."

I watched her as she began poking the coals, and a plume of smoke and cinders twisted into the air as he strode over and squatted down to wait for her to serve him.

"They say you getting to know the way the strangers live," she said. I understood enough to realize she was probing him for something, so instead of coming closer I ducked behind his burra, sat down in its shadow, and pretended to plait some grasses together.

"Yes, that's true."

"They say, you stay and camp with her." The woman kept her face from showing any emotion.

"She teaches me her language so we understand each other."

"You learn fast. Djingalu hunt for me but he got no time after, 'cept to eat and do stupid stuff… you pretty good to get all that and hunt too."

"She's a good teacher." I smiled as he complimented me. I caught only broken parts of Yidinji speech, but I understood what she said and what she implied as any woman would.

The woman shook her head as she piled some white meat and wilted leaves onto a bark platter. I saw her flick a glance in my direction but she ignored me, no doubt thinking I could not understand her conversation. "You be careful. This woman might have magic you do not know and you will get trapped like that goanna you are eating."

"I shall be careful."

"Take a wife… then be careful."

He grinned and shook his head. They were all trying to marry him off and never let an opportunity slip by to remind him.

"So, you gonna stay with this woman again?"

"Sometime."

"Sometime, when?"

"Before the dry season starts."

"Tomorrow then."

"You are nosey… Do you want to come too?"

The woman erupted in dismay and horror with the thought of going anywhere near me in my camp.

She picked up a stick and threw it at him. He smiled, stood up, and thanked her for the meal, and then I saw him turn and walk back to his own shelter without acknowledging that I had been there for some time.

He squatted down in the grass in front of his burru and I stood up quietly behind it and walked around its girth.

"Mulley, I have been looking for you."

"Before or after you sitting behind my house listening?"

"Oh, yes, well I had to finish this little cord for my teacher, so I thought I would just wait for you."

"We should go or it will be dark to cross the stream."

"Yes, I suppose so."

I could hear the crackle of fires and the muffled voices of the thirty or more gathered together in the camp in the shadow of the mountains behind them.

He gathered up his spear and we walked out of the circle of dwellings to where my mare was tethered. He helped me mount her, and I pulled her head around in the direction of home.

He walked with me in silence for a long while, and then I spoke. "What were you talking about? I… heard my name mentioned."

"She warn me about you—didn't you hear?" He looked up after a moment or two, and then said a little shyly, "But I know your magic. You like a quartz stone, wet in the river. One on its own. You got eyes, green like the pool when sunlight gets under the weeping trees." He swooped his black hand down through the air, almost in time with the horse's stride, to demonstrate. Then he said, "But you got a strange heart, burning like a cooking fire that been forgotten and catches the dry grass around it. It run with the wind, spread a black trail through the undergrowth so new grass will grow next season for wallaby." He shook his head, "And when I walk through the long grass, I remember you. I feel you on my legs… when I go hunting."

I suddenly felt shy, and heat seemed to rise in my belly. For a moment, I lost the sense of where I was and only his voice touched me.

Now he admitted, as might any man with those ancient passions of old that draws him to the side of a woman and away from the manly joys of all other things. He told me how he could not keep his mind from me. He said when he went to sleep his dreaming eye touched every part of my dress, my hair, my slippery, foamed body he had seen behind the "hard water" of my window months before.

I could not reply. He had revealed the intimacy that I also felt, but frightened me more than any horror this land could throw at me. I sat atop my horse in a trance and his revelation seeped into me like the dusk light falling all around us.

When we arrived at the cabin, he left me for the burra he had built a little distance away in the shade of the trees on the plain.

I lay in my bed, thinking about what he had said, and I replayed his words over and over. All the while, a single question kept pounding in my ears. Where is Edward? Is he dead? Surely, he is dead.

As time went on, we dared not speak of such revelations but we carried on learning more fully of each other's way of life. This joint discovery and the familiarity I now had with the clan, created a new world for me, a world that included both his ways and mine. But when we were alone, the knowledge we shared formed some kind of hybrid that was entirely our own. A magical and private place no one shared but us.

He stopped calling me Margaru, which was his pronunciation of my English name. Now he called me Gubaguba—the Yidinji word for the rare natural pearl found in these tropical waters that is revered by the Yidinji. He knew it to be and the meaning of Margaret in my own language and he said my father had known that I would be desired and rare and had named me for it just as the Yidinji do for their own children.

Often, he led me through the forest on trails the Yidinji had walked for thousands of years, and he taught me all the names of the animals and plants, their meanings in the dreamtime and their uses in the present. I learned how to catch and cook all manner of fare, and how to make a burru if I was caught in a place when it rained. The forests were far from empty, as I had thought at the beginning. The jungle and the plains were alive with provision and I soon became confidant that I would never face starvation again, nor sickness either.

The days became dry as the Gurraminya Minya season took hold.

One morning he took me up the track that led to the high peak that overlooked the whole coast. He would not tell me what new thing I should learn but we followed the same path he and second boy had used when they went to collect eggs.

About halfway, we split off from that track and onto a path along the rock face and up the side of the mountain. Higher and higher we climbed until a flat shelf provided a resting point. Behind it, a huge section had slid from the rock, and a small, gently sloping floor of grass in a canyon of granite walls strewn with boulders on each side nestled in the heart of the mountain. It seemed to me to be a natural Cathedral and I marveled at its beauty.

Looking about, I said to Mulley, "This place is magnificent. Is it special?"
"Is sacred."

We walked into the breast of the mountain enclave and I could not help but think, 'Lord, this is where I would best wish to worship you …'

The journey had taken some hours and I amazed myself by how strong I had become for such exertion.

"We rest," Mulley said and smiled as I dropped to my knees and looked out at the beautiful coastline. He gathered a selection of supple bows, bent them over, and speared them in the ground at either end, tying them into a curved shelter. Then, layering wide leaves of palm fronds, he covered the frame, and then he filled the floor with wide leaves. Finally, he lowered himself beside me, and in front of the instant dwelling we sat in awe of the view. It seemed we were on the edge of the world as we looked on the turquoise Coral Sea and along the coast that I had once traveled past. That memory seemed so far away as to no longer be mine as I sat next to my native owner of this beautiful land and bathed in peaceful delight at where I now found myself.

As the afternoon closed and the sun fell behind us, he stood up and offered me his hand.

I took it and rose to my feet, wondering how I would summon the energy to go any further up the mountain.

He led me away from the main track and through the tussock grasses of a clearing to a wide outcrop of black granite and huge boulders clinging to the mountainside in shallow soil.

Suddenly he dropped to his haunches and swung his arm back to stop me dead in my tracks. He turned slowly and put his finger to his full lips. Then he moved quietly and carefully forward, and I followed a pace or two behind.

He came to the first of the boulders and leaned into it, looking over its top to the area beyond. A small forest fire in some season past had cleared the ground of thick undergrowth, leaving the burnt stumps of trees and some new-grown grass ferns that shivered in the breeze.

At the base of two fallen trunks, a dark earthen hole could be seen. He pulled me to the rock and rested his upper arm over the top, pointing to the grass in front of the logs.

Suddenly, I saw what he was pointing at. A small animal about the size of a house cat, with a light russet-colored coat, was meandering around in the grass and thrusting its snout into the crevices between the rocks. It had white spots evenly spaced over its fur and a long, furry tail.

Sharp black eyes were placed in the center of its flattened head, and it looked forward as it hunted. It spied a large grasshopper and in an instant pounced on it, devouring and chewing it with its spike-like teeth at the side of its mouth.

I thought it looked somewhat like a weasel or a stoat but much bigger and beautiful in its spotted coat.

When it had wandered around the side of the boulder, dragging its tail behind, and was finally gone from view, Mulley smiled and told me I was lucky to have seen the elusive quoll at last. It was a solitary animal and generally hunted at night and only one or two inhabited each peak.

When we returned to the resting place, evening had all but come.

I watched him as he started a small fire. He gathered dry leaves and then placed a special dry stick into a short piece of wood that looked like a small canoe. He dropped a few dry filaments of grass into it and then he quickly rolled the stick between his palms until it sparked and he blew on it, transferring it to the pile until a quick flame appeared.

I sat and tended the fire while he disappeared for a short while, returning with a bush turkey clasped in his hand by its throat.

Before long, it was plucked and roasting in the coals, and we ate under the growing array of stars in a crystal-clear night.

When drowsiness overcame me, I crawled inside the green shelter and lay on the cool, smooth bed he had made for me. He lay at my doorway with his back to me and I could hear his breathing, finding my own soon matched. The rustle of the forest and the cooler air of our altitude were wonderful, and my heart filled with happiness. The silent quoll hunted somewhere in the darkness, and my faithful aboriginal protector guarded my door. No life could have been better for me and as I slipped into a peaceful sleep, my heart gave way to the secret wonder I had found and I determined I should live no other way before God as long as I lived.

Well into the dry season, which is the time of gathering, I learned daily the way to live as Yidinji. Their link with the land and all the living things made them part of the creation and the spirit of their people dwelled peacefully among it. They were indeed, no less human for having rested their souls from the clamor of striving known by my people. But they had, in their way, understood better the way of our Lord, yet having never been taught a single matter about him.

It had been over nine months since we had first come to the land where Notre Maison farm was cut into the landscape and Edward had left.

Mulley was my constant companion. He led me through the forests, taught me to collect fruit and nuts, how to leach the poison from those that could not be eaten without being processed, and where to find and dig out the bush turkey eggs buried in huge mounds of rotting vegetation. I learned how to catch fish using traps that Mulley showed me how to make. We built shallow walls from stones and stacked them in scallop shapes across the shallow part of the river that fed Notre Maison farm. The fish would gather in the pools in front of the walls, and it was easy to catch them with our bare hands.

He taught me how to spear a wallaby by crouching silently in the grass, and how to make a raffia trap strategically placed in the boughs of a tree with fruit as bait to catch pigeons or fruit bats.

I learned how to catch and cook the small bandicoot marsupials, which were only a little bigger than a rat and liked to dig small holes in the grass looking for worms and grubs.

Some foods I learned to preserve, and I knew how to find honey and where to find barramundi fish and mangrove jacks in the slow bends of the river.

The maize flowered, the tomatoes fruited, and my life was good.

We laughed together and talked of many things, and we never noticed time slipping by. His face and touch became familiar to me, and his nakedness ordinary and I rarely wore more than my camisole or underskirt and gave up my pretentious ways. The simplicity of the Yidinji's ways led me to desire such a state for myself, and I began to understand the true spirituality of life they had discovered. It seemed to illuminate those lessons from my own world and the discovery delighted me. The Lord himself seemed all about me, and a joy filled my heart as I understood his gifts.

My skin had become plump and healthy, my face and limbs tanned, and my golden hands, once so wretched, now could weave.

Once only did I think I heard the sound of a gun and the crack of a whip echoing off the mountains, but I never saw anything of the new settlers, who must have continued to fan out from the town far in the distance. If they occupied the territory up beyond the mountains on the Atherton tablelands or south toward Herberton or north to the goldfields, I didn't know it and Edward had become a distant memory I had all but convinced myself, was long dead.

Mulley was never far from me, and if I called, he mysteriously arrived. If he hunted, he always brought fresh meat for me to share first. His visits to his people's camp were infrequent, as they had moved to the higher land closer to the sea for the change in season.

We went together to the new camp a few times during those months, but as we became inseparable friends our own company pleased us best.

The weeks went by without being remarkable, and I began to feel like I belonged to his world, and the way of the Yidinji.

Then, on a clear day in March, Mulley arrived as usual.

It was afternoon and I had been harvesting the second tall maize crop, which now stood tall above the fence I had made months before.

I was hot and my bonnet shielded my face only enough to stop it burning. The sun's heat blazed on the top of my head, and I was perspiring heavily. The fabric of my clothing, was damp, and I was thirsty from all my work.

He appeared behind me without a sound. I was used to this now and smiled happily at his return to me.

I wiped my brow and he shook his head, marveling at the constant work I did, even in the hottest part of the day, when women of the clan would have long since retreated to the trees to sit and laugh and gossip among themselves and to rest the heat of the day away.

He grabbed my hand and pulled me from the row I was in. I did not mind.

We walked through the grass to the big waterhole that had carved itself into the thick fringe of forest trees. A cool oasis lay before us.

The shores of the stream sparkled with the full heat of the day and a host of yellow butterflies, fifty or more, drank at the sandy edge with their wings tightly clasped together and upright for a moment, as though praying. Milky-colored under wings yawned in perfect unison with each sup they made. As we came down through the trees to the water's edge, the creatures scattered into the air, and their canary yellow fluttering was carried on the current of the breeze up into the leafy canopy.

Mullegadajawara reached back to hold my hand as I descended the small slope to the river. He didn't let go I found my footing but instead we stood hand in hand looking out over the jade pool bathed in the dappled light of the forest.

There was something uniquely uniform and perfect in the myriad of leaves that jostled for space in the chaos of the disorderly collection, and I let out a sigh of awe at the beauty before me.

"It's perfect, ..." I whispered.

The water was trickling through its course and the deep pool fanned out to the other side where ferns draped like fine shawls into the water, lazily stroking the flow with their fronds.

Mulley turned and smiled at me as though we hardly needed words to understand the thoughts even a glance could express.

I smiled back. The comfort of his hand holding mine made me feel safe. I could smell his now familiar scent. His was the scent of the forest, the earth, and all the light that was in this land, but mixed with the smell of a man and I delighted in it.

He walked me to the pool and nodded to it. "We swimming?" He asked me and I looked at him quizzically.

"No! No, I cannot! There will be eels in there. I caught one just the other day."

He laughed a laugh that was perfectly honest and came from the innocence and the humor that had made its home in his people.

"Night... They out, come in night for hunt, not now, Gubaguba."

I corrected the way he had said the sentence and he repeated it back to me. He could see on my face I was pleased with him, and he pressed me, "Come... swim!"

He pulled at me but I continued to resist, leaning back from his hand as I tried to escape. He was much stronger than I was, and it was not long before I was standing in the shallows, my skirts floating up and away with the water and our laughter joining the sound of the rapids as they danced through the gully.

"Take off covers, Guli." I knew this name meant "mother of pearl shell," a more reverent name than Gubaguba, and I saw a strange look pass over his face.

He reached out and clutched a handful of my petticoat.

I was hot but some misgiving remained though I knew not why. I had long since learned to ignore the nakedness of his body and mostly dressed only in my underthings even in public among his people.

For a moment, my mind seemed to calculate what it might be like to be completely free and naked in the stream with him. I knew the Yidinji had neither shame nor judgment; it was only some small memory of the conventions of my own people that kept me from such freedom and some inner knowledge of he as a man beside me.

Mulley watched me, knowing I was at a turning point.

Without warning, I spun around away from him, went up to the bank, and sat down on the sand.

He stood looking at me with some question in his expression. I sat with my knees pulled up, my wet skirts clinging to my legs, and my flushed face resting on my crossed arms.

Without speaking, he simply turned and dived into the pool. The water spangled as it twisted and fell from the air to reassemble with the main body, flowing clear and gently through the scene as he disappeared into its depths.

When he arose from the water and shook his head, his matted black locks spread an array of droplets all around him. He wiped his face with his two large hands and puffed a great sigh of air from his lungs at the pleasure the water had brought him.

I sat on the bank and watched him. The heat was stifling and the sight of him soothing his body in the cool water made me envious.

"Oh what nonsense!" I muttered to myself, and with that, I removed my boots and stockings and cast them aside. I stood up, dropped my skirt, and stepped out in just my thin cotton undergarments, quickly staggering over the stones. My bare feet, pink and tender, carried me into the water as I waded toward him.

He moved forward to greet me. Holding up his hand, he led me deeper and I dropped smoothly into the water that enveloped me like a cloak of clear velvet. My senses instantly renewed under its cool and silky skin and my hair drifted around my shoulders.

We didn't talk but lazily held onto each other's hands and swung around in the pool. Without a word, he pulled me closer toward him and I could feel the warm breath from his lips on my face. The birds sang intermittently in the trees and the leaves whispered as they jostled in the breeze above us.

I lifted a hand and stroked his shoulder as though I was discovering the reality of his person for the first time. The scars of his initiation flowed under my fingers, and I explored each one as he quietly studied my face and allowed me to touch them. I smiled and searched his face.

His dark eyes looked into me tenderly, and he began to gently pull me to the shore as though he knew an appointed time had come.

We rose up from the pool and he walked me across the stones to the beach of river sand stacked up under the roots of a giant tree, where the butterflies had been. He sat me down and lowered himself to sit beside me.

With his forearms hanging over his knees, and his hands locked together, he began to speak in a quiet but firm voice.

"Mullegadajawara choose Guli." He said the words almost apologetically.

I leaned back and lay down on the sand with my eyes closed, digesting the words, untangling them from my quickly beating heart.

Suddenly, everything seemed strangely clear to me. I lifted my hands into the streaming sunlight and twisted my wedding ring from its finger. A white line showed where the thin gold band had been and spears of light pierced between each finger as I studied the empty hand.

As the ring slid off and I clasped it in my fist, I felt sure I was no longer married. The act of removing it signaled my acceptance of the black man's words as he sat beside me in the pristine beauty of the stream. I dropped the gold band in the sand and marveled at how easily I could return it to the earth while Edward had so earnestly desired to find such metal in some river far away from here. He had craved it and had abandoned me for it, perhaps at the cost of his life.

Forgetting this entirely, I slid my hand up Mulley's back.

"I know …" I replied, "I choose you also …"

I waited for him to look down at me. As he understood my words, he turned to face me lying beside him. A happy and subtle smile spread over his face as his eyes took in my small body.

My nipples were cooled and prominent under the sheath of fine cotton, and I could feel them tingling. I knew he could see the curves of my stomach, dimpled where my navel lay, and my flesh was shivering with excitement.

I had one knee propped up and I watched him as his eyes flowed down over me to the darker triangle of pubic hair beneath the thin film of cotton.

"Never... not never, Mullegadajawara leave you, alive or dreaming... Never."

I lifted my hand and stroked his arm and it left a wet mark on his drying skin.

As he stared back to the water for a moment and it reflected off his face he said, "Mullegadajawara feel... deep water inside, an' happy, tears ..." His voice broke a little as he tried to find words. "Inside Mullegadajawara feel for no other like this. I break, like waterfall and thunder, inside... you understand?"

I sat up at that moment, and he turned to me, his growing maleness suddenly visible on his thigh, and I did not shy away or feel self-conscious.

"I understand ..."

"I choose Mar-ga-ret."

I swallowed in surprise. His use of my proper name and his touch made me shiver, and I could feel the heat of desire rush into my stomach.

Gently, he began to peel the gauze of my underclothes from me as though it were the skin of a pallid snake, its illness stripped away to uncover fresh new skin.

He stared into my eyes, holding me in the trance of the moment, and then I lay back in the sun, free at last. Its warm fingers caressed my stomach and my breasts began to blush with its heat. He was breathing quickly, and my chest rose and fell in time with his and the rising excitement of us both.

His hands began to stroke me until every inch of me came alive, mesmerized by his gentle black fingers touching my shivering white skin. I could do nothing to break the spell that he wove over my body, and I did not want to.

Finally, his shadow fell over me as his torso lifted up and onto me, blocking out the sun. I felt his weight press down on my thighs, his full body weighing on mine, his heat blanketing me as I looped my arms around his neck and drew my lips up to kiss him.

Without a moment to consider what I was doing, I let his weight part my legs, and within moments, he thrust himself into me powerfully. I felt entirely as a woman should, as though this was all I was made for and nothing in the world could be more natural.

His strong forearms held himself up over my breasts and I lifted my hands to hold onto his shoulders that were hard with muscles naturally and perfectly used.

His head sank down between them and his lips found mine. They were soft and full and I felt as though we melted into each other, locked in that ancient dance.

Forgetting all, I let the moment have me and writhing in pleasure, he rhythmically drove me into the sand. Passionately, we rose together furiously, and the air of the clearing was filled with our moans.

With one final thrust, he welded himself to me and disgorged the mature seed of his life inside me... and I knew I should love no one else in my life.

The events of the afternoon changed us both and we knew we must make certain the magic that had now made us one.

Before the shadows of the mountains could change our minds, we fed and watered the animals, Mulley saddled the mare, and we threaded our way back through the bush toward the winter camp of his clan.

When we arrived, the evening fires were already glowing and we could hear people talking from some distance away.

When he entered the clearing before me, the women looked up.

Instead of giving their usual greeting, they glanced at him sheepishly and then looked away. Almost as quickly as they recognized him they ignored his entry to the group, and myself along with him. The cold glances spoke a message of its own long before he reached the men.

"Mullegadajawara, you return to us!" one of them called. He pulled me to a spot some distance away and made me sit. I waited there, wondering if I should join the women.

A young man sat cross-legged, chewing on a bone left from the evening meal.

"Mullegadajawara, we thought you had been killed and eaten!"

A second man, Djanaba, sat down and pulled Mullegadajawara down beside him to sit in the circle.

"So, how is your trial with that woman going? The trees have told us that you are enjoying your lessons!"

I suddenly felt sick to my stomach.

Djanaba had kept his head down as he said it, pretending to be focused on the comfort of his hips in the grass.

"I suppose teaching a female, even an ugly one, is better than hunting or climbing trees," one of the other men in the group offered.

Mullegadajawara looked down into the embers of the fire as he listened but I knew his mind was on the waterhole and the bliss we had experienced there, and he was not concentrating on their comments.

He remained silent and all began to wonder why.

Finally, Mully's old grandfather mumbled while he picked something from his toe, "The wind says you have more on your mind, Mullegadajawara." He shifted his hand and rubbed his knee lazily while he stared at his grandson. His black, rope-like locks, straggled down the sides of his face and his shining skin glistened in the glow from the fire. He looked regal and was an accomplished man among them.

I could see from his expression that he struggled on the edge of what he wanted to say but could find no words, even though he ached to speak openly.

The old one waited silently and then with care, he raised himself from the grass and brushed himself off. "I go for a walk down to the stream."

Mullegadajawara took the hint and he immediately raised himself from his place and left the group. He did not look back at me but followed his grandfather.

I stood up quickly and all the men turned and looked at me without saying anything. I felt like a criminal or some woman of ill repute as I turned and fled through the trees, skirting the light of the campsite. I followed the sound of the old man's humming and Mulley's near-silent footsteps following a good way behind along the trail to the stream.

Though it was dark among the overhanging trees, I knew they were aware I was there. The women of the clan were often not permitted to discuss things openly, but they were permitted to observe and to listen from a distance to matters that concerned them. No matter on earth could concern me more than this, so whether permitted or nay, I pushed myself through the undergrowth to keep up with them.

The old man walked to an open space by the place where they fetched water.

When Mulley came through the trees, he saw his grandfather already seated and staring into the forest, his arms clamped around his knees.

Mullegadajawara sat down beside him. Being his paternal grandfather, he was as close to him as any person in the camp. He had been taught the ways of the forest from this man and had learned the protocol of the clan and the Yidinji tribe. His grandfather had been the first to take him on walkabout, because his father had died. Striding out from the people as a young boy, he had returned from the wilderness months later, a man.

For all this, I could see Mulley was seated in a way that offered honor and was in the style of a formal meeting, and he began to speak shyly as though he was not related at all.

"Wise one... I am ..." He could not begin. "This woman has ..."

"Bewitched you?"

"No. No, I cannot say that!" I heard the tone of his voice and it showed he felt caught out. "She has my flesh in her soul, and I have hers." He looked back in the darkness and I could feel his eyes on me and I smiled. "No, this is a dreamtime thing, wise one."

"This is a hard thing. A woman is one who should be loved and desired... but should not live inside a man or the man shall give birth to strange ideas."

"She is as the moon is to the sun, Grandfather. She is... my spear and my shield."

The old one waited as he thought about this.

"So you wish her to be your woman, your wife?"

"I do."

"This is not what our women will want. They will fight you on this."

"I suppose so."

"I know they will. Not one of them hasn't already lived your life for you and decided which way your river will bend."

"Perhaps, but I have become a man who knows his own river and I do not bend to anything but the time that eats me."

"This will bring no good, Mullegadajawara. She is the property of another tribe and they will not give her up. They will send warriors and take her back."

"Her tribe has forgotten her."

"What tribe forgets its own?" He turned and his voice carried disbelief in its tone as Mulley replied.

"Her tribe does."

The old man digested what had been said, and then he spoke very carefully. I listened as though every word was to me alone.

"It has not forgotten. It has only put her away in a dilly bag to soak in the river till her poison is leached out... and if you drag it up and take it for yourself, they will suddenly say you have stolen her, and they will make war on you and on all of us."

"Then I shall stay near her, camping near her shelter that cannot be moved, and I shall be her hunter and the man who keeps the shadows off her."

"So you will leave us?"

I could hear the frown in the old man's voice even though the darkness hid it from my eyes. It was not their way to ever leave one another. He spoke as though a spear had pierced his liver and the pain of it was coming on like a flood.

"This, too, will bring harm. Shall you be her husband and yet not live in her world? No... No man can own and yet not possess. Your hunger will make you like the dingo, and before long you will try to live as she does. This will kill you long before her people do... and leave you for your own people to bury."

"Grandfather... what way is there? I cannot be parted from her, she must be made safe among us then."

"This cannot be... and nor can the other." He looked up at the moon and sighed deeply.

"Are you joined?" Again, my stomach went cold, and I felt suddenly ashamed.

Though the warrior Mullegadajawara spoke, it was the voice of a small boy who replied to his grandfather. "We are one, grandfather."

"Ah, this is a great trouble for me, Son... Go. I shall commune with the ancestors, and I shall ask the black and the white cockatoo what shall become of us."

Mullegadajawara lifted himself from the ground and, without a word or a sound, left the old man alone in the silence.

For a moment, he disappeared, and I felt lost in the dark and as silent as the beautiful quoll alone on the high peaks. Then he came up alongside me and I felt his hand grasp my elbow and his lips bury themselves in the nape of my neck.

I whispered, "Mulley, take me home ..." For there was nothing else to say.

Chapter 13

MY FRONT PORCH was bathed in early morning light and I leaned against the pole at the end looking toward the big fig tree.

Lately, I had let my hair hang loose each day instead of tying it on top of my head, and this morning I had brushed it out so that it fell in golden tinted sheets of silk in the morning sun.

As I stared up the incline toward the big fichus tree, I saw three kookaburras squabbling over a small fish that one had in its beak. The other two stalked the lucky bird and harassed it, growling away in loud kookaburra language and hopping from branch to branch, heavily puffing their feathers out to intimidate their successful companion into letting go. He did not, but caught the fish up in his beak and swallowed it whole, to the consternation of the others.

I'd returned from the camp in the darkness with Mulley the night before. I knew he was worried, as silence followed him just as I had. As though given some unearthly prediction that we would be pulled apart, he was troubled for the first time since I had known him. I denied such hovering thoughts and clung to the notion that nothing in the world could spoil what we had found in each other. I consoled him and said it didn't matter that the clan wouldn't recognize us; we could quite easily go on forever as we had quite apart from both his people and mine.

Mulley had looked at me somewhat blankly as though there wasn't anything he could or wanted to say to this, and instead turned back toward the camp in the dark hours. He kissed me sweetly and stroked my cheek and then set off to wait for his grandfather's wisdom to come from some ancient being embodied in the flight of the black cockatoo or the screech of his white cousin that only the old man could decipher.

In the light of the crisp new morning, I put their deliberations out of my mind. I'd woken calm and happy, as though I'd found a jewel and had buried it in a field where only I knew where it was. I'd found love in a man, and his touch was still alive on my body from the delight of the previous day.

The breeze lifted for a moment, and a strand of my hair wafted up and licked my cheek. I smiled to myself as I waited for Mulley to come back to me and thought about him, warm against me.

"Margaret!"

When I heard the voice, ice flowed into my heart and threatened to stop it beating.

I swung round and below me the figure of a tall man dressed in a dirty shirt and trousers stood beside a huge gelding.

"Madam, you are a feast for my eyes!"

Instantly, my mouth went dry and my eyes focused and refocused on the face of the man as though unbelief worked hard to expunge him from reality.

"Well? I've returned… where is your greeting, my dear?"

"Edward!… I'm shocked—it's been forever."

Struggling to clear my throat, I instinctively looked beyond him to the trees to see that Mullegadajawara wasn't there.

"Edward, please… please come in and I shall fetch you tea." I moved to the edge of the step and held onto the rail with white knuckles.

Edward tethered the horse and patted its neck as he stepped past it toward me.

"The maize looks good." He turned his head toward the field swaying in the breeze, its flower tops browned off and ready for harvest.

"Place looks in good order …" He looked down on my face as he rose to the final step, "You look wonderful …" He cupped my cheeks and I felt as though a stranger had moved far too close and I fought the slight recoil my body made as his rough hands pulled at me.

"Beautiful Margaret… how I've thought about you almost every day. I've ached for the day I would be here again." He leaned down and kissed me.

His lips were hard and I could sense his shaking body was held back like a steed with mares on his mind.

Struggling to still the cold in my stomach, fear began to rise in my heart.

"I thought you were dead! It's been almost a year and not a word."

"Yes, my dear, I know… the rains locked us up there for at least four months, and… well… Look Margaret, let me show you!"

He had already swung the wooden chair made from tree boughs out from the table. It screeched and he thudded it down roughly before seating.

"Look what I've got for us …" He pulled out two tin boxes. With blackened nails, he pried open their lids, and the sun caught the contents and they glowed with the fire that had lit the heart of the man who found it.

"My God, Edward!"

"We have enough here to replenish supplies and build a fine house for you and get our first cuttings of cane …"

He looked at me, and his face transformed into the expression of a child who had done well or had won the best marble at school and proudly displayed himself to a parent for approval.

"I… I… I'm not sure what I can say, sir." My face lost its luster and I swallowed hard. "I hardly know what to think, Edward."

"What to think? Hell, madam, I have returned the victor with the spoils! We are on our way at last to fortune, and I'm here at last… with you." He paused, perhaps a small measure of guilt creeping into his thoughts. "… You know I agonized the whole time. I wasn't sure how you would fare. I worried… that I'd come back to a ruin, but you have turned out to be a pioneering woman indeed!"

"Not so, I had a great deal of help."

"Oh yes, the Kanaka and the Chinaman."

"No sir. The Kanaka stole all the money you left me and absconded the day after you went. And Jackie …" I looked across to the grass and my eyes welled up with tears, "… he was accidentally killed about three weeks later."

"My God! How did you… manage, my love?"

"I could do little more than my best and all but starved …" I looked toward his face and smiled shakily. "But as luck would have it, I killed a big snake and dried the meat!"

"I can hardly believe it!"

"But Edward, my best help has come from the natives here." I smiled and my eyes widened as though waiting for him to relieve the pressure I felt by being pleased that the Malanbarra Bama had been so accommodating toward me while he had been away.

"Natives? My God, Margaret… they are reported as killing settlers everywhere!"

I thought about his reply.

"Edward, these natives have neither harmed me nor stolen from me. They have given …" I paused as the image of Mullegadajawara came into my mind, and I was momentarily shaken by his presence. "… They have given me much knowledge of the bush life and have protected me."

"Well, that may be so, but they are savages. They cannot be trusted, just as you might not trust a pet shark or the snake you killed. Margaret, I forbid you to encourage them. They must be driven back into the bush and made to vacate our farms and our towns. I tell you, they cannot be taught civilization, and they are mindless idiots. I've seen it myself. The only good black is a dead one… or one far enough away that he can't be tempted to become the leeches that they are."

"Edward! I'll thank you not to speak in such a way!" I swung round on him and the fear I felt turned to anger. "The aboriginals are as well-equipped in mind and conscience as any one of us!"

"Margaret, I'm home now and you have no need for heathens anymore. Come, my dear, let us not break out into discord at my first return. Why

don't you see to that tea, and then perhaps we shall rest for the afternoon …"
He smiled gently, perhaps realizing I was still a little shocked at his
unannounced return.

I forced a smile and turned to go inside the cabin.

"Tell me, have you seen any of the settlers of the surrounding area?" he
continued nonchalantly, and began to undo his boots.

"No, I haven't… I'd quite decided that the rest of the world had packed
up and gone back to wherever they had come from."

"The port is awash with new arrivals and land is being settled everywhere.
In Smithfield, a substantial town has grown, though they fared somewhat
badly in this wet season too. They were twice flooded, I'm told. I happened
upon a cedar logger coming down the gorge and he told me most had begun
to relocate to the port township because of it." He was speaking loudly to
me through the door opening. "I'm astounded that no one has come upon
you here."

I appeared from inside with a tray carrying a teapot and cups and
placed them on the table, then poured a cup for Edward and one for myself.

"I suppose I look a mess." I touched my hair, feeling somewhat self-
conscious in his presence and reminded of my former ways.

"You look very fine my dear. I imagine it is I that look unmentionable in
polite company." He stared at me, overly fascinated by my face, my slender
neck, my shoulders.

"You are quite the most well-looking I've ever seen a woman… For all
your time separated from me, I should say you are suited to the settler's life
after all, and are well ready to start a family …"

I could feel his eyes on me, and I suddenly felt ill at ease.

"Edward …" I changed the direction of the conversation, acutely aware
that Mullegadajawara might appear from the brush. "… I've very little to
offer you in the way of food. You see, I lost the flour in the rains, and I've
only a little of a smoked lizard, which is quite good in the absence of bacon,
mind you." I paused, sipping my tea. "I could put together some eggs perhaps…
But it occurs to me, I should go to this place along the stream where there
is fruit perfectly ripe at the present, and then I shall make you a good tart

with the little jar of flour I've kept sealed all this time for just such a day as this." I smiled beguilingly.

"All right, we shall take a ride to this place together and fetch your fruit if that's what you want to do. Tomorrow, we should ride to the town and fetch more supplies and some labor. Your days of deprivation are over. What do you say to that, my dear?"

"Edward, you have all but killed yourself to get here, I suggest you have a little something to eat and then a rest. That is more important. You must regain your vigor. I shall go and get the fruit and be back in time to have a nice meal for this evening. If you have a mind to, you can go off and get supplies, it will certainly suit me if you do that."

"Well, my dear... I shall do as you bid. But mind, I plan to keep you by my side every minute... and you will pick out a good new dress from town too." I shifted my gaze and he caught me searching the bush line.

He looked at me with a slight frown as though he could see something hidden under the innocuous speech I had made and my glance had given me away.

Suddenly, he stared into my eyes and placed his hand over mine without letting it go. "But madam, all plans are of no account until I've had you in my arms ..."

I grimaced with the thought that his remark evoked but knew I couldn't refuse him.

"As you wish," were the only words I could muster, and he dropped his head sadly as he realized my enthusiasm of the past was absent from my tone.

He looked up at me, and his expression changed as his ardor was ignited by my nearness and the desire for my body overcame his sensibility. I could see he would have his rights with me, no matter how my heart refused him, and I felt suddenly small and alone with this stranger.

"I wish indeed, madam... and I hope that this will be your wish again in time."

I saw him look away, a frown forming on his forehead with obvious disappointment, and I paused as though considering his proposal, yet knowing he had every right to expect my body and my kindness to be returned to him according to my vows.

"Edward... I'm sorry. I'm a little lost in the events." I turned to hide my face. "But in time sir, I shall be as I was, I suppose." I knew even before I had released my words to the air, that I had lied.

He stood up with a rush and I saw him move toward me with a certain determination. My hands suddenly let go of the enamel mug and it fell with a clatter to the deck.

"Edward, please... such haste!"

"Madam, you forget yourself... I've seventy ounces of gold that is the measure of my time away from you and I mean to get its worth in your embrace this very minute!"

"Please... I'm not ready for you, sir ..."

"The hell you are, woman!"

His hands were rough over me as he pushed me through the door and flung me upon the bed. It creaked with indignation and I clasped my breast as he undid his trouser buttons with shaking hands. Without a moment of gentleness, he lifted my thighs, forcing my skirt up out of the way and I felt his palms scrape over my skin. He tore at my bodice and my chest blotched with red welts as his fingers robbed me of my decency. In frenzy, his tongue rasped over me, and his bristling jaw feverishly scraped over my cheek and neck like a steel file until he found my breasts and devoured them in a manic fit of hunger.

I began to stiffen and step away in my mind from this shocking intrusion that had come upon me after my former peacefulness.

This man's breath wasn't the scent of fresh water, clean food, the almond nuts of the forest, but the smell of fat and liquor and the wild dog.

The bed groaned as he did also. I lay in silence as his heavy weight rose over me rhythmically and the pallid skin of his gaunt shoulders passed before my eyes. He drove into me and a muted squeal escaped my lips, which excited him even more.

Not a flicker of even the smallest flame of desire rose in me. I winced as he hurriedly thrust himself upon me, grunting loudly until he reached his end, and I lay still as death beneath him when he had finished.

Silently, I wandered through my memory as he lay on me, panting heavily. I distanced myself from this rough man that I no longer knew.

Sparkling water and Mullegadajawara's white smile spirited me away from the hot interior of the cabin and this stranger who rolled from me and now lay beside me.

I wrestled with the desire to run screaming from him. Just as the strangler fig coiled itself up a healthy tree and choked the life sap from it, so did this day to the peace of my life I had had before the dawn. It had delivered the end of my happiness in the form of this man.

Mulley... I called in my hidden silence and waited desperately like a spring pressed down into its box until I could be free from this confusion and be alone with him again.

I closed my eyes tightly and a tear squeezed from between the lids, rolling inexorably down my stinging cheek to blot away in the linen of the pillowslip.

With blinding clarity, I knew that the months of purest joy had turned in an instant to a mere dream. It had no substance at all in the light of my husband's return.

I waited patiently in the warm cabin. Finally, Edward's breathing slowed, and I realized he was more exhausted than he had admitted and had fallen into deep sleep.

I lay very still, waiting to be certain.

Desperation finally overwhelmed me and I slid from the bed and dressed quickly, barely buttoning my blouse or tidying my hair. I had to find Mullegadajawara and warn him that the spirit of chance had already decided... I was no longer free.

In a daze, I rode the mare to the head of the river, to the flat plain that rested at the base of the mountain. I followed the path that led to the new camp.

I dismounted and ran toward him and then I stopped dead.

Mullegadajawara could see I was distressed, but when he came near, he stood a little from me. I felt sure he could smell Edward on my skin, and if not that, he could see the shadow of him in my eyes.

"Mulley…" I whispered shakily. "Edward has come back and he has… demanded me as his wife again."

"Man cannot give away wife and have back when he chooses."

"Our custom is that… marriage is for life unless unfaithful with another man or woman."

"So you are unfaithful? Say that you are free."

"If I am unfaithful and he knows… he will kill me… and you and your people."

He took a deep breath and frowned. He turned his back then completed the circle to face me again.

"You are free… but now I am not."

I looked into his face to see if I could fathom what he meant.

"I don't understand."

"I am not free of my people. I cannot live without you, but I cannot kill that man that does not own you anymore …yet you say he does? I can't condemn my people because of this man or because of you." He shook his locks and the shells round his neck chinked with the movement. "I am not free, Gubaguba. You have made me a prisoner …"

"We cannot see each other again… or he will know, …" I said.

Mullegadajawara took my declaration silently. His face fell into the despair that comes when devastation has eaten its fill and only scraps of a man's heart are left still raggedly beating. He simply turned and began to walk away, announcing by his action that he understood. Just as he reached the edge of the trees that opened to the camp, he stopped and stood still with his shiny back facing me. Then he turned and I thought, 'He has an idea… surely we will be saved.' He returned to where I stood and stopped a pace or so away.

I stood with my hands clasped together, desperately hoping for an answer. He reached around his neck and untangled the strings of shells that hung from his neck. He took one strand that had a small woven raffia bag hanging from it. He pried it open and dropped something out, concealing its contents in his palm. Suddenly, he stretched out his arm and pulled my hand from my skirts. He held it for a long time it seemed, and I began to weep. Holding me by the gaze of his brown eyes, he opened my hand, dropped a peach-colored pearl into my palm, and let me go. I looked down at it. It was the color of the summer dawn and except for a small crease, perfect.

"Mulley… I cannot …" But when I looked up he had already turned, and without looking back he walked away. And I did not follow him.

As I rode back, I sobbed until my rib cage felt bruised and my eyes could not focus even upon the head of my mare.

When the tears ceased numbness settled into me, and I plodded along the grassy meadow back toward the cabin as though I had merely been out for a stroll and the life I had led was a novel I had finished reading and set aside.

Edward knew something had changed in me. He was attentive but his manner was aloof. Just as it is the prerogative of a woman to ignore her husband's infidelity, it was the duty of a man to know his territory no longer had one master, and he seemed to stew with some unspoken doubt over me.

Edward went to town on his own the following day to sell his gold and get supplies. I feigned sickness and claimed I had need to do some chores in the garden, as I wanted to avoid being with him. He reluctantly allowed me, thinking no doubt it would take some time for me to forgive his long stay away.

When he returned a few days later, he brought back three laborers. They began at once to till the fields that had lain fallow and then planted short cane sections that would grow into tall stalks of green sugar cane.

Almost a month went by. There was not one day that I did not think of my life alone with Mulley. But I slowly resigned myself to my duty and hoped I could, at the least, have some influence in protecting the Malanbarra Bama.

When next we needed supplies, I agreed to go with Edward. My curiosity was somewhat whetted to see what had become of the outpost port now called Cairns Township.

We rode in on the dray on the new track our labor had built; across the river and over the land we had first traversed. Even so, it took the best part of the day to reach the new thoroughfare the settlers had cleared all the way to the place called White Rock. As we arrived I was shocked at the development that had occurred in my absence. Though I should have enjoyed the adventure and the chance to buy all manner of necessary things that are the trappings of civilization, the affair was empty for me. I merely watched on like a player who stood in the wings, claiming participation without applause, a mere patron who had not paid for his ticket.

Wide roadways now swarmed with carts, horses, and a population of women in white with their parasols twirling in the heat of the day. They punctuated the new town with civility and propriety and I could not have felt more separate from them.

Edward's gold had bought fresh Queensland legal tender and he had a healthy sum in an account opened under his name at the Bank of Queensland on the corner of Abbott and Aplin streets.

At a little after midday the following day, he excused himself to go off and find more labor and cane cuttings for planting the west field, and I was released to attend to the necessities I had all but forgotten and to find a suitable new dress.

At the end of town, the two-story School of Cairns had been established, and one street before it, a new millinery store had been opened, so I began to walk up the covered path toward it.

I could see the general store remained just as it was when we had first arrived, and curiosity led me to pause and turn into the shaded interior.

The storeowner, Mr. McKenzie, was serving someone, but I could hear his Scottish accent as he loaded up the man's arms with a brown paper parcel full of items. When he had finished and the man departed, I walked through the merchandise stacked in rows and came to the counter.

"Good day to you," he smiled broadly, and I nodded back politely.

"What is it I can help you with, ma'am?"

"I've a list... my husband shall collect these things presently."

"Aye... Quite a list it is, Mrs.... Bermingham!"

"Yes, I suppose it is, though I wonder if I shall ever find a need for some of these things, as now I've so long been without, that I've completely forgotten the use of them."

"Oh? Where have you been Lass?" He looked up quizzically.

"My husband has been up at Thorn Borough and had a good deal of luck, but it was a necessity that I be at our selection down by the pyramid, and I found myself alone thanks to the disagreeable conduct of my help."

"My, my. I had heard of such a woman, and this is you? How long were you out there, Lass?

"Well… There wasn't the bank here when I first arrived."

He looked up with a certain poverty in his face as though neither concern nor amazement were allowed to give me any clue as to his thoughts.

He turned and collected an item from the shelf behind him. "Indeed… then it is the providence of God that you have managed so well." He smiled sparingly. "I've rarely seen a young woman so glowing and in such good health."

I smiled a little shyly.

"'Tis a wonder indeed that the natives did not concern thee." He gathered up his receipt journal and began to write as a small packet of linseed was added to the bench top. "Hereabouts, they have raided almost every farmer, and even just this month killed a gentleman in Port Douglas. Speared him they did, and he was left in the roadway where he fell."

I suddenly felt a rise of indignation that I couldn't prevent my lips from voicing. "Unfortunate indeed, but I would wager that no settler has given even the courtesy of the day to one of them, nor considered what they shall eat if their lands are taken from them. I should say that I've no doubt that the Malanbarra clan that are upon the area we live, are free from such trouble, as we have gladly left them to their normal way and are happy to keep our land separate from their hunting grounds and camp sites."

I saw his look of surprise, and I couldn't help but see his expression as an affront whether it was or not.

"And sir," I went on, "I also say, since I have knowledge of the aboriginals, they are certainly more kind, well-mannered, and civilized than most of my own countrymen!'

He paused and then a creeping smile touched his lips. "Well Lass, I'm glad you have such a good report to offer. Between us, I suspect you are indeed right. Aye, it is a sore point to many, but in me heart; I think they are more than likely an honorable lot, if managed fairly. I wish I had occasion to know them better, as I'm certain they are greatly misunderstood." He nodded in agreement with himself, and the turn of his moustache and the creases around his eyes gave me the feeling that he was as genuine as any I had met.

"Sir, I'm sorry if I burst forth somewhat harshly for a lady ..."

"No apology is required nor sought." He leaned forward and patted my hand affectionately. "Consider me a friend to you on the subject."

"Well... Thank you, sir. I've naught to say but thank you. 'Tis really because none know of them that they are so ignorant and treat them so badly, I suspect."

"Perhaps not, Lass. There has been ample opportunity for peaceful conduct. But as it is, many are too hungry for their future comforts that they should warrant such a group with any kind of consideration, and none have any intention of altering their plans to accommodate a native."

"I see it is a poor situation, then."

"Ah yes, but it bodes ill for such men as these also, mind. As our good Lord has said, Lass, 'What does it profit a man if he should gain the whole world and lose his soul?' And such are some, that by their actions, are set to do so!"

"Indeed." I looked at the goods gathering on the bench top and his words reminded me that I had been a good while without the need of many of the frivolous items that I had chosen.

"I think not to take so much on that list as I had first thought. Would it trouble you if I should set aside the rose water and these ..."

"No trouble at all. Whatever your need is, I'm happy to oblige."

I had, at that moment, felt the first sense of trust and pleasure in the presence of a man of my own race, and I smiled sweetly as we concluded our business. I waved happily as I left and made a certain commitment in my heart to see him again.

That night we stayed at the Imperial Hotel, and Edward excused himself from me and went to frequent the drinking men who quenched their thirst at the bar below. He closed the door, and I felt the hush of the room tell me I was alone both in my material world and in my heart.

Staring quietly from the window, I watched the sunset close the day and the street lamps begin to light, one by one, against the backdrop of the mountains. My mind wandered to the Malanbarra, knowing they would be sitting around their own fires and Mulley with them, and I longed for him.

Below me, the sound of carts and busy activities ceased for the day, and I took the lamp, lit it, and sat down to write a short letter to Martha to be mailed in the morning.

Dear Martha and My Dear Liz Beth,

I send my most heartfelt best wishes and also beg you to forgive me for not writing sooner, but I had not occasion nor opportunity to write thus before now. It was a long time before I should be able to come to town, but I've survived well and have learned to be "civilized" in a good deal better manner than I had hoped upon my arrival at this new settlement.

Edward has fared well and returned from Thorn Borough quite a man of means, and we shall have a fine crop of cane in before the season is too late. Edward now wants to begin a family and hopes I shall have a child within the year...

As I wrote the words I frowned slightly. I had already missed twice those monthly trials a woman bears and felt sure that Edward's wish would come to pass.

After I had finished writing the letter, I washed and put myself to bed. I did not hear Edward come in, and thankfully, he slept soundly without so much as touching my person.

In the morning, I dressed quietly, left a note for Edward as to my whereabouts, ate in the saloon below, and set off to the milliner's to pick up the plain but suitable dress that had been altered for me.

A short while later, Edward found me. He led me to where the cart had already been loaded. Two men were loitering near the trunk of a large tree where the cart was standing in the shade, the mare quietly grazing at her feet.

"Shall we be off home, madam?"

I did not reply but nodded with a smile and climbed up on the cart. The two men hauled themselves up and sat at the back with their legs dangling, but I did not speak a word of congeniality to them and they stayed silent also. It took most of the day to return down the clay roadway back to where our newly cut track now crossed and led home to Notre Maison, and darkness was well upon us when we arrived.

Edward saw to the workers while I closed myself up in my little cabin for the night and waited for him in the silence of my thoughts that was a s torturous as any trial I had endured.

There wasn't a moment my body did not ache for my Mulley, and I grieved in a silent way every night, every day. However, just as quickly as I had fallen from grace, I now turned my life to the new grace extended to me by the fortunes made by my husband's return.

In the silence of my cabin, I lay thinking about the turn of events. I knew my "real" person was but a ghost and mirage of a Margaret, who only played her part. My true self still wandered in the afternoon with her aboriginal in the cool shade of the forest or across the grass plains in the low lands. There, the silken strands would brush against her legs and life flowed through her veins like the rivers and Yidinji trails that crisscrossed the land. Whatever secrets I had learned now lay hidden deep inside me. I wondered if they should ever again see the light of day. Indeed, like a mirage, I feared that they too, would melt away and the hard truth of my real life would banish them one day, even from my memory.

Edward busied himself planting his precious cane cuttings, and I had flour again.

We had labor and a track we could come and go on to the town. The maize had been harvested again, and the quiet days of the past slipped away behind the busy days of plowing and weeding, cooking and washing, banal conversations and orders to laborers.

New settlers were arriving. We often met our neighbors and sometimes saw people moving south to take up land all around us. Mounted police accompanied by aboriginal rangers from New South Wales patrolled the growing municipality. They had twice called upon us and we were able to declare that the Malanbarra had caused no trouble and had rarely been seen.

Edward and I went to church three times. The Lord opened my wounds in that congregation and I wept, disguising my tears as some effect of the cane flowers now spreading like a pink and white haze across the tops of huge fields. I found excuse not to go again and instead we busied ourselves at Notre Maison farm.

Edward probably did not care whether we went to church or not, except for our standing in the community, but I consoled myself that I was still a believer by giving thanks at the evening meal and knowing in my heart, the truth of Him. Indeed, I had faith enough that the Lord knew my hidden pain and was good enough to forgive me for all my foolishness.

I saw Mullegadajawara in the trees just three times. He remained as still as the crane just before it strikes a fish, and it took all my strength to turn away from him.

The final time I saw him, we watched each other for some minutes, then he turned and disappeared into the trees.

The dry season roped in the land like a wild heifer, branding it with sunburnt grasses and stranded waterlines of shrinking creeks. For some months, I might have almost forgotten the one beautiful day under a fig tree and the best part of a year in the tender friendship of my rainforest aboriginal. Though my life appeared to be happy in my husband's care, try as I might, I could not forget but best managed my sadness by becoming a woman of such industry that I might well have rivaled Martha. Alone and in darkness, the ghost of Mullegadajawara in me could do nothing but stay silent.

Yet, I could not ignore my husband's intentions to start a family, and a little after ten weeks from his return I began to be sick each morning.

Edward did not suspect, as he rose early every day and disappeared to the fields, only returning for breakfast much later and avoiding any real conversation with me.

One afternoon he arrived back at the cabin early, and I wondered if he had amorous intentions in his efforts to ensure I should fulfill his plan. I in no way felt I could suffer his attentions this day, so I pretended to be busy folding and refolding washing.

"Margaret, please, sit. I want to speak candidly and find we are disposed not to speak more than a few words..."

He was very formal.

I obeyed but looked to him with a blank expression.

My face had become pale and thinner than it had been and barely a smile passed over it of late. He was tired of it but had left me to my sullen disposition. He rightly guessed, that neither a beating nor a rose bud would lift it from me.

"Margaret, in these three months we have indeed managed quite a bit, I think you would agree."

He looked up at me and I nodded. "The new maize is in, the cane cuttings planted." He smiled as though trying to encourage me to be pleased and hopeful. "We should have a fine time in the autumn after the cane has got to full height. Once it has flowered we can burn off the fields, get rid of the outer leaves and cut it ready for the mill. Those will be hot days and heavy work but there aint a smell alive that beats the caramel of burning cane." His gaze drifted over the sea of green that fanned out away from where we sat. "Yes indeed, we will need some good labor then!" His hands slapped his thigh like a strike of lightening before the voice of thunder. "At last my dreams are materializing and we are getting Notre Maison farm into shape, are we not?"

I realized he was waiting for my agreement so I said, "This is true, sir."

"I know I was away a long time before, and mind, you did more than well in my absence ..." The turn of his conversation told me something coiled, drew back its head, and prepared to strike. "... The weather is good now." He licked his lips and I looked up with trepidation.

"It is my wish, before the fields are cleaned out, to rejoin Mr. Daley at Thorn Borough and get what we can before the gold is gone. Some have said it will be totally finished in less than a year."

My eyes had widened and I felt the blood rush to my cheeks and neck as he went on.

"I know you are well set up now to manage, and there is help for you, with the Chinese fellow, Sung, and the field hands he looks after. And there are neighbors now. The mounted police patrol is all about this area, so there is nothing to worry about concerning your safety. I see no impediment to my leaving you, say, for a month or two." He looked up brightly. "What say you?"

I was dumbfounded at this sudden turn. "Edward… it is not my wish that, having returned to make a life with me at last as a proper married man, you should again abandon me after just three months!"

I was angry. It welled up, asking for justice, claiming unspoken wrongdoing, demanding to be free to cry, how long will you ruin my life and give me not a moment that is sure?

I sucked in a breath of air shakily. "Is it your intention to get rich at the expense of your obligations to me?"

"Margaret… You have no rein on your emotions! We have a lifetime to suffer each other, to grow old and wonder what opportunities we missed. I talk of just a small amount of time away with Mr. Daley so that you, Margaret, you shall have a substantial home to raise your offspring in and I shall have some comfort for my labor!"

"Edward, if it were not for the fact that your voice wavers every time you hearken back to your association with that uncertain gentleman, Mr. Daley, I would almost believe your intentions were good and for me. I think it more likely, sir, that the gold fever has you!"

He stood up to full height and poured a look that resembled black molasses on me. At any moment I felt sure he would strike a flint and set me on fire.

"Madam, I presume you have forgotten your deficient days here and are innocently ignorant of the comforts my near starvation and labor have bought you since… and quite because of that 'fever' you say I have for the simple business that you now seem to despise." He stopped only to catch his breath and continued with vehemence.

"Do you not realize, madam, that had I not shared the ordeal with Mr. Daley, we should have long since packed up our suitcases—and would not have had even so much as the fare to return to anywhere, save the poorhouse or the morgue!" He was spitting the words at me, his tone a mixture of defense and defiance.

"Well perhaps so... and I don't say I'm not grateful. But I was in perfect harmony with my lot and my surroundings for those long months of your absence... and, in fact, I enjoyed them!" My voice caught because my words barely hid what those times had truly meant to me.

I rose from the table and slammed my palms on the tabletop and choked away my sorrow to glare at him.

He jumped up and I flinched as though his hand might strike me.

"Well, you shall 'enjoy' them again!" He yelled and began to stride from the porch. "I shall be packed and on my way two days from now and that will be the end of it!"

"Edward!"

"What is it madam?" He turned and stood with his fists jammed into his hips, one leg thrust into the dust of the yard path while he leaned back on the other.

"Wait, there is something I must tell you."

"Then speak... I've things to do."

"You must not leave me now... I'm with child!"

There, it was out.

He stood frozen for a moment, considering and weighing the news. For a time, it seemed he would do nothing then he skipped up the steps and pulled me to himself in an unusual moment of tenderness.

"This is good news. How far along?"

"I think, three months, to the day."

"So there is a way to go." He released me, turned, and rested his hands on the rail of the deck, staring at the outer fringe of the clearing.

"I shall come back before the ah... young'un is due. I will make sure I'm back before the wet season even looks like beginning and in plenty of time to see that you are safe in your delivery." He turned and began to skip down the steps while I stood close to the door in shock as he went on seemingly talking to himself more than I. "You are in good health, you are strong. I shall make sure the mission folk take a look in on you. And you have a track to town now." He began to walk away and slapped his thigh as he put voice to his thoughts. "What a turn of good luck! I am certain it is an omen for our fortunes at Thorn Borough. Yes indeed!"

With a broad smile, he turned to look at me standing alone on the deck above him. "Oh, my dear, you shall be as big as a house when I get back!" Then he said quite sharply, "Mind, you are to take care and see to it you eat well, there are plenty of supplies and money for more, so you have no excuse not to look after my... son... in your belly."

I stood dumbstruck that my revelation had not shifted his resolve to leave me for the goldfields in the least.

"So you are determined," I frowned, searching his face for some glimmer of remorse as I walked to the rail and leaned over. He knew what the tone of my words were intending to do. I wanted him to condemn himself or be wracked with guilt and hence, change his mind.

He sucked in a long breath and sighed. He would not be backed into it, nor pressed into staying, and quickly turned away from me. I heard him call out, "Things will be all right, Margaret. Mark my words. Daley and me will finish up and I'll be back in no time—and a good deal richer too!"

He had shaken off my stare and strode boldly over the yard toward the shed to prepare his saddles and equipment for the journey back to the fields.

"You are callus, sir! Callous! I would be just as pleased if you did not come back!" I yelled with more anger than I had ever felt in my whole life.

He paused for a moment but did not turn, and then he strode forward and disappeared from my view.

I adjourned from the porch and sat on the end of the bed inside the cabin. The heat was easing for the day but it was still blisteringly hot under the tin roof of the room. My husband's behavior did not surprise me. I ignored it, deep in a turbulent stew of thought. I had already begun to stretch my mind out beyond Edwards' leaving, to the weeks that followed after that, and I found myself perpetually returning to Mullegadajawara's face.

I sat on the cover of my bed and wondered whether he was still to be found or whether the camp might have moved with the new settlers invading the landscape.

I wondered whether he would know when I was alone again and whether a day would come when I might see his dark body, conjured up in the forest shadows, appearing again in my sight.

As I thought of him, my stomach turned and I found myself filled with a chilling excitement, as though my anger toward Edward's leaving had been a mere show.

I looked up and out of the small square window that glinted in the afternoon light. A slight smile bloomed on my face like the slow bud of a rose that couldn't deny the warmth of spring, and I let myself hope I might see him again. Though my belly was filling with my husband's child, Mullegadajawara still filled my whole soul.

I took a deep and long breath in. Surely, with my husband gone, he would find me again.

After Edward left, I settled into the daily routine of managing the farm.

It wasn't as it had been the year before. My workers were faithful, if not because of character but because they could be tracked down and charged if they absconded.

They weeded the fields of cane and tended the new maize crop, sweet potatoes, and other garden vegetables that were in for another season.

Every day, I scanned the tree line to look for Mullegadajawara, but he did not materialize. I began to despair that I should ever see him, and that filled my heart with a kind of sickness that was far worse than the illness I had every morning. I was tempted to go to the camp and see if they were there, but the observation of my workers and what they might report to Edward prevented me.

Two weeks after Edward had gone, I instructed Mr. Sung to harness the mare for a trip to town. I intended to get a sack of flour, some lard, and borax.

The morning was clean and bright and Mr. Sung hummed some Chinese song I had never heard before. Occasionally he commented on some aspect of the fields or the garden as I chatted happily with him on the way to town.

As we arrived, Mr. Sung asked, "You be right to set down here, missus? I go get Mr. Edward's timber... come back for you?

"Certainly, Mr. Sung. Everything shall be as it normally is, so get whatever the master would have you get. I shall go to the general store and see to the supplies I need."

I got down from the cart and nodded in the direction of the store. "Come and collect me from there, and we can go back at a good hour. I would rather not have to stay even if we shall be back well after dark."

He tipped his cap and said he would, then the horse and cart moved off toward the lumberyard.

I crossed the dry clay street and into the shade of the overhanging awnings of three small shops, dodging a dog that crossed my path and a long-legged drover who bowed slightly and said, "'Scuse me, ma'am."

As I walked along the wooden planks of the pathway, I saw Mr. McKenzie spinning a small barrel around and along the front of his shop to place it with some others displayed for sale.

"Mr. McKenzie, good day to you." I called out and he looked up and smiled.

"Ah Lass, you have returned to us again, I see."

"Indeed. I'm in need of supplies so I may feed my labor in suitable fashion."

"Will your husband be fetching later?"

"No sir, I'm again tending my own affairs. We have agreed he is to spend yet another few months up at Thorn Borough. He is hopeful to be as lucky again so that he can see to a house for us... and for such new children as may come."

"Ahh, well, 'tis good news you have for me I suspect."

I looked to my hands, which had momentarily fallen in front of my skirts where the secret child lay, not yet visible to the casual eye.

"Is it to be a new child, and born an Australian!" He said and I nodded shyly.

"So your man is storing up some wealth for ye?"

"That is his hope."

"He is a man indeed, to suffer that endeavor twice."

"Yes, I suppose he is." I turned my head from Mr. McKenzie, pretending to be interested in a teapot that sat forlornly behind glass and had a pattern of daffodils on its side.

"I've heard a man's language turn to a mule's at the hardship they have had up there."

"True, but I find a man's language is often akin to a mule's at the best of times."

He grinned at me, "P'raps so, my dear, but this last wet season, as you know, had them cut off for most of it and begging for even our Lord's help." He was talking and working at the same time as he recounted the tale of the Thorn Borough gold miners terrors' in the year 1878.

"Even horses couldn't get down the track. Sections were torn away in rainfalls so rapid as to be a million buckets of warm water just tipped straight out of heaven... And the subsidence's were big enough to wipe away whole hillsides and any cart on it! And that, not all, they said 'twas need for rebuilding the pass more'n seven times! But even so, they is still heading to that field to this day, knowing it be likely to drown 'em or flay 'em right to the end."

I watched him as he walked me indoors and continued. "Anyone who has a mind to stay just a little too long is nigh on destined to become a citizen of hell this life and, as they live it, in the next too, I'd wager!"

"I presume, sir, you do not approve of the venture."

"Well Lass, 'tis an old vice and the tale of every gambler that ever pitted himself against the malice of the bet, I'd say. Eventually, it's always a sorry story and what's won is good enough lost, with just time being the only question." He smiled, but I could see he was quite serious. "And if that normal course is not enough there's been some wicked superstitious rumors of late around the camp up there and the town down here." He looked up at me and I frowned slightly.

"Oh, what say they?"

"That fate has outsmarted most, lured all with a promise, but is set to stab the greedy from behind!"

"Really!"

"I'd say it has good as run its course... but they still go! He finished adding up my goods, then he looked up and a shadow of concern crossed his face. "Lass, I beg ye, take care in the town on yer own. There is a multitude of miners that are hauled up in the tent city because the track has slipped again week 'fore last and none can get on their way back to that ungodly place. 'Tis humid, too, and them that are about are mightily frustrated and are getting to the grog, and by afternoon are not a sensible lot."

"The track has slipped, you say?"

"Aye, might be five hundred men stuck on this side and perhaps a thousand up beyond.

I listened as my sacks were shifted to the door and Mr. McKenzie droned on. "They say it is being cleared as we speak, but it has been a troublesome time, I can say—for them and us about the town."

"My goodness ..." I trailed off, looking about for Mr. Sung and wondering how Edward had fared.

I said good-bye to Mr. McKenzie and began to walk down Abbott Street. I suddenly noticed that there were in fact, a good many bedraggled mining men, thin and gaunt, wandering about or sitting on crates talking with each other.

My curiosity now quickened with Mr. McKenzie's report, I decided to set off in the direction of the tent city to find someone who might know of Edward or Mr. Daley's condition.

Skirting the post office and walking through the alleyway that led behind the second street, I strode through the grass that led to a sea of tents and boxes, crates, carts, and horses tethered or grazing around its perimeter.

I could see to my left quite a large wooden shed that could have been mistaken for an empty stable were it not for the cast iron pot belly stove at one end and its chimney with a twirl of purple smoke twisting overhead and being wafted inland.

A large gathering of men sat around rough-sawn timber tables and on wooden stumps or crates. A lone woman seemed intent on stirring something in a cauldron, and I could smell a mixture of hops and meat cooking amidst the sultry heat of the area.

Raucous laughter made me halt, as it was most certainly not a place a decent woman should be comfortable.

Suddenly, a loud laugh drifted over to me, quite separate from the others, and I thought I recognized it.

As I rounded the trees and came within eyesight, I could clearly see it was Edward and, with him, Mr. Daley.

"Edward!" I called out and walked as restrained as I could, to the edge of the group.

"Margaret! What do you do here woman?" I could see he had obviously been drinking strong liquor.

"Sir, I'm told the track has been blocked more than a week, why did you not take it as an omen and turn about and come home?"

"Come home? What manner of man do you think I am? Turn about?" His voice was slurred. "... There is gold to find, madam, and what is there to dig for at your farm? I've already ploughed that field and planted the crop. Now I've a mind to get comfort where it can be found in the bottom of a river bed, and that's a certain comfort indeed!" A few of his companions nodded with agreement. He lowered his head and muttered under his breath, "And better that madam, than look for any warm comfort in your bed."

The men began to murmur, and some perhaps, felt embarrassed for me.

"Sir! I beg you. Can we speak of this privately?" I moved one step toward him. "I should like to have you home until the track is clear and things are decided."

"Be off with you! Go spend my money and get a crib for my newborn to come... and while you consider yer duty, best you buy some perfume to entice me homeward or a man might well forget what bed he ought to have!"

An old man raised his jug and laughed as he spoke in a heavy Australian accent, "Now mate, why do you find fault with this little girly, eh? And she's gone done ya service in getting with kid!" He swigged on the rim of the jug and a trickle of amber liquid spread through the gray whiskers at the corners of his mouth. He shook his head, "Can't say as I understand ya wanting to spend your gold with them Kate house girls up there when ya got a perfectly good little girl like this one 'ere at home." He raised his jug again and called out loudly, "Raise your beer mates, to the good little women waiting at home. May they all be ready to do their duties like this good'un here so we don't have to spend our gold on hoars!"

Horror filled me and I felt sick immediately. I could barely speak but looked at Edward's back and stuttered my last word with as much courage as I could muster.

"All right, Edward… Go to your beloved 'goldfields.' I should not wonder that you might never come back. But I warn you now, I shall have my property rights as a married woman and… I shall make room for you in the shed if you do not end this folly!"

The men roared with laughter as if something funny had been said, but I had said it with perfect disgust and had meant it. I watched him sway slightly but he did not move a muscle to respond.

"So be it!" I whispered and turned on my heel to flee. It was all I could do to gather my skirts and run back through the trees out of their sight, then sickness was upon me and I retched into the grass.

Breathlessly, I held the trunk of the huge fig whose dark shadows hid me. Slowly I recovered against its solid comfort. I wiped my palms on my skirt and took a long look back in the direction of the tent city, but there was no sign of Edward, so I found my way back to the main street.

"Missus, I been looking for ya. We is all loaded but is going to be very late for getting back!"

"Sorry Mr. Sung, I had… an errand I had forgotten." I hid the shame of my husband's manner and his avoidance of returning to me and looked toward the cart.

"You ready now?"

"Indeed, let's get on." I climbed up and Mr. Sung clambered up and sat next to me with the reins in his hands. The mare obeyed his "Gee up!" and we set off down the track toward home.

I looked back to see if Edward had thought better of it and followed me to give some commiserating explanation or deny the accusations of the old man.

Mr. Sung saw me and said, "You forget something more?"

I did not reply. I turned my head back toward Notre Maison and determinedly away from the vision of Edward and the man he had become.

"No. Nothing forgotten, and never will be."

Mr Sung frowned and flicked the reins a little harder to speed us on toward home.

As the rocking and jolting cart picked its way along the flat track around the foot of the mountains, I began to pine for Mulley and the pure life I had lived alone at my cabin and in harmony with my lot—and away from the excesses of my countrymen and the civilization they embodied—and away from that man that dared to call me wife.

I began to justify my relationship with my aboriginal, extinguishing all my guilt and imagining that I could simply leave all and find myself safe again in his arms. I could see the clan camp in my mind, the happy faces around the fire and Mulley coming home from hunting.

Like a jolt of some strange lightening that woke me from my delusion I realized my error. The reminder of my unborn child swelling in my belly seemed to stir me back to reality. In an instant, I knew there was nothing in the world I could do but fulfill my duties at the farm, manage the workers Edward had hired, and wait for the day I should be a mother. Any dream of escaping to my beloved Mulley was as futile, as it was dangerous.

I sat in silence for the entire journey and thought about the revelations the chance meeting with Edward had made known. I felt cold at the thought that he was visiting with common prostitutes and had no genuine interest in me whatsoever. His heart was consumed with the torrid life of the fields and the fever of finding more gold.

By the time night had fallen and we arrived at the cabin, I had reconciled myself to the fact that my unborn child was all that was important. As

I hauled my tired frame up the steps and closed the door of my cabin, I resolved that I could never be tempted to think on the life I had so loved nor my desire for my darling Mulley again.

Chapter 14

THE WEEKS ROLLED on, I closed my eyes to anything but the task at hand.

The police commissioner had visited and asked if we had any troubles with the blacks of the area, and I'd assured him that we did not.

He said the other settlers, too, had been left in peace, which was to all accounts a surprise to him. In the north and to the east, the aboriginals were very troublesome. Several homesteads had been raided, and some settlers had been killed.

More police had been brought up from the southern state where aboriginals had been trained to subdue their own kind, and authorities intended to do the same in our districts with the help of black trackers and force.

Nevertheless, the local police chief was opposed to the vigilante tactics of so many of the northern district settlers who would, in the course of reprisals, kill and force into near starvation many of the clans of the Yidinji and the Djabuganjdji north of the Barron River.

In due course, my new neighbors, the Richardsons, came to visit complete with oatcakes and kind acquaintance. They discussed their new endeavor and their wish to create a cooperative for our cane production and one day build our own mill to process the raw cane so we would not have to ship it in crates to the mill further south in Townsville. The idea was admirable and I promised to tell Edward of their plans should he arrive home. They were somewhat surprised that I had been left alone to manage, as it was now quite clear that I was with child.

Mrs. Richardson made me promise I should come to them if I needed any help, and Mr. Richardson suggested he would call from time to time to see if I needed anything mended or fetched. Although I was thankful of their kindness, my desire to stay alone was strong because I still remembered the days when only Mulley and myself lived at the farm and had need for nothing.

Mr. Richardson wanted to arrange a meeting with the other small farm holdings around us that now encompassed all the land from the headland to the Mulgrave. He commented that the aborigine in the valley, were still somewhat undisturbed and he should very much like to see it remain that way, and I quickly agreed.

I said, "Might we not halt this desperate condition that is happening elsewhere by petitioning the police chief to leave our aboriginals at peace, as they have done no harm to us and seem content to leave us well enough alone? Surely it is better for all if they are left undisturbed and will therefore, do likewise for us."

"Indeed Mrs. Bermingham, I do believe you make good sense. I am going to meet with Misters Connolly, Matthews, and Sterling this week concerning the mill proposal. I shall indeed speak to them about what you have suggested. If all agree, I shall write a petition, and we shall all sign it and present it to the commissioner."

I was greatly pleased by this and my isolation seemed less by the knowledge that such kind people lived only ten miles away and were of such a mind, that I could in some part, help protect Mulley and his people by our cordial association.

We spent a pleasant afternoon, and I was greatly engaged and on occasion sported a fleeting smile that I had barely had occasion to do for many months.

My greatest pleasure however, was the thought that our petition may well protect my dear Malanbarra bama for a little longer.

I was sure Mullegadajawara still guarded me from his own people too, and in so doing, kept the warriors of the clan from the other settlers also.

Daily I would go to the places where we once wandered on my farm when there was no one but ourselves, still hoping he would find me, but he did not appear.

One afternoon in July, I walked slowly up the track from the stream where the waterhole was. As was my custom, I had stood at the top studying the trees for some movement, some hint, that Mullegadajawara's glistening eyes were upon me.

Nothing stirred. Only the screech of the ever-active and playful rainbow lorikeets brought the forest alive.

As I stepped up the last part of the incline, puffing slightly, I felt the wind on my face and a shadow move to my left. I turned quickly, and there he was.

"Mulley! Oh, my. I've so wanted to see you again!" I whispered in a shaky voice that mimicked the shaking in my whole body.

He turned and walked up quietly beside me. Without replying to me, he swapped his spear to his left hand and reached out to my skirt.

I felt his hand rest on my stomach and I could feel the heat of it through the fabric. Gently, he lifted it off again and without any comment to suggest he was interested in my condition, he walked up the track beside me to a clearing where he sat down, cross-legged, waiting for me to do the same.

I struggled a little to find a place and with my skirts falling between my legs, I sat opposite him, my belly cradled between my thighs.

For a moment neither spoke. I plucked a dry grass stem from beside me and began plaiting it between my fingers.

He watched me and I looked up straight into the man's face as though I knew the exact spot my eyes would meet his.

It was painted with white stripes down his nose, and feathers had been tied into his hair along with shells. Several necklaces looped in a gentle curve over his scars onto his glossy, hairless chest. Nothing was out of place; every muscle was contoured under the black onyx skin. He was quite the most beautiful man I had ever seen.

"I've missed you." I looked down to my plaited grass as though ashamed.

"Have I left you?" He smiled a little.

I did not know what to say. "I thought you might never come to see me."

"I never leave Guba guba." He looked down at the mound sitting like a hidden egg in the skirts covering my thighs and repeated. "Guli... I never leave you." He looked up at me inquiringly as he corrected the familiar name he usually called me to the more reverent name of "mother of pearl."

"He leave you?" His question unsettled me. I wanted to say, yes, and he will never return. But I knew I could not.

"No... He is only gone for a little while to get gold."

"When back?"

"Ah... before... before the rains come."

"Ahhh ..."

A stillness settled in the space between us and time seemed to stop.

"I cannot ask you to be my friend, but I so desire it." I looked up, tears in my eyes, and an innocence that comes from having lost all and having nothing left to conceal, showing in my face.

"Mullegadajawara and Margaru is forever. What good is for you, that is all I can think." He stopped and considered his words before adding. "What good is for you... and your young... is all I can think." He sighed heavily and looked down at his feet lying still in the grass.

"Please, I value you beyond what I should... shall we at least preserve our friendship?... I will still teach you English, and perhaps I can help if you have trouble with the... new people."

Mullegadajawara stood up with the ease of a gazelle and hovered above me.

I looked away from his nakedness now, as he held out his hand to help me up from the grass.

He grinned and shook his head. "You not pay me in lessons. I happy anyway." He did not let go of my hand and I left it there as I stared into his coffee-colored eyes. Then he said, "Tomorrow, come to the place where blue plums are." He turned and pointed down the stream with the tip of his spear, back toward the mountains.

I knew he offered a private place where we could meet far from the gaze of my laborers or other prying eyes.

"I shall come," I smiled. He was near me, and I could smell his warm, musty scent. It filled me with longing to have his arms again around me, but I resisted, knowing such times had passed.

Instead, I put out my hands and gently grasped his. I held them for what seemed an eternity, and together we remembered each other as though we had never been apart.

Edward again broke his promise to me. A man on horseback, traveling south, delivered a letter from him.

He had trotted up to the yard and, without getting off his horse; he leaned down and put the letter in my hand when I came out of the cabin to greet him. He was Irish, and his heavy accent rolled off his tongue accompanied by the smell of whiskey and tobacco.

The note was scrawled in pencil and stained with red-earth fingerprints.

It said that they had, "… begun to struggle for gold" but having recently found a "good and untouched vein," they felt sure they would come out on top. But it would take at least another three months, "to be sure" to clean it out.

If he returned as he said, I would be very near full term.

I screwed up the note and tossed it on the table beside the bed. It rolled and landed against the wall. It announced that I had no more feeling for my husband than the letter he had written and from that day forward, I gave him little more thought.

Mullegadajawara was again my daily companion and that entertained me far beyond my husband's uncertain activities or absence.

I continued to give Mulley lessons, and he continued to teach me all kinds of herbal remedies and the spiritual way the Yidinji understood their world and the "dreamtime."

The days went quickly and before long, I felt the nearness of new life stirring unstoppably within me.

Midnight had come and gone. A nagging stomachache, like that of eating too many green apples, had disturbed my sleep, and I lay in the darkness wondering and dozing.

Just after two, I woke fully with sharp pains cramping my stomach and my belly was hard like a drum. The bed was wet and I gasped as hot, searing knives pierced me from within and I began to feel the tight pull of labor.

"Oh my Lord... not now!"

The darkness was thick with the heat of a still night and my groans filled the cabin. I got up tentatively to find the water pitcher and light the lamp. My nightdress clung to me wetly and I tried to find another, but the searing cramps and strong contractions forced me back to the bed.

I wiped my face with the cloth I had dipped in cool water and I cried out as one after another of the agonizing pains came in waves.

An hour went by, and then two...

At last, the force of the contractions overwhelmed me. I raised myself up and began to push, nature taking over as midwife and I became consumed by the task of delivering my own child.

With one final and determined effort, the child slid from me and lay between my legs. I hung my head back in relief, sweat pouring from me, and recovered for a moment.

Then suddenly, I heard the muffled sounds from the wet bundle between my thighs and I scrambled with my nightdress to uncover the babe.

He was shakily waving his arms and spluttering into a cry.

I wiped him with the sheet in the half-light, pulling the wet newborn infant up into my arms and close to my breast. The umbilical cord stretched between the babe and myself, and I was suddenly at a loss as to what I should do. I held the child in the crook of my arm and stretched to try to reach the kitchen knife that lay with the utensils on the cabinet against the wall. Not having thought to prepare it for its task when I lit the lamp, I reached over, the baby coughing and crying in my arms, but could not grasp its handle. My fingers just touched the tip and it unbalanced, fell, and skidded onto the floor with a clatter, disappearing somewhere in the dark.

I am not sure what prompted me, but I placed my newborn between my knees, picked up the cord, and tore it in my teeth until it broke. I wiped my mouth on the corner of the sheet and then leaned forward and collected the baby under his arms and pulled him close into the crook of my arm.

Looking down, I studied his crinkled body, the darkness of the room masking his features. I could make out a wide little nose and a round dimpled face nuzzling me, and I opened my garment and guided him to my breast.

The light played over the covers as I waited. Soon nagging contractions began again, and in a few moments, the afterbirth was delivered.

I gathered up my baby and lifted myself gingerly from the side of the bed I had birthed on, and staggered around the end of the bed to the dry sheets on the far side, nearer the lamp.

I lay down and in a half doze, rested until exhaustion claimed me and I slid into unconscious sleep with my child still in my arms.

I slept for a brief time, then awoke with a start, as the babe moved.

I raised myself up a little and opened the sheet he was wrapped in, and looked down at the baby in my arms.

I was nearer to the lamp and in the full light it shone in us, a sudden shock of the truth struck me.

"Oh no! My darling… no!" Tears began to flow as I held the baby up in my hands and looked on him clearly in the lamp light.

There was no mistaking it: he was dark-skinned.

I cried and shook my head in despair—not that the child was Mullegadajawara's, but that he announced my infidelity.

I knew Edward would explode in a jealous rage. He would never accept either the child or myself and would evict us into the wilderness, if he did not kill the child and beat me within an inch of my life.

He would hunt Mullegadajawara down and destroy the clan along with him, with none to halt his vengeance just as the the Yidinji elsewhere were being persecuted without remorse or protection of law.

Still, this was my beloved baby, and I pulled him to me, stroking his cheek and studying his face one way then another. Between my tears, I smiled shakily and my mind leapt from one thought to the next, searching and wondering what I should do while the child nuzzled with gusto, unaware of his inconvenient and dangerous existence. Exhausted, I fell asleep without intending to as the lamp burned softly and the night shielded us from the fears of the day to come.

When the dawn broke, the infant began to cry, having slipped from my breast.

I woke with a clouded mind, and as I looked down to the child, I began to weep again as my little son spluttered and grunted, hungry again for my new milk.

As my tears subsided I smiled at him, as a mother cannot help but do. With my cheeks wet and shiny, I lifted him to my breast as his demands grew louder, and I nursed him while the birds sang their opening chorus and the early light oozed through the waking landscape.

My eyes could not leave him and I studied him as the light grew. He could not be mistaken as not having aboriginal parentage. Perfect, coffee-colored arms and legs, plump and warm, kicked out and wriggled now that they were free from the confines of my womb and his little brown eyes remained tightly closed in the folds of his lids.

I surveyed him; holding his little fingers and marveling at the small, perfect fingernails and the pink palms. He was healthy and beautiful.

Little by little, it began to dawn on me that his birth must be concealed and he must be saved at any cost. I knew I must protect him and his father, his people, and myself. There seemed only one course of action.

As I thought about it, I cried, realizing what sacrifice I must make. But soon my emotions gave way to necessary sense.

As the minutes ticked by, I became more and more certain of what I must do.

It was Sunday, and that brought one mercy, I thought. The laborers would not come that day, so I had just a little time before discovery to make good my plan.

I summoned my energy and my courage and painfully raised myself from the bed. A piece of sheet served as a shawl, and I wrapped the baby tightly in swaddling clothes, just as I had seen my mother do with a neighbors child she had cared for, and then I placed him in the egg basket.

I washed myself with cold water, not bothering to waste even the time to heat it. Then I dressed, wincing with pain. Gingerly, I gathered up the basket and crept out of the cabin.

The Torres Island doves were cooing across the yard, and the distant sound of the kookaburras called from the stream. Even my chickens clucked loudly as they saw me but none of these could distract me from my task.

I limped slowly to the shed and found the sidesaddle. Summoning my courage to make up for what I lacked in energy, I saddled the mare.

I knew I couldn't climb up in the state I was in, so I carefully placed the sleeping baby in his basket on the top sack of a pile that was stacked along the side of the shed and stood the mare quietly beside them. I stepped up on two crates until I could reach the saddle easily, then I reached down for the handle of the basket and tied it to the front of the saddle with the sheet.

Slowly and painfully, I rode out toward the track and across the stream.

I could not tolerate anything but a slow walk, and the journey up the river through the trees was agonizing. Barely keeping my balance, I headed the mare along the trail as the saddle soon became slippery with blood.

Though I faded in and out of consciousness, my white fingers clung with the grip of death to the baby and the basket as I urged the horse onward.

By the time I had reached the path that led to the clan's present camp, I was hunched over the basket perched in front of me and though my thighs were locked in the sidesaddle, I lolled and swayed with every step the horse made.

When the horse could smell the presence of the clan she slowed and stopped, dropping her head to the grass on loose reins. The baby began to cry and his voice echoed in between the trees though I barely heard him.

Mulley told me later that it was the old woman, Menge, who looked up first from her new cooking fire, lifting her nose to the air as though she could sense from where the sound was coming.

"I heard a baby... Kamerunga, do you hear a little one?" she had called out.

From within shelters, the Malanbarra appeared. Men and women began to gather and walk toward the sound.

Mullegadajawara came from his grandfather's shelter and he listened with a frown. He told me a cold sensation crept into his stomach with the distant cries. At first he felt only some vague recognition and then began to run full tilt along the path as he realized what the sound must mean. He scrambled between the others and pushed himself out in front.

When he came upon the place where the horse stood grazing, he could see I was lying over something and the muffled sounds of the distraught baby came from beneath me. He said I looked small, and that blood, thick and red, blanketed the side of the horse and a cloud of flies had gathered.

"Margaru!" He leapt across to the horse and leaned up to pull at me.

I roused and fought to hold my basket but he pried my fingers away and took it from me handing it to the women who had gathered around us.

He grasped me around my waist and pulled me from the horse, my skirts wet and red, and he could see I was gravely ill.

The clan's women, immediately cloistered around the basket. They stared in at the baby and looked at each other with both curiosity and concern.

"He is our own, ..." the old woman whispered. "This is the mother?" She frowned with amazement and dismay. "Mullegadajawara, what story is this?"

"Old mother, the story will be of his young mother's death if we do not do medicine on her now!"

He yelled for some of the men to help him, and soon I was carried carefully between them, with the clan's women cradling the basket and a young boy leading the horse.

When I later awoke, Mullegadajawara was seated behind a medicine man and a woman was washing my face with damp leaves and moss that smelt like rosemary.

The darkness of the shelter was cool, and the scent of the people in it with me mingled with the smell of blood.

"Mulley, I found you ..." My voice was rasping and dry.

The woman leaned over and placed a gourd to my lips, and I drank cool, fresh water greedily.

"My little boy... my baby... where is he?" I held out my hands to Mullegadajawara and he moved between the medicine man and the woman and clasped them tenderly.

"He is well, Guli."

"Thank my Lord!" I rolled my head back and sighed as though the trauma would leave my body with the escaping air.

"Mulley, he is ...your child."

"Yes," He looked down tenderly at me. "I knew from time I see you at stream." He smiled slightly because he could see my fears even in the half-light as clearly as if showing outside in the bright daylight.

"I cannot keep him ..." I broke out in tears and took one hand from him to cover my face. "You understand? Mulley, it is not safe for him ..."

"He is my son... I will keep him and you also."

"No, you cannot! I cannot stay. I would love nothing more than to leave that world, but they will not let me. Edward will come looking and he will kill you all and take me back."

I stared up at him, my eyes hollow with fear and longing. "He will not accept the truth. He will say you raped me, and he will make sure you are all destroyed." I shut my eyes tightly. "No one will come to stop him." I whispered as though I hid a terrible secret about my kind.

"Mmm," Mullegadajawara nodded and pulled his hand from me. "The child is Malanbarra ...we will keep him."

He stood up slightly, bowing under the low ceiling of the dwelling. Then he stepped away from me toward the doorway. Just as his dark body filled the opening, he turned and I could see a stern and determined expression on his face.

"When you are well, I take you back."

"Mullegadajawara ..." He stopped at my call but did not turn to face me again.

"His name is James."

Mullegadajawara stepped out of the opening without replying and disappeared from my view.

I lay quietly and thought of my child somewhere in a hut such as the one was in, and I wept until I fell asleep to the voices of the two remaining aboriginals discussing unknown things in their own language beside me.

I awoke in the dark, a darkness seldom known by the people of civilization.

The hut wasn't silent, though. It resonated with the rustling of the breeze through its leaves and the creaking movement of its frame.

I could hear the sound of breathing and feel the cloistered warmth of a sleeping body beside me.

"Mulley?" I whispered in the darkness.

"Guli, I'm here. Are you well?"

His voice was deep and reassuring. In the darkness he sounded more like the echo of a heart I had known for a lifetime, and our intimacy seemed greater for the removal of the sight of our surroundings or ourselves.

"I've got to get back... before the workers arrive."

"No."

"I must. I know what I'm going to do."

"You stay and heal... Then we decide."

"Mullegadajawara, please, I know you understand. Don't make this harder for me."

"You don't know... Harder has not yet come. Stay with Mullegadajawara and I will protect our family."

"We can't live like this. I know what will happen. No matter how you protect me... he will come and destroy us all. Please... get me back to my cabin."

"It is dark ..."

"Please Mulley, I must go, with or without you." My voice began to be tinged with determination. It is Sunday night ..."

He thought about it for some minutes, then silently got up and left the hut. I heard him speak as he ducked out the entrance, "I get the horse."

I sighed a sigh of relief.

I carefully pulled myself up and leaned through the opening, "Mulley, get me a wallaby, a small one. You must bring it with us."

Everything depended on the deception I had conceived, and to do this, I knew I must get back before dawn.

I pushed aside the desire to find my child, even though I was suffering from full breasts that desired him also. The women had tied a raffia cord around my swollen stomach and a net of dry leaves and moss between my legs. I looked about for my pantaloons but couldn't find them in the darkness so I struggled with discomfort and exhaustion to crawl from the burru.

I found Mullegadajawara as he led the horse through the camp. When he reached me, I summoned my strength, and with his help, climbed atop the mare. We set out and he led her through the dense brush land toward my home.

By the time we reached Notre Maison, the distant dawn was still some time away, but the sky began to herald its future arrival with a slight lightening of the night sky. Stars had retreated in the haze, and I could see the outline of the riverbank, the spinifex grasses, and the roof of the cabin thrust up into the night air.

"Come, I will show you what we will do." I spoke breathlessly as he helped me from the horse and I limped across to the shed.

"Help me." I slid out a wooden box about the size of an apple crate that had held the precious cane cuttings when we had shipped them from the town.

I emptied it of the sacks that were folded and stacked inside.

Mullegadajawara carried it over his shoulder behind me as I walked back to the cabin.

When I opened the door, the smell of blood and rank air struck us in the face. The small room had been shut up for a day and the dirty sheets lay as they had been left, rolled on the side of the bed.

I lit the lamp and opened the window so the fresh air could filter in through the screen.

Lifting the sheet, I emptied their dry and shriveled contents into the crate and carried them outside.

"The sheets will have to be soaked, the saddle will have to be washed too." I turned and looked at Mullegadajawara who was staring at me perplexed.

"Get me the wallaby. Hurry… the dawn will come and the workers will arrive. They are always prompt on a Monday."

He obeyed, collecting the small marsupial that had been speared the day before from the flanks of the horse where it had been tied.

"Thank you… Lord, let it fit!" I gathered the wallaby and folded its back legs into the box. It seemed about the right weight, though its shape was ungainly.

I pulled the long tail around and forced it into the box. For a moment, I paused, realizing the enormity of what I was doing.

"All right …" I calmed myself, not really speaking to Mullegadajawara, though he might have thought so. "May our Lord have mercy on us."

I gathered up Edward's hammer and began to strike a small nail into the lid of the box then hammered it home. I repeated this with several more nails until the box was fully closed.

A kookaburra called and I looked up.

Mullegadajawara's eyes did not leave the box, and as he saw the light of the oncoming dawn appear, he walked to me and rested his wide hands on my shoulders.

"We finish now."

I looked back at the box sitting forlornly on the table. "Soon …"

I made him carry the box up to the big fig tree and set it down as I dragged the spade behind me to the spot I would choose.

Silently, I began to break ground and dig the surface layers of a hole.

He watched, and when he understood my intention, he took the spade from me and continued.

"That's deep enough, Mulley …" I whispered.

We put the box next to the open grave Mulley had dug.

"We'll leave it here until my workers come, so they'll understand what I'm going to tell them."

Then I turned and walked behind him until we reached the cabin. There I reached out and held his shoulders with my small hands and rested my cheek against his damp, black, back.

"I will always love you, Mulley ..."

He turned to face me. "Long time in the desert... my people come to here in dreamtime... When the sun love the moon and they together... Then spirit of jealousy take the moon and hide her, but they love still... Jealousy stand in their way and separate... Keep it night and day." He stared out at the dawn light. "They cannot see each other but they know ..."

I understood his meaning.

"I know. We will be like the sun and the moon, Mulley, but no one can ever know."

"When earth is gone, in dreamtime place, you my woman."

"In dreamtime place ..." I whispered back.

We sat quietly in each other's arms on the steps of the "shelter that could not be moved," and we hid the last moments we had together in our hearts like jewels that had been stolen from a rich merchant who would come looking for them at any moment.

"You have to go ..."

"Mullegadajawara come back with son and visit?"

"No... No, you must not. I will come to you when I can." I flustered a little with the lie because I knew I could never risk going to them.

He nodded and his eyes went dull as though he knew this would be farewell and he was neither willing to allow it nor able to prevent it.

For a moment, the agonizing sadness seemed to pull the curtain of dawn that was rising up, back down, and we clung to those last moments before the determination of the sun broke free and dawn was upon us in a new day.

We said our good-byes, and he disappeared into the forest. I limped back to the cabin, gathered up the sheets, and put them to soak in the barrel by the bench outside.

The water swirled red, and I thought of my baby, waking to the breast of some other mother, an aunty or a cousin, in the camp by the river.

My heart sank as I struggled up the steps back into the cabin. I closed the door, lay on the bed fully clothed, and drifted into the buzzing haze of desperate sleep.

Chapter 15

"MISSUS... MISSUS? YOU there? We ready to work."
I heard the distinctly Chinese voice and roused drearily to its call. "Go to work... I'm sick. Missus sick. You understand? I will come out soon."

I lay back staring at the ceiling of iron corrugations that was already beginning to transmit its morning heat onto my face.

I lifted myself gingerly, washed my neck, and grimaced as I walked to the door. My stomach was aching and felt bruised but the bleeding had eased, so I opened the door and let the new morning air freshen my hot skin.

"Mr. Sung, please, can I speak with you?" I leaned over the rail of my porch as he stood, hat in hand and his head respectfully drooping. "Missus has had her baby, it has come early... and it did not live." I uttered the words shakily, half expecting the lie to reveal itself in my voice.

He looked up with genuine sadness on his face. "Oh missus, that very sad... Missus okay?"

"I will be... but, well, we need to bury him. The heat you know... There is no time to arrange anything in town. Too far away." I rested my hand on my stomach.

"Oh… Shall Lou bury it, missus?" he whispered, and his eyes flirted with the soil and grass at his feet.

"Yes, we must. Can you call the others? We should have a service. I want him buried under the big fig tree."

The man nodded and backed quietly away.

I could hear him calling the three workers who had already started to weed the first garden where my new maize had begun to sprout vigorously.

By the time I arrived, they had walked up the hill and stood looking at each other, the small crate sitting next to the hole forlornly.

Mr. Sung frowned as he looked at the hole. I could see him wondering if I had put the babe in his box and dug this hole all by myself. I saw him shake his head and mutter something, no doubt thinking me a strange woman.

As I walked up to them he whispered, "Missus, no need do this. Sung could have dug hole and… put in crate."

I shook my head and stared at the little box beside the hole.

For some reason, though I knew what lay inside, I felt loss and sadness as though it were truly my baby going into the fertile soil under the huge, twisted fig tree.

"Can you put him in the ground?" I nodded toward Mr. Sung and the other Chinese man standing nearby.

"Oh… Oh yes, missus," he stuttered and quickly shuffled toward it.

They lifted the box and together placed it in the bottom of the hole. The weight rocked slightly as they manhandled it in, though without dropping it. The smells of blood and death must have wafted up into their nostrils as well.

Mr. Sung stood up and said, "Sung say something, missus?"

"If you like," I replied.

"Okay… I say funeral poem for Chinese… Okay?"

I nodded, and Mr. Sung began to sing his dirge. The other Chinese sang along with him, their voices together sounding to me more like the howls of cats than the hymns I was accustomed to.

When they had finished, he looked across to the other workers and called out in a loud voice.

"Here is missus' baby... an' gone to heavenly place. We say good-bye. Amen!"

They all said amen and stood like statues with their heads bowed waiting for me.

I made a small sniff and put my hand up to my mouth, and a tall Kanaka named George took it as a sign to begin to bury the forlorn container with its grisly contents. He lifted the spade and began to shovel earth over the sad little box, and I feigned a tear and stepped back from the burial site.

"Thank you, Mr. Sung... that was very nice. I'm going to rest today. Please can you see to the men, and we shall go on ..."

He nodded profusely, concerned for me as both his employer, and therefore the source of his wages, and as a woman to whom kindness and pity were owed.

I exchanged courtesies and shook each man's hand in turn, and then Mr. Sung walked me back to the cabin, where I quickly slipped inside and shut the door. I had seen him frowning at my manner and could sense him still on the porch, standing, looking at the closed door.

I knew his Chinese heritage would think that a woman should be in the care of other women: mother, sisters, or her husband's other wives. He would be worried now, but I hoped he would do nothing about it.

I lay on my bed, dizzy and with no further thought but to close my eyes and fell into a deep sleep.

For many years, I told myself I had no choice. I suppose I had "choices," but they all involved telling the truth and facing the consequences, which I rightly knew would be brutal.

At the time, however, languishing in my growing illness, such thoughts and worries were far away. I did not even dream. Finally, voices broke in on me, and they seemed to float in the air before my eyes.

Margaret... Margaret, are you in there?" The voice was deep timbered but young.

"Your man Sung rode to find us. He says you need help!"

I drifted for a moment, dizzy, lost in the fog of heat that had dehydrated me and the onset of infection that sweated through my pores and made the room seem like another world.

"Ahhh …" I couldn't muster words and my spinning head began to make me nauseous.

"Margaret, it's Pastor Daniels, from the Methodist congregation, and Mrs. Steadman. We have come to see if you are all right." Silence replied to his pleading.

"Jonathan, help me. We will have to break down the door. Shelly, get round and see if you can see in the window!"

I distantly heard a "One, two, three!" and they struck the door, which did not give way.

Finally, on the third try, the hinges parted at the top, the door skewed in its frame, and an opening appeared.

The two men pulled at it with a mighty effort and with the squealing and creaking of all parts giving way, the door was pulled out and laid on the porch.

"Oh dear!" One of the men let out a cry of exclamation as he saw me lying on the bed, my clothing wet through and I barely conscious. He rushed to my side and stroked my forehead.

"Margaret, Margaret… Can you hear me? It's Jonathan, Jonathan Stanford… Do you remember, from Cook Town?"

He looked into my face as the woman whom I came to know as Mrs. Steadman came rushing in the door.

"You know her, Jonathan?" The pastor looked up.

"Yes. We lodged together at the Cook Town Hotel when she and her husband and I first arrived. I thought they had already selected land up there to settle." His eyes were shocked to see me so depleted from the once-bright girl he had first known.

"Quick, we must get her to town and a doctor. She looks very poorly." I could hear the high-pitched voice of Mrs. Steadman speaking, but it was like a dream.

They lifted my small body and carried me down the steps to the waiting cart.

Mrs. Steadman had bundled up blankets and a pillow and climbed on to receive me into her arms, and I moaned as the pain of crumpling my poor body into the cart roused me.

"There, there, dear. We shall get you help you can be sure …" She soothed my brow but her face showed the deep concern she had for me.

For hours, the cart hobbled over the rutted track that was used continually by horse and dray, cedar loggers, and settlers on their way north and south to Cairns for supplies. Every jolt made me wish I had already died.

By the time we arrived, I was unconscious and couldn't be roused any longer.

They took me to the newly built infirmary, called the Cairns Hospital Building, and there I was placed in their kind care.

White-dressed nurses busied themselves around me and the doctor administered quinine and various tonics. All waited that first night to see if yet another woman would find herself silent and buried in the settlers' cemetery.

I held on, however, and day by day, through raging fevers that came and went, they tended me never knowing whether the next fever would finally take me.

Two weeks after my arrival, I woke in the morning, and for the first time felt almost human.

I ate breakfast and even raised myself out of the bed to sit in the chair beside it. There I sat, resting and wondering about my baby and how I had come to be there.

A nurse came and was amazed that I had got up, promptly admonishing me and insisting that I get back into bed. She tucked me in and without a word, sped off to fetch the doctor.

He entered the ward with a broad smile and stood beside me.

"Well, young lady, it seems you are a very lucky woman. You have survived a good dose of septicemia, and few manage that. It was lucky, I have to say, that you were in good condition from the start, though it will take some time to recover and you must be careful not to overstrain yourself. I suggest you stay in town for a while. Leave your laborers to tend your farm and rest up here."

I looked up at him and said in a rasping voice, "Sir, I thank you for your courtesy, but it is my wish to get back to those things that have need of me as soon as possible."

He smiled gently. "Madam, it seems you have had a very… isolated existence, but regardless of your wishes and the tasks you observe have, 'such need of you', you are all but brought back from the brink of death! I see no need great enough that you should risk it again and are certainly not obliged to let you go."

"I am sorry, sir, I must return …" I had little or no interest in my duties. My concern was solely nearness to my little James, but before I could summon the strength to resist the doctor further he firmly said, "No madam, I must insist!" He patted my hand reassuringly. "I think the pastor will be up to see you today," he went on, "and he is a fine man, a good sort. I suppose, when you are feeling better, he will want to discuss with you the internment of your son and Christian burial arrangements here in the town cemetery."

"Oh no, sir, I don't want that! He… is buried where he shall lay… and that for as long as I live!"

"Oh my dear, but do you think that wise?'

"In what way?" my voice rasped. "Is he any less loved by the Lord if buried with respect by two Chinese and three Kanakas in the shade of the exquisite work of a fig tree by the Almighty?"

"Well, of course not, madam. It is just there are certain proprieties …"

"There is naught so proper as where he is, sir. And there he shall remain!"

I must have announced my immanent recovery by my outburst, and I could see a look of surprise creep up his face with the flame of passion in my every word.

Looking away from him, I went on somewhat distantly, "I only wish I could escape the pomp and ceremony of such things and find for myself a tree to be buried under." I looked out the window wistfully, my sorrow unable to be, concealed.

Given my husbandless and now childless state, he probably wondered if I might truly desire such a thing earlier than it was destined for me. Frowning a little because such melancholy was in no wise a matter openly admitted to, and no doubt concerned he said, "Well, I suppose there is nothing more to say about that since we are all destined for many troubles. Indeed, there is nothing for it but that all must cheer up and think on better times." He stood up and smiled politely. "I've already contacted your friend Mr. Stanford, and I think he is arranging for your care when you are well enough to leave us."

I looked up with surprise, "Jonathan… is here?"

Patting my hand gently where it rested on the bed, the doctor said, "And, my dear, perhaps you should know, in case it bothers your mind at all, you shall be able to have many more children… All right?"

I took in his words and tossed them about in my mind before deciding what they were and where they belonged.

"Ah… I see. Well yes, that is… comforting," I whispered, though in my mind I was screaming, But what husband shall oblige me? And please, dear Lord, I should never wish to have him do so!

After he left, I rested, and the day droned on with the hollow thud of nurses' steps on the wooden floorboards and the sounds of patients being wakened and fed or tended.

I wanted to get up and walk, but that wasn't allowed, and as the afternoon wore on, I decided to write to Martha in Cook Town and to Sally in England.

Just as I reached to gather the paper and pen the nurse had left me, a familiar voice drew my attention to the door.

"Margaret! The Lord in Heaven be praised!"

"Oh, Miss Margaret, you look a fright!"

"Dear Martha, Liz Beth… I was just about to write, and here you are!"

"Well, looks like the week spent to get here was not wasted by the look of you." Martha pulled up the only chair and it screeched lightly across the floor.

"We been all the way down the track soon as we got word by Missar Jonathan, 'cause Miss Martha won't go on them 'grubby ships'." Liz Beth stood by my head and held my hand firmly in her own, and her eyes glistened with tears.

It was odd to have her near, and a pang of longing filled me as I looked on her smooth dark face and bright coffee-colored eyes sparkling in the light reflecting through the window slats. A tear welled up in my eyes that I simply could not stop, and a reply in Yidinji threatened to slip from my lips with the sight of her aboriginal form, but I choked it back and instead stuttered shyly, "I couldn't want for any other persons to visit me."

"Mr. Stanford sent word of your plight and that ...Mr. Edward is not to be found, so we bundled up and left Old Henry and came down with some others going south. We have come all the way through the Daintree to be with you. My, we have worried so, all this long time since you were with us ..."

"Oh, Martha, you had naught to worry. I managed and was well-schooled in the ways of the wilderness ..."

"No, dear one, wasn't the wilderness we knew you had to fear, but that man ..."

"Martha, please... Mr. Edward might be harsh from time to time, but he is as he is, and no real trouble for me ..."

"Lovey, I'm not sure how we should tell you of this... being as you are not yet recovered and have had such a sad time... We should have wanted to come to you sooner, 'cept the hotel held us fast, you know. 'Tis a frightful distance, and not knowing where you be out there... So we just had nothing else of it but to pray hard for you ..."

Liz Beth piped up very seriously, "'Tis true, Miss Margaret... She be fair troubled, an' no doubt Miss Martha want to drop 'n trot all this way to warn ya... But we just ask 'im that 'tis Lord 'n heav'n to keep ya from expirin'!"

"Liz Beth, I'll mind you to let me ..." Martha leaned forward and patted my hand, and then almost whispering, she began.

"You see, no sooner had you left than Wongoree, that black fulla... Well, Wongoree's body floated up and was caught in the mangrove swamp, and the whole town was wondering who killed the poor soul.

Even so, the police had no interest 'cause many a black fulla gets in a scrape but they handed the carcass over to the mission people and he got buried up there. Then Liz Beth's people came to her because there was a payment due and they knew from whom it was owed, and she knew of Mr. Edward at the hotel."

"Edward owed it?" I gasped a little.

"Yes Mr. Edward owed it …'

"An' that not all he owed, Miss Margaret. He owed them Wongoree's life, too!"

"Liz Beth, I shall not warn you again!" Martha leaned in. "They say that Mr. Edward was seen after he had been down at the West Coast Hotel with that Mr. Daley fellow, drunk as a possum on bush bee honey. Evidently, Mr. Edward, he went up to the docks for some reason, no doubt looking for a ship to get away on… and in the dark …"

In the light of the hospital room and in hushed tones, the two women told me that Edward had left me just after our meal, as I remembered, and after he had seen Dayley at the West Coast Hotel, he had walked up to the dock in the black of that strange night.

He was not alone, however, and he had heard a voice come up behind him while others watched from afar.

Liz Beth tapped her finger in the air as though knocking on Edward's shoulder and mimicked a deep aboriginal voice. "'Hey boss, you still alive?'" Her eyes caught mine and were wide and her expression was certain as she said, "That just what he say, Miss Margaret! True as true, Wongoree come out of the dark like them black ghosts that have no skin and likes to afrighten us people who is a fearin' Lord A'mighty!" She shook her head and went on to replay her relative's description of the events, no doubt told her in Guugu Yimithirr, which she was 'not 'llowed to 'member.'

Martha sat listening, occasionally correcting Liz Beth, while she tutted in horror at what Edward had done.

I could see the picture before me as Liz Beth acted out the scene.

She squeaked in her vibrating voice, "Mr. Edward, he yell, 'My God man! We heard a shot… Thought you were dead. If we had known, we would have fetched you.'" I could imagine him turning to face the dark figure standing near him.

"'No boss, I still alive... I need me pay and me horse.'

"'Pay? You didn't do the job, man... We didn't build anything and ...'

Liz Beth frowned deeply and said, "An' our Wongoree, he say, 'Oh no, boss... that no good. I take you out there, you need to pay me and give me back me horse, eh?'

Liz Beth shook her head and I could see the anger in her face before she mimicked Edwards voice and said,"No sir, I made a deal with you to take me out there, mark out the boundary pegs, build a cabin, and clear a market garden ...'

"'No, no, boss, you pay me! I take you out there... it not my fault that you not check to see that land already taken!'

Her face flicked back to her own and she said in a small voice,"Then he say, Miss Margaret, 'What? Did you know it was already cattle station land?'

"An Wongoree say back,'Well boss, me cousins might've know but I 'aven't been out there, long, long time ...'

"So Mr. Edward, he say, 'Why didn't you say something man? It's hardly my fault we couldn't do what we went out there for.'

"But Wongoree know'd Mr Edward was tryin' ta sneak outta payin' an' he say, 'I not your boss, mate. You say me to go out there with ya, and I went! Now you have to pay me.'

"'Well you can forget that ...'" Liz Beth replied in my husband's deep voice as she played both Edward and the aboriginal's parts.

I could almost see the scene. In my mind's eye, he would have spun round and stepped away from Wongoree with the arrogance I had seen in him for the natives before. Wongoree would have followed him and stood very close, not wanting to let him get away without paying him.

Liz Beth continued to tell the story her watching relatives had passed on to her.

"Wongoree not dumb an' he say, 'Boss, you have to pay me, cause you agreed—and I know what you did to them fullas... Yeah boss, I know what you did wiv them bodies. You and that China fulla did a bad thing to them whitey's, eh boss?"

"You bastard... How dare you threaten me!"

"I not threaten you, boss. I just want me pay an' me horse back."

"I cannot believe it—it's extortion! How dare you! You think you can contend with me? You are no one, I say, no one ...!' That what that biigaarr say!"

"Liz Beth!" Martha leaned forward and slapped her on the arm and the small girl looked back as fiercely as I had ever seen her. "I thank you not to use such language. We is polite society!" Martha paused and then she whispered to me, "But she is right lovey, that man is true enough a taipan snake, like she says in that heathen tongue she is not supposed to know, I might add—if ever there was one!" She shot a piercing glance at the girl and Liz Beth sucked in her lips and looked away shyly.

Then Liz Beth turned back to me and went on,"Wongoree was not gonna give up so he keep pressing that man, 'Pay me, boss, and I go away and remember nutt'n I see.'"

Edward apparently stood in the dark, staring at the corner of the dock. Then he must have seen a long line grapple hook left there.

In an instant, Edward would have swooped down and grabbed the grapple hook. As quickly as he grasped it, he had swung it around and ploughed it into the black flesh of Wongoree standing in the shadows, and the strike sank deep into his chest.

Liz Beth's eyes were as wide as they could be, and she assured me her relative had "seen it all, Miss ..."

She feigned the blow to Wongoree, "Argggh!' he not even able to scream Miss. He was gurglin', an' his hand was graspin' the iron rod and they was sliding down its shaft with all that blood ..." she said as he looked for a way to remove it. But as he did this, his power left him.

"Oh my!" Martha whispered and shook her head.

Liz Beth said his hand let go of the rod buried in his upper chest and only his middle fingers hung from it like a hook. The weight of his body pulled on the rod and as he slumped to his knees, the weapon was pulled out of Edward's hands. It clanged loudly as it hit the dock planks and the man crumpled over it.

Her relatives had cowered in the darkness, perhaps shocked at what they were seeing but too afraid to confront Edward now that the deed was done.

Edward had stood over the humped form in front of him. For a few moments, he waited.

Wongoree did not get up. He lay still and lifeless, the last of his breath hissing from him.

Standing up, Edward had held up his hands, sticky and wet with blood in the moonlight. He had quickly leaned down and wiped them on the dead man's shoulders and hair.

He had been breathing heavily and paced back and forth for a moment or two before deciding what to do. Then, with arms linked under Wongoree's shoulders, he dragged the body to the wharf's edge.

The aboriginal's head had flopped forward, and his legs dragged along the planks, leaving a trail of black drops that would, the following day, be thought of as only some sign of a fisherman's catch. Edward pulled the body the few feet to the water's edge, and with one heave he rolled it over the side and into the darkness of the incoming tide. A loud splash sounded as it struck the water, and then it gurgled down into the depths with the weight of the iron rod still pierced through him.

Liz Beth sucked in her lips, and cocking her head to one side, she said, "That be 'xactly how it happen, Miss Margaret! 'Xactly!"

That night, he had come up to our room freshly washed and told me to start packing. He had wanted to be as far away from Cook Town as he could get, and as fast as possible. Mr. Daley had been his opportunity and the beche-de-mer fishing vessel had been his means.

Indeed, I recalled it clearly. In my heart, I knew the story was true. It explained so many things.

"But what was Wongoree talking about, that he knew about what they had done to some other men?" I asked, suddenly wondering how the confrontation had come about.

Martha's eyes widened as though the worst was yet to come—as though the death of the aboriginal would be eclipsed by something far more serious.

"Well lovey, you remember a cattleman was found, killed, they said, by natives,... Well it was Wongoree that did it!"

"I don't understand... If he did it, then why was he accusing Edward?"

"Well lovey, soon as Wongoree's body turned up and all knew he had been murdered, Lee Tong 'fessed up to me what had happened up there. Yes indeed, when he was found half rotten in the swamp... the Lord take him ..."

Liz Beth squeaked with a noticeable catch in her voice and then she quickly echoed, "The Lord be good 'n take 'im even if he be not all a good'un, an' he be a black fulla too!"

"That's right, Liz Beth, the Lord's mercy is for him, just as well ..." Martha consoled the young girl with unusual compassion. Then she went on: "Lee Tong was scared right out of his yellow skin, and when I took me washing down to the laundry women, he grabbed me by the arm—and I got a good fright myself—before he sat me down and told me what he knew and how it had all happened."

"Frighten' to bits, she was! Come back whiter 'n cockatoo feathers!" Liz Beth had her eyes fixed on Martha, and I felt her grip momentarily tighten on my hand.

"He was afraid the police would come knocking for him because Mr. Edward had absconded south and that they would never believe him on his own, on account of him having poor English and being a Chinaman. Still, as he knew me well and knew I could speak up for him. He told me all, so as to make a record in case the other bodies were found too and so they would know that it weren't him alone that had done it, nor no abo."

"Not none of Guugu Yimithirr do that... Not none!" Liz Beth said very soberly.

Martha began to tell me what had really happened when Edward had left for our first selection inland.

Edward, with Wongoree riding ahead, and Lee Tong straggling behind, leading a mule laden with provisions had set off to find our land on that day as I remember well.

By afternoon, they had traversed the wooded plain and threaded their way up the hills toward the Black Mountains.

Wongoree had become agitated as they got nearer to the strange pile of black rocks that made up the mountains. "This place kalcajagga. Boss... we should go round. Men go missing here, boss."

"It will be all right. I've been here before. Just stick to the track. If anyone goes missing here, it is because they have fallen into a cave, nothing to do with native mumbo jumbo."

"No boss, it no good place ..."

Edward had stopped his horse and turned on Wongoree. "You want to be paid?" he said angrily, not liking the aboriginal questioning him.

Wongoree had thought about it for a moment and looked up at the foreboding rock pile ahead, and then back to the man who had already been through this track and lived.

"If I die, I still come get me pay, boss... You be a sorry man not hearing me, boss. Kalcajagga not to be messed with."

Edward ignored him and turned his horse back onto the trail. They passed through the strange pass with rocks as black as coal that tinged if you struck them. When they came over the hill and crossed the stream there, Edward stopped.

"Hey Wongoree, I think the first marker for my land will be down in the far corner. There's about ninety acres of flat here and another, say, one hundred, round about the corner there, further down the valley. Do you see?" Edward had pointed from a standing position in his saddle.

"Okay, boss... I go down around that way and we take a look." He'd swung his horse around, pulling on his reins to bring the mare's head to the new direction, and then cantered off through the grass and the odd eucalyptus tree that had grown back from some long distant fire that had left the land relatively clear.

"Lee Tong, take the mule down after him. We can set up a camp down on that flat." Edward pointed to a more level section of the valley, and as he did, his eyes were caught by the look of it, bathed in the air and light after the big storm.

I'm certain his excitement would have mounted as he trotted down the incline but the moment would have been short-lived as Wongoree called out from the scrub ahead.

"Hey boss, you better come here." Wongoree's voice echoed against the opposite hill.

Edward sped up and trotted down to where Wongoree was standing beside his horse that was grabbing a few mouthfuls of grass at his master's feet.

"Been men and cattle here." He was pointing to the ground, where little could be seen but new grass. "See here, grass clipped by cattle and a man over here ..." He stepped aside a little and pointed again in the grass, "... and here. And the marker, it over there by that fern." He strode off to the spot. "See boss, some bugger gone and pulled out your marker!"

Edward smacked his hand on his thigh, loudly cursing. "Damn them! Damn them all to hell! Lee Tong, get that marker and put it back in, and we will go down to the one on the bottom corner and see if that one has been pulled out too."

He had frowned and spat the air from his lungs angrily. "Those bastards... they aren't going to get away with it this time!"

He pulled hard on his horse, which bared his bit, opening his eyes wide, and flattening his ears with the sudden cruelty. "Well, come on man! Get a move on! "

Edward kicked his horse and cantered off down the slight incline toward the bottom corner of the valley.

"He got a bad spirit that one... Bad spirit!" The Chinese man frowned as he watched Edward speed away.

Wongoree nodded but spurred his horse on to follow after his employer, not replying to Lee Tong's observation.

When he got to the corner where the trees of the opposing hill swept down to meet the valley plain, he dismounted quickly and began to look about for the marker and whatever other signs were there.

"Been here too, boss. Four men been talking here and one been smoking ..."

Edward had already dismounted and was searching the grass for the marker. He finally found it where it had been thrown and had landed in the bush some distance away.

Wongoree could hear him slashing the grass and then striking a tree trunk in anger. The hollow clunk reverberated through the glade before he crashed through the undergrowth to come back down to where Wongoree was.

"I imagine the whole lot are out." Edward had mounted his horse as he spoke and then rested both hands on the saddle and pushed himself upward. "Well, they take them out, we'll put them back. This is my valley, and that is a fact, so no matter... And if we find their cattle, we will drive them off."

He slumped back into the saddle and gathering up the reins, he trotted off in the direction of the next marker, leaving Wongoree still studying the signs in the grass.

Suddenly, Edward saw a group of about twenty dune-colored cattle crackling through the undergrowth as they grazed.

"Shhh...!" he spoke quietly to Wongoree and pointed around a eucalyptus tree to the steers beyond.

Wongoree had already seen them.

"They are from down country, I'll be bound, and they're running them up here now. Those are shorthorns." He whispered to Wongoree, who held his horse in tight so that they did not disturb the cattle until they were ready.

"What we do, boss?"

"You go round over that way. I'll go this way, and we will herd them out of the valley up there. If we push them over the stream, if it isn't too full from that storm water, we can get them out that way and they probably won't come back for a while."

"How you gonna keep them out, boss?"

"I don't know but they aint staying on my land a moment longer."

He started walking his horse around in a large circle so he could get behind the cattle, and Wongoree set off the other way.

As soon as they were in position, they let out loud whoops and yowls and began driving the steers through the grass and between the trees.

The cattle took off quite naturally, their backs vibrating as they thundered through the scrub.

Water and sticks flew up from around their hooves and their smell filled the men's nostrils as they herded them up the valley.

Edward had his hat off and was whooshing it through the air and Wongoree was slapping his thighs and letting out great howls and whistles, and the cattle obeyed, moving up through the valley toward the stream a little way down from the campsite.

Suddenly, just as the men could see the stream in front of them and the cattle were heading for the lowest bank to cross, a loud call broke their concentration.

"Oi! What the bloody hell do you think you're doing!" A man on horseback rode fast toward them from the campsite."What the bloody, God-damned, hell!... Stop what you're doing right now!"

With that, the man fired his rifle and the sharp bang echoed twice across the valley and startled both the cattle and Edward. Edward and Wongoree pulled up their horses and the other man, sweating and red-faced, soon appeared bedside them, his horse snorting and breathing hard.

"What you think you is doing, eh mate?" He spoke menacingly.

"I presume these are your cattle, sir."

"Agasey Station Cattle... Who the hell are you?"

"My name is Edward Bermingham, and this is my land... We were driving these trespassers off."

The man interrupted him rudely and with much indignation.

"Well I'll be dammed! You got some guts, I'll say that." He lifted his hand up to his hat and brushed the front rim. "This is all Agasey land, right through to the ranges."

"I'm afraid not, sir. This is registered as my selection, over nineteen months ago, at the Cook Town courthouse."

"Is that so?" He stared at Wongoree, while speaking to Edward. "Well, you got your wires crossed, mate. There's no one made a selection here, and nothing been registered but Mr. Agasey, and he's got the surveyor's papers to prove it."

The man dropped his rifle a little and turned to look at two other horsemen coming down through the trees to join him.

"Well sir, as I know you are very much mistaken, I suggest we go and speak with your master and sort this thing out like gentlemen." Edward's voice was heavily laced with arrogance and sarcasm, which did nothing but serve to enrage the man with the gun.

"No need for that, you pommy bastard! We can settle it right here." He turned his horse again to face them. "How 'bout you get off those horses and we'll have a little discussion?"

Edward looked across to Wongoree, who had, for a black man, become quite pale, as all knew there was no law against murdering an aboriginal in this region.

"Come on now, I said get off your nags." The gun was lifted hastily to his shoulder, and it was clearly pointing at Edward's head.

"Now sir, you can't do this." Edward was shaking his head, knowing that out here they could very well do what they liked. Still, even as he protested, he and Wongoree began to slide from their mounts and stood with their hands open in surrender.

The three cattlemen dismounted also. One had pulled out a shot gun from his saddle bag and the third had an aging handgun shakily held in his right hand.

"So mate, you gonna admit you been trespassing here and harassing Mr. Agasey's prize new cattle?"

"I say again, this is my legal land …" Edward barely had the words out, when the younger man holding the handgun shakily, yelled, "Shut up mister!", and it fired, striking Edward in the forearm.

He let out a loud cry and instinctively fell to the ground. Blood was pouring out through his sleeve, and although it was only a flesh wound, it was painful. He held it, groaning, as he rolled from side to side until the first shock of pain subsided.

"Idiot!" the first man yelled at the shooter. "You may as well have killed him… 'cause now you gonna have too!"

Wongoree was now shaking badly, and his black hair glistened with the shivering body beneath it. He walked up menacingly toward the aboriginal.

"So, what you gonna say about this, munga?" He shoved him to the ground and taunted. "Anything? Eh, eh, Abo? How 'bout you say you saw this man harassing Mr. Agasey's cattle and he was way onto Mr. Agasey's land, and he tried to attack my good mate here and grab the gun and it fired accidentally. How 'bout you say that, eh, black fulla?" He leaned his fist down on Wongoree's jaw, "Or maybe we just shoot you out here and you rot in the ground and no one goes looking for ya?"

Wongoree started stuttering as he spoke. "I not see nuttin', boss, nuttin' at all. I not even here. You say what you like. I don't know this man at all. I was just doing a track to go see me family inland. I got lost, and I see nuttin' at all."

The man burst out laughing. "Typical bloody black shit! All cowards—ain't that right, Mr. Pommy? But who's gonna believe an Abo could get lost?"

As the man turned his attention to Edward, Wongoree took the opportunity to explode from his kneeling position and run.

He darted through the trees like an agile wallaby, and before they could target their guns on him, he was gone like a shadow in the dappled, scattered trees of the valley.

"Shit! Like a bloody kangaroo! Ben, get after him quick. Don't let the bastard get away!" The man stood full height over Edward as he turned his attention back to their captive. "So, what are we going to do with you now?" He hissed menacingly, angry that the aboriginal had escaped so easily.

"Long way from anywhere, Jacko." The man who had shot Edward now spoke, no doubt afraid of the consequences of what he had done. "Who's to say he didn't get lost or gone walkabout in the storm and disappeared in them black mountains?" The walked over to Edward and from behind, pointed his old gun at the back of his head.

"Yeah, well, since you shot him, looks like we've got no choice but make him go missing, eh?" The leader Jacko looked across the valley as though checking that there were no other witnesses before seriously considering the deed.

Suddenly yelling pierced the air and the sound of a shot rang out distantly through the trees.

"Sounds like Ben's got the abo, so that's one down."

"Should do this one too, Jacko, so there's no one that says nuffink,… Then stick a spear in him so if anyone finds his body they will think it was the blacks."

"Yeah, s'pose so." Jacko replied and slowly began to raise his rifle.

Edward started to fully realize his danger as soon as he heard the shot that he supposed must have killed Wongoreer, and as they threatened foul play, he appealed to them. "Sir, sir, please, I don't think we need to go to all this …"

"Too late for that mister, you got about a shit show in hell. If you got anything you wanna confess, better do it now before you meet your maker."

Edward's face drained of color and he began to scramble for words. "I'm sure we can come to some arrangement… I could just forget this whole affair and return to where I came from …"

The man thrust out his arm and struck him in the face with a hard blow. "No one forgets. After the fear is gone mate, you will suddenly remember everything, including what color our buttons are." He stepped back a foot and raised the rifle to his shoulder. "Sorry mate, just nothing better we can do."

At that split second, there was a gut-wrenching scream as though all the cats in Cook Town had, at the same time, caught their tails. It echoed and reverberated in their ears and caught them so off guard that both men jumped and momentarily lost their footing.

"Yewaatcha ling tou!!!" Lee Tong bounded out from the trees where he'd been watching. Brandishing his machete, he leapt on top of the man holding the rifle.

The man raised his arm to protect himself and Lee Tong caught him across the forearm, opening it down to the bone and releasing a shower of blood that splattered all over the grass and his clothing.

The second blow was launched within seconds and came down hard between the man's shoulder and neck. Again blood spurted, but this time the man could do nothing but crumple to the ground on his knees.

The rifle fell from his hand as he clutched his neck and shoulder, but the blood poured in pumping bursts. His face grew pale and quickly took on a slightly blue tinge. His pupils dilated to full size and he fell forward onto his face in the bloody grass.

The second man had already jumped to a defensive position with his gun pointing out in front of him. A terrified expression distorted his face as he peered at the mad Chinese man standing over his companion. HE pulled the trigger but the old gun was empty.

The empty click ignited Lee Tong. He lost no time in preparing to hack at the second man, but before he came within striking range, Edward kicked the young cattleman's feet from under him. He toppled onto the grass, and before he could stand up, Lee Tong loomed over him, machete poised to strike.

He dropped his gun and began to stutter. "Listen mate, I didn't want none to do wiv it, eh. Was my leading hand. He was the one… I just played along."

Edward, behind the young man's back, picked up the dead man's rifle and slowly raised it to his shoulder, as the cattleman continued to plead with Lee Tong. "Mate! I'm just a drover… I don't know nothing but cattle, and shit, hell, I'm only sixteen …"

Suddenly a violent gunshot cracked from behind, so loud that Lee Tong dropped his machete and covered his ears.

The young man's chest exploded and blood and tissue soaked his shirt as he fell face forward to the ground.

Edward stood behind him, the rifle loosely hanging in his hand.

"Mister! What do that for?" Lee Tong screamed as he picked up his machete and stepped back several paces from the body and out of the way of the smoking rifle in Edward's hand.

Edward was quiet, not acknowledging that he had heard or even seen what he had done.

Lee Tong and Edward stood for a moment in the face of the carnage, and then Edward said very slowly. "They're not getting away with it this time …"

"But he very young one, mister... it be an accident he shoot you."

"The other one was right... He would have talked." Edward turned away and walked up the grass to collect his horse.

Lee Tong yelled after him, "We go look for Wongoree?"

"We had better do something with these bodies," Edward said, ignoring his question. "I suppose we had better load them up and take them back."

"Be a lot of explaining, mister. There be a court. I don't wanna go no court, mister... not me. Lee Tong don't do nothing with no court or policeman. He thinks I murder these white men and I go to jail! That one I kill, it just self-defense cause he gonna shoot you... but you shoot that young one in the back... that be murder mister... that be murder!"

"But I need you to back my story against the one that is out there." He pointed back down the valley.

No, you take them back if you want, mister, but Lee Tong not go anywhere near. Ohhh nooo! Lee Tong shook his head determinedly. "Maybe you say I shoot that young one! No one believes Lee Tong!"

"Well, we can't just leave them here."

"No problem! We take 'em down to the big river, take bullet out, put a spear in 'em, and let the crocs eat 'em up!" His hands were waving about and his whole body was shaking, sweat pouring off his face. "Anyone find, they say, the black fullas do it ..."

Edward realized that Lee Tong was probably right. It was cattlemen that had had him beaten for lodging his selection nearly two years ago. These men had obviously removed the pegs, and their employer had claimed the land for himself. Lee Tong's idea suddenly had merit: the law would not necessarily take his side even if he had a story backed up by Lee Tong.

He paused as he digested the consequences. "All right, man. Get the tent and we will wrap them up before their mate comes back ..." His voice trailed off.

Sometime later, they had wrapped up the two bodies and between them manhandled them onto the mule and Wongoree's horse.

"It getting dark soon. We better walk down this stream long way so no one track us from here, eh boss? We follow it round the back of Black Mountains and stay off the track." Lee Tong was puffing from all the exertion and pointing down to the swollen stream where the cattle had crossed to the other side.

"Yes, I suppose so. We could have done with Wongoree now."

"No need, I know way. I been to goldfields lots a times... Me, I like homing pigeon!"

"Well, don't get us lost."

"No, we be all right. We just get to big Endeavour River inland and the crocs will do good job for us."

They started out. The horses gingerly climbed down into the stream's fast water and walked, thigh deep, in its flow. When it got too dark to see, they made camp while their grisly cargo was dropped to the ground beside the mule and the mare.

The following day, they began to thread their way through dense bush near the river and plodded through the beginnings of marsh bog where mangroves spread out around them with their air roots spiking up from the mud.

It soon became impassable for the horses, so they unloaded their cargo and tied a rope to each. They dragged the first body over two hundred yards to the riverbank.

They left it there and slogged back to the horses to repeat the process with the second body. The mud clung to their feet, and each heavy step sucked at them. A deep, twisted trail was trodden between the trees. Finally, both bodies lay in their shrouds on the riverbank.

Together, they unwrapped the corpses, and Lee Tong stripped off the clothes. He had wrapped a torn shirt around his face as some protection from the smell, and Edward hid his nose in the crook of his arm.

Lee Tong made a rough sling of reeds and attached rocks to the bodies. Then he pulled out his knife and looked down at the hole in the center of the young man's back. Edward nodded that he should dig out the bullet.

Lee Tong shrugged before leaning down and sliding his knife in, twisting it and digging out the bullet. He washed it in the muddy water and handed it to Edward. Edward looked at it in the palm of his hand before casting it far out into the middle of the river.

After weighting the bodies, they rolled them feet first into the river. Then they roughly folded up the tent pieces with the clothing and carried it back to the camp to burn.

The following day, after they had saddled the horses and packed up, they took a last trip down to the mangrove burial site and stood almost knee deep in mud to survey the water's edge.

They did not venture any nearer, as Lee Tong's predication had come true. The water periodically swirled with underwater activity too large to be eels or fish life alone.

"Let's go ..." Edward looked down at his feet as though he had crossed some invisible line and had surprised himself with how easy it had been. "We should get back to Cook Town."

Lee Tong did not reply, only shook his head very slightly. Then they turned and plodded back through the mud until they found where they had left the horses.

"We should have seen where Wongoree was." Lee Tong spoke with little gusto in the rising humidity.

"No, if that fellow got him, he will wonder what happened to his partners. We don't want to bump into him. I guess they will order some kind of search party. Let's hope they don't find our tracks."

"We need more rain, mister, lots and lots of rain."

"Looks like we may be lucky there." Edward looked up and pointed ahead to the sky that met the plain sweeping off toward the distant ocean. Purple clouds were again building on the horizon.

Half a day later, they had found their way back around the Black Mountains onto the Palmer track. They left their ordeal behind them and headed to Cook Town through the endless tracts of grass and woodland. The journey was made in almost complete silence, with only the rhythmic thud of hooves accompanying them, each lost in his private thoughts.

Facing an uncertain future, I'm sure Edward's mind was consumed with what he would do next. I realized now it had rarely been turned towards me.

Liz Beth's face suddenly appeared again before me, as though the horrors I had been told had been seen in my dreams.

"… He done collected them bad spirits in them Black Mountains, thjat be sure what happen Miss Margaret… an' he be no good for never now!"

"Liz Beth, please!" Martha was looking intently into my face as I seemed to break from my trance and the enormity of the situation dawned on me.

"My Lord …" I shook my head, realizing that if Edward was ever identified, they might very much question me, and my own secrets might surface.

I leaned forward and whispered to Martha, "Did the bodies ever get found?"

"No lovey, has been quiet from that day to this."

"You must swear to me you will never tell anyone about this."

"Oh lovey… What you ask of me …" She shook her head.

"Swear to me!"

"All right, don't upset yourself now. I see how it is, but you must promise me you won't go back with him. I don't wish to find out you have upset him and he decides to find a fourth wife. No indeed!"

"… an' how we know them uva ladies died as he says?" Liz Beth growled.

"Quite right, Liz Beth!" Martha nodded vigorously and said, "Dearest, promise me you shall stay in the town or come back to us when you can travel and have naught to do with such a man as he."

"I will. And anyway, who knows, perhaps he is already dead or run off. We have had no word at all, and he was supposed to be back well before now."

"Well, that will be good of it, if he has, I can say. 'Tis never lucky to stand too close to one who has offended God and not paid his dues by the justice of earthly men. So you stay well away from him."

"… Miss Martha is right as right! Them ghost snakes soon do the judgment, you can be sure, Miss Margaret… But you can come right home to us 'cause you part of our fambily," Liz Beth caught up my hand and purred into my ear.

"Gimu rigimarawalla yirmithay ..." I replied, then suddenly realized my error.

Liz Beth stiffened, her eyes widened, and I quickly distracted all by speaking again in English. "I mean, thank you my dear friends. I should not know what life would be like without you."

"'Twould be a business best not done," Martha replied, not interested in my use of the Yidinji tongue. "You know we shall always take it that you have a home in Cook Town at the hotel. You just see to it that you get well, and if needs must, you can send word and we shall get Old Henry to fetch you, quick smart!"

They stayed with me for some hours and promised they would visit again on the morrow before they must set off to return to Cook Town and the hotel.

When I was again alone, I couldn't stop thinking of the events now revealed. The man I had found so warm and caring in London was a common murderer and of such poor character that I feared I should never believe anyone like him again, no matter how charming or decent they might appear.

I eventually took my leave of the infirmary, and Jonathan arranged for me to board with Mrs. Steadman, who was the kindest of people. Mr. Sung stayed out at the farm, keeping it going for me. It was Mr. Sung that took it upon himself to get word to Edward that I had delivered the baby, even though I should have preferred not to see him again. Because he was informed, I had no way of knowing if he had planned to come back for me or not.

When Mr. Sung came to tell me that Edward had finally returned I thanked him, sat down at Mrs. Steadman's kitchen table, and clasped my hands together as tightly as if iron straps were welded to my skin, and my lips followed suit.

When Edward arrived, he greeted me so softly that I was undone by his demeanor. I looked upon his ragged face and I wondered how such a man could have done what they said he had. He brought out of his heart such a sorry tone, and repeatedly reassured me that his times of abandonment of me were over and he was certain that we could begin afresh. But I knew that no matter his repentance, I should never find a feeling in me for him.

As though courting me anew, he brought me flowers and visited me every day for a week, and a little of the man I had seen in London reappeared.

By the time he broached the subject of a return to Notre Maison, I had already decided to break my promise to Martha and Liz Beth. I knew that I could be in no other place than Notre Maison because the call for nearness to my son and his father was so strong as to possess me even though I knew I must never allow myself to see them.

When I agreed to go with Edward he seemed suitably pleased. No doubt he thought he still had some place in me, but the truth was far from this.

The first days back at the farm were somewhat strained. He was unsure, I suppose, what he should say. He must have considered himself responsible for my troubles and, I suppose, felt guilt for his long absence. Perhaps he realized how easily he could have lost his third wife along with the child and his past fears for the loss of yet another wife probably ate away at him.

I did nothing to comfort him nor to relieve whatever guilt the man had. I was empty toward him. I felt nothing but the intrusion of his presence, and I encouraged him to hunt, fish, explore, or work somewhere on the farm as long as it was some distance from me, and he willingly obliged.

He had not had the great success of his first foray at the Thornton goldfield. He blamed the Chinese that he said were like 'rats', digging even around their own tents and beside paths to get even spilt gold dust. But it was clear from the start that the field would never be as good as the Palmer and had a limited life.

Now, faced with the prospect that only hard work would make our fortunes on the land we so thankfully occupied, he soon returned to being cold and surly and quick to find fault with everyone.

Having naught but our tiny cabin, we suffocated each other, and before long I wondered if it would be better for me to return to the town and find employment, perhaps teaching at the mission school.

Edward, of course, would have none of it, so I plodded out my sad days hoping upon hope that I could slip away and visit Mullegadajawara and my darling little boy.

The weeks passed and I began to feel the despair that comes from seeing nothing of the hope our little farm had represented. Now it seemed destined to fall short of any good thing, and my countenance became deeply morose.

Then one day, I saw a familiar shadow that brought back light to my soul.

Edward was nowhere to be seen, having gone hunting for the day. I knew Mullegadajawara would have made sure of that before he came, so I ran out joyously to meet him.

He had in his arms my little one, and I looked on his beautiful chocolate face as though he were the only thing in the world that could keep me alive.

Mullegadajawara wanted me to leave this cage of mine and return with him to the camp. I suspect he brought me little Jaimie, even against my instructions, to lure me.

Still, I argued with him and pushed him away, and he stood in the trees with our son in his arms until I urged them to leave for fear that Edward might discover them and all would be lost.

I returned to the deck of the cabin, and for a while my heart was euphoric at the sight of them both. Though my hands continued to complete whatever chores they seemed to know to do, my mind was playing in the long grass with Mulley and little Jaimie.

Then suddenly Edward was there.

"Margaret, what in blazes have you done?"

"Edward... What are you talking about?... I don't... You're back early."

"You think I'm blind, that I'm not a man who knows his own wife... Or are you my wife now?"

"I don't know what I can say ..."

He stormed up the step, and before I had any time to react, he hit me hard on my cheekbone and I flew back against the wall of the cabin.

"My Lord, Edward... what are you doing?" I screamed, and the sound of my voice returned from the surrounding trees as though it had been sent out to cut its way through the undergrowth to find help only to find no one and so return pitifully.

"I was coming through the woods, but even at a distance, I saw you with that black savage. The man was carrying a creamy." He spat the name the locals gave to half-cast children into my face. "Woman, that... that 'baby' had your features showing in its face... I saw how you were standing there with that mongrel holding it. Anyone would be a fool not to understand your rushing to him like that!"

He spun round and thrust out his hand to grab my arm, and I cried out at his pincer-like grip. "I say again, what have you done?"

"Edward... I think you have gone mad!"

"So, you would have me believe that the child and the mongrel with it, fawning all over you... has nothing to do with you?" He dragged me off the step. "Well, we shall see, shall we?"

The dust sprang up from my feet as he hauled me over the grass.

My skirts flopped and flowed through the heavy footprints he jammed into the soil in front of me and I cried out repeatedly as I was dragged over them.

My shoulder stretched out of its socket and I squealed. "Edward... please!"

He forced me with him to the shed and collected the spade.

I instantly understood his intention. "No! Edward, I beg you. Don't do this ..." I screamed through the foam forming in my mouth, terror gripping me as he pulled me hard behind him. When we reached the fig tree, he threw me to the ground and I fell backward, landing heavily on the palms of my hands. They stung with the impact and my left wrist felt as though it had snapped like a twig.

He picked up his spade and plunged it into the slight mound of the little grave. The flowers that had been laid there spun in the air momentarily and then scattered on the ground in all directions.

"I'd wager no one saw your dead baby go into this grave! I want to see my son!" he yelled as I sat in the grass, fear beginning to spread over my face like a disease.

Shovelful by shovelful, the ground opened and finally, the box lid appeared from under the red soil. He yanked the box out and sat it hard on the ground in front of me.

"So, this is our son?" He stared at me, his hands on his hips, towering like a giant ready to devour his prey. "Well… is this our son?" It was as though for a moment, he doubted himself and he waited, not willing to open the box to look. A moment passed, caught on the chasm of momentous revelation.

"Edward …"

With my one word, he knew the truth.

He grabbed up the spade and caught it on the corner with his boot holding the box down. He pried off the top until the small nails squeaked and the wood flew off like a jam jar lid that finally let go.

The remains of the wallaby, shriveled and dry, confronted his eyes. A second or so ticked by and his face turned from pink to dark gray.

"Edward… It's not what you think. Please, you have to try to understand!"

He did not reply but turned and ran from me down to the cabin. Within moments, he had appeared again with his rifle, and I began to scream.

He ran up the incline and raised it to his shoulder, leveling it directly at my head and I was sure I would die.

He paused. Seconds clicked by, but at the last moment he stopped. He raised the gun in the air and yelled at the top of his lungs before discharging it into the wood of the old tree.

The cockatoos screamed and the rainbow lorikeets screeched and scattered from the surrounding bush in a rush of panic. The echo of the shot spilled out over the land until it hit the mountains and distantly faded away.

"There is nothing to say. He raped you …"

"No… no, please, I beg you. However it happened, you cannot blame him. He saved my life, you have to try and understand, I was alone …"

"Really, well I understand just one thing… He's an animal, plain and simple."

"He's aboriginal and a man like any …"

"He raped you… And you… you were pregnant with it." His rage was barely contained. He lifted his gun up to my face and pointed the muzzle at me. "I'm not finished with you madam… nor your bastard."

Before I could say another word to dissuade him, he had stormed off to the stable, and moments later he sped off on the gelding.

I sat in the grass, my heart pounding so that it might have been in danger of bursting, then as the fear gave way to anguish, I wept.

My sobs stained the dust on my face, and I dropped my hands to my lap in utter defeat.

Suddenly, in the midst of my tears, I began to pray. "Lord, if there were ever a prayer you can hear of mine, let me ask now. Please protect the innocent and preserve their lives!"

The fig tree shushed with a breeze that blew in from the sea far away. The cane waved, and the crickets began to sing again. All but my small body seated in the dust moved on in peace, sure, I suppose, that the Almighty would do as I had asked even if I was not.

Chapter 16

A s SOON AS Edward had ridden out of sight, I gathered myself from the ground and ran back to the cabin. I pulled my hair back and scrambled to saddle the mare. She could feel my agitation and shifted backwards and forwards, but I hurled myself up on her and took off at a great speed to follow him. I was terrified at what he might do. The mare clattered over the stones of the stream and flung herself up the other side, her flanks streaming and my skirts wet off her sides.

I followed the trail of dust that Edward's gelding had thrown up and realized he had set himself a course to town, perhaps to drown his sorrows or to muster a gang to exact his revenge. Whatever his plans, my heart pounded as I turned the mare toward Cairns and pressed her as fast as was sensible without running her into the ground.

A little, ahead of me, I could see the dust haze of his ride along the track but by the time I reached town he was some half an hour ahead of me.

Riding down Abbott Street, I headed straight for the Empire Hotel, and sure enough, the gelding was tethered on a long rail beside the building with many other horses dropping their heads into a trough of water or nuzzling the horse beside them.

I pulled up alongside, my face wet with a cold sweat and my hands shaking uncontrollably. Sweeping the loose strands of my hair back from my cheeks, I peered over the deck rail with the hopes of glimpsing Edward through the wide door that led into the darkened interior.

From inside, I heard the sounds of a great ruckus and I could hear Edward's voice above the rest.

"Look, I'm telling you, these abos are plain dumb animals, and I swear, they have troubled my farm for the last time!" Edward was stirring the gathering men with the passion of his own frenzy. "I'm not going to stand for my wife to be mucked with—nor handled in any way that a man's property should not be handled." He stopped short of saying I had been raped but implied that danger. "Not one settler would thank you for preserving this group of reprobates. If wolves got on your land, you can't tell me you wouldn't just shoot them."

"Yeah, track 'em down and shoot 'em. They're no better than roos and twice as stupid," one high-pitched voice twitched with excitement in the din.

"And they damage the grass just as bad I say. They are just a pest and they don't belong 'mongst the civilized, taking up valuable land they got no way of making use of," a man yelled from the crowd, and a rise of agreement followed.

Mr. McKenzie from the general store had heard the uproar, as had half the town, and he walked along the sandy path toward the Empire.

I saw him and ran forward. "Oh sir, please, sir... Help me, I beg of you!"

"Lassie, dear Lord, what ails ye?"

"It's Edward... he,... he blames the Malanbarra Bama for my trouble. He thinks that they must have... interfered with me, and ..."

"He is distraught over the child's death I 'spect." He patted my shoulder and I looked up into his sharp eyes.

"I know it is not considered seemly to have been in such a friendly state with aboriginals, but as you know, I managed a good deal of sensible contact, and I cannot bear the thought that their goodness to me is to be repaid with whatever madness he inflicts." I stared deep in his eyes pleadingly. "And I confess I fear his hatred is really a guise to remove them from our land. He will not be satisfied 'til every last one is not just run off, but dead."

"Oh no! Well, that is not right!" He pulled away from me and said reassuringly, "Go to Mrs. Steadman's and calm yourself. I'll find out what's a foot and try to put a stop to it."

I thanked him, but as soon as he strode off in the hotel's direction, I returned to where the horses were tied and waited, not certain at all that Edward could be pacified.

"What goes on here?" Mr. McKenzie asked a patron leaning in the doorway, nodding as he listened to Edward's tirade in the center of a gathering crowd.

"He's from south, near the pyramid, and his missus has been threatened— some say interfered with. She narrowly got away with 'er life, they say ..." He bent his head down and whispered, "an' they say she lost her first kid in childbirth 'cause of it. Man's rightly justified if he shoots them all. So says us all, I'd wager."

"There's no crime in shooting vermin," a man called out from the edge of the group. "No sir, they been raiding all of us, and I been in fear it be our womenfolk was at risk next. Can't go nowhere to do nothing without worry for what's hap'ning at the home front."

Many voices agreed.

"Too right!" the man beside Mr. McKenzie added his approval.

Edward's voice rang out amidst the crowd. "Well, each man knows his own duty, but I'm going to see to it that those black bastards never raise so much as an eye to my farm or my wife again!" He slammed down the beer jug and strode from the hotel, his back slapped as he went, and a cheer of encouragement sending him forth to exact his rage.

"I say, sir... A little calm might be in order ..." Mr. McKenzie tried to catch Edward by the arm as he strode by.

"Leave him alone, McKenzie. He's got to clean out them vermin, and I'm going to do exactly the same." A man snatched Mr McKenzie's arm from Edward who ignored him nd continued out the door. A parade of men spilled out onto the walkway behind him.

Mr. McKenzie watched the tall man mount his horse, and I ducked down behind the barrels against the wall behind the last one in the row to remain unseen.

He spun the gelding around angrily and yelled at the top of his voice, "I'm seeing to the mongrels on my land... If you do the same we will all be the better for it!"

Several of the patrons that had followed Edward out, somewhat worse for drink. They whistled and yelled agreement with fire in their bellies for Edward's cause that they would not be so certain of in the sober light of another day. But fired up by my husband's rant, they now seemed intent on burning and shooting whomever they could and some staggered toward the horses as though they might try, even in the state they were in so late in the day.

Mr. McKenzie gathered one by the arm and laughingly headed the man back inside, declaring loudly that, "'Tis no time for that kind of thing, but surely you will all have another drink on me." The men erupted in cheers, and it seemed that in no time, the would-be vigilantes were soothed into their normal afternoon activities of raising a beer mug and toasting Her Majesty repeatedly.

I watched as Edward, atop his gelding, swung round in the roadway, throwing a last glance at the hotel to see if anyone had followed him. He could see Mr. McKenzie had turned them back in, and I saw him slap his thigh angrily and turn to gallop off toward the south track.

Quickly, I gathered up the mare and headed off inland via the inlet stream, to cut him off.

I shadowed my husband all the way from the township. He turned off the track and followed the trail beside the mountains where he thought the Malanbarra would be at this time of the year, until at last, he found the clan camp.

As Edward arrived on his gelding, the younger aboriginal boys ran full tilt toward the elders in the camp to tell them he was coming.

Rounding the corner of the last bank of trees, he was confronted by six warriors, spears and shields in hand, glaring at him in front of the clan, who watched from the background.

"Where is he?" I heard him spit the words out in an enraged scream.

None could understand him, yet they knew why he was there. I heard them say to each other, "This is the man that is the white woman's mate, I would guess."

"He is here to lodge a complaint."

"I don't think they know how to do that, nor do I think he is going to wait until coroberee at the season turn."

"Nah, this man has got blood in his eyes... He is going to fight him right now."

Edward was oblivious to the remarks, not understanding a word of the language. He kept hauling on the horse's reins and pulling it back and forth as he yelled repeatedly, "Where is that black bastard?"

When no one moved he raised his gun and shot a round into the air.

"Shit!" Djanburra dropped to his haunches and looked up in the air where the crack of sound had come from. "What was that?"

The others had fallen back and now assumed defensive positions.

"This is the stick that blows holes in you without a spear being thrown. Up north, they are talking about it. They point this stick, and then you die."

"Shut up! Tell this mongrel to get off our land. I'm not scared of him or his stick... See he doesn't even get off that animal to fight!" Julladnji raised his shield and spear and shook it in the air so that it vibrated and made a hollow sound against the wind.

Edward kept yelling. His eyes had, in fact, turned red with blood, and his throat also. The sweat poured from his brow and his mouth frothed at the corners.

They could see he was engulfed in rage, and none came any nearer to menace him, not willing to attack a man with a true grievance nor one as mad as this.

"Someone should find Mullegadajawara." A woman yelled from the barrage of howls now streaming from the camp where the women and children stood, shaking their fists, and stamping their feet.

"He is across the river down in the plains, hunting. Send someone to get him."

When I heard them say this I hoped upon hope he could not be found, but I knew he would have heard the shot and would know the direction it had come from. I kept whispering to myself, "Stay away my love. Stay away ..." I held back amidst the trees hoping Edward would realize Mulley was not there and calm so I could try to speak with him, perhaps find some new lie to explain.

Dust began to obscure the outlines of the people in the clearing as it filled the air, yet still Edward sat his horse, pacing back and forth, and screaming.

Mullegadajawara must have started running the instant he heard that distant shot because suddenly he burst through the trees. When he saw the men shaking their shields and spears and the big man atop his horse, yelling words he understood, his blood drained from him, and he stopped dead with his spear jammed in the ground at his side. He saw me, and my expression of terror, and he must have known what had happened and that now, no one was safe.

As soon as Mullegadajawara appeared, Edward hauled the horse around and gouged it in the ribs hard so that the gelding reared slightly and laid its ears back before darting forward as though from a starting gate.

"You black mongrel!" The horse had moved forward barely ten feet before he had raised his gun to his shoulder and fired it.

The bullet slammed into the ground inches from Mullegadajawara's left foot and he ducked reflexively, then turned and ran into the bush.

Edward forced the horse forward and at full speed, crashed through the bush after Mulley.

I ignored the howls of the tribe behind me and cantered off after them, not knowing what I could do.

Edward kept up with Mullegadajawara, who evaded the horse with quick, twisted maneuvers through the trees along the banks of the Mulgrave. I struggled to find my way, and the mare was jostled and hit the trunks of trees as I tried to keep them within sight.

Finally, Mullegadajawara led Edward into the mangrove swamp where the river began to fill with estuary waters from the sea.

There, Edward could no longer ride, and as he saw Mulley dive through a clearing he jumped from his horse and scrambled into the dense undergrowth after him.

Edward thrust his way through like a madman possessed, and indifferent to the gouges and scratches inflicted on him as he followed just behind Mulley, who darted through the branches like a lizard.

I dismounted and dragged myself behind desperately trying to keep up and by the time I could see them clearly I was exhausted, my chest exploding with the effort of trudging through the deepening mud in my long skirts.

At last, I saw that Edward had almost reached Mulley in his frenzy and he dived forward, catching him by the heel and tripping him headlong into the mud at the edge of the water.

"Edward... No, I beg you!" I screamed, but my voice seemed muffled by the dense undergrowth.

"I'm going to kill you, you bastard animal!" Edward's panted and wheezed.

"No...!" I screamed again but my voice dissipated into the trees and was lost in the frantic hiss of splashing water, slipping mud and trees being pulled apart, their leaves shaking, with the men falling through them.

Edward reached forward as the Mulley's skin slipped from his hands, grasping for something to hold onto. But with no clothing on Mullegadajawara, he almost got free and might have escaped.

Edward, possessed with rage, flung himself fully forward again and caught Mulley by his rope-like hair.

Mullegadajawara struggled, his hands reaching up to pull Edward's fists from him. They rolled and fought and mud flung up and covered them as the two puffed and spat, struggling desperately with one another.

The brush and mangrove shoots crushed under them as they cut a swath along the water's edge with their momentous fight. Wrestling with all their strength, the men thudded together, skin on skin, and bone on bone. Edward used his weight to force Mullegadajawara into the water, and the estuary tide made Mulley even more slippery so that Edward lost his grip.

For a moment, he was free. I saw him frantically try to stride away in the mud and knee-high water, only to stumble and be caught again.

Edward grabbed him around his chest, and being heavier and much taller, threw his weight on the smaller man's back, and they tumbled with a splash into the river. The mud underfoot swirled and was dragged away in the current and I pulled myself through the mud in their wake.

Finally, Edward managed to grab Mulley around the neck and his forearm locked tight under his jaw.

Mullegadajawara struggled to free himself, coughing and spluttering through his white teeth, but was clamped tight by the other man's grip. His eyes rolled and he tore his head around to try to face Edward and for a moment, I saw the whites of his eyes and fear on his face. I screamed, "Edward... You're wrong! Let him go... I beg you!"

He ignored me as though he was entirely deaf. I saw him struggle to hold Mulley. Edward could feel his throat slipping under his arm so he forced Mulley down and they fell together into the water. Being twice Mullegadajawara's size he threw his body over him, and locked himself heavily on top of him.

Mullegadajawara kicked and thrashed but Edward had pinned him beneath the surface. He held him under until, little by little, the struggle abated. Eventually, there was no movement at all.

Mullegadajawara lay still, and I likewise seemed to be held in the frozen grip of those moments. He was dead, drowned in the river of his homeland, and as it dawned on me, I began to shake uncontrollably, as though the scream I could not voice in my horror was forcing its way out of my very skin.

Finally, that agony refused restraint, rose up, and erupted from my throat. My knees and joints seemed to give way, and I dropped like a small puppet with its strings cut, into the mud. My skirts flooded around me and my hands fell loose on my lap.

"No... no, no, no... it cannot be!" I began to shudder convulsively as I cried. I looked out to where Edward had done this terrible thing and screamed, "Murderer!"

Suddenly, I leaned over and vomited into the mud. If I could have stopped my heart from beating, that terrible moment would have enabled me to leave this world of my own accord. I wiped my mouth and stared like a blind woman in the direction of that dreadful man.

Edward lifted himself to his knees, his arms in front of him, his hands pressed against the back of my dearest love, laying still in the muddy water, the late afternoon sun glowing on his smooth, dark skin.

He dropped his head as he panted to recover from the fight. Then very slowly, he raised himself from the body and dragged himself to the mud of the shore. Grabbing a small sapling, he pulled himself out and up through the trees. He did not look back, nor did he look to me, my muddy form still lost in the horror of what I'd seen.

My eyes could not leave my beautiful Mulley's body as it floated quietly out into the current and slowly began to drift downstream.

Then I stared at that terrible man who stood for a moment, his hands propped on his knees while he caught his breath. His hair had flopped over his face and he kept his eyes clamped shut as he restored his composure.

I was weeping and shaking in the mud as the wind suddenly came up. It pushed the leaves and they hissed above men as though they were an angry crowd furious at the acts of this interloper just as I was.

"If I had your gun... I would turn it on you ..." I whispered as Edward turned and looked back out into the river. Mulley's body had already moved some twenty yards west, and he watched coldly as the small hump of his back, buttocks, and heels slid even further toward the distant mouth of the river.

Suddenly, we both heard the sound of movement in the trees behind us and he turned quickly.

I watched as nine Malanbarra warriors paced quietly through the trees, each with his shield and spear and their faces painted. They were spread out and stepped through the mangroves as though the trees themselves had suddenly grown legs and come to join the attack.

"Djanburra …" I called out shakily, but not one head turned to look at me. They walked past me so near that I could smell the salt on their skin but gave no sign to acknowledge my presence. Steadfastly, they moved silently through the trees ahead and into the light glittering off the river.

Edward saw the young warriors at a distance and scanned the trees but there was no way out or back to his horse without being caught. He must have realized there was no escape, so he stepped back and slipped into the water where he could conceal himself. He dropped into the cool current and eased himself out and along the edge of the trees until the mangroves thickened and the air roots showed where the sea was beginning to mix, carrying its mud along the bank.

Gently, he slid low and let the current carry him along the edge. Very slowly, he moved along the bank as his adversaries' voices searched for his marks. They seemed to be confused, and their voices began to head off away from the river. Then, suddenly, there they were. They stood still and silent in a group and Edward's stomach must have turned to ice, because I could see he froze where he was. I sat dumb and dazed barely wondering what would now happen to us.

Then, all at once, they dropped their spears to their sides. They seemed no longer ready for attack, but were watching him. One nodded towards the river and they all turned and looked past Edward and I thought they must have been searching out Mulley's yet they looked upstream. Like a gathering of stone statues, they simply stared and then they turned in unison and stepped back into the trees.

I watched them and I wondered if it was because of me that they seemed to have lost their interest.

For a moment Edward's breathing eased and I saw a look of confidence cross his face as though he might have thought he had evaded them. Yet, it was obvious they had seen him as clearly as I could.

Just as Edward began to relax a little, a sudden rush of water flowed up and over his shoulders. Before he could even get out a cry, I saw his eyes widened to the sharp pain and sound of cracking bones in his legs. He was pulled backwards from the bank with such speed that his head created a wake for some ten feet or more before he gurgled out a cry and was pulled under the green water.

I jumped and my eyes widened in shock as the unearthly wave took him.

A second or more passed, then the surface broke. I saw the upward swing of his torso, and the rolling body of a fifteen-foot estuarine crocodile. It must have been attracted by Edward and Mullegadajawara's splashing in the river shallows as they fought.

The patterned white underbelly of the monster swelled in the water, and his olive green tail flicked across the surface like a jagged snake as he tore Edward's legs from their hip sockets.

Edward would have seen nothing more than his own blood filling the water and his arms flailing about in the bubbling swirl of the river before the sound of his screams died and his vision sank into darkness along with his life.

I could barely breathe as I watched the water become quiet and the stain of red drift away.

Edward was dead. He had murdered my dearest Mulley and now had himself, been killed. I knew his body would be dragged to some deep hole to rot and be eaten, and I would now be alone with the horrors of my dreams with all that had happened.

"My dear Lord... both dead?" I whispered to myself. Then some strange refusal overcame me. "Mulley... you cannot be dead!"

I struggled to my feet, hauling myself up with the help of a mangrove trunk and waited, staring out beyond the ominous spot where Edward had been. I strained to see if Mulley might rise from the bank on the other side, wet and sleek and alive, his would be murderer now gone from between us.

The Malanbarra warriors were walking back toward me. I could hear them speaking to each other quietly, and I expected them to greet me. Instead, they walked past with their eyes focused on the way back out through the mangroves. Not one looked up.

"Djanburra... I want my son back. Please, I must come with you. I want my son!" I yelled, but still no one would pause or look to me. As I watched their backs disappear amidst the trees, I heard an emotionless voice speak out of the shadows. "Mullegadajawara dead... His son have no mother. His son is ours."

"No! I want my son back... You cannot have him!" I ran through the trees, slipping and falling to my knees again and again as the warriors disappeared.

By the time I had escaped the swamp and found the mare I was whispering frantically to myself over and over, "They cannot have him... Mulley must tell them, they cannot have him."

I mounted and kicked the mare so hard that she cried out in a piercing whinny and reared, but I forced her forward, and at breakneck speed rode back to the Malanbarra camp.

As I held onto the reins, my arms thrashing over the saddle, my mind fought with me. As I tried to believe he was not gone, it kept raising the image of Mulley floating away. With the trees thrashing around me, I felt my sanity gently float away with him, my soul still caught in his lifeless arms, and we drifted silently down the estuary to the sea.

The only thing that held me tight to my saddle and the stinging reality of my frantic ride, was the thought of my dear baby. I determined that whatever the world would think or might do, I would have him alive in my arms, and no one would separate us again.

Chapter 17

THROUGH THE TREES and across the grasslands, I rode. My tears came and went in fits and the mud on my skirts dried quickly and the crust crackled and fell as I went, leaving pale, powdery streaks all over my skirts.

When I arrived at the clan camp, I dismounted hurriedly and threw the reins into the bush, not even bothering to tether the mare properly.

As I walked into the open area before the burrus, I saw several people I knew, and the old woman was seated near a cooking fire ready to prepare the evening meal. Tears welled up and I cried out, "Menge, he's dead… Edward is dead! I'm free at last! Do you hear, free?"

The old woman shifted slightly and stopped sorting a pile of green leaves and vegetables. I walked quickly to her and expected her to greet me. Instead, she lifted herself wearily and hobbled into her burru, ignoring me.

"Please, where is little Jaimie?… I need to see my son."

The younger women also paused in their work and walked away, and I dimly saw several of the warriors hanging back in the shadows of the trees, watching but not acknowledging that they knew me.

"Please… where is my son? Someone tell me where he is!"

As I turned and took a step toward a young man, he turned and disappeared into the undergrowth and I was left alone in the clearing.

"Answer me... I want my son!" I cried out loudly.

For some minutes, I looked about in desperation. I went to the first burru and peered in, a rude and clumsy imposition that no Yidinji would commit. A woman and a young boy stared blankly back from the darkness. I pressed her to tell me where Jaimie was, but she turned her head away and refused to utter a sound.

I scrambled to two more burrus, searching for any sign of my child, but no one spoke and he was nowhere to be found.

When I reached the burru of Menge, I went to crawl in, sure she would see my agony and take pity on me, but as I kneeled and began to crawl in, pleading with her as I went, a spear came down sharply in front of my eyes from behind me and barred my way.

"You have no part here... go!" Was all the old man would say as he stood outside Menge's burru.

I looked up into his hazy old eyes, milky with time and sun, and whispered, "My son... He's mine."

"Go!"

He raised his voice and hit the earth in front of my hands with the spear tip. A puff of dust scattered on my fingers.

Suddenly, I felt cold and frightened. I got up slowly, brushing the dust from my skirt and turned quietly to leave the collection of dwellings. I mounted the mare and sat atop her for some time, leaving the reins loose, while she grazed among the trees just outside the clearing, oblivious to my distress.

I stared toward the camp and cried silently, hoping upon hope that someone would bring out my child.

For a long while no one ventured forth. I saw an occasional face peer from a dark shelter and then retreat hurriedly.

After what seemed an eternity, a darker shadow appeared in the trees beside me. It was Djingelagar. He had his shield in his hand and a spear already raised at his shoulder.

"Get out of here, 'she-dingo'… Go back to your crazy kind. Don't come here again!"

I got such a fright at his outburst that without thinking I grabbed up the reins, swung the mare around, and galloped off through the trees, bouncing and swaying wildly as I went.

The low boughs swatted my face and body, and I choked on leaves and tears as the mare dived headlong through the scrub and the growing darkness, in no particular direction.

Finally, far from the camp, she slowed and stopped, and at last I was alone. I wept in agonizing bouts of misery, flopped over her neck in the middle of nowhere.

Eventually, I ran out of tears and was left numb. I pulled myself up and wiped the hair and tears from my face. I couldn't think what I should do. I looked around to see where the mountains were and picked my way in the direction of the peaks I knew until I came out on the track leading to the town.

When I reached our roadway, I stopped and waited at the junction as though some part of me was deciding if I should carry on and seek the comfort of my own kind or bury myself at Notre Maison. I looked up the long roadway and then down the track to my farm. It's call made me pull the mare's head around and in a daze, I set off in the direction of home.

I slept that night as if I had also died, and woke the following morning to the realization that the day before had not been some terrifying nightmare, but real. The emptiness of my heart made me feel entirely alone even though the workers busied themselves about the farm because it was Saturday. I sat on the porch and stared out at the mountains beyond the stream, trying to think what I should do.

I could not summon the motivation to attend to anything and so languished in the shade of the porch watching the grass shuddering and the trees gently swaying in the sea breezes as I rested my soul.

The sun was quite high already when a sharp cry pierced my trance and a man's voice wafted up from the direction of the stream.

"Go on 'round. I'll see to this one."

I looked toward the sound of the voice, which came from the direction of the track that disappeared down to the stream crossing. Soon, a man's head, then his body leading his horse behind him, appeared as it came up the incline. I stood up and watched him as he waved out and walked toward my cabin.

" g'dday missus. Name's Peter Mathieson. We is setting out to visit all the settlers in these parts to warn 'em."

"Oh, what do you mean sir?" I replied dreamily.

He frowned at the sight of me. "Well, you best head off into town for a while and send your workers home. There's been quite a ruckus in these parts. It's said a man's been killed by the natives who are harassing and causing trouble all around this area. They is saying that they're molesting women now. Best you set off into town, and you tell your husband he can join us to sort them out, good an' proper."

I knew instantly how this rumor had begun, and I should have spoken up then and there and let the truth be known. I suppose my mind was fixated on nothing but my dear little boy and I had no thought to be truthful. Even so, some part of me whispered to preserve myself in front of this man who would condemn me as worse than a harlot if he knew how I had known the Yidinji. So my eyes drifted off to the distant mountains, and with a voice as innocent as melting butter in a child's mouth, I concealed the truth.

"My husband is… away hunting, and I cannot leave for fear he will not know where I've gone. There is no trouble here, sir. Best you go on your way." I turned away nonchalantly, and the man shook his head somewhat angrily.

"Well, as you wish, missus, but be it on your head! We're set to drive them black fullas off this stretch and deal to the men that have done these crimes, so you better be looking out for any that run off this way. Stay close to your buildings and go down to the river only at noonday. We'll look in on ya, if we can on, our way back."

I did not reply. My mind was drifting and dizzy, and I simply went into the cabin and closed the door. I heard his horse gallop away, and then

I moved about the cabin without purpose, shifting the odd ornament and smoothing creases from the coverlet.

Finally, I sat on the bed with my hands clasped tight on my lap. The hours seemed to merge into one, and the whole day moved about me while I sat still in its center, unmoving. At almost dusk, I heard Sung call out that he and the rest were going home and he would see me Monday. I did not reply.

As the night began to fall, I heard many gunshots rebounding off the mountains. I stood up and went out on the porch and listened curiously, but it did not register what the distant gunfire might mean.

As the light faded, I wandered into the cabin again, singing a Malanbarra song about the seasons changing and the wallaby grazing near the river, and lay down, possessed by a waking death. I fell into a cold sleep, still in my muddy clothes of the day before.

When the morning woke me, my body reminded me that I had not eaten for two days but no morsel could tempt me. As I drew a cup of water from the barrel beside the cabin, again a volley of shots rang out somewhere in the distance.

I looked up in surprise, and as though awakened abruptly, I realized the sounds were coming from the clan camp area. A shudder took hold of me and I dropped the cup on the ground and ran to the stable.

The mare was not there but wandering about on the grassy incline, still saddled and caked with dust and dried mud.

"What on earth? ..." I whispered to myself, as I realized time had gone by and I had not been aware of it.

I walked over to the mare, gathered the reins, and led her back to the stable. I checked the saddle's girth strap and mounted, then set off for the camp. As I took the incline down to the river I wondering if I should be turned away again or whether I could bargain with them. Perhaps they would accept my help with the vigilante settlers in return for my son.

As I rode, I could hear periodic shots ring out in different directions, some on the hills north, some higher in the mountains.

When I came closer to the path that led to the camp, it had an eerie quality and the mare shied several times and flattened her ears.

I too, had a sense of foreboding, and as we walked through the silence, I was suddenly stopped in my tracks by the sight of a dark body lying in the grass to the side of the track. It lay face down, spread-eagled, and a warrior's spear and shield lay on the ground some distance away.

I had to urge the mare to go forward as she was not at all inclined to go near, but soon was near enough to see if it was someone I recognized. The young man had been shot and the blackened wound in his back where a bullet had entered caused me to cover my face with my hand in shock. Several flies buzzed over it. I swallowed hard, and the mare stepped back a pace or two. The shield that lay fallen in the grass had been split and the clear imprint of a horse's shoe showed where it had been trampled underfoot.

I forced myself to look at the body, not registering who it was but realizing he was indeed Malanbarra, and my heart sank. A chill filled the pit of my stomach as I remembered my dearest Mulley.

Moving on, I summoned up my courage and trotted down the path quickly to the campsite, terror growing with every step.

When I arrived, instead of the hum of activity of women working and singing, stillness greeted me.

The camp was deserted, the burrus were torn apart, and several had been burned. I dismounted and walked into the clearing, my whole body shaking. There was no one to be seen. Suddenly, I looked up and then, inexplicably, I felt drawn to walk beyond into the fringes of the forest as though someone had called out loud and I followed the sound of their voice.

I never reached the trees.

As I walked past the circle of destroyed dwellings, I stopped. All around me were strewn the bodies of children and those of two women who had been beaten and lay face up, their legs apart and their faces black with blood and debris.

I screamed and dropped to my knees beside the first body. It was the young girl who had first laughed and then helped me learn to make my first dilly bag.

"No... no!" I cried as I lifted her cold hand in mine and clasped her stiff fingers in my own.

A buzzing sound filled my ears and the daylight faded to an inky blackness. I coughed a little and struggled to take a breath as I dropped back on my haunches and let go of her hand.

"What have I done? ..." I choked the words out and looked up into the hills hoping some had escaped and would hide themselves in the forest, my son with them.

For hours, I sat in the grass unmoving and barely breathing amidst the dead in the heat of the sun. All seemed too terrible to me.

Finally, a huge flock of cockatoos landed in the trees above me and their screaming cries seemed to rouse me.

I got up and stood looking at them, and one bird from among the fifty or so others dropped from his perch to the ground and began to search among the grass for seeds. I watched him distantly as he began to wander toward me and I stepped forward away from the bodies to look at him. He continued pecking at the ground, and then stopped. He cocked his head and looked up at me with one black eye. We both stood still, studying one another.

In my madness, I was certain he would speak and give me some of the wisdom he had shared with the old man, but he did not.

Suddenly, I yelled out angrily, "Jahan-gu mahan dilk-ga, ginggu-nanda-n-ngana?"

At the sound of my voice, the bird flicked his yellow crown up with a sharp movement of his head. I felt shame overwhelm me at having spoken to him in the Yidinji tongue as though I now had no right to speak it. I repeated my question in English, whispering as my heart broke with his silent judgment, "Please... why are you staring at me?"

He let out a loud screech and lifted off the ground in a flurry of wide, white wings, and flew back to the tree of his noisy companions.

I dropped to the ground defeated and sat dumb in the dust.

Then with a flurry of brilliant feathers and loud screeches, the flock broke my daze as they lifted off to forage higher in the rainforest canopy.

I took their departure as a sign and said, "Oh yes! Quite right! I must go home... Mulley might come with little James... I must wait for them," I whispered to myself, lost in my distorted world. My madness dangled dreams in front of me of Mulley swimming free once he had disappeared around the river bend and that he was not drowned at all.

I got up as though rising from a pleasant picnic, turned and strode through the bodies as though they were not there.

When I returned to Notre Maison, Mr. Sung was there to greet me.

He held the mare by her head and said, "Missus B., police been here. Come, I talk to you 'for they come back ...'" He frowned deeply as he saw the disheveled state I was in, my hair streaming out and matted with twigs, and my dress torn and muddy.

I suddenly felt obliged to reassure him and said quite stiffly, "Mr. Edward has gone missing... I have been searching for him... He's gone missing you know."

"Ah, Missus B., come, come, sit down here. Sung will get tea for you... You sit here... Be al' right, okay?" He disappeared and in a little while reappeared with a full pot and a cup.

As I drank it, he sat with his gnarled hands under his chin, propped up on his elbows on the table watching me.

"You better now?"

"Thank you, much better," I said dreamily.

"Bad news, Missus B.... Police come. They say Mr. B. has... been killed by them black fullas. I so sorry, missus. Sung so sorry. But you not worry, Sung not leave you... We stay and keep farm going, and you rest up." He went to pat my hand but then thought better of it and withdrew it to rest in front of him. "You want Sung to fetch Mr. Jonathan or churchy people?"

"No thank you... I feel a bit tired, actually. I must get some rest... I'm waiting for ..." I trailed off, and Mr. Sung frowned again, no doubt noticing my fractured state.

"Sung will get bath for you, an' better get some food, eh missus?" He stood up as I did, and I smiled for the first time in what seemed like a lifetime.

"Thank you... A bath. Yes, a bath."

After I had become more composed in the care of Mr. Sung, several days flowed by with little to tell one from another. The stream of time was only punctuated by the return of the police officer for the district, and he repeated what Mr. Sung had already told me.

I did not divulge what I knew, I simply let them announce that "savages" had 'most likely' killed Edward because they had found the tracks of a large warrior group and Edward's horse caught in the mangroves. They had not found his body but had found a shoe and his belt.

He told me to be careful if we traveled away from the farm. Vigilantes had been active in the area, and the police could not guarantee anyone's safety until things settled down a bit. He told me furious reprisals from angry settlers had erupted throughout the district to "clear" the area of "troublemakers." It seemed uncontrollable now: these renegade men were determined to live uninterrupted by the aboriginals also trying to live on the land. He also told me the parishioners and mission people were working feverishly to get the remaining aboriginals to "come in" and had offered them safety, but that none had thus far been found.

I listened somewhat disinterestedly, my heart cold and switched off and I continued to hide the truth. Whenever I looked up to the mountains covered in deep rainforest, all I could think about was little Jaimie in the arms of an "auntie," safe from the madness down here on the plains. In the blink of an eye, everything had changed and I knew down inside me, deeper even than the dark green pool, that it would never be the same again. Everything beautiful, good and pure, was over.

After the officer left, the days turned into weeks and those into several months. The world around Notre Maison seemed to settle. We ceased to hear gunshots, and dawn and dusk came and went as though what had happened might have only been a misprint in the annals of history. The earth absorbed the bodies of the dead, and emptiness filled the bush and creeks and wide expanses of grasslands. The wallaby returned to foraging, still looking around warily for the hunters, but none came. I retreated into the silence of my mind and lived like I was already dead.

Mr. Sung burnt off the fields and then cut and bundled the cane stems. Edward had been right. The smell of caramel filled the air along with a strange purple haze that made it look as though it were the end of the world, as the sun dimmed and turned orange as it passed overhead.

At the end of the season he brought in the maize crop and cleared the fields and another season ended and waited to begin again.

I ate little, laid about lethargically, and did only what came upon me at the moment and with no recognition of the days. I was consumed with the idea that I must wait and that something would bring about the return of the Yidinji and my son with them.

Every night, I languished in fits of inconsolable grief, and in the day, I wandered about desolate and heartbroken. My skin became pallid, my eyes dark and shadowed, and my skirts could not disguise the thin frame beneath from even a casual glance.

Mr. Sung watched my degenerating condition with concern and soon could bear no more, going into town and again seeking out Jonathan Stanford to come and see to me.

He visited me perhaps three times, and each time he begged me to abandon life at the farm.

"Margaret, dear lady... I urge you, please come into town and let the good people of the fellowship care for you. Surely, you cannot deny that Notre Maison is no place for you at present."

"I have renamed it Ulmarra." I looked up at him and smiled somewhat falsely, "It's the name the Malanbarra had for this place before we came. It means 'a bend in the river,' and the deeper meaning is 'a place that changes your direction.'"

"Really, Ulmarra, you say. Well that is somewhat curious, but whatever pleases you. Surely you cannot still think that you should stay out here alone?"

"No, Jonathan, I simply cannot leave now."

He swung around toward me, and with a deep frown of consternation he said, "Margaret, please... I beg of you, hear what I have to say!"

"No, no... no! I cannot go... They might come back. Don't you see? I have to be here in case they come back."

"I don't know who you're talking about, but my lady, take a look at yourself!"

He swept around as though connected to my skirts while I twisted to avoid him.

"You cannot live out here and not take a care for yourself ..."

Finally, he stopped me and grasped my upper arms, pulling me around to look into my gaunt and white face. "Margaret... please. Come into town with me. I shall watch over the farm and... well, if anyone turns up, I shall be obliged to tell you. What do you say, Margaret? Come now, you can trust me—you know that! I just cannot bear to see you like this a moment more. It's not natural."

"Jonathan, I thank you... I do. But there are things I cannot say, as I'm sure you will not understand. I must stay in case they come. They have... children that will need my care and protection. You see, they helped me, and I cannot now abandon them."

"Ah! I see. You're speaking of your aborigines. Oh, you are most noble, but Margaret, have you not heard, they have all been packed up and taken to the mission at Yarrabah? There's nothing you can do for them now."

"Yarrabah? Jonathan, I didn't know!" I suddenly began to move with renewed animation. "When... when did this happen? I must go to the mission at once!"

"Margaret, please you must consider matters sensibly. These are savages and not for you to concern yourself with."

"No Jonathan, you don't understand. I have an interest in them... They helped me stay alive out here... I simply cannot abandon them."

"Well madam, if you must... I shall go with you."

"Jonathan... you do not need to do that."

"Margaret, there is a whole district to cross, and I can't imagine that you would go there without an escort. There are still some wild ones loose out there."

"They know me. I have nothing to fear."

"Perhaps it is as you say... But they're also now angrily aroused, and who can say if you would be safe even among the friendlier ones."

"I shall go this hour, sir, whatever you say!"

"Well madam… This is certainly unplanned… What if we should go on the morrow, instead?"

"No sir, I mean to go now, this very morning!"

"Well, if you must… you leave me no choice. I shall get the horses ready, and a packhorse, I suppose."

"Thank you, Jonathan… I am indebted."

He turned to go to the stable to saddle my mare while I turned to gather some provisions, but before he disappeared from my view, he called back. "Indebted you are, madam… and I mean to have you truly consider what I have offered and come away from this farm and into town directly after this visit to the mission—if only for a while. What do you say?" He paused and looked back to me as I busied myself with renewed energy.

For a moment, I stopped and was caught by his gaze. "We shall see, all right? I won't say more than that."

"Well all right then, madam, we shall go on this wild goose chase, and I will be happy to have at least the consideration of my idea until you come to your senses."

The trip to Yarrabah was a hot and strangling affair. We took the horses around the end of the inlet, across the wide plain of dense bush and over the other side to the headland.

A track had been cut for the mission and it followed several rocky bays. Unlike the interior, the headland was dry, strewn with spinifex grass and fallen leaves from the rock-hugging eucalyptus.

I stayed silent on the journey. My mind was on Mullegadajawara and our son. I hoped upon hope that we would come to the mission camp and find the remaining Malanbarra Yidinji standing there, my son among them.

Jonathan tried for a time to hold up a conversation single-handed, but by the time we reached the base of the track that led over the headland, he had realized the effort was futile.

We rode side by side, the packhorse behind, but I avoided letting him see my face. Knowing he watched me as I rode sidesaddle beside him, I was sure he felt pangs of compassion for my solitary state, but I was not sure that this was entirely the result of Christian affection alone, and I berated myself for allowing him to accompany me.

When we rounded the high ridge that guarded the beach on the eastern side of the peninsula, the mission camp appeared below us. It had come about when a bedraggled group of some thirty aboriginals had fled their lands looking for somewhere safe to live. They had been discovered by some parishioners of the Anglican Church, who had built shacks for them, and a priest now had oversight over them all. More had been added until quite a village had grown on the shores of the Coral Sea. Without concern for tribal boundaries, the missionaries gathered aboriginals from the whole coast, so that every clan and even tribes not of his own territory now mixed together.

As we rode down the track, we could see the sad collection of dusty dwellings and canoes hauled up on the sandy shore. A group of dark men and women gathered under the trees or sat nearby.

As we entered the camp, a dog greeted the horses, raising its nose into the air to interpret the new scent that had been brought into its domain.

Dark faces appeared from rough-made tin shanties. Straggling grass fringed the pole foundations that raised the shacks slightly above the clay-and-sand ground.

"How will we find them?" I was scanning every face as we passed and soon, a line of aboriginals seemed to fan out either side of us as though we were the only attraction in a parade.

"I suppose we must find the priest in charge of this place. It looks like there is a building of some kind ahead."

Jonathan trotted a little in front of me.

"They will hate it here," I whispered to myself and to my horse's head.

The faces that peered at us did not smile, and their clothing looked heavy on their shoulders. Children peered from around their mothers and aunties, and I felt a pang of desperation for the baby I had abandoned to the clan that had lived under the mountains beside the river.

"Sir!"

A voice in the center of a swarm of white linen–garbed aboriginals and sisters of the faith called out.

"Good day, father." Jonathan dismounted and led his horse forward to the rail as he began to speak directly to the man who stood among the aborigine and women.

"I apologize for arriving without a letter of introduction, but I have brought this lady, who has a great deal of Christian conscience, and ..." he turned back to me to help me dismount, "... seeks to find the aborigines who lived on her land, as she has a special compassion for them."

He lowered me to the ground, and I smiled and nodded to the group.

The priest clasped me by the hands and looked into my face. Then he smiled and turned back to Jonathan, who continued to explain as I stood silently in the gaze of the priest's clear blue eyes.

"I believe that they, rightly or wrongly, have suffered in a matter of judgment against them by various vigilantes, and have thus been removed from their place and brought here."

The priest nodded knowingly and let go of my hands as he turned to address Jonathan. "Well, that is most likely so. We have been the open house that has preserved what remains of this childlike and un-endowed people, and if they have been moved off, they will be here. What clan does the lady know them to be?"

The priest rested his hand on Jonathan's back and ushered us toward the open door of the house.

I finally spoke, saying, "They are from the river Mulgrave, the river people called the Malanbarra Bama ..."

I had turned aside at the doorway, not eager to be moved into the building, which made of timber and iron and seemed designed to capture the heat of the coastal sun rather than repel it.

"The Malanbarra Bama camped at the western end of our acreage," I continued. "There was some trouble, and they have been wrongly dispersed. I hope to find any of them and hope they might tell me of certain individuals who... were very kind to me. I owe them a certain debt of concern."

The priest gathered me in the small of my back and I walked reluctantly through the opening into the shadows of the interior ahead of him.

"Ah, my dear, I shall attempt to assist you, but I warn you now, most do not come in but lose themselves deeper in the jungle. They have want to carry on their heathen life and trouble the new settlers with disastrous consequences to themselves. Your Malanbarra bama may well have disappeared into the Lamb Range and live by raiding and theft."

"Well, that may be so of others, father, but these people were nothing of that sort. They were peaceable to all of us who settled in that area."

"Well, not all are so willing, it seems, to let them live in peace, daughter. Instead, I think they're of a mind to annihilate all trace of them, which is why we have formed this enclave. I don't say that it's ideal... no ..." He seemed to lose his concentration as offered us a seat at a wide, heavy table and seated himself.

"But," he continued, "this is our service to God, and we make every attempt to teach them, convert them, and prepare them for what life they may have as law-abiding persons." He shook his head as though he understood this was an impossible task, and then called over a young woman whose face was as black as ink in the dark room.

Slowly and carefully, he spoke to her in a kind of broken English to explain that we searched for the river people.

She nodded with wide eyes and quickly darted from the room, keen to oblige the man and his new visitors.

My eyes followed her and I leaned forward in my chair as though to launch myself in pursuit. "Father, if I may, I would like to go with her and see if there is someone I can recognize."

The priest frowned and looked across to the door, then deciding to accommodate my request, he called out the woman's name.

A few moments went by, and when she did not reappear he raised himself from the chair with a screech and walked to the doorway. "Mary, Mary... stop girl! Take this dear lady with you."

My heart lifted. "Oh, thank you, father, I'm much obliged." I stood, barely glancing at poor Jonathan. Then, realizing my discourtesy, I turned and gave him a shaky smile.

"Jonathan, thank you. I don't know what I can say. I'll go and look, and if I can find them, I'll come back and get you. Is that all right?"

He sighed, shaking his head slightly, but smiled back. He looked at me as though I were as delicate as the wing of a dragonfly. My face must have showed the anguish that comes from trial and tragedy, and his face reflected this in its pity.

"Of course, my dear… Do as you wish."

I ran from the porch and flew across the dry clay roadway toward the waiting Mary, who had stopped and turned when she had heard the priest's call.

Quietly, I walked alongside her, and nothing broke the silence as we moved to the side of the road and stepped along in the late afternoon light coming through the overhanging trees.

I watched as we passed the small shacks that we had first seen entering the camp. The faces that glanced curiously from the doorways seemed a shadow of the happy people they ad once been. Their black skins were clothed in European garb as they had been in Cook Town, but these people were not yet converted to that halfway existence that I had seen there.

I began to speak to Mary in Yidinji that I had learned from Mulley. "There is a child, Jaimie, the son of Mullegadajawara, and I want to find him."

Mary stopped in her tracks and swung round, grasping my hands together and giggling in spontaneous surprise at hearing her native tongue from the mouth of this small, white Englishwoman perhaps only a little older than she.

"You know us!" she replied in Yidinji. She smiled widely and her coffee-colored eyes sparkled between the black lashes, oiled and long, that ringed them perfectly. "You got Malanbarra accent. Me, I's a Mandigalpi Yidi." A shadow passed over her face. "I only one of my's family here …"

"Do you know if the Malanbarra are still in the mountains or have come here?" I asked.

"Not all that clan come in to us but I know of the old one, Menge, and some of her lot that's here."

"They're here?"

"Some here. Some, still in mountains and… lot been killed 'cause they not come in and they blamed for stuff they not do."

I dropped my head and did not disguise my sadness. "Are there any children?"

"A few. No little ones."

"Oh …" I felt my heart drop.

When we arrived at the area where the remainder of the river people now lived, I could see a small shed and a dark doorway. Seated on the boards inside the doorframe was the outline of an old woman.

"Who is it?" She called from within in Yidinji Yidi, and the girl called Mary approached in the style of protocol that asked permission to speak to her.

"It's Mary. Mother… I come to bring a visitor. She is looking for someone."

I stepped forward and lowered my head.

"Ahhh!" The old one let her cold gaze rest on my head and shoulders. "You're too late! No more Malanbarra Bama for you to steal with your witchcraft. You brought all this on us, and we've lost our world, our lives, our people …" She poked out her tongue and removed something with her fingers. "See, we too, now live in shelters that cannot be moved."

Mary translated for me but I understood Menge and replied slowly and Mary listened and frowned. "Forgive me… I cannot bring back the time." I looked up and the old woman could see my sincerity and the pain scarred in my face as if by the claws of some monster that had ravaged me and left me permanently marked. "The message man? …" I stuttered.

"You're seeking a dead man," she said with cold indifference. "He is still walking around. He has no dreaming place because of you."

I swallowed hard. I knew she referred to Mullegadajawara's ghost and that now, she or, any aboriginal could not speak his name. They believed that if he was called by name he would haunt them and never go to his rest. She looked up into my eyes searching the glaze that my madness had left there.

"No, mother, I seek his child. Is he still alive? Where is he?"

"He is not with us. He's been taken to the town where those men with no rules come from. They are nesting there like bush bees always ready to sting."

"He has been taken to Cairns? Why?"

"Because he's tainted with your color, foolish girl."

"Who has him? Where?"

The old woman lowered her head and stayed silent.

"Wherever he is, I must find him. Surely you understand, mother... he is my son."

"Now you want to find the one you threw away and would not give milk to?"

"I had to. It was the only way I could save his life... Menge, you cannot understand the way of my people."

"Silly girl! If I do not understand, I wonder why I sit here in a place that is the land of Kunganji and mourn the spirits that once laughed with me and wove the split cane into baskets at my left and my right.

"If I do not understand, why do I cry for the cassowary that does not speak except in secret and the canoes that only go out from this place now to take fish without sharing rights being given?

"If I do not understand, how is it that I'm old and can remember what was and the story of our people and am not allowed to teach it?"

She finished her speech on a loud, high-pitched note. The words spilled out angrily and her frown deepened every line in her face.

I felt the cold hatred in her and her deep inconsolable sadness, and I backed away from the door without responding. I turned and began to run down the roadway and back to the mission house. Strands of hair came loose and fell around my shoulders and my eyes blazed with stinging tears.

When I arrived back at the house, Jonathan was standing to the side of the door smoking a pipe. He saw me as I rounded the bend and took his pipe from his mouth and struck it against the wall to empty it. Then he quickly came down the steps to meet me. He could see I was greatly troubled and he reached out for me, clasping my limp arms to pull me to him.

"Margaret, for Heaven's sake, what is the matter?"

"He's not here... They're not here."

"Oh… Well, that is unfortunate." He looked down at me and frowned quizzically. "What shall we do then?"

"I suppose I shall… I shall have to consider your offer. I think I shall have to go to the town after all." I carefully concealed my real motive and refused to look directly into his eyes.

His eyes widened and he exclaimed his pleasure at my words. "Well, that is good sense talking!" He let go of me, turned toward the building, and smiled modestly, "I suggest we stay here for the night and head back tomorrow. What do you say?"

"Jonathan, I thank you… I know you must wonder what I do, but… I want to go now. I just cannot bear this place. To see it like it is here," I swung my arm around in a wide arc. "It won't be dark for a couple of hours yet, and we can camp along the way somewhere… I'm used to it, it is no bother for me… I simply must get away."

"Well… I suppose so. I don't know what the father will think, but if you insist I shall say our farewells. We can't get more than a few miles, though, before we will have to make camp… But if this is what you want, I will oblige."

He frowned as though for a moment he could see a shadow of insincerity in my face.

"Thank you, Jonathan… I am much obliged, you shall never know how much." I ignored his examination and turned to walk with him to the building to tell the priest our plans. I crossed to the mare as we arrived at the steps. She was tied up at the rail, and I collected the strands of my hair that had fallen and tucked them back in under my bonnet as I waited.

He sighed and turned to go inside.

I climbed up onto the horse and once seated there, I waited for Jonathan to come out from inside the mission house. He appeared again with the priest following him.

The priest came along side my horse and looked up at me. "Well, I'm sorry we could not help you, my dear. Please feel free to come back. We do so like visitors out here." He smiled, and I nodded politely as he went on. "I should have liked to suggest that you stay and eat with us, but as your companion is insistent, we bid you farewell and… bless you." He smiled in such a way as to hint that he could feel the unusual nature of the visit and that he could discern my demeanor as someone deeply troubled with sorrow and guilt. "You know …" he whispered, "God always has a plan. It is true, my dear, for you, as it is for all of us… these people even more so. We cannot always see it… but time has a way of declaring it. We must only have the courage to continue and the faith to believe it will all work out in the end."

I guarded my eyes from the man's penetrating gaze and thanked him as I stared at the saddle and without looking back. Then I turned the mare around gently and walked her back down the roadway.

Jonathan waved good-bye and followed me.

We rode back the way we had come. Back up the track and away from the mission village and the poverty of soul that hovered over that place.

When Jonathan and I arrived back at Ulmarra farm the next day, I packed up my belongings and set off with him to town.

Jonathan Stanford became my new champion. He arranged for me to board again in Cairns township with the accommodating Mrs. Steadman, as I had when I was ill, leaving behind the farm and my little cabin. He also organized Mr. Sung to plant and maintain the fields and introduced me to his fellowship. I confess, it was a comfort for me to be away from the memories of the bush, Mullegadajawara, and Edward.

Little by little, I healed under the comforting habit of prayer and worship and the kindness I received from Mrs. Steadman and the congregation there. My return to health was somewhat spurred on by the promise that little Jaimie might be among the half-cast orphans and dispossessed at a mission created by that fellowship to house these "creamies"—the offspring of local men who had taken advantage of the displaced Yidinji women. As the clans had been dispersed and broken up, many of the surviving women camped near the town in the bush, and unscrupulous men gave them supplies in return for the use of their bodies. The weekly tithes of the parishioners paid for the orphanage and a school built some distance from the township.

A few of the Gimuy-Walubarra had been put into paid employment to care for the orphans, but since they were not permitted actual money they were paid in food, supplies and even tobacco. Mrs. Steadman told me of the mission, and I ached for some pretense to go there and search for Jaimie.

I soon convinced Jonathan that I was well enough again and asked him to find me a starting position at the mission school. He took this to mean that I had a Christian conscience for those people that lived there and for the children, who needed the English language for their futures. In truth, my motivation was far from such noble things.

"Margaret, Pastor Daniels tells me they would be pleased to have you come and mind the smaller children three days a week if it pleases you."

"Jonathan! What can I say? How marvelous! When shall I start? Oh, I shall have to see to my bonnet, it's very much worse for wear... It will not do at all!" I bounced about with excitement at the thought of perhaps finding Jaimie at last.

"Margaret, they're only children, dear lady, I doubt they shall even notice if you have a bonnet."

"Oh Jonathan, you know nothing! Children always notice one's bonnet!" I playfully tugged at his coattail, and then came around before him. "I shall forever be grateful to you sir... Indeed you have been a wonderful friend to me."

I glanced up and caught the faintest look of disappointment in his face. "Something troubles you?" I said as I swept around the table to hold his hand, which lay limp at his side.

"It's just that I fear I shall lose you to the endearing qualities of those little creamies, as I know you're besotted with all things aborigine."

"You know I shall never do that, Jonathan... But it's my calling, if I can say such a thing. I know they must have our help and they have suffered so much already, having no family or clan. So I feel compelled ..."

"Yes, I know." He leaned forward and kissed me on my forehead, and for a moment I felt a slight lightening of my heart and a feeling of safety with this man who had saved me twice over.

I took a deep breath to speak, just as Mrs. Steadman appeared through the door.

"I have wonderful news," I told her, "I shall be allowed to teach the small children at the mission orphanage three days a week. I'm overjoyed, Mrs. Steadman, overjoyed!"

"Well, I can see that, Lass." She grinned and held my hands as I bounced in front of her.

"Best you have an early tea and be off to bed at a good hour. You must see the dean at ten tomorrow to get your starting orders," Jonathan quipped. "And I must take my leave, ladies. I'm off to Ulmarra tomorrow to see what progress Mr. Sung has had with the south field."

I turned. "Oh, are you, Jonathan?... Can you see that my nanny is still all right? Mr. Sung was going to take her to a he-goat so she could kid when the Gurraminya Minya begins."

"Oh my!" Mrs Steadman sucked in a deep breath. "I had quite forgotten how well suited you will be to teach those dear little children some decent language." She turned and nodded to Jonathan as he shook his head at my use of the Yidinji yidi and replied.

"Of course I shall see to it. As always, I will give you a full report on my return." He smiled broadly, touched his forehead politely, and let himself out into the hall.

In the morning, I was awake and up by five, as bright and clear-headed as one who had slept a year. I felt so thoroughly rested as to be able to run against a prime racehorse. The streets at that hour were only just stirring, and I sat and wrote in Mr. McKenzie's journal for a while, then saw to breakfast.

Mrs. Steadman had the cart brought round for me, and off I went to find the mission north of the town on the only road that headed toward the pass between Cairns basin and Smithfield on the other side. The track was smooth, and the trees gave way periodically to fields of tall cane or market gardens laid out in the rich, brick-red soil.

I was excited and slapped the reins on the horse's back until she laid her ears back at me indignantly.

When I arrived, a number of small houses showed where a settlement surrounded a church. A two-story house painted yellow against the green of the surrounding hills stood off to the side. A stream marked the boundary of a good-sized field, and two horses and a milk cow grazed quietly in the morning sunlight.

I pulled into the gravel roadway that swept around to the main buildings and a man walked across toward me as I rode in. He held the horse while I put on the brake and dismounted.

"G'dday, fine morning aint it?" he smiled, and three spaces in his teeth greeted me.

"Good morning, I'm here to see the dean. He's expecting me. I'm Mrs. Bermingham... I shall be here three days a week to teach the little ones."

"Oh, that's very good of ya. I heard they was looking for more help. Seems the little mob grows every week. The creamies are being rounded up and brought here from all over."

"Shall I go in?"

"If you have a mind to. I think the master is down by the stable. If you want, you can walk in the garden over yonder while you wait... got some lovely frangipani out at present—right nice."

"Oh, thank you! I will do just that."

I strode across the yard, through the gate in a low picket fence, and into a small garden area where vegetables grew in one section and a number of roses, now somewhat dwindling, in another. As the man had said, a stand of some seven or more trees spread their shade over the mown grass and several shorter frangipanis grew in a raised garden in the center. Their heavenly scent filled the air. A seat had been strategically placed right in the center of the garden at the end of a little path, and the blossoms were scattered over it and onto the grass like a small snowstorm.

I walked toward it and as I did, I heard laughter and it drew me toward another fence with a similar gate to the first, at the back of the garden.

Suddenly I saw a group of small children, some eating sandwiches or fruit. A white-dressed nurse was watching over them as they played.

At the back of the group a blanket was spread on the grass, and several small babies and toddlers were seated there. A young aboriginal woman, also dressed in white, was tending to them.

In the midst of this handful of tiny children, I saw a child with Mulley's face.

My heart stopped and I gasped. My belly began to shake uncontrollably and my throat flushed and became hot.

"Jaimie," I whispered, and I found myself fumbling with the latch of the gate and scrambling to open it as fast as I could. I stepped through and the first nurse yelled out sternly, "Shut the gate, if you please!"

I did so and composed myself as I walked forward tentatively.

"Are you the new one?" she said.

"Ah... yes. I shall be starting with the under-fives."

"Oh, that is good. We're shorthanded." She looked up at me and smiled.

"May I? ...?" I pointed to the babies on the blanket, "While I'm waiting for the dean."

The woman smiled and nodded somewhat knowingly. "They're rather lovely, aren't they? Just sweet as caramel."

I hardly heard her voice, my eyes were fixed on the little boy I had seen only twice in his life, at his birth and in the arms of Mulley under the trees.

As I sat down on the edge of the rug, quite unconcerned for etiquette, my little son gurgled and crawled forward. He climbed up on my skirts and grasped handfuls of it, pulling it toward his mouth.

I leaned down and hugged him, and for a moment, a kind of cog dropped into place inside me. I had to use every ounce of my control not to cry out with utter joy.

The little boy pulled himself up, and as he did, I grasped his little hands and he held them tightly, tottering on his little fat legs, and smiling broadly at the sensation of standing upright.

"Oh look, Mrs. Lynch! He standin' up." The young aboriginal nurse, seated above me, grinned widely.

"Well I never! The older woman looked up, nodded, and turned back to a little boy who was being a bit rougher than she liked as he played with a wooden horse.

"You gonna be good wiv 'em, lady," the girl said kindly to me.

I couldn't reply. My breath was all but taken away. At last, I had found him, and my misery seemed to fly off into the trees, frightened off by the singing in my soul.

Chapter 18

AFTER I MET the dean, I accepted my new role and settled into my wonderful task.

While some of the children were true orphans, as one might have thought, many of them were the children of aboriginal mothers who, having borne them to unknown white fathers, were not permitted to raise them.

As the mission people found the children playing in the dust or still on the breast, they gave them Christian names and marked them in a register, then came and collected them when they turned three or four. The mothers often tried to hide them, but in the end, the children were taken away.

Little Jaimie was not as they were. He was one of a few children who had survived the slaughter of his clan. He had been discovered and rescued by a logger, who dropped him off like a lost kitten. He was also the only one who had a mother who was of this same infernal breed who had come in conquest without so much as a passing glance for what they destroyed in their wake, though only I knew this.

So his parentage remained hidden as he lived there with the kind missionaries at the orphanage, and the ache in my womb was consoled by seeing him frequently.

I could see my mother in the shape of his eyes and my beloved Mullegadajawara in his face and body. I delighted that at least I could be with him a little and guarded my secret in the disguise of a teacher at the school.

As the weeks and months rolled on, I found Jonathan Stanford beside me at every turn.

He began to call me Maggie, and I realized then that the warmth between us was not entirely platonic. His personality was such that I could indulge in a playful banter which seemed quite natural, and I remembered we had had this comfort from the very start of our meeting in Cook Town. He sometimes seemed frustrated by this light limitation in our relationship, but I had long since separated myself from that part of my heart that was permitted to love or feel those deep yearnings I had with Mulley so I was careful never to encourage him.

One day Jonathan collected me from the school, and on our way back to Mrs. Steadman's he took a turn down a clay track to the stream that followed the road through Smithfield.

"Jonathan! Are you determined to rock me off this cart?" I hung to the rail and lurched from side to side as we rolled down the track with the horse stalling from time to time as she felt the cart come up from behind.

"I have only a mind to wake you to the loveliest of spots... Whoops!" The cart hauled to a stop. "There, we made it!" He declared and after lifting me down, he said, "Well, what do you say, is this not the most delightful place to take a small detour?"

I looked about, and it was true that it was lovely. Though the view did not compare to the sunny afternoons Mulley and I had spent along the rivers of our territory and the waterhole of Ulmarra, I had no wish to disappoint my dear companion. "Perhaps so... It is indeed a pretty place," I said.

"'It does not have half the beauty of you, my dear ...'" He took my hand and then stood beside me looking out over the gentle stream that attracted hovering dragonflies and reflected sunlight onto our faces.

"Jonathan ..."

"Please, Maggie... I simply must say something."

"I beg you, do not."

"It must be clear to you that I am unreservedly fond of you, and ..."

"Jonathan, I beg you do not think of such things. I am clearly fond of you, too, but I have something akin to a 'presence' in my heart that does not permit that kind of affection."

"I know it is nigh on only ten months since... that unfortunate business, but can you not see how well suited we are? ..."

"My dear friend... Such as you would be the pleasure of any young woman, but the things that have happened to me have left me... without that feeling for anyone. Indeed, I do get great pleasure from your company, and I know I shall never be able to repay you ..."

"Maggie, do not say such a thing. You think I am at your side to be paid? I do this as I will, and all I now ask is that you consider me... us. And perhaps one day that 'presence' will be gone and you will learn to love again." He smiled the sort of disarming, humorous smile that took all tension from the air. "I only hope that such a recovery would see me the winner of your affections!" He broke away from me playfully and grinned, "After all, you must let me win at something!"

I did not have the heart to tell him such a thing might never happen, but an odd feeling had come over me as he said the words "you think I am at your side to be paid?" Mulley had said something similar. It had the effect of making one side of me recoil, as though I could not have any other man in my heart as Mulley had been, while another part slightly warmed, even against my will.

The months went on and the subject was not again raised until the wedding of a couple from the church. We all came together to celebrate the happy occasion, and as they said their vows, Jonathan looked across to me. I knew immediately that he had not forgotten his desire. I was a little slow at turning away from his smile, and I suppose that gave him hope to ask me outright the following week as we walked along the esplanade just as the pelicans were walking up the estuary sands to rest on the higher banks out of the tide for the night.

"Maggie, I can wait no longer but feel compelled to ask …" He stopped and pulled me from my stride so that I also stopped between the trees of the walkway. "Please, do me the honor of being my wife …"

"My dear friend… I would have been so pleased to have said yes in another life, but I cannot."

He dropped his head between his shoulders and took two steps to the grass verge, then he dropped to the ground to sit with his arms across his knees. He looked up at me in consternation and nodded to the place beside him, so that I should come and sit with him as he went on. "Why ever not?… I manage well your affairs. I am the sort who is a man of prospects… and I love you!"

I was quite dumbfounded, I confess. I knew these things, but as soon as he said those words, I felt the clouds part and confusion descend.

"What can I say to you? …" I turned out of the pathway and moved to sit beside him with my skirts lightly brushing against his legs. "I confess, I am more inclined to consider… such things. But I still grieve. I still… dream."

"You ask me to wait?"

"I cannot ask you that… But if I shall ever find myself free, I would desire you to ask me again."

"And when should I do this—when we are forty?"

"No, my dear sir… perhaps next year."

"Next year!" He rubbed his forehead, and I knew I asked an unreasonable thing of a man who was strong and well ready for marriage.

"You would press me, sir, and not be sure that your chosen loves you fully in return?"

"No, of course not." He got up quickly and held out his hand to pull me up. "I am in the unenviable position of being in love with you, woman, and therefore it is your wish that is my command.

"You leave me with hope only, that you will find your way to me eventually and put me out of my misery."

"Sometimes… a part of me wants to be convinced." I smiled and gently looped my arm in his.

"Such is my plan," he grinned. Then he changed the subject of conversation, and we walked back to Mrs. Steadman's. I was left wondering, for my part, whether or not I might one day change my mind.

The months went by, and almost eighteen months had slipped past since my love and my husband had departed this world. My little Jaimie was a toddler and had begun to talk, and I delighted in the days with him and the other children at the orphanage and school.

The farm began to present a good profit under the care of Jonathan and Mr. Sung and his workers. I gave them a fair share and frequently went out to the farm to see my nanny and walk about the grounds. Jonathan had built a much larger cabin conjoining the first, with a door through from my bedroom. The new room had a desk and table where he would work and often stay at Ulmarra.

At the end of the Gurraminya Minya of 1880, Jonathan and I visited Ulmarra, and I walked down along to my favorite place in the world and listened to see if I could hear the echo of those happy times with Mulley. Hearing a step behind me interrupt my thoughts, I looked up through the trees as Jonathan appeared.

"Ah, here you are," he said, "like a butterfly hiding in the shade."

"And you… a quick bird looking to catch me out and chase me into the sun to peck off my wings," I said back with a laugh.

"No, I should not like to do that. I should like to gently take you in my hands and make sure no such bird could find you and feed to its babies, but instead you could fly across the flowers of my garden as free as you like." He grasped my hand, and I laughed as naturally as I had in the beginning in this place. Suddenly, he pulled me to him and I felt his lips press against my cheek.

"Jonathan, take a care. You will spoil me."

"Marry me, Maggie… I beg you," he murmured.

I stood still, waiting to hear some whisper from the ghosts of love past. But only the sounds of the weeping fig that shushed in the cool shadows and the quiet riffle of the waterfall through the fern leaves at its fringe filled the space around us. The voice of my beloved was still and I paused and stared down to the water. A leaf floated past my gaze and I let my eyes flow with it until it was out of sight then I looked up at Jonathan.

"Ask me tomorrow... this day is too lovely to answer in. I feel sure I might say yes and I am not certain that I should ..." He shook his head and released me and for a moment, I saw an uncommon expression of annoyance pass his face as he turned and walked back up the track without replying.

I slept in my refurbished cabin that night alone as I once had for long months and stranger times. Jonathan had made up a cot in the sitting room addition. As always, he handed me the key to the door between us and excused himself, and as always I locked the wooden door and he, from my heart.

I lay in the darkness, listening to the sound of crickets outside my paneled walls and the sound of the night birds calling across the darkness. Jonathan's proposal reverberated in my mind and I played out the life I thought I might have with him.

Mulley came and went from my visions. His face shined in my memory and I knew he would have no judgment of me for a single thing I might do.

By the early hours I knew I would never have the love that I'd had with him with any other man, even one as endearing as Jonathan. But I knew the world I now lived in required that I have a husband to protect me, and it was unreasonable to engage Jonathan and prevent him from pursuing another course whilst still desiring his help at Ulmarra.

When I thought of him I found myself "approving" of his qualities. His goodness, his kindness, his humor and his tenderness were admirable, and I realized I could not, in truth, find a fault to displease me. Above all, he had a certain way of giving me leave to pursue my own affairs, and I felt sure, after so long a time, that this man would not turn or become someone I should fear as Edward had done.

By morning, I had decided.

He did not raise the subject even so, and we set off for town. He was somewhat morose and quiet all the way, as I had not shown any clue of my decision.

When we reached Mrs. Steadman's, he led me to the door, and his face showed he was resigned to yet another rebuttal.

"I suppose I should not ask again... for I now fear the answer and have a mind to stop putting myself through such disappointments ..."

I took his hand in mine and very carefully, I placed the key of my bedroom door in his palm.

"Maggie... this is your key!"

"Yes."

His eyes widened and he seemed to take a moment to realize what I had done, then he said, "My God, at last!" He swept me into his arms, and for the first time I allowed myself to feel the comfort and desire one should have for one's future husband.

Mrs. Steadman was delighted with the news and brightly declared, "I had no doubt that you should be wed, children,... but only prayed every night that it should happen before I am too old to enjoy the day!"

And so, Jonathan Stanford and I were married. All the mission people were invited, as well as the church fellowship, and in front of the pews, the children of the orphanage were seated on a woven mat. Seated in the first row on one of the aboriginal nurse's knees was my dear Jaimie. The day was all but perfect as a new part of my life began.

While Jonathan had a proper house built for us at the farm, we boarded in a small upstairs room above the town jeweler, and I carried on working at the mission school.

I taught little Jaimie English daily, along with the other infants and toddlers. He seemed to learn all manner of things quickly, and as he did, I began to hatch a plan.

By the time Jonathan had finished building our new home, I knew what I would do.

The homestead Jonathan built did not resemble those humble and meager beginnings I had known so well. I was well pleased with the wide "Queenslander," with its verandas almost all the way around, facing the stream and waterhole. It entirely consumed the area I had once known as my home, and that helped the memories of my sad days to be eclipsed by our new beginning.

The land stretched out silently now, uninterrupted by trees, and great harvests of sugar cane began to build our wealth. Jonathan purchased new land and expanded our holdings.

It was a great sadness and disappointment for me to have to finally relinquish my teaching position at the mission to move home to Ulmarra, but this departure was also a crucial part of the plan I had been plotting for some time.

I had asked Jonathan to build me a schoolroom attached to the study on the house, which he did gladly, presenting it to me as his belated wedding present along with a magnificent new bed that he had shipped from Sydney.

The schoolroom faced the wide fields and the river boundary, and when the sun set each day, it was the last room to lose the light. He had framed a large blackboard on one wall and set out a collection of tables and chairs. It was wonderful.

"But whom shall I teach, dearest?" I asked mischievously.

He smiled in that gentle way of his and said, "Our own children of course... and any such needy ones you may manage to round up!"

It was typical of Jonathan to consider the children of our workers and those of the neighboring settlers. There was yet to be a state school nearby and wages were too low to allow children to be sent away for such education.

It was my Jaimie that I had counted as the most important student I might have, so I insisted that Jonathan arrange for him to come to the farm and be taught and raised by me, citing that the child had "much potential among the aboriginal children" and needed to be trained in an upright family environment. I made the excuse that he was, by all accounts, one of the last of the Malanbarra, and I desired to do this for them since they had done so much for me.

Jonathan did not once resist me. Being of sincere faith, he was kind enough to do this for Jaimie and for my conscience.

Leaving the mission and the lost souls of his kind, Jaimie came to live with us, and with that, at last, it seemed my odd life had become almost perfect.

We soon gathered a good half dozen of mostly Chinese and South Sea Islander children and began a happy little school that filled my days with satisfaction and joy.

I was acclaimed as a good and kind lady who had considered it no trouble to exercise my Christian duty by bringing this half-cast boy into our very home and educating him along with the local workers' children.

All the while, I kept my secret and guarded my own reputation carefully, and enjoyed my Jaimie, safe with me alone, at last.

It was not long before Miss had other children. Jonathan added to his house a future that poor Edward had never realized, so that by the time Jaimie was six, he had three half-siblings.

Augustina was the eldest. She was headstrong and confident and a natural leader. John, her younger brother, was quiet and mild mannered, and Amelia, was a pretty and pleasant girl who delighted everyone.

I admit that as each pregnancy progressed I would feel a growing fear, and the memory of my first delivery alone in my little cabin would haunt my dreams. A strange distance and loneliness would invade me just before their births, as though Mulley were trying to break through from the place where I had hidden him. However, as my family grew and my days became happy, he receded far into my deepest parts, and I was permitted to almost forget him. Each of my babies established me in the world of my husband, and I loved them all, each in the way they most desired.

Nevertheless, my first child held me in his eyes often, and I shared something I cannot express with him. This silent bond did not bother John or Amelia. They were warm and kind children, whom I rarely needed to rebuke, and were happy to give their love. But Augustina found the presence of Jaimie a thorn in her side, and her jealousy, coupled with my control of her outbursts, exacted secret retribution on her older half-brother. I suppose this tension tended to make our relationship somewhat cold. I tried so hard to teach her the ways of peace, but peace was not what her heart desired.

Each year, Jaimie grew and learned just as the others did. He called me 'Miss', and I called him Jaimie. I never once allowed myself the pleasure of calling him 'son', and no one even once suspected that the increasingly fine features and green eyes of his parentage could be attributed to me. He remained a hidden member of our family and only Jonathan had the luxury of speaking to him thus, "Come and help me saddle the horses, son." Or, "Son, take these inside to Miss Margaret." I envied him. It is true that a hidden burden seems light to begin with, but seemingly small things make a secret, grow heavy with the years.

Oftentimes I would see them playing in the garden under the fig tree and marvel at my brood.

Augustina would march them about, as was her way, though John was frequently distracted by some new creature or other, much to her consternation. Jaimie was always, it seemed, happy to be tethered to a play cart or made to fetch for Augustina even though she was more than three years his junior.

I thought of the life they would each lead, and I considered my firstborn and the unique life he must live as a party to two ways and two worlds.

Until he was six, I took him to Yarrabah on the third weekend of every month to see Menge and the last of her people.

Jonathan had no qualms in taking us on the long journey by cart so that I could see to it that Jaimie had lessons from the old woman in what it was to be Yidinji and part of the Malanbarra Bama.

For his part, Jonathan took the opportunity to take a load of supplies to the mission and whiled away his time there by chatting about such things as men do with the priest, or wandering along the shoreline, talking with the aboriginal fishermen, all of whom were from different clans and tribes.

I would entertain myself with lessons for the girls while Jaimie learned such things, as Menge would teach him. There was a huge outdoor communal table and I would sit there with the aboriginal girls and teach them conjunctions and adverbs, nouns and contractions while showing them how to make dilly bags that they would likely never use except to hold a hairbrush, some ribbons, or a sea shell necklace.

Then one day, in our little classroom at Ulmarra, on a day when the other children had to help their parents in their home gardens, Jaimie seemed to arrive at a crossroad concerning his understanding of the world.

I remember the day clearly.

A new church building had been built near the cane crushing plant that year, a mere three miles away. A small roadside community had been growing there, sporting a general store, a drapery, and a public house. The inhabitants had named it Gordon Vale.

Jonathan had urged us to fellowship there, and he was insistent that the children go to Sunday school and learn the ways of Our Lord.

Augustina had gone once and been quite adamant that the hour of sitting and behaving like a "good little Christian girl ought to", was not her cup of tea at all, but the reasoning for Jaimie's distaste was far more troubling.

As I had finished telling him that he should have to grow to like it, I saw the boy's face had become noticeably distressed.

His eyes were pink, his lips quivering, and he said boldly, "I don't want to go, miss ..." he had looked up pleadingly. "I might never get to see Menge if I got to go to them churchy people all them Sundays. She miss me so bad already. Look! She making magic an' crying in the sky!" He had pointed toward Yarrabah in the east, where the sky had turned red after the sun had risen. "I have to go get taught by her... don't you know!" He frowned with sincere admonishment.

"I know you will miss them at the mission... Perhaps we will still go out, but not as often, that's all. You are a big boy now and you have to understand, Jaimie. Things have changed so much from your Menge's day, and now the good people at the Sunday school are going to teach you other things you need to know too, new things.

"They don't know nothing 'bout things! That churchy man there, he don't even know how to find bush fowl eggs or nothing! We'll all starve and have no magic things, I just know it!"

His small fawn face quivered. His little heart could not contain the sadness caused by the threatening prospect of no longer going to see Menge, nor the anger he felt at the utter ignorance of this new world around him. A world, which had no interest in even the simple things of the forest.

"I know what you mean. But you see there are things you must know, like the way of Our Lord and how good people are supposed to live… Those things will make you wise and strong."

"I don't want to learn that!… And how you know it's right anyway?" He stared hard and defiantly into my eyes, and for a moment I could see myself looking back.

"Because, my little Jaimie, they're truthful things that cannot be wrong."

"But how you know?" He shook his head, and the way he did it recalled Mullegadajawara, and a shiver passed down my spine. Then he said with utter clarity, "How you know dreamtime not the truth and people should learn that way?"

He frowned and wickedly pouted his lips for effect. "I don't see none of this lot doing one thing that they know nufink of right living, that's what Menge say!"

"…Nothing, Jaimie, not nufink." I stood, looking out at a sky that would reveal its promise of rain later in the day.

He pressed on, "Menge say that they're 'dumb idjets'… I s'posed to shut my ears, miss… real tight!"

I sat near the boy for a moment, suddenly realizing the source of his conflict.

"You must learn, Jaimie… don't you want to be like Mr Jonathan and me?"

"I'm… not like you. I like the 'dinji way best, miss. An' them churchy people's they don't know nufin-g, they just making up them stories an' they got no dreamin' in them 'iva!"

I felt a shadow of fear creep up from behind and whisper, "You would call him your son? He is a savage still!"

I fumbled to find an explanation for why he must learn.

"Jaimie,… it's like some men who stand on a high hill and look out to the sea far away and see a great ship in the distance."

The boy suddenly stopped, opened his mouth, and listened, because he loved my stories.

"They remember that the Captain of that ship was on the docks just a few mornings ago and that Captain did all kinds of wonderful things, but he had to go. He's too far away to see from the hill but they still know the ship is out there, and standing on the deck of that ship, giving orders, and looking back to the land, is the Great Captain. They believe he's there, Jaimie, because they know it, even though they can't see it. And if he says he will come back, they know he will."

The boy's face was still and he was imagining the scene that my words evoked. The child breathed shallowly as the story took hold and his mind focused on it.

He added very knowledgably, "... He come back just like the whale shark and the dugong?"

"Yes that's right... When the season is finished, he comes back around." I smiled and his little eyes blinked, hungry for the next installment. So I went on.

"Now, although the men on the hill stay behind, and they're quite silly men, cutting down all the trees and killing all the animals and doing many things that are not sensible, they still look out to that ship, knowing it's out there somewhere."

I touched the tip of his little nose and said, "Now, if you asked them, they would have to tell you so. Yes indeed, someone would have to tell you about it even if you hadn't seen it for yourself."

"Ahhh ..." The small boy had nodded in childish acceptance of my explanation.

"Now, on that ship everything is being done correctly and the Great Captain can't tell a lie at all, not even one. So he will come back just as soon as it's the right season, just as he said."

"Oh!" he said curiously, "is he 'dinji too?"

"No dear, he's not like anyone... So anyway, the people at the church are like those men on the hill. They know about the ship, even if they don't know how to get bush fowl eggs... and it's their duty to teach you about it and the Great Captain."

He frowned, somewhat let down by the ending.

"But why does the ship have to be going... How come Menge doesn't know about it? We have canoes and we been here from dreamtime, long, long time ago. She doesn't know about that big ship."

"Lots of people know about the Captain a little bit, and that big ship that came, but not everyone knows it the same way... "

So it a bit like them big whale sharks?

"Whale sharks?"

"That's right miss... They got dots and stripes, too. Menge showed me one that been washed up an' was all stinky an' dead as anything."

"Really, I didn't know you had seen one."

"Yep. Menge teached me 'bout it."

I looked up to the ceiling and wondered what new superstition she had imbedded in him.

"She say, the way things are 'tween all of us... is like when two people swim on the reef an' a big whale shark goes between them. Well, the first man counts the spots on his side and he says, 'There are fifty-four spots!'

"Now, the other man counts the spots going by on his side and he says, 'There are fifty-five spots, and sixteen stripes as well!'"

"Oh, is there that many?" I smiled and he went on.

"Now when the fish is gone, the two men fight 'bout it an' say, 'I'm right!' and the other fulla says, 'No, you're wrong, I didn't see any stripes.' Neither work it out, it's just one shark! He looked up at me with his clear green eyes, "Silly men eh? They just see it from different sides an' in different ways." He slapped a small palm in front of him with glee. "An', an'... I tell ya som'ink else too! That shark got a big, big tail, and he can swallow a whole fisherman you know. That's what Menge say!"

"Yes... I see. Menge is like that, Jaimie. She tells it her way, and the Yidinji people were not where the Captain was when he first visited... That ship had to go a long way to see the first people so it could tell the whole truth about the Great Captain and the things he brings with him."

"I wish I could go on a ship like that." The boy propped his chin up on his plump little hands as I went on.

"Yes, well, it went first to a place called Israel, a long time before Menge and even before Menge's great, great, great grandmother. When he left that place, the Captain said to the people who had seen him and all he did, "You people go by yourselves and tell the English people, and they can go and tell Menge and these people in Australia because I have to go and get ready somewhere else for when the season changes, and I come back for you. If they believe you, then I will certainly come one day and take them on my ship too and we will go to the biggest forest of all, where the trees never get cut and the bush fowls lay all year round."

The boy's eyes widened, and I could see him threading together the story.

"So you see, Jaimie, that is how people who know about the Great Captain came here. We took another big ship and it sailed over the deep ocean all the way to Australia." I added thoughtfully, "Menge hasn't heard about it properly because she covered her ears when the silly men on the hill told her about it, because she didn't like what they were doing to all the land. But it doesn't mean they haven't told her the truth about it, and... I want you to know the truth too."

I watched him as he thought about this. The boy was joining the dots together as do the aboriginals when they see the end from the beginning and can trace the path of any place or animal back to the present.

"So that Captain is coming back here after, and them churchy fullas is going to tell us all about it?"

"Yes. One day, Jaimie, one day it He will come back to us just as he promised and the ministers will teach you. I just know that one day that good Captain will come and shake your hand, Jaimie, and say, 'Well done good, and faithful, Jaimie... Come on over here and stand with me on this ship of mine!'"

I smiled, although I was not sure that what I had said was quite the way to say it, but Jaimie loved the story anyway.

"That be an 'citing day!" The small boy's face lit up at the prospect and a white smile gleamed. "You know," he said thoughtfully in his six-year-old way, "we should get up Bundadjarruga Mountain and keep a look out in case he comes while I'm stuck in that Sunday school place." He was staring at an odd angle up toward the ceiling as he worked out how this fitted with what Menge had been teaching him. "And I better go out to Menge a few more times and make sure she knows about this prop'ly, or she might not be lookin' out for it ..."

He shook his head and his little green eyes focused on me sharply. He dropped the corners of his mouth and frowned sternly. "Be no good if my Menge miss the boat, she too old to swim out to us!"

I smiled as I thought of men sitting atop Walsh's Pyramid waiting for the Lord's return at the little boy's insistence and old Menge looking out from the shore waving her stick.

Jaimie was pondering deeply, just as his father was apt to do, then he said very seriously, "You know, rainbow serpent, he must have been on that ship long time before too, an' he must have swum ashore and begined all this land... That's how Menge know some of this." He swept a smooth brown arm through the air, and his voice took on the drama of the storyteller's voice just as I had heard on a still evening in the camp around a glowing fire. "... And I bet he's waiting for that ship to come back too and wake him up at Double Island so he can meet that big Captain again!"

Jaimie's voice returned to that of the six-year-old boy he was. "So... when is the ship coming, miss?"

I could tell he was keen to distract me from the book I had picked up, heralding a return to our lessons. "When the time is right and everyone has learned their lessons!" I stood up and patted the boy on the back and turned him around by his shoulders toward his books.

"You should teach me some more 'bout the Captain on that ship, miss, 'cause that would be a gooder lesson."

"A better lesson!" I corrected him. "I will, but not today. Today we're going to learn grammar, which you're sorely in need of, young man. And anyway, you can learn all about it at Sunday school." I smiled and continued to push him along toward his writing desk. "Then you can teach me what you have found out."

"All right miss, I'll go… but I not that keen 'bout it!" He cocked his head on its side and raised his eyebrows. "But I know you need me ta teach you 'cause I know Yidinji way too. That other side of the big shark, eh,… An' you got not right 'mount of spots and stripes in your mind 'bout the whole thing eh? I teach you the dreamtime part." He said matter-of-factly.

I suppressed a smile and the urge to grab him up and cuddle him. He was so clever. I felt the swell of pride just as a mother should even though I was dismayed that he seemed determined to hold onto the Yidinji stories he had already learned from Menge.

I knew he must learn the ways of our civilized world, or be no better than poor Liz Beth. I determined we must stop the long trips out to the mission at Yarrabah to see Menge and the last of his people altogether because he was becoming confused, caught between our two worlds. I was afraid my indulgence of Menge and her teaching would spoil his chance to live in the new world that had come, where the Yidinji ways were abhorrent and irrelevant to all but those of us who had touched it closely and could understand it. And, I confess, I wanted him for myself alone and I had all but returned to my former life as though I had never left it.

As I watched him slap his books on the desktop, I saw the last remaining part of the world of his father fading with my decision. It was being buried forever under the whitewashing of my own people, and I felt a tiny pang of remorse as though I betrayed them.

His beautiful eyes looked up at me, ready for their lesson, and I was held for a moment on the brink of some invisible decision by those green pools. The war raged for a few seconds though it felt as though an eternity fought with the question and then my heart spoke and silenced all. Without the right education, he will be nothing.

For all my love of the Yidinji way, in my mind I knew that unless he could be as we were, he would be swept into the gutters and never become the man I wished him to be.

I heard the distant whisper from my memory of a now long dead, Malanbarra warrior who derided my decision. He had warned long ago, that his people would lose their part in the dreaming by taking on the white man's ways. His voice unsettled me but I brushed it aside.

What use is there for a dead Yidinji? I thought. Even without his soul, he is at least alive.

Years later, when life played out all its cards, I came to see the wrong of my selfishness. As time showed me my error, and when age permits one to hear that ancient voice, I would learn the wisdom that comes from the great white cockatoo that counseled the old Yidinji. I would come to understand that it was not only his blood that made Jaimie entitled to the life of his people but the truth of their ways and their love for one another. Christian training could not replace it nor give a full understanding because the Christ was in the ways of the Yidinji, too. Even in the flying fish and the forests. He could be seen as one stripe or dot by all manner of people just as the giant whale shark, smoothly gliding through the oceans of his world.

But before such wisdom had settled in me, I followed the very course of those I had so criticized for their destruction of such a precious people. And I did this myself... to my own son.

By the time Jaimie had turned seven, his beautiful Yidinji heritage had all but been wiped from the land. Of the nearly four thousand natives that had lived in this region when we arrived, less than five hundred individuals remained. The forty-thousand-year occupation of the rainforest aboriginal was over.

I began to think about Jaimie's place in the world and what should become of him if I was unable to protect and care for him. Though Mr. McKenzie had first put in my hands my precious diary to record my impressions and the ways of the Yidinji for posterity, I had always known its true purpose would be to reveal to my son who I had really been to him and what part he had in his father's Yidinji "dreaming." even after I had done so well to destroy all memory of it.

I kept the diary closely guarded even from my dear and kind husband Jonathan because, though he was a wonderful and generous man of great character and compassion, he never had that place in me that my precious

Mullegadajawara had had. I knew he would realize this if he ever read my words. I could not bear to see him thus hurt, so the existence of this book was never revealed.

Knowing that I too, would one day go to the dreaming place, I prepared an appendage to my will and wrote my private wishes that Jaimie should have an equal share of Ulmarra farm with his half-brother and-sisters, and attached it to the legal document. I placed it inside the leather cover of this diary and carefully concealed the book and contents in a panel of my writing desk.

For many years, I have added to this account, keeping the history of Ulmarra as accurately as I could in the hopes that one day, my son should be the recipient and guardian of it for the future.

But my most precious gift to Jaimie, was his name. Being aboriginal, he had no surname and no record of his birth.

Jonathan and I agreed he should be named after the place that had once been his people's land and where he had grown up, a place that had brought our family much peace and prosperity.

We had him registered at the Cairns Courthouse as James Ulmarra on the ninth day of April 1889, though he was ten years of age.

His new birth certificate had his father's name boldly printed: "Father: Mullegadajawara of the Malanbarra Bama …Mother: Unknown."

Jonathan frowned, no doubt thinking it peculiar that I should know his father was an aboriginal or know his name. Jaimie was clearly half cast and the mission had been filled with offspring from their unknown white fathers. I quickly whispered as we signed the certificate, "Menge told me who his father was… but no one knows the other."

He had nodded and smiled in his gentle way, and the subject was not raised again until Jonathan was on his deathbed, some thirty years later. He looked up at me and whispered, "Did you know the mother …?"

I said, "I don't remember her, but I know she died when Jaimie's father did." He smiled at that. His last words to me were, "You're a good woman …"

On that day in April when we registered Jaimie, we returned as a happy crew on the back of the cart from Cairns. Young Jaimie held the paper proudly and in such a tight grip as to leave his fingerprints permanently etched in the stiff certificate, as though it were the most precious thing in the world. His face beamed with pride and he stared in a strange and knowing way up to the rainforest mountains all the way back to Ulmarra farm.

As I watched him, I felt a certain sadness that I could not quite define. My secret hope was that he would grow to be a man who not only represented the "bend in the river" of his new name, Ulmarra, but who would inspire himself and others with the deeper meaning of the name, "a change in direction."

Whatever Jaimie's life would be, I had done all I could for him. I knew the future would determine where it wanted him to go and reveal its plan. I hoped it would be for the betterment of all in my countrymen, and my true home—Australia.

A letter addressed to the young aborigine in her mother's distinctive hand lay in Augustina's hands.

Her mother had struggled with the last of her waning energy to find it in her bedside drawer and enclosed it tightly in her gnarled fingers on top of the bedcovers for them to find.

Augustina read out the part that had her so agitated to the others in a whisper, her face cloudy and dark.

… I have left the desk and its contents to you in my will, my dear Jaimie, so that one day you will discover the truth about yourself in the words I wrote of you and your people. When you find it, and read it, you must understand that love brought you into this world, and love must be what guards and guides your life always.

It's my wish that you have a share of Ulmarra. A permanent ownership in law, of the land that was your father's for longer than anyone can imagine. You will find this document inside the book if you look in a place where the "fat grubs" might be, and only a Yidinji would know how to find one.

I have left these instructions to guide you to the truth and to ensure the appendage document finds its way into your hands alone.

I trust that Augustina, Amelia, and John will love you and keep you near, just as I have done... and you will understand when you read the diary, why... I now beg you forgive me—and us all ...

Augustina shook her head and screwed up the letter, blowing short breaths from her mouth with nothing short of hatred on her face. The others looked at each other, knowing she had despised Jaimie even as a little girl. She had a fierce will and could show it mercilessly and he had been the brunt of most of it.

With their mother Margaret's descent into age, Augustina had had a free hand to push Jaimie far from "the love" her mother had written of in her letter. She had long since made him a mere worker who was now rarely near the house and lived in a tiny cabin at the edge of the southern field.

Amelia raised her eyebrows, thinking, Jaimie hasn't got a hope. However, she would never cross her older sister, and John, too, had inherited his father's amiability and was happy to let things play out as they will, enjoying the company of the animals far more than the drama of his sisters.

"Mother, you must be mad!" Augustine muttered to herself, almost ignoring her siblings and ensuring her voice was low enough not to wake the old lady far on the other side of the room. She turned fiercely to the others, "You shall never say anything about this to a single soul... Do you hear me?"

They nodded obediently and looked at each other as if to say, who would dare?

Augustina went off to the schoolroom, where the desk was, scrambling furiously through every drawer but finding nothing in the old piece of furniture that had been made from single cedar tree, felled when they had expanded the farm and cleared the land. Somewhat battered, it was carved along its length with a totem design of the Malanbarra. Augustina had always hated the look of it.

Unknown to her, the carved edge she so despised, concealed where her mother had carefully hidden the documents and the diary. The solid piece of furniture that she wrote her lessons on was like her very body, and in its heart, she had hidden her most treasured and secret things as she had also done in her heart.

While Augustine angrily slammed drawers and rifled though the desk, up in the old woman's room the wind slightly ruffled the curtains. With its gentleness, Margaret slipped dreamily and peacefully into the long sleep that heralds the gateway to the dreamtime place. The future would have to carry out her wishes for her. It was clear Jaimie's siblings would not.

"She has gone... I'm sorry, she has gone." The doctor patted the old woman's still-warm hand. The skin was paper thin and marked with purple stains and spots. Her white hair flowed like strands of spider silk, lazily lifting from the pillow in the breeze that blew through the window she had asked them to open so she could smell the air of the countryside and see the dark green ranges in the distance.

"She had a full life ..."

"A pioneer's life," John said. "The times she saw will never be seen again. The world has got too small already. I wish I had been here then." He shook his head as he looked down at his mother. "There were lots of birds and animals back then but a lot of them are gone now."

"What a beautiful day." Amelia looked out the window, turning her head from her mother, fighting back tears, and looking for a distraction.

"I agree, beautiful... Do you think her spirit will fly out there and take one last look?" John put his arm around his sister.

"No, she will have just closed her eyes and gone to Dad in heaven," Amelia replied.

"Yes, indeed," Augustina nodded.

The day rolled on. One child or other sat with the quiet body lying in the bed her long dead husband had bought for her. Those not sitting with her walked quietly through the house and spoke in hushed tones.

The undertaker came and arrangements were made. The family solicitor arrived around midday, and they discussed her wishes and her will. But the letter with its cryptic message for Jaimie about the missing addition and the diary was not mentioned.

On the third day after the window had been opened and Margaret had flown on her way, she was laid to rest on the lower field where the stream and the river met, just as she had asked.

The day was again perfect, as it always is in the dry season in Cairns. Around the grave, the dark-clothed mourners met and remembered her.

It was a peaceful affair, although most of those she knew well were long in their own graves and only the young surrounded her. She would not have minded.

John and his sisters held each other and grieved for the old woman who had been teacher, counselor, and friend to them all.

Behind this group, a little back from the family's friends and town notorieties, stood a lone man.

He had aboriginal features somewhat fused with European descent. His worker's hat was held in one hand, while his black, curly hair dangled free around his jaw. His broad shoulders harkened back to times of plenty and hard work.

He watched and waited.

She had always been kind to him, even when some of her offspring had not been.

The old woman never allowed his aboriginal heritage to be a reason for him to be disadvantaged, and she had been his teacher and champion as he grew up at Ulmarra. She had given him his name.

Today, he watched her slide into the earth as peacefully as a turtle drops into the water to be hidden in the deep. He knew in his heart that her passing was a signal for his own life also, that he was to be cut away from the past she symbolized. A tear for "Miss" rolled freely down his coffee skin.

After the wake and the cordial funeral, the grave stood quietly.

Three days later, two workers were commissioned to create a cement-and-stone surround with a wrought iron fence, and a headstone was set in place.

Jaimie helped them bring up stones from the river to set in it. When an acacia seedling that Augustina had supplied, was left sitting forlornly in its pot waiting to be planted at the head of the grave, he took it and threw it discreetly into the river.

Leaving Ulmarra farm, he went in search of a sapling of a native fig tree from near the place where the old people had told him his ancestors had lived. The giant tree grew where the mountains' dipped their feet in the big river as it poured through the gorge and onto the plain. It twisted and flowed in the wake of the mythical rainbow serpent that had gouged it out a millennium ago before he had found his in the heart of Double Island to sleep.

Margaret's son stood in the morning light and stared across the wide, open field of cane that was now planted there. He imagined those days when the sound of his people wafted through the trees that once stood there. Silence spread her cloak over the view and only the field finch sang his brilliant trill in that place now.

He followed the river up to the rocks that jutted out from the mountain. The river flowed through the polished rocks and above him the old tree shaded it so that its dark green depths seemed so clear that it might have been the eye of God he looked into.

He searched until he found a new shoot from the Great Fig tree and carefully dug its roots free of the soil that belonged to the Mallanburra bama.

He knew she would have liked that—not some pretty foreign tree that meant nothing.

He brought the tiny sapling back to the place where she lay.

An iron grid fence of lacework had been erected in his absence, and he stepped over it to her head and planted the little tree.

Standing, looking down at his work, he had a strange feeling that something had been completed, and he smiled. He took it to mean the old woman was indeed, pleased.

Stepping out from the grave, he strode off to the workers' huts to wash his hands and begin work. And with that, the passing of Margaret, was over.

Chapter 19

Now I will tell you how I came into the picture all this time later.

Auntie Sal told me that the old woman's children began to take their place as the custodians of the estate, and life carried on.

The will was read a little while after and the writing desk was declared as Jaimie's. No one was surprised by this, as they had known that the old lady had a soft spot for him. It must have seemed a wasted gesture because he had nowhere to put it, and they wondered if he would ever use it.

Margaret wasn't the only one who had kept a diary. John liked to record everything too and letters of Augustina's, said that she had suggested to Jaimie that they keep the desk at the house where it was. She didn't like it but for her mother's sake, she said he could use it whenever he liked—as long it was a "convenient time" for him to come and visit.

Sal had kept everything about that family and between the various accounts, it was clear what had gone on after Margaret Stanford had died.

The oldest of the white kids, hated Jaimie Ulmarra, and he knew it would never be "convenient" for him to come into the house to either use or get the desk. Still, he agreed with her and, there it stayed, untouched ever after.

Within six months, the new masters at Ulmarra farm had Jaimie hankering for life with others of his own kind in the town, and he finally packed his belongings and left the farm.

He met and married a girl from the very mission where he had been placed before he was spirited away to live with Margaret and her new husband.

He was well-educated, for an aboriginal, and he became a clerk for the railway in Smithfield.

He and his young wife lived in a two-room house rented from the railway for some thirty years. They had five children, and Jaimie lived out his life in his own way, as the leader of his family clan, respected and loved, wise and reflective. He died in 1955 at age 77.

His funeral was surrounded by the faces of the last of the rainforest aborigine—and no one from the people of Ulmarra farm.

Augustina and John had families of their own, and the farm continued in its cycles of cane harvesting and cane planting, and a short railway led from the farm to the main line that bought the crop to the crushing mill in Gordonvale.

Amelia took her leave for Sydney with a "somewhat obtuse young man," Sal said, whom Augustina thoroughly abhorred. For that reason, no one heard from Amelia again until her death some seven years later, when she mysteriously fell from a train.

Each generation of Jaimie's descendants, oblivious of the desk or the diary and his share of Ulmarra, dispersed into the growing population of Cairns. The settlement had officially become a town in 1903, with thirty-five hundred people, and became a city in October 1923 with over forty thousand. It had a variety of industries along with the huge agricultural development in the region, and eventually became a tourist Mecca with its warm climate, beautiful coral reefs, and the mountainous rainforest standing guard behind it.

In the streets, a few of the descendants of its first inhabitants could be seen from time to time. They would wander across the forecourt of the Cairns Central Sun bus terminal or hang out at the protected heritage building of the Empire Hotel, which still peddled a cold beer after more than a century, only now it had sports screens and a TAB betting booth.

Who knows if the indigenous fullas were real Yidinji. I did see one day a really small girl dressed in an orange dress with white flowers on it. She had skinny little arms and legs and was as black as the ace of spades. Her frizzy hair was tied in a bun that looked like a rabbit's tail stuck on the back of her head, and she was as blotto as you could get, twirling a white daisy in her fingers and singing something at the top of her lungs. As she staggered aimlessly across the hot concrete pavers with bare feet, I thought she looked like she might be pure Yidinji or pretty close.

Even though my grandfather used to tell me stories of his how his great-grandfather was the first of us Ulmarras and he reckoned he was all Yidinji, I thought he was about three-quarters. He was too tall anyway, and he didn't have brown eyes like the rest of our people, so I thought there had to be something else in us. He had small moles covering his face, but he used to harp on about how he came from the "first ones" and "we had all the land in those days."

I thought it was all bullshit. We could have come from anywhere, and who cared anyway. We were poor and may as well have come from Woop Woop for all the good it did being able to say you were Yidinji.

My granddad was sort of shy and quiet, and he was employed in all sorts of laboring positions when he was young, not that I knew what they were. It didn't matter to him because Nanny Liddy said he wasn't too bright and he didn't care what he did so long as there was a cold beer and a TV at the end of the day.

By the time I remember them, they lived in the suburb of Earlville. He never married my real grandmother but lived with Nanny Liddy, a woman older than him by four years. Nanny Liddy wasn't my dad's mum—I never knew her. She was a drunk, they reckon, and disappeared somewhere. No one knew where she'd gone.

My dad always called Nanny Liddy "auntie," and I liked her because she always gave me a teaspoon of condensed milk when we went to visit and said I was her best boy.

Actually, I was her only boy—my dad only had me and dad was an only child, too. He never knew if his real mum had any other kids somewhere else. Nanny Liddy didn't have any kids to old Grandpa, so there was just my dad and then me.

Our house was a government house two streets over from them. You weren't allowed to have mixed sexes living in government houses if you were an unmarried abo. Regardless, my mum and dad never got married and lived on their separate unemployment pensions, both received at the same address, and we always thought how dumb the government must be not to notice.

My father had brown eyes, and he looked like a full abo.

He used to say I was nothing short of a miracle. My mum reckoned I had been conceived when she was drunk after New Year's Eve, but I don't think she really knew because they were almost always drunk, as far as I can remember. Both my mum and dad liked a good drink or two anytime, sometimes all day, and I'd come home from school to a house that was a mess and the air blue with smoke all the way to the floor almost.

Anyway, my birth happened on the way to Cairns base hospital in the back of a taxi. My mum would tell me over and over, through the years, that my cord was wrapped around my neck and stopped me falling off the seat. And my dad said, "Your mother was screaming bad bloody language, eh, so bloody loud it near deafened the driver and he was in shock for days!" Well, that's not a surprise to me.

My proper name was James, after the guy on Star Trek that they watched on Thursday night for years, and it was about the only time they weren't fighting about something.

Anyway, they called me Jimmy, and mostly my name came up with some instruction attached to it, like "Jimmy, walk down the road and get us some bread and a bottle of milk and some ciggys, eh?" I've probably walked ten thousand miles backwards and forwards to Woollies in the Earlville Plaza getting something for her. I didn't mind though, I always mucked about down there with my mates, and when I'd finally get back, she would say, "Thank bloody God, I was hanging out ...Where the hell you been, Jimmy? Don't you know I was on my last one, bloody little bastard ..." And she'd storm off, lighting her cigarette while she was walking away and muttering to herself.

So that's what I remember about them.

I had a girlfriend last year, she was into some kind of poetry, and she said I had a look that was "like the deep water in a slow river." I admit, I always thought I was strange because my skin is dark brown but my eyes are clear and just like the color of an olive python's skin, green as green. She didn't hang around long and I didn't care because I'd rather go walking by myself up the culvert at the back of our road, where there is a bit of land with a lot of trees and the inlet mangroves are nice and cool. It's quiet.

I didn't get much out of school. Actually, it wasn't cool to be smart anyway. I learned more about how to break into houses and how to get free ciggys from the tourists down at the esplanade when I was growing up. The best place for cadgin' a cig was in front of the night markets. I'd been picked up by the cops a couple of times down there, but I didn't care, they couldn't do much. And my mum and dad didn't give a stuff, so it was all good.

My dad dropped dead at the Centrelink office on a hot day in November. It was really hot that day and inside they had the air conditioner on too high, we reckon, and it was bloody freezing. We all thought that is what did it, the shock. They said he had the heart attack because he had diabetes and cirrhosis of the liver—and he was fat. But I think it was lack of booze that killed him. He always went cold turkey if he had an appointment with them for a renewal because if you were drunk they would threaten to cut off your benefit and arrange an idiot counselor for you, because abos weren't allowed to drink on the dole—though I can't say that rule ever applied to us.

After he died, my mum didn't do too well, and I had to move out just after my fourteenth birthday because I just couldn't stand it. Soon as he was gone and she didn't have him to fight with, she started on me.

I used to go round and visit once in a while. Then one day I turned up, and the place was empty. A cop visited about two months after that and said she had died of mixing booze with prescription drugs in Brisbane, and I thought, Wow… I'm an orphan.

I'm not sure if I cried or not, but he said some people were going to come back to pick me up and look after me. My mates said I should get out of there, because I was under sixteen and the child protection people would get me, and that was worse than jail. It never happened though—they never got me.

I lived with me mates down Murry Street, but none of us had much to do, just the usual, mucking about. We didn't have much money either, so we used to bum around on the esplanade or down at the Rain Trees shopping plaza.

Sometimes though, when it was still on a hot night, when everyone else was asleep or passed out, I would walk down the street while the asphalt was still hot and look up at the stars.

I felt as though I was meant for something, but never could put that into words. I just knew something wasn't quite right for me and things were not happening as they were supposed to. I had no idea what I was meant to do but, and no one cared to give me a clue anyway.

I would stand in the light of the streetlamp at the corner of Hutchings and Mulgrave Road and watch the insects gather around it. And I wondered if that was what I was doing, just being a dumb human insect, mesmerized by the light in a pointless life and beating my brains out for nothing—until one day, I would drop dead of a heart attack like old dad did, and have meant nothing important to anyone.

I felt like I was waiting for something to "light my match," point me somewhere, anywhere, for whatever I was made for. But it just didn't come.

Then one day it did. My match was lit by some crazy stuff that had waited over a hundred years to find me.

Auntie Sal was a descendant of Margaret Stanford. Her great-great-grandfather was one of the kids, John, and her family still had the farm down Gordonvale way, over all these years, right up to 2001.

I met Auntie Sal because her mother, who had been living at the place for years, had finally died, and she and her brother and sister had decided not to keep the farm because they all had homes of their own and other jobs. A big company had bought the farm for the land to build houses on it, so they were going to demolish the old house. And that is how they found out who I was and what I had to do with them.

Auntie Sal told me the old house smelt of decay, like it had already long since died, when they went there to take a look for anything good to keep before the wrecking crew came. The dust was so heavily caked on everything that you did'nt have to touch a windowsill or a wall to feel its presence.

When they walked across the floor it creaked because the beams underneath were rotten and the whole thing just wanted to fall into the ground and finally go to sleep like the people who had built it, already had.

"I don't think we will find anything in here worth having. It's been sitting here too long," Sal told her sister, Caroline.

"So, it's definitely sold then?" her sister asked.

"Yep, and the guy who has bought it is going to build brand new homes all the way to the highway. He doesn't care what we take out cf the house. I think he would be just as happy to have us move the whole thing away, but it's utterly rotten." She looked up at where the ceiling had dropped in places. There were water stains everywhere.

"What's this?" Caroline called from the study. Her voice echoed because the place was more or less empty.

Auntie Sal walked through the opening between the rooms—the door had long since disappeared. "I really don't know—an old writing desk, I think. Is it okay?"

"Looks okay. Maybe one of the others will want it. It won't go in my house."

"Nor mine, but I guess it might be nice to have something of the old family, you know. Someone might want to keep it."

She ran her fingers over the top of it and a line of dark wood appeared from underneath the dust. "Look at this, it's got an abo carving right across the top." She flicked the dust off it to look at the markings. "You know, it's amazing to think that we came from this house. The first one of us, maybe, sat right here."

Auntie Sal said she was going to arrange the removal of the desk and then the Chapter would be closed, the house demolished, and the memories would fade away like mist on a cool morning in the dry.

When Auntie Sal came back two days later, she brought her cousin Steve and his son with her to move the desk out for her brother, Peter, who liked doing up old things. He said he wanted it but couldn't get off work that day.

"Careful, Steve!" Sal said as the two men hauled on the old writing desk with its scratched legs and dented top.

"Sal, this thing weighs a ton," Steve panted. It's rubbish—can't see why your brother wants it."

"Well, he does, so be careful you old duffer." She backed through the doorway and onto the veranda, which sloped at the front. Its rail had collapsed at the far end.

"I hope it fits on the ute," Auntie Sal said.

"Should do," Steve puffed, and his teenage son strained a little. "Can you hold that end up, son! Come on!"

The doorway was almost too small for the desk to fit, and the two wrestled to get it through. Then, just as they began to clear the opening, the boy lost his footing on the uneven floor and for a moment he wobbled.

His father, not ready for the shift in weight, did likewise, and with a resounding curse, he dropped his end and the desk was ripped out of the boy's hands and smashed hard on the floor.

The legs splayed out and dust sprang away in swirling clouds. Sawdust sprayed from the splitting timber, the top skewed and parted from the sides, and more sawdust scattered and landed at their feet.

"Oh look!" Auntie Sal growled. "You've broken it!"

"Sal, it's rubbish. Look, it's full of termites!" He pulled a little of the wood away and revealed the cream-colored interior, crumbling and riddled with small tunnels and white insects here and there. "Bloody 'ell—it's lucky we did drop it. Pete wouldn't thank you for bringing these into his house! He'd have to fumigate, eh?"

"Oh dear, he's going to be disappointed."

"Well, I suppose we'll have to just move it aside and leave it here."

They started to pull off the bits of wood that had come loose, and as they did, the body of the desk started to fall to pieces.

Suddenly, the boy noticed something. "Hey look, there's something tucked in here." He was pointing to a gap where a small sliding panel was hidden in the frame. "Looks like it's a book or something."

"So it is. What a find!" They carefully pulled out the leather-bound diary, which was wrapped in thick camphor paper.

Auntie Sal told said they walked it out into the light and together they opened it, peering into the handwritten pages.

"This is my great-great-great-grandmother's! Look, it's signed 'Margaret Stanford.' This was her house."

"Wow! The family is going to be interested in this," Steve mused. "I wonder if it's worth anything?"

"Steve! It's priceless. We can't sell it—it's part of who we are, for God's sake! I swear you would sell your own mother if there was a buck in it."

She slapped old Steve on the arm, and he chuckled. "Nah, I'd never do that. Might give 'er away, but!"

"Can you read it?" His son was peering over Auntie Sal's shoulder.

"I think so. The dedication is 'For Jaimie.' Oh dear—God knows what's in here!"

She carefully flicked through to the last page. "Look here—there's something tucked in the back sleeve. She pulled it out and unfolded a thick legal document and several pages of a long handwritten letter.

As soon as she looked at the document, she whispered, "Oh my Lord, look what we have here …" She told me she closed the book with the loose leaves sticking out from the center and said, "We gotta see someone about this."

The very next week, Auntie Sal went to her lawyer and spoke to her brother, as well, who went off to his lawyer too. They decided to have a meeting of all the beneficiaries of the family trust so they could decide what to do.

She said they had a barbecue first, with some pretty good wagyu beefsteaks, and then afterwards Auntie Sal brought out the book and Uncle Pete started telling them what it was all about.

"Seems our ancestor, Margaret Stanford, had a bit of a life no one knew about. Before she married our great-great-great-grandfather, she had been married to some fulla called Edward Bermingham, and he was the one who brought her out from England. Looks like he was a bit of a bad character, and he left her on this land in a shack for nearly a year while he went gold mining. The local abos looked after her because the help ran off with her money and she almost starved to death.

"Seems she got a wee bit too friendly, putting it mildly, and had a half-cast kid. If you read what she wrote, it must have been terrible for her, and what happened was bloody cruel. Still, she survived and it turned out all right in the end. She married old Jonathan Stanford and that is how we all started.

"Now before she died, she had a proper appendage made to her will, and hid it. I guess she was scared to tell her family lawyer or make it known to Jonathan's kids, in case they put a stop to it. She hid the diary and the extra bit of the will in her desk, and when it collapsed, that's how we found it. So poor old Jaimie Ulmarra, her first son, never got his part of the farm, and no one after him either."

"Abos?" Catherine spoke up disbelievingly, "You're kidding!"

"No. We have a whole other side to our family, and they might be still living here in Cairns. Who knows?"

"Well, it doesn't matter. They don't know anything, and who's going to tell them?" Catherine's daughter spoke up.

"The original will left the Ulmarra estate to 'all my surviving children,' quite cleverly not naming who those children might be," John spoke over the top of her. "All Ulmarra had to do was turn up with the diary, his birth certificate, and the appendage—and he was in."

"Was lucky he never found the diary and we did," Steve's teenage son quipped.

"What do the lawyers say now that it's this late in the piece?"

"Well, almost a hundred years later, we sort of don't have to do much, I suppose. But if it's found out or someone comes forward, they can make a claim through the indigenous land settlement courts, and we will have to pay it if they win."

"So what do we do to get out of it?"

Auntie Sal told me she was pretty upset that they were so greedy about it. She said, "Look, seems like you're all looking for a way out of it. Shouldn't you be thinking about the fact that there's plenty in this estate for everyone, I mean it's sold for nearly five million dollars—so what if we have to give a bit away?"

"Hey Sal, don't get all goody-two-shoes on us. That five mill has to be divided by seven of us. What if there are fifty of them out there all looking for a handout?"

"We learned in school, their life expectancy isn't that high, Uncle Steve. There won't be fifty." Catherine's youngest son offered his know-it-all comment and tried to settle his uncle down, who had become red faced with beef, beer, and bother.

"We should set up a trust and wait and see," Aunty Sal told them. "You have to remember, these aren't just any abos, they're the descendants of our great-great-great-grandmother, Margaret. They're part of our family!" Aunty Sal was quite annoyed, she reckoned, and said it so forcefully that a few of them jumped and everyone went quiet.

"Look, we're lucky to have anything from the old farm. Pete, me, and Catherine are the main ones, and my mum's brother's kids: Stephen, Mike, Jenny, and Pearl. Our mother had that life tenancy, and when she died, she wanted us to keep this old farm intact. She wanted us to keep it whole, even though it doesn't make any real money anymore. We have gone and sold it against her dying wishes just so we can all get a bit more for our own lives.

"Why shouldn't the people who owned it first, the real owners, have a cut of the pie to help them out too? It was theirs to start with, and this Jaimie was equally entitled because he was Margaret's first child and son. It's what Margaret Stanford wanted back then, and it's what's right—now!"

"Okay, I guess we can see your point," Uncle Pete had said.

So, Auntie Sal got her way, and she was given the job of tracing anyone that was a descendant of old Jaimie Ulmarra.

She took details from his birth certificate that had been in the desk and did a search. It took more than six months, but finally she found out that I lived in Manoora and was the last one left of the Ulmarras. And I found out at last where I got my green eyes from.

Chapter 20

WHEN AUNTIE SAL got in contact it was a bit of a shock. I wasn't sure what this plump woman in her forties, dressed in nice but boring clothes, had to do with me.

She had gone to the Ministry of Aboriginal Affairs after she found out I was alive and where I lived. They had put her in touch with this abo elder called Willie Butterworth, and the two of them came to visit me.

Me mates buggered off as soon as they rang the doorbell because they thought it was something to do with the cops.

I let them inside. The place was a mess, with a ton of clothes over the chairs and pizza boxes and cans of Red Bull and Four X everywhere, but Auntie Sal didn't say anything about it because she's a nice person.

Willie introduced her and said it would be okay for me to talk to her but if I wanted, they would arrange an aboriginal lawyer.

I didn't care—I just wanted to know what it was all about.

She was a bit shy but not half as much as me. Then, when she bought out this blue file with a ton of letters and official stuff in it, I thought, Shit, the people that grab underage kids have caught up with me! My heart was pounding out of my chest and there was a lump in my throat. I just sat there like a tawny frog mouth bird, dead still and scared stiff.

"Do they call you James?

"Nah, Jimmy," I said.

"What a coincidence. The first Ulmarra was a James, too. They called him Jaimie.

"I didn't know that. Only know my parents and my granddad and Nanny Liddy."

"Well, this goes a long way further back than your grandparents. There was a… 'mistake' made with that first Jaimie Ulmarra a long time ago, and we want to sort it out. Even though it happened almost eighty years ago, in the early nineteen twenties. The first settlers here were my ancestors that came out from England, and we found out one of them is your ancestor too."

"Nah, Can't be nothing to do with me. I'm Yidinji—I know that."

"Yes, but it turns out Margaret Stanford who owned Ulmarra Farm down Gordonvale way, she had a child to a Yidinji message man and warrior before she married her husband Jonathan. And that person was your ancestor."

"I don't believe it!"

Willy leaned forward and smiled. "No boy, this is a true case—and I have to say the best one I have ever heard of. This family, the Stanford family, sold the farm and they found the documents …"

"And a diary …" Auntie Sal whispered.

Willie smiled and shook his head somewhat disbelievingly, "… And the family want to right the wrong done way back then. Since you're the only remaining descendant they're going to create a trust with a share from the sale of that land, and you can use it for property or education …"

I stood up, put both hands round the back of my head, and laughed. "This is a joke, right?" I looked at Auntie Sal and could tell right away that it was true. She wasn't kidding.

"So how much is it?"

"Well, it's about half a million dollars."

"Bloody hell! …" I'd barely had more than a fifty in my hand in my whole life. "When do I get it?"

"As soon as a settlement is arranged and a trust account is set up. There will be two trustees, one from the aboriginal land courts and one appointed by the family."

They smiled, and I could see Auntie Sal was really feeling pretty good about it.

"You can use the money for whatever you want—within reason," she grinned.

"I don't know what I want to do …" I shook my head and suddenly thought how weird it was to have this happen and not have a single idea how to take advantage of it.

"I guess it's a shock, but I think there is one more thing that will help you."

"Yeah?"

"Yes, how 'bout we meet somewhere for a coffee, and I will bring you the diary and the letter Margaret wrote to James Ulmarra? I think when you have read that you might have some ideas what to do."

"Reading isn't really something I like doing."

"Maybe not, but I'm pretty sure this is one book you're going to want to read. Anyway, it might give you a pointer as to what direction you should take from here, what change of direction is right for you."

When she said that, I felt kind of funny. I thought maybe this was what I had been waiting for. When I looked into her eyes, they were green like mine, and for some reason I liked and trusted this kind woman.

I agreed to meet her down by the esplanade under the big frangipani trees in front of the public lagoon pool. She said she would be there the next day.

I almost didn't make it because I couldn't sleep all that night and had to knock myself out with half a bottle of Jack Daniels. And then I slept in and missed the bus to town.

When I got there, she was sitting on the picnic table seats under the trees and staring out to the estuary flats where you could see the sea grass because the tide was out. A bunch of spoonbills and pelicans were preening in the sun out a bit. And green-and-orange rainbow lorries were screeching in the trees overhead.

" g'dday," I said shyly, and she turned around to greet me.

"Thought I might have missed you. I was late and I couldn't find a park," she said.

"Nah, I'm sorry I'm late, eh. Missed the bus."

I went to sit down, and as I did, I looked up into the big tree there and spied at least fifty black-and-tan flying fox bats hanging upside down."

"They don't seem to care about the cars or any of us down here," she said as she looked up at them too.

"Nah, they know they're protected."

"Well, I'm glad they were. It's a shame we hadn't done that for some of the people that used to be here."

"I guess so," I said.

"You should call me Auntie Sal—because we're family, you know. Distant perhaps, but we're related and that is good enough for me."

"Okay, that's cool."

"I've brought the book. It's very, very old, so you have to understand you can't keep it. Instead, I had a copy typed out for you. Margaret's writing was very elegant but it's too hard to read nowadays." She looked at me but I didn't blink an eye. "The letter to her son is the same, and I guess maybe you should read that first." She slid the book, which was in some kind of special plastic, across the tabletop so I could see it. I picked it up and unwrapped it.

The leather was sort of dry and pretty knocked about. When I opened it, the pale blue ink sprawled across each page evenly and looked like the fine curls of hairy palm leaves when they peel off little green threads. I turned a few pages and, I admit, it was a weird feeling, going back in time that far and realizing that this woman from England was in my blood.

"Have you read it?" I asked.

"Yes."

"What is it about?"

"Well, it records a lot of how the Yidinji lived, their customs—even their language, which is good because there are only eleven people who can actually speak it nowadays, and a lot of it has been lost." She looked a bit sad, and then said, "Some of the people in the tribe are in there and your great-great-great-grandfather. He was a good man. A clever man."

"Yeah?"

"I think you should get to know him. It's hard for a young person to know who they are or should be—when they don't know who they came from."

"I guess …Well thanks, you didn't need to do this for me, eh."

"Yes I did."

"Well, whatever. I'm grateful. I'm going to try to read this—least I can do, I guess. But it might take a while."

"Well I hope you do, because I think she would have wanted you to find your roots and have a life that is equal to your potential."

"Potential? Sounds like them teachers I had at school. That is only good if you know what to do with it, eh?"

"I don't know about that, young man. I believe the genes in you means you will find out what you are and know how to get on with it. And not just for your own good—for lots of people around you."

"You're a nice lady."

"And you're nice, too. Call on me anytime, my door is always open to you. After all, we're family."

"Thanks."

I slid the old book into its plastic cover and picked up the white printed copy.

"Hey, you want a drink?" I said, feeling like I should do something back for her.

"All right, how 'bout a milkshake? I'll pay."

"No way, I'll pay this time… Auntie Sal. You can get it next time, eh."

And that is how I started.

Auntie Sal was a great lady, but I guess that printed copy she gave me sat around for a week while I summoned up the courage to even try to read it.

On the day I decided I had stuffed around long enough, I took the bus to Cairns Central then the one down to White Rock and on to Gordonvale, where the old farm was.

I had to walk maybe two kilometers until I found the place, and finally walked down a long gravel driveway toward the old homestead, which was deserted.

There was a wooden railway sleeper bridge that crossed a stream. The roadway stopped on the other side at a gate and it had an old sign hanging on an angle that read Trespassers will be prosecuted.

The house was still there. Sal told me later the developers had a glitch getting approval to subdivide and local cane growers had lodged an objection. It was up a bit of a hill, and a huge, old tree stood behind it and its leaves were all over the roof. The whole building leaned slightly on its foundations.

I climbed the gate and jumped from the top rail onto the dust of the roadway on the other side. I stood looking at the house that was almost a ruin, waiting for someone to put it out of its misery and demolish it.

I noticed a sign hanging from one nail that still held fast to the verandah overhang and I whispered under my breath, "Wicked!" when I realized it was my name up there: Ulmarra.

I felt strange and started shivering in my guts as I walked around through the long grass looking at the house and the stuff lying about. I headed up the front steps to the front door and tried it. It was nailed shut. A plastic sign was pinned to it: DANGER: TO BE DEMOLISHED WITHOUT FURTHER NOTICE.

I jumped off the end of the deck where the hand rail was missing and skirted round the side where there was an add-on bit of the building with windows looking down to the stream. One of them was broken, so I climbed in.

It was just an empty room, but there was an old blackboard attached to one wall and someone had scratched graffiti all over it. I stood there thinking about it, wondering why they had it there.

In the next room a pile of broken pieces of furniture were scattered on the floor and I realized this must be the desk where they had found the book and other papers. I stopped and pulled a few bits of wood away in case there was anything else they had missed.

At the top was a long edge that was carved and had white and red ochre in the grooves. I recognized the design as something from the Yidinji because old granddad had a wooden bowl a bit like it, so I thought I should get it off and keep it.

I pulled it back and half the top came with it because it was rotten. A pile of white termite larvae fell out and onto the floor. When I looked down the hole, I could see where the space had been for the book. I also saw a small tin nailed to the back of the drawer. You wouldn't have been able to see it unless you pulled the top off, so it must have been put in there when the thing was built and closed up.

I twisted the frame apart and got my hand in to wrench the tin free. When I pulled it out, I could see it was a tobacco tin, and looked as good as new. On the front was a man dressed in a red coat and he had a huge moustache curling up. The lid was tight but I pulled at it, and eventually it flew off and something jumped out and hit the floor. It rolled a bit on the slope of the boards and I dived and caught it just before it disappeared down a hole where the floorboards were rotten and a draft was coming up from under the house. I stood up and opened my hand carefully.

In my palm sat a pearl. It had a small crease on one side but was otherwise round, and I looked at it wondering whose it was and why it was there. The tin had a tightly folded up hanky stuffed inside, with a corner of fine lacework and some initials on it, so I put the pearl back in the dent in the center of the hankie, closed the lid, and stuffed it in my jeans pocket to show my new Auntie Sal.

Getting upstairs was not easy. The main stairs were close to collapsing, skewed over to one side with the sway of the house, and the fourth step was missing altogether.

At the top, the floor was on a bit of a lean too. I walked down the short hall toward the window that was missing at the end, and when I got there, there was a door missing to my left. A big room with windows that faced the mountains opened up.

I walked over and stood in front of it, staring through the broken panes to the dark green of the rainforest in the distance. You could look down from here to where two streams met, and there was a big tree a bit to the left hiding the bottom part of the land.

A slight breeze drifted in and the old tattered lace curtain lifted and floated over to touch my cheek. I was so focused on the scene outside, I got a fright when it touched me, thinking it was a spider or something. I jumped and tore at it and it disintegrated in my hands.

I decided to get out of there before the place collapsed on me.

I climbed out the side window again on the bottom floor and walked down toward the bottom of the land that spread away from the house. I could hear water so I knew there must be a waterfall there amongst the over grown trees.

Sure enough, I found a waterhole and a track down to it. I didn't bother to go down but instead turned back to see if I could find somewhere to sit, take a rest, and have a drink.

Between the water hole and the house was a big tree and beneath it a bit of old iron filigree fence low to the ground that looked like there must have been a grave there. The tree roots had pushed out and the head stone had fallen over and broken in the grass.

I swung off my backpack and slung in on the ground. Then I stepped over the ironwork that was still standing upright on one side and spread the grass with my hands to look at it.

The top bit of the head stone was in one piece and it read In loving memory. The bottom bit was broken in half down the middle and I could make out beloved wife of and Mar on one side and gret on the other and under it Guli. Stanford was on the other side.

Auntie Sal had told me the guys that had been surveying the boundaries had backed into the grave accidentally and they were going to dig her up and shift her to the pioneer cemetery in the middle of Cairns. I'd walked around that place, and it was quite cool looking at all those people that started Cairns off, but I didn't think the old girl would like it.

Still, no one had a choice because no one wanted to build a house on top of her—until Uncle Pete got on to his lawyers and they put a condition on the sale. It was agreed to make a park area around the waterhole to include the tree and Margaret. Someone was going to erect a plaque and fix up the grave, but for now it was still broken.

"Here she is," I whispered. "This must be the old girl ..." I felt a bit weird and for a moment I traced my finger over the name Guli, not knowing what it meant. Then I leaned back on my haunches with my palms propping me up on my knees and thought about her lying under me.

The wind shifted and I heard the leaves above me rustle. A big cockatoo screeched and I looked up. It was high in the top and hidden by all the big leaves.

"Okay, I hear ya," I said to myself, and I climbed out of the gravesite and sat down with my back up against the tree. I pulled my backpack forward, dug deep into it to get a Red Bull I had stashed in the bottom, and then pulled out the printed book with the folded letter in its inside cover.

For a moment, I leafed through the pages, thinking about how hard it was going to be to read it all, then I unfolded the letter and started.

Time sort of stopped.

A kind of coldness hit me and I felt like someone had yanked me back in time and I was sitting in that old classroom in the house and everyone was gone except me and her.

What bothered me was what she had to say, the old one that started it all. It was like she was talking to me—as though she had just been down the road and left this letter in my letterbox, addressed to me, Jimmy Ulmarra, not Jaimie.

My dear son, it's time I spoke to you from my heart. I'm very old now, and although you have known me, it is unknown to you who I really am.

It's time to know the truth. The diary I give you will let you know my story, but I know the story alone is not enough. It tells the facts of my life and the facts of your being, but only that. It does not reveal the secret things that matter, beyond the circumstances of your birth.

I want to show you what I discovered in the time I was free. I have told no one because I could not bring myself to say where I learned it.

When I left England, my beloved England, I knew not, that I searched for more than just a new life away from my drudgery. A need was in me—from my very birth, and it made me open to the offer of marriage to Edward and caused me to come to this strange land.

I was looking for something because my soul had not believed all that I had been taught in my own world and rightly so, because in this place I discovered I only knew in part, the secrets of life and here I found its completion.

I left the bindings of my home and ways to wander the open land of my inner country. And there, I became a woman who could aspire to dwell in the dreamtime place of your people. And such is the first lesson, that to find such a place, you must first open as a flower and be as innocent as a child.

I didn't know that I would find that innocence in the teachings of a native message man and warrior.

I found in him, my keys to freedom. He took me away from all that I had been trained to be. He showed me a way that I had never experienced but knew must be there. He stripped away the trappings of the busy civilization I had come from and showed me a true man, the one who can walk with his God in peace.

The rainforest and the wildness, thousands of miles from my home in England, made it possible. It is there and only there, that I found a nakedness that is found in the presence of my Lord, and it was your father that showed me this.

Your father's way was one of order and tranquility, not of lust and the marching of a plague across the land. Even now, my own people transform the green world to one of dead dwellings and dead people, treading on dead paths set to be devoid of life in their race to subdue and own all things.

My son, learn from me: His way is easy, His burden light. I saw it in the laughter of the women as they sat under the trees and in the young men practicing their spear throws.

But the way of the other world makes a man run and chase as though he is ever hungry and always in fear of loss. That world is without the partner of life. The work of those hands, do not weave baskets for food that is plentiful—but works destruction to other living things. Such men are unwilling to discover that they are not 'God' at all—far from it. For all their endeavors, they only spread their disease, and that is death to their own lives and souls—and many others along with them.

The ways of your father's people did not lead to this. Their understanding was of abundance and a place for all. It held them in a happy state as the jungle, the rivers and the ocean never depleted and never withheld their bounty. It provided for them like a good husband and did not desert them, for it promised to feed life into them for as long as they stayed married to it. And would still do—had not we come and chained them to our foolishness.

For a brief year in my life I lived in the care and kindness of those who by countless eons of time, had learned this freedom.

It never occurred to me that I would lose what I had found, caught up as I was in the glorious pleasure of each bright and fascinating new day.

I reveled in the pretense that nothing could touch us and I gave myself over to the delight of each new discovery as though I was a character in a play. I dwelled in a secret theatre where the only audience was the light flutter of leaves clapping their approval in the breeze above us. The orchestra accompanying us, was the chatter of cicadas, and the sound of a whip bird calling out for the curtain call.

Then one day, I was cruelly awoken to the reality of my folly. Joined to your father in spirit, and one with him in the world of the rainforest, still I could not prevent the truth from claiming me. It shattered all illusion and declared that I still belonged, legally and culturally, to my first husband, Edward.

I learned what hell was after that—because I saw what I had done.

Still, I cannot say I regret one moment of my discovery with my beloved Mullegadajawara in the time we had, nor the transparency of my naked being in the beauty of its creation. I would not have missed it for any earthly thing, save pleading for his life. But having no power to change a single moment,

I thanked God ever after, even while I denied my awakening outwardly to return to my former life. I never told a soul what I had seen or known. It was a secret I kept along with who you are —but cannot remain secret, still.

Now I have come to know that everyone will make their way to a place that has been appointed for them to learn the truth. I am sorry I took from you the chance to learn it fully when you were but a boy but as you come of age, I urge you to seek it for yourself where you are most likely to find it, amidst the land itself, the land of your own people.

You will find as they did, the cathedral for your worship is not made by your own hands, nor any man who has set himself up in the place of God. It is provided for you in the mountains and the rainforest by He that knows you.

The choir is made from the voice he chooses: a multitude of splendid birds. The organ is the sound of thunder. The trappings are real flowers growing where they will, the mists of the forests his incense, and the altar of worship can be no other thing accept the 'the rock of offense'. But for you, it is a rock of safety.

You will worship, barefoot and clean from the mercy of His rain, not coming with any sacrifice of your own and you will stand in that place in awe of the gift you find there.

Yes, this is the place where you will find the truth. The rainforest cathedral must be the place you hear His voice.

When you come back down from that holy place you will be changed. From this inner holding, this "secret," you will be ready to be who you must be, yet no doubt misunderstood. Having been reborn, you are beyond judgment because above all, He has accepted you and that is your complete justification and what man can question that?

I knew this full well for myself. But when all seemed torn from me, I stood at a gate that asks, "Decide". I stood there, and to my shame, I lost my courage.

I could not bear my starvation of soul without your father, desiring to be part of others once again and in doing so, I turned my back on all but faith. I went into hiding, grasping the edges of my shawl and pulled it across my face so that none might see what I had done nor what I knew as right and good. There I remained as though my awakening had never been and I willingly put my soul back in chains.

That is what happened to me, my son. I denied my newfound grace and freedom and returned to the conventions I first knew. Having learned to lay down my fruitless work and accept the gift as perfect, I then ran back to pick it up again.

But the years have taught me well my folly, and I have returned to it at the end. I urge you from my heart, not to make my mistake or you will regret the time wasted and the truth denied.

So I plead with you to walk again the pathways of your people and your father. They are places where you might walk freely, unashamed and unafraid. Relearn the "dreaming" and remember the way that is compatible with a good and wholesome life, bringing back light to your eyes and health to your body.

And dear son, it grieves me to say, that all of this you will have to learn for yourself, for there is no one of your people left to teach you. Only the great forests, the open deserts and the rivers as they flow, and the open ocean breathing beneath— only these things can teach you now.

If you will quiet yourself, you shall hear His voice inside creation itself and it will show you again the ways your people knew and passed down for thousands upon thousands of years. And not your people alone. Many have known it, but I fear that in these times, some do not desire to hear anymore.

My son, search inside yourself where no one can go, and be innocent, willing to believe. Into that fire you must reach and listen carefully as the sparks twist up into the night. One day, you shall be made whole by those words you hear and you will understand the true name of the rainbow serpent of old. He knows the way.

We cry out to you from your past, warning you to make new what is not yet born and to plant, in new fashion, what has been torn up—so that your journey will be greater than ours and you will live far better than we. Hear that great voice and decide if you shall be the beginning of the new Yidinji and form a bridge for our two worlds—and heal them both.

My people say that a time will come when we shall know all things, there will be judgment, and we, and the world will be made new. I know I shall see my beloved Mulley again. I cling to this as my only hope, and the proof is the shadow of it we had in our short year together on earth.

I shall ask them to bury me on the very spot where I first met him, as I don't have the bones of your father to lie with in any other place. Yet I shall have his memory and his words on that day, his laughter, and his first touch on my hand in that spot.

On that very day when I met him, I had you set in my future, and I will ask them to plant a new fig tree that shall be the symbol of that future outlasting us both.

In it, the white, and the black cockatoo will stand guard and the rainbow lorikeets will chant praise to our Lord in the upstretched arms of that tree that ever worships him. And when it is that tree's turn to return to the red soil of this place, then the land itself will remember us and write our names in the history of the dreamtime. Yes, our names will be written in the book of life as people who have known the author of the dreamtime, each in turn, but in His name only.

Son, this is my farewell to you, but farewell with a hope—a hope that this great thing we call life has a purpose and that purpose is greater than our understanding of it.

You must learn the secret that is the foundation of all happiness, and when you have, hold fast to it because it will keep you when the storms of life come and you are lost in the loneliness and wilderness of its miseries and troubles. It will keep you and guide you when nothing or no one can.

When I am nothing more, absorbed by the roots of that great tree, you shall go on to discover what you must for the day that we will again see each other—as we really are. On that day, there will be joy for us all because we will be together at last, 'midst the giants that cannot be felled nor ever pass away—the Cathedral of his making... in the eternal rainforest.

When I finished reading this letter, I folded it up and put it aside. I sat still under the big fig tree she had foreseen. After a few moments, I picked up the diary. I sat there holding it and thinking about it. Then I began to read.

The whole day went by and I kept reading. Every page washed over me and through me. I kept reading about her life and the life of the Yidinji until it got too dark to see.

When I stopped and looked around at the grass beneath the tree and the broken, rusted wrought iron fence disappearing into the shadows, I started to realize that I knew what I would do with the money, and what I would do with the rest of my life.

I folded over the corner of the page I stopped on and took one more look at the headstone lying in the grass.

"Thanks," I said. "Good-bye."

I looked around to see if I could find something to take with me to remind me of her and what she had done for me. In the grass there was a small sapling growing off the root of the main tree that had poked its head up because the grass had been un-mowed. I got out my pocketknife and cut it out of the soil and tucked the roots in the empty Red Bull can, and then I left her under the tree to sleep.

I walked back down the road in the dark, got a bus at Gordonvale near the BP gas station, and headed home. I was the only one on the bus. Sitting under the lights inside as the dark road flashed away between street lamps, I read eleven more pages of the journal on the way home.

It took me a week to get through it all, but by the end, I felt like I had been through the initiation rites my great-great-great-grandfather would have done and I was ready for a walkabout of my own.

I took a trip to Auntie Sal's a week later. Standing on her tidy front step, I rang the bell.

"Hello love, I thought you might get here one day. How have you been?"

"I've read it."

"Ah. So, what do you think?"

"Can I come in an' talk to you 'bout some ideas I've got?"

"Of course, of course ..."

She showed me in, got me a drink of orange juice, and we sat down in her leather lounge suite.

"Nice place ..."

"So, what are these ideas?"

"Oh, before I forget, I found this in the old house." I leaned forward to hand her the tobacco box I had found.

"Well that was lucky. They demolished it all a few days ago."

"It was right inside the desk,... I pulled the top off because I wanted the carved piece on the front. I think that was a Yidinji design."

"Well, well... Look at this!" She pulled open the lid and the pearl glowed in its handkerchief nest. "Ah... This was hers. It was given to her by Mullegadajawara, I remember that in the diary."

"Yeah, I know. I thought you might want it."

Auntie Sal fingered it for a few moments then put the lid back on. "No dear, this is for you. One day give it to someone you love as much as he did her."

I couldn't say anything back. I took it from her hand and said, "I think you're like her."

"No denying genes, you reckon?"

"Nah, but they aren't no good to you if you don't want to make use of them."

"So how do you want to make use of yours, young man?"

"Can you help me get back in school? I want to learn about the land."

"You want to be a farmer?"

"Nah, I'm thinking about becoming a guy that protects the trees and the animals—you know, one of them."

She smiled, and after a moment or two she said she would find out what I needed to do and what courses I should take if I wanted to start at the beginning of the next year, in the last week of January, the week of Australia Day.

I said I needed a bit more time than that. I would have to start the year after, because I had one last important thing to do before I began the rest of my life.

I thanked her and went home. For the first time in my life I was excited, and everything looked greener and brighter than I had ever noticed before.

The next day I packed my bag. I went down to the pub that we liked to go to in the afternoon sometimes, even though we were underage, and sat down for a tall glass of orange juice for a change. Auntie Sal had helped me put the little tree shoot in a pot, and as soon as we watered it, it took off and grew. I brought it and the copy of the diary to the pub because I was going to take it with me on walkabout.

I sat there in a sort of daze, and I don't mind admitting I felt scared shitless. Despite that, I knew I was on the edge of something big, a turning point. Just like I always knew a storm was coming when the bats took off from the trees by the library on Abbot Street. They would fly away to hide in the inner forest on the distant mountains that rose from the plains of Cairns City, and now I was set to do the same.

The doors of the pub swung wide and a guy I knew named Steve'o strode in looking for a seat.

"G'dday mate." He was much older than me, and his voice woke me up a bit.

"Been alright?"

"Yeah."

"Hey, you want a beer?" I didn't reply but took a sip of the orange and put the glass back down on the bar top.

"Seen Amber?" he asked.

"Nah."

"I heard she went down to Townsville with Gabby an' that lot."

"Dunno."

"What you got there?" He lifted his glass and tilted it toward the stool beside me where my pot plant sat. Its tall, single stem rose about two feet out of the dirt with green leaves clinging to the fine stems branching from the stalk.

I looked across at it and then looked back to my glass. "The future." I said.

"Shit, that's deep. You going to be a bloody tree hugger or something?"

"Might do."

"Bloody hell. What's brought this on?"

"Dreamtime story."

I drank the dregs of my glass before he had a chance to answer, put it down carefully, and picked up the pot and the diary. "See ya, mate. I gotta go walkabout. Got a tree to plant."

I strode out of the pub, the pot under my arm, but when I got out onto the footpath, I stopped.

I looked down at the concrete under my feet, staring at the white-hot hardness of it and then up to the incandescent blue of the Queensland sky.

Suddenly, I leaned down, put the pot on the concrete, and undid my shoes. The heat of the footpath burnt my soles as I stepped from them, but I didn't care.

I picked up my grubby runners with their dirty gray laces flopping like dank hair and stood full height, breathing deeply.

Then I hurled my shoes up in the air, one after another.

My breath boomed out of my lungs with the effort—I put everything I had into it, and the shoes turned and tumbled high up as they crossed the road, sailing in a wide arc to come crashing down on the roof of Cairns Central Plaza.

I looked at them there for a few moments, lying a little apart at odd angles on the river-gum-colored roof.

Then I leaned down, swept up the pot plant, and strode off down the street toward the bus stop, barefoot.

I padded silently along the concrete, my heels merging up to my skinny, dark brown legs, all shiny in the bright Cairns sunlight.

My left arm was crooked tightly around the pot and the tree waggled along with my stride. A white lady walking the other direction noticed my plant and then looked into my face, with a curious look on her face. I know what I looked like to her: One of those indigenous boys, that drink and steal and live under the edge of their world. But my face, shiny black, and my green eyes shaded by my heavy brow, was set like flint in the direction I was going. My mouth, full-lipped, tipped out and down to greet the slight stubble of my chin where I hadn't shaved and I kept my mouth tightly shut like it held back a dam.

'The mountain rainforest must be your Cathedral,' I thought about her words.

Slowly, my lips opened to reveal my broad, white-toothed, abo smile.

I knew right then, I was the new Yidinji.

Jimmy disappeared for nearly a year. When he returned he told Aunt Sal that he had gone walkabout through the Great Dividing Range and had explored the mighty Daintree Forest, thought to be the most ancient in the world. He wandered barefoot through Kakadu National Forest in the Northern Territory, with its huge canyons, and the Yellow River that was the last bastion of the really big crocs.

The young man was not the same when he came back. He had left a boy and returned a man, and she knew he was ready to take on his future.

Aunt Sal had a pre-fab granny flat put in the back of their home so he could stay, and he went to school for a full two years. Every afternoon she had shortbread fingers and orange juice ready for him and helped him to complete his homework when he needed it. On the weekends, he would take off and visit Yarrabah, and sometimes Willie would look in on him.

When he turned nineteen, he entered James Cook University and studied biology, land management, and environmental studies along with computer studies and microbiology. He joined the Cairns Conservation Society and became an active participant in their projects in the region.

On the day he graduated with his degree, Sally wrapped her arms around him and said amongst a flurry of tears, "She's proud of you, son—and so is he."

By the time he was twenty-four, he had applied for and been granted funds for a foundation that began a movement that would see thousands of acres of trees replanted and returned to the forests it had once been. He helped create far-reaching legislation that would see corridors of native flora and fauna spread out between farms and roads like the fingers of a green net forming over the previously damaged landscape. His team would create new solutions for land use and food production and transform the lives of many.

It's said that when Jimmy led the first wave of planting in the reclaimed areas, up on the dark mountains in the distance behind Cairns, a breeze swept up the valleys and hurried the leaves out of its way.

The cicadas stopped their incessant clicking and rasping, and the birds froze and stared out from their branches as though startled.

A tiny whisper could be heard, if one listened closely, so small as to be mistaken for just the wind or the creak of a forest giant moving.

Guli... I feel the breath of the quoll coming home.

The trees seemed to sway in satisfaction as the breeze passed and listened for an even more hushed reply.

He's learned the secret... We are free at last ...

THE END

www.ingramcontent.com/pod-product-compliance
Lightning Source LLC
Chambersburg PA
CBHW051434260626
47162CB00001B/86